Enhanced Gravity

More Fiction by Washington Area Women

Edited by Richard Peabody

Some of these stories and novel excerpts have been previously published: Kate Blackwell's "The Secret Life of Peonies" first appeared online in *Carve* (July, 2005); Patricia Elam's "Young Boyz Drinkin a Forty out the Bag" appeared in *Mid-American Review* Vol. XV, No. 1–2; Colleen Franklin's "Piece of Cake" appeared in *Penn-Union* Vol. 5, No. 1; Susan Land's "The Somewhat Point" first appeared in the *Florida Review* Vol. 30, No. 2; E.J. Levy's "My Life in Theory" appeared in *Bloom* Vol. 1, No. 2; Julia Slavin's "Last Rights" appeared online in *Pif Magazine* No. 45 and is also available from www.pifmagazine.com in an audio version read by the author.

ISBN: 0-931181-20-8
First Edition
Published in the USA

Book design by Nita Congress.
Cover by Jody Mussoff, © 1988, "I Burned the Planet, Dear"
(colored pencil 57¾" x 34¾").
Printed by Main Street Rag Publishing, Charlotte, NC.

Paycock Press
3819 North 13th Street
Arlington, VA 22201
www.gargoylemagazine.com

For my first writing teachers:
Shirley Graves Cochrane and Ann Darr

Writing the lives of women is politics.

—Grace Paley

Contents

Acknowledgments

Special thanks to: Nita Congress for her editorial skills and desktop wizardry. I couldn't have done either *Grace and Gravity* or *Enhanced Gravity* without you; I also owe a huge debt to M. Scott Douglass for being both printer and independent press magnate. You do good work and wear as many (or more) literary hats as I do. Tons more thanks to: Doreen Baingana, Ron Baker, Sophy Burnham, Robin Ferrier, Sunil Freeman, Robert Giron, Emily Hancock, Derrick Hsu, M.H. Johnson, Wendi Kaufman, Mary Ann Larkin, Jerry Leonard, Nathan Leslie, Richard Luck, Robin Alva Marcus, C.M. Mayo, Leslie Pietrzyk, Joel Pollack, Kim Roberts, Naomi Thiers, Julie Wakeman-Linn, Jackie Walker, Steven Waxman, Tim Wendel, and Elly Williams.

Introduction

Publishing and promoting works by women has become a new calling for me. A lot of people think my attention to so-called "Women's Issues" begins with the projects my literary-partner-in-crime Lucinda Ebersole and I have been creating since 1993. Fact is, I owe a lot to Lucinda, but the initial nudge in this direction begins with *Garfield Street*, the Pacifica Radio show I hosted weekly on WPFW from 1978 to 1979. One week we did a show that focused on local women involved in publishing and I spoke with Helaine Harris of Women in Distribution, Candyce Stapen of *Sibyl-Child*, and Wendy Stevens of *Off Our Backs.* That show was a real education for me. All three women were dealing with unimaginable issues—from printers who wouldn't print their work, to mailings that never arrived. Their courage and resistance in the face of so much flack impressed the hell out of me. I don't pretend to step into their shoes, nor do I tread more than lightly on their turf. I've assembled the first two volumes in this Washington Area Women Writers project because the best thing about being an editor is discovering people. I hoped only to energize, anthologize, promote, and cross-pollinate the Washington literary scene. Maybe bring some attention to writers who weren't known enough outside of town.

Plus, I had so much fun assembling *Grace and Gravity: Fiction by Washington Area Women* in 2004, from contacting the contributors, asking for names they'd recommend for a possible second volume, and the magical night of the launch at the Sewall-Belmont House on Capitol Hill, that I knew I'd have to assemble a companion volume if only as an excuse to stay in touch with everybody from the first book.

This book was almost as much fun to assemble but the results this time created a much darker collection, more reflective of these grim times. Not that the other book didn't have dark moments. But this book just seems less sad and more violent, with more women writing from the male point of view, more writers trying to dissect just what it is about violence and madness and death, and revenge, and misogyny.

For *Enhanced Gravity*, I asked fifty women to participate and heard from forty-three. This second volume doesn't feature as many big names, doesn't have as many writers with books in print, but does indeed feature more multi-ethnic writers than the first book, as well as more examples of experimental prose. There are short-shorts that are almost prose poems, there are long macro stories, plus five novel excerpts, and more newbies and up-and-coming authors then the first go-round. And I think this new mix is just as powerful and unforgettable, partly because a lot of these younger writers were willing to take a risk on a book like this one. I'm particularly pleased to have Stephanie Allen, Patricia Elam, and Julia Slavin in this volume, as I'd hoped to include them all in the first book only to lose them to other obligations.

One of the suits at the *Grace and Gravity* launch asked if the women considered the male reader or audience when creating their work. The answer was a rapid-fire No. Not really. Writers write what they write. I don't mean to create a Women's Fiction Ghetto with these books. I hope instead to be illuminating the many fine fiction writers in the DC area who just happen to be women.

In these days when the *Washington Post Book World* is focused more and more on nonfiction books, when *Paris Review* fired their woman editor and replaced her with a man more invested in nonfiction, when the Corporate World that runs the media, the publishing world, informs me that fiction is to be discounted, disregarded, placed on the back burner, ignored, left unreviewed, when agents tell me No, No, No, I see this volume as a battle cry for fiction in the Nation's Capital. A rallying place for books that actually matter because they do more than just focus on the same old same old. The women in this book aren't afraid to take on hate, fear, death, love—taboo subjects in these days of complete control.

Fiction is after all the lie that tells the truth. And in these days when the people who should be telling us the truth lie about everything and fiction often seems more and more like thinly disguised memoir, it's great to have a book that revels in storytelling.

Jody Mussoff's wonderful color cover drawing is ironic because it's what men think women would do if they controlled the world when in fact it is men who are destroying the planet. Jody's satire on how men see women and how women see men seeing women hits right to the heart of what this anthology's all about.

Want to know what women think? Read this book. Read these women.

—RP
Summer 2005/2006

Stephanie Allen

The Kind of Place for Us

STEPHANIE ALLEN is the author of *A Place between Stations: Stories* (University of Missouri Press, 2003), a finalist for the AWP Award Series in Short Fiction and the Hurston-Wright Legacy Award in Debut Fiction. She is at work on a novel in stories tentatively entitled "Behind the Black Curtain."

I should start with the parties. My parents had a large circle of friends and it seemed, for a while, as if one of the couples in it threw a party almost every month. Since most of my parents' friends had children, too, provisions were made for us at these parties. The upper floor of the host and hostess's home became the children's domain. If the party was in a finished basement room, the adults packed us off to the ground floor of the house. If party guests swirled through the ground-floor living room, dining room, and kitchen, they ushered us to the second-floor bedrooms where, in winter, piles of coats, a riot of textures from silk linings to poplin to serge to wool, lay thrown across beds, waiting for us to dive in and roll around in them.

When we tired of rolling, we lay still and listened. By this time the music seeping up from below had slipped along that invisible line that connected funky dance numbers to mid-tempo R&B, Spinners, and Main Ingredient songs, and these to the slow-drag tunes, Lou Rawls and balladeers who addressed their women as "lady." We'd sneak down the stairs, just far enough to see them. Men in smallish afros and loud sports jackets embraced women in shimmering gabardine dresses and platform shoes, the wisecracking banter left over from bid whist games stopped, and couples moved like silent ships across the floor. Their eyes closed, their faces relaxed in the absence of a need to speak, they did not so much look younger as they did older, serious with a kind of gravity that transcended scolding, stern orders to finish homework, and complaints about messy bedrooms. The paradox, of course, was lost on us.

After all, we had heard how loud they could get. Not long ago had come that moment during the party, a moment every party reached eventually, when the conversation and laughter and rattling of glasses had reached a crescendo. And at the top of that crescendo we would hear the sound of my mother's fruity, contralto laughter as it rose above the roar, ricocheted along the ceiling, and then submerged itself again in the noise of the crowd. By then we children were half-asleep. Stuffed with food stolen from the kitchen, we lay dazed among the coats, inhaling the grown-ups' scents, our eyes tingling from the cloud of cigarette smoke that had risen from below. That moment: every party had one, when the separate vitality of the adults, and the sleepy, contented weight of us children, hung in an impossible balance.

It seemed only moments later, far too soon for that slow dancing to have finished, our parents' hands were rousing us, shaking off the sleep, bundling us for the ride home that we thought was still hours away.

They met, my parents, five or six years after my father was discharged from the Army after serving in Korea. My parents' courtship was no silly tumble of one young person into the arms of another. It was neither a game nor a swoon. My mother, working the register for a Cleveland pharmacy, and my father, hired to drive its delivery truck, discovered one another. Each was, for the other, the one thing that remained to be found after youths spent in the chasm of the Great Depression, the early deaths of parents, work, rent parties, friends lost track of over the years, books, beer, the self surrounded by the empty rush of the city.

My father approached the counter as my mother rang up the purchases of people in line. Clevelanders of the lower working class, they waited patiently in their blue shirts or white blouses, passed bags and parcels from one arm to the other, and fidgeted only to ease their tired feet. They paid for their purchases in coins and spoke their genuine thanks.

When the line was gone, there was my father, standing in front of an end-cap full of mouthwash, toothpaste, gum powders, and patent toothache remedies. Spence, his running buddies called him. They were Tomcat, Whistle Stop, Ken Eddie, but they reserved for him the most mundane of appellations. He wore no eyeglasses, but had a face built for them, cheekbones made to look prominent by a peppery sprinkle of black freckle-moles and eyes set back deep in his head. And he stared. Stood there in that Wentworth's uniform, its overlarge pants taken up with a safety pin that would open sometimes and prick him in the back while he was driving, and stared at my mother.

She had the beauty of spoon-swirled coffee and smelled of unperfumed soap. Her hands, treated daily with baby oil, sparkled in the wan fluorescent lights of Wentworth's dingy ceiling. Her bottom lip swelled just slightly at its center, where the lips of others made a cleft, having healed over in an extra bit of flesh after being split years before. It didn't change her speech, or lead her to avoid lipstick, or make her laugh with her hand over her mouth, my father had noticed.

Here's what he said to her: "Cleveland ain't the kind of place for us."

She looked him over. "Us who?" she asked him.

Instead of answering that, he said, "War built up the factories and plants, but that's gone now. This place got no future going for it."

He had to show her what he meant. The GIs from WWII still lazing around on street corners and in bars, out of work. The enormous war-parts plant on the edge of the city, quiet as a grave.

"Come with me," he said.

She laughed at him. "Look, Buster, I don't even know you."

She was wrong. She did know him. He showed her that, too. They listened to her radio shows together, *The Shadow*, *Bergen & McCarthy*, *Fibber McGee*. They ate in the coffee shop, Rex's, a block down from where they worked, as the shapes of people hurried past them in the dark outside the plate-glass windows: liver and bacon, split-pea soup, lamb shanks, butter beans, pop. He came around, and they sat on the couch flipping through *Life* magazine. Or he came around, and they rolled the pennies she had been dropping into a grape juice jug for years. He waited on the stoop of her building until she came down, and they walked around the block, getting what she called "the jumps" that had built up as she stood all day at the counter out of her legs. And then they sat on the stoop looking at the stars and laying out, each in turn, every bit of their pasts that they did not wish to perpetuate into their futures.

"Glo, you ain't gone out in a month!" one of her roommates said one morning before they both left for work. "When's that fool gonna take you on a date?"

"Me and that fool are getting married," my mother said.

That, at least, is how I imagine my parents coming together. That is how I am sure it must have happened, give or take a word or a deed, the name of a person or a diner, here and there. I don't believe it could have been otherwise.

The rest is a matter of record, for I have seen the photograph with the date scrawled in my mother's looping script on the back: the two of them, a few pieces of luggage collected at their feet, standing in front of the bus station. After that, they were on a Greyhound coach laboring east into the rising sun.

In Winnikee Falls, New York, they started with one girl, added another, and then surprised themselves by having a third. They moved out of their cramped apartment and into a house bought from a widow overwhelmed, finally, by her own home and its tendency to disintegrate. By the time the house passed into their hands, the pipes leaked through the ceilings and the wiring behind the walls routinely gave out.

27 Therogrand Avenue was, however, a house made for children. In its attic lay a treasure trove left by the widow: an antique aluminum meat grinder with a clamp to grip tables, a washboard with ribbed and pebbled surfaces, a storm lamp, a rusting bicycle. These prizes lay not on top of the piles of debris that littered each of the attic rooms, but below it where they needed to be picked at and pried loose, an activity that could consume hours of a school-less summer day. A hall closet tucked under the main staircase was a perfect hiding place. And decay provided my sisters and me with endless possibilities. We might pick loose flakes of linoleum where it was curling up behind the kitchen stove or tread on loosening floorboards that gave up creaking notes like giant

piano keys. We could jolly along a tear in the wallpaper until it revealed a whole new pattern underneath or trouble a wobbly cut-glass doorknob until it dropped loose in our hands. There was no end to our home's everyday fascinations.

My father managed to arrest the floods and blackouts and to stay the effects of his children's mischief. He wetted down and stripped away roomfuls of dim Victorian wallpaper full of flowers and trellises and maidens tending gardens and painted the walls with Montgomery Ward flats. He ripped out an inset china cabinet and the wall behind it, opening a breezeway from one end of the house to the other and allowing light and air to flow freely through the ground-floor rooms. He laid new flooring over varnished wood so old that it was turning black.

Still, whenever we came back home from a family outing, a trip out for ice cream or fried chicken, or an expedition down to the riverfront park, and stepped through the front door, all of 27 Therogrand Avenue's past came rushing back to envelop us, taking away our breath. The shadows, the ancient dust in the air. The floorboards that creaked no matter what you laid over them, the primeval formations of those radiator ribs, bones of long-gone beasts.

My mother would put down whatever she was carrying, walk into the living room and open the blinds, admitting light. She'd sit in the easy chair and kick off her shoes, relaxing as if she were enjoying the most palatial room in the Vanderbilt mansion.

My sisters and I would find her there when we came in for the night later. Cold Nehi grape in hand, she'd be sitting there as if she'd been waiting for us. She'd let out a long sigh, nuzzle one of us, and tell us to go get our father. It was our habit to spend the early evenings watching baseball games or old movies together.

"Aw, Ma," we'd moan.

We knew where he was: in the dank, spider-webby basement. We didn't even have to look. If you called him from the top of the stairs, he wouldn't hear you. You had to go in. He was down there prowling around, looking for leaks or droppings, testing the bricks to make sure the foundation was holding up beneath us.

In time, my mother took a job doing assembly work for a small electronics firm. She brought bits and scraps of her work life home with her. My sisters and I incorporated the pieces of colored wiring, the plastic disks, and castoff punch cards into our Barbie fantasies as if they were nothing unusual. And if we ever sat examining a punch card, fingering the neat columns of numbers, observing the way light made a pin-shaft through each of the small holes where a number had been, we never thought to regard it as anything more than a sheet of paper—certainly not as the artifact of her absence that it was.

We were sated, full of the milk of her, buried in comfort. With my mother we spent Saturdays shopping, first in the department stores, where we pulled out and talked over far more shirts and dresses and pairs of pants than we could have carried, and then at the grocery store. Usually we stopped in between at the Kresge's lunch counter for hamburgers from the grill. Weekday afternoons, when we came home from school, we clustered around her, chattering about the school day, watching her apply her makeup, which she kept in a lacquered black box decorated with a bucolic country scene in its top so remote from our small city lives that I doubt we ever regarded the place as really existing somewhere. Then she was off to work, catching a ride with a neighbor half an hour before my father arrived home from his job in Montgomery Ward's shipping and receiving.

My father had not wanted her to take the job. In the weeks leading up to the day she started, we heard a change in the tone of their evening conversations, which drifted up to us in our bedroom from the kitchen where they sat talking. They didn't raise their voices. Instead, long patches of silence began to interrupt what had been the steady hum of their voices, silences bracketed by words that broke off from their sentences and floated free: Paycheck, borrow, expensive. Mortgage, dentist. Afford. Deserve.

With my mother away, my father was left to look after us girls. Alone with my sisters and me nights, he was not lulled by the sound of our antics from the upstairs bedroom. He would yell for us to quiet down, and if we did not comply quickly enough, he would stalk upstairs. When he appeared in the doorway, he usually issued nothing more than a gruff "Shut up and go to sleep," but not before we saw the briefest flash, in his eyes, of a frustration out of all proportion to the minor nuisance that we posed.

Not long after she started working, my mother bought herself a car. We also started taking an annual, two-week summer vacation. Our destination, every year, was Cape Cod, Massachusetts—not the shore towns along the Cape, Brewster, Dennis, Sandwich, but Provincetown, a long, leveled sand dune at the tail end of the land speckled with trinket shops and seafood restaurants.

Each time, my father strapped himself into the driver's seat and drove the seven or eight grueling hours it took to get us to Provincetown. It took us another day, at the end of the two weeks, to get back home. In between, the days opened out in movements of the tide. We collected ourselves on the beach: my mother and sisters, who couldn't swim; my father, who didn't swim; and I, who swam so badly I ought not to have ventured in at anything but low tide. By early evening, with the shadow of the motel creeping down the sand toward our beach towels, my father was usually dozing, a straw hat over his face, my sisters and I were bartering items from the mound of seashells we had collected, and my mother sat in our midst, holding open the paperback novel she somehow managed to read as she chatted with her daughters and fanned the flies away from her husband.

On those days when my sisters and I grew tired of the beach, we cajoled my mother into a visit to downtown Provincetown. She would change into her yellow halter top, slacks, and flip-flops and, shaded by sunglasses that made her as glamorous as any movie star relaxing on a day off, oblige us. Down the main street we went, weaving in and out of shops selling seashells and lobster figurines, gorging ourselves on fried clams with bellies, grabbing at tie-dyed T-shirts and caps with "Cape Cod, Massachusetts" emblazoned across them. We wanted everything: jewelry, clothes, toys, kites and souvenir shot glasses, carved white whales, clams with goggle eyes and plastic lips glued to their shells. One day's drive removed from home, we became like pirates suddenly washed up on the steps of a glitter palace.

By the end of the day, exhausted, we walked to the car for the drive back to the motel, each of us clutching two or three bags of booty.

"Carol, let me see that necklace," my mother would say to my sister, or, to me, "So, Linda, that's a cowrie shell? Lessie, save some of that candy for when you get home."

And we'd rifle through the bags to hold up the treat or the bauble she had just laid down her money for.

"It fits OK? You have room for it on your dresser?"

Oh yes, oh yes. On we chattered. Behind the dark glasses, my mother seemed to be looking at the other tourists, the white-gloved officer directing traffic, the little storefronts, the sun in the sky, the way before us, and us, too. We held up a box of saltwater taffy, a scrap of plastic scrimshaw. It was, somehow, enough to absorb our greedy love.

After one of these raids on Provincetown, we returned to the motel room to find my father gone. His clothes were draped neatly over the back of a chair.

He was outside, swimming in the ocean. We stood on the beach watching him, staring as if we'd found a whale that had lost its herd. My father moved through the choppy waves, coming up at irregular intervals for air, then diving down again, down there where you carried your thoughts like your air, tight against the confines of yourself. For half an hour, he swam back and forth along the shoreline. Then he stood up in chest-deep water and walked back to the beach, pouring streams of water from himself.

That night, as we ate a fried dinner at an outdoor seafood stand, he didn't mention where he'd suddenly acquired a taste for swimming. He sat on a bench, looking out over the sand dunes where the sun was setting, not saying much of anything at all.

After about a year, my mother was able to switch to the day shift. For a while it was a little awkward to have her there in our midst once again at dinnertime and afterwards. It was as if she were a different mother from the one we girls saw off in the afternoon and spent all weekend with. We gazed at her, surreptitiously, trying to figure it out.

With my father, it was even worse. They bumped into each other, spoke at the same time, gave us contradictory orders and then, when this was pointed out to them, sheepishly canceled both sets of instructions.

Exactly how long this went on, none of us girls could have said, because the year of my mother's return also marked the season of a collective growth spurt for the three of us. When we weren't fighting over the telephone, my sisters and I, we went tearing through the house, tumbling restlessly from one room to another.

We filled up all the space in the house. Our shoes and sneakers lay all over the place. The telephone rang off the hook with our callers. We ransacked the refrigerator, leaving swaths of empty space, jars and bottles with mere puddles at the bottom. We frayed the couch and pounded hollows in the front porch floorboards. And then summer rolled around and added long, long days powered by near-endless sunlight to the frenetic mix. My sisters accumulated cuts and sprains. I sneaked out and sat in my mother's car, put the keys in the ignition, and contemplated the places that I, the oldest, thought I was so very close to going.

In the midst of this whirlwind, my parents retreated to their bedroom. On weekend mornings, instead of rising early as they had always done, they closed their bedroom door and remained behind it until lunchtime or even later.

Sometimes, approaching noon, we'd run into my mother padding through the kitchen in bathrobe and slippers still, and she'd smile drowsily at the horde of children, some her own and some her neighbors', that streamed around her. Or the horde roiling around in the hall would send one member springing up the stairs, only to be stalled at the closed bathroom door, from behind which my father would emerge in his slow and plodding way, smelling sweet with steam and shaving cream.

I am sure we did not consciously decide to flush them out. Why would we? Caught up in our own affairs, we were only dimly aware of their retreat, and we didn't sit still long enough to wonder about its purpose. Nevertheless, our bodies began to knock over lamps and our hands managed to shatter plates on the floor. Somebody left a pan smoking on the kitchen stove for an hour. A stray dog got in through a door carelessly left wide open, and ran barking up and down the hall. Lessie, or perhaps it was Carol, or maybe even me, let the bathroom tub overflow with water.

And then Lessie came screaming home with—what to call the thing?—a chunk of wood half the width of a baseball card driven into her palm. It was green, still, with park-bench paint. My parents drove her to the hospital and carried her home hours later, a drugged and bandaged rag doll. For days my mother watched her for signs of infection, until I broke curfew and came home at eleven at night when I lost track of time at a party. Someone had told my mother, when she called, that I'd left at eight. My parents were combing the streets with an army of enlisted neighbors when I walked up the block, puzzling over the commotion. After that, I had to sneak out to the next party, and after that, run off without permission after my sullen promises to stay put. Carol fractured her arm. And Lessie failed the second grade.

Ensconced on my mother's lap, she cried about it for at least an hour. We all happened to be gathered in the living room for the performance. My mother petted and stroked her nappy little head while she howled, and then hiccoughed, and finally sniveled. I looked at Carol, and Carol looked at me, the two of us wondering how on earth she could be such an idiot as to fail the second grade. My mother said, "These things happen. They're just part of growing up."

My father, who was off a ways in the easy chair, reading the *Winnikee Falls Journal*, nodded without looking up. My mother kissed Lessie on the top of the head and pulled her away to speak to her. It was a bright, hazy Saturday morning in June.

"Think of all the new friends you're going to make," my mother said gently. "Think of all the new people you're going to get to know."

Lessie didn't look convinced, but at least she stopped crying.

"Don't summer school run all the way 'til the end of August?" my father asked.

"I think so," my mother said, and winced at him a little.

That canceled our summer trip. But before summer school even rolled around, my parents closed-door mornings had ended. My mother began, once again, making weekend morning breakfasts for us all. She'd wander out as soon as we were up, a beat-up old bathrobe lashed unevenly around her body, and check Carol's cast and Lessie's hand. My father didn't follow her.

All of us girls helped with breakfast. Lessie cracked eggs, getting most of them into the bowl; Carol heated up the griddle, which I thought she let get way too hot just for the pleasure of watching it spit and crackle like something about to explode; and sometimes I gallantly waved my mother off from the stove and cooked the flapjacks themselves: oval cakes golden brown on the outside, and more often than not gooey with raw batter inside. She ate them without complaint and without comment, her fingers absently teasing out uneven tufts of her graying hair as she chewed.

We didn't go to Cape Cod that summer, or the summer after that, though Lessie passed the third grade. Whenever one of us girls asked about it, my mother or father simply said, "Not this year," and changed the subject.

During a heat wave, perversely enough, my father disappeared into the attic and moved every piece of junk in the smallest room into one of the other rooms. Then he went off to a lumber store and came back with a pile of Sheetrock and bags of plaster of paris, which he hauled up into the attic. For several weeks he spent entire evenings after work up there, banging and pounding, dragging and sawing. My mother told us that he was doing the room over so he could rent it out to a boarder. We girls couldn't wait to see who this new addition to our household would be. One of the dashiki-sporting, black-power-saluting militants from the neighborhood? A friend of ours had a whole family in her attic, farmers tending a roomful of marijuana plants.

One day while my father was at work, after the heat wave broke, Carol, Lessie, and I sneaked up into the attic against his orders and surveyed the progress. There wasn't much to see: two smooth, white rectangles of Sheetrock nailed into the beams of the low-sloping ceiling. The rest of the room had the same maidens-and-trellises wallpaper it had always had.

Late in the summer, my mother announced that she was returning to the night shift at work. No nighttime conversations between my parents had preceded this. Once again my mother fixed dinner early, put on her makeup in front of the aromatic box late in the afternoon, and left for work at three-thirty. The three of us whined and wailed and pleaded with her to go back to the day shift. It was only temporary, she assured us, and mentioned something about better pay from a shift differential, something none of us really understood. That she deemed it necessary was enough, in the end, to get us to stop nagging her.

The summer nights remained, for us, a mere coda to the long, lazy, heat-drugged days. Lessie played with her friends in the backyard while lightning bugs put on their usual evening light show, and I congregated with my friends in parking lots and driveways, flirting with boys. When we finally came home, the three of us, we fell in bed and drifted off to sleep to the smell of Downy-rinsed sheets and the muffled sounds of my father banging and dragging on the floor above us.

One night he came into my room, and what woke me was not the noise but the mingled smell of plaster dust and sweat and something, a tension, in his movements. I sat up in bed.

"Linda, look after your sisters. I gotta go get your mother," he said.

I was still half-asleep, but this wouldn't have made sense even if I'd been awake. My mother had her own car and drove herself home every night. So I said the most sensible thing I could formulate.

"Where's her car, Daddy?"

He hesitated for a moment, gripping the doorknob.

"They got some kinda mess out on Route 17," my father said. "Traffic all stuck. I'll be back as soon as I can."

Then he was gone. I heard the rumble of his Impala starting up in the driveway, then the rough purr of it rolling into the street in reverse, then the blast of it shooting off down the street. He was not driving slowly. By now, I was fully awake.

I tiptoed down the hall to the stairs, cursing the noisy floorboards as I tried to sneak past my sisters' room without waking them. In the kitchen, I sat and listened to the silence. It wasn't silence, really. The house gave off its usual creaks and groans, whooshes of water running through pipes, settlings. I didn't know what to think, what on earth my father had been talking about. Whatever it was, I thought he and my mother would be back home soon. Eventually, I put my head down on the table and fell back to sleep.

My sisters awakened me. Carol yanked me by the shoulder until I opened my eyes and blinked at them. I looked at the clock. It was five a.m.

"Where's Mom and Dad?" Carol asked.

She had Lessie by the hand.

I told them what my father had told me, which seemed like much less information now, with the first chirpings of birds trickling in, than it had a few hours ago. My mother got off from work at midnight, and usually, by the time one of us awakened to pee or get a glass of water, she was home.

"You mean a traffic jam?" Carol asked.

"I don't know," I snapped.

I got up and got Lessie a glass of milk to have something to do, but she didn't want it. She settled into Carol's lap and waited.

We all waited. Six a.m. rolled around, and with it came daylight, but still nobody came.

By this time, I thought I was supposed to do something, call the police or one of our relatives, but I could not believe such a need was upon me. So I reached over and turned on the transistor radio my mother kept amidst the clutter on the kitchen table, and wheeled the tuner dial until I found music. For a few minutes, we half-listened to pop songs. Then Carol picked up the radio and tuned it to a station where a man was talking.

"...still a backup of several miles. Jim, can you see anything moving out there?"

A staticky voice answered, "Teddy, there is just nothing moving out here. The rig is still blocking the road where it jackknifed. It looks like—wait a minute—"

Silence, briefly.

"Yes, there's some police cars just arriving on the shoulder now. There's been police here all night, so I'm not sure what these officers are going to be doing."

The first voice picked up again.

"Thanks, Jim. That's Jim Salkey reporting live from the scene at Route 17 at that—that chain collision that happened a few hours ago. We've got reports of a lot of injuries, and they've been taking people to St. Ignatius Hospital all night. They've taken about a hundred people there, we're told, and—"

The front door opened, and my mother stepped inside. She carried the same assortment of clutter she carted off to work, a jacket over her arm, her enormous purse, a plastic bag full of magazines, and her coffee thermos. She turned and spoke to my father, who was stepping through the door behind her, in the hushed voice you use so as not to awaken sleepers.

Lessie bolted off Carol's lap and ran to her. Carol followed, and I brought up the rear.

My mother, as she always did, found a free hand somewhere to put around Lessie.

"What are you three doing up at this hour?" she asked us. "You all scoot on off to bed, you hear me?"

"What happened, Mommy?" Lessie asked.

"Go on to bed," my father said, unusually gruff. "Let your mother get some sleep."

"The radio said there was a big accident!" Carol said.

It was still buzzing in the kitchen, where we'd left it running.

"Lordy, I am tired," my mother said, and made her way to the couch, all of us trailing her.

She pulled Lessie up into her lap and settled Carol next to her.

"Well, I was just driving home, just like every night, and all of a sudden, *wham*, I hit the car in front of me. Thank goodness we'd already slowed down. Then, *wham*, the car behind me hits me! And I hear another crash behind that. And the same thing is happening in the lane next to me."

She laughed a funny, fluttery laugh and pulled Lessie closer to her. My father, who had not sat down, was standing over her, listening like he hadn't heard any of this before.

"Gloria," my father said. He didn't usually call her by her full name.

She waved him off with a strange look.

"Come here, Linda," she said, beckoning me closer.

I sat on the floor, the only space left near her, and put my hand over her knee. I could feel the muscles in her leg twitching.

"Are you OK, Mom?" I asked her.

"I'm fine now," she said.

I put my head down on her knee, and listened to her talk, her voice so calm, so normal, while the man on the radio in the kitchen went on squawking shrilly without any audience to hear him.

She didn't go back to work the next night. Or the night after that, either. And on Saturday, instead of taking us shopping, she sat at the kitchen table, chain-smoking and drinking black coffee.

I sat with her. She finished a cigarette, leaned over, and mashed it into the ashtray. She didn't put it fully out, though, and I sat there wondering whether I should reach over and finish it, or point out that it was still smoldering, or just say nothing. She lit another cigarette before I could decide.

She was talking about the accident out on Route 17 again.

"Here your daddy is, looking all over the place for me, and where am I?" She huffed a humorless little laugh. "Sitting on my can in my car, watching everything like I'm at the movies or something. And ain't a thing wrong with me. But there I am, sitting like a bump on a log, not saying a word to all those policemen out there taking people's names and everything."

She squashed out her cigarette with half of it still unsmoked and lit another one.

"I'm a damned good driver. Your father will tell you that. But I never saw it coming. One minute I'm just driving, not even much traffic on the road. Dark out there, too. You think you can see fine until you find out different." She laughed again and looked at me as if she were just noticing I was there for the first time. "But if you fall off of a horse, you got to get right back up on it, don't you? That's what I'm always telling you kids."

I didn't know what to say. I nodded.

She looked down, flicked her cigarette at the ashtray, and sprayed red ash on the table. It went out almost at once.

"Right back on," she said.

She didn't go back to work that Monday following our weekend chat, though. Or that Tuesday, either. On Wednesday, while we slept, she rose early and went in for the morning shift with my father. We saw her little purple Pacer in the driveway when we got up. She rode in with my father the next day, and the one following it. By the weekend, though none of us asked about it, and she didn't say a word, we understood that the night shift, and the differential, were gone for good.

We never went to Cape Cod again. I was too busy, at the time, to miss it, or to wonder about the reasons why. I suppose Carol and Lessie were, too.

Though my parents, over the years, had gradually dropped out of their party circuit, they decided, one year, to accompany some of their old friends on a trip to Myrtle Beach, South Carolina. It was to be a weekend trip, a brief getaway for the adults.

It was Labor Day weekend. The beach that far south stayed warmer than the chilly New England water. Even on the cusp of fall, when Massachusetts would have been cool after sunset and cold at night, Myrtle Beach allowed barbecues on the beach and strolls along the boardwalk long after dark.

My parents returned after four days and three nights. We helped them cart in their overstuffed suitcases, the cooler they'd stowed sandwiches and iced coffee in, two or three atlases, a fistful of maps, a packet of tourist brochures, several blankets, a pile of beach towels, assorted floating rings, and an inflatable raft. The raft and rings were still in their plastic packaging, the brochures were glossy and unused, and the towels and blankets had no sand in them at all.

Their only souvenirs were the coral necklaces my mother gave each of us.

"Take a picture of me," Lessie squealed as soon as she got hers on. My mother always saved a few shots on the last roll of film for homecoming photos, the final chapter of our vacation adventures.

She rummaged through her enormous shoulder bag, the one that seemed to contain everything anyone ever needed, and said, "How about that?"

My father, the cooler under one arm, trudged past on his way to the kitchen.

My mother sighed. "I guess I left the camera home."

When I was a little older, eleven or twelve, I began hanging around my father as he went about his projects. He didn't seem too eager for my company at first, and he mostly ignored me. Then he sent me off from time to time to fetch some or other tool for him: awls and ball peen hammers, Phillips screwdrivers and levels. As he worked, he explained what he was doing.

"This here outlet," he'd say, "I'm going to leave an opening for it because you can't cover them up. It's code."

Code? Like Morse code? I didn't know what he meant, but I didn't ask, because after a while, with some repetition and close listening, I found I began to understand most of the things he was talking about. His grunts and mumblings made sense, finally, too. And I saw a dexterity in his hands, a strength in his arms as he drove the hammerhead home again and again, that I had not noticed before.

Sometimes he worked late into the night, past the time that I, and he, most likely, should have gone to bed.

One evening, I sat on the floor in the kitchen, watching him paint the radiator a warm, chocolate brown. Neither of us spoke, as usual. It was summer, muggy, the house around us almost finished with the thumping and groaning of settling in for the night. From above came the thin, watery sound of the pipes emptying, and my father stopped what he was doing and leaned his head back against the wall. The faraway look in his eyes told me he'd forgotten I was there. I wondered what he was thinking of. And then the sound came again and I realized it wasn't water at all. It was the sound of my mother's laughter, leaching down through the floorboards of the upstairs room where Carol and Lessie surrounded her, as they did every night, demanding story after story before sleep.

Christina Bartolomeo

A Winter Thunderstorm

CHRISTINA BARTOLOMEO is a Washington native whose first novel, *Cupid and Diana* (Scribner, 1998), was set in Cleveland Park and was a 1998 New York Times Notable Book of the Year. Her other novels are *The Side of the Angels* (Scribner, 2002/ St. Martin's Press, 2004), and *Snowed In* (St. Martin's Press, 2004). Her short stories have appeared in *Cosmopolitan*. Bartolomeo began writing novels through classes at the Writer's Center in Bethesda, Maryland. She lives in Bethesda.

What I regretted most about coming back to Wilkinson, Pennsylvania, was the certainty of seeing Lucas Greeves again. When I'd been a self-pitying scholarship student and Lucas a truly golden boy on campus—and he was one of those golden boys: haloed, glowing, unapproachable, the kind of person I detested then and still detest—I'd dreamed of returning in triumph someday, successful and elegant and kindly condescending. In those days, the idea of elegance meant a lot to me. Now I know that I will never achieve it, which saves a lot of work.

Instead, I came back to Wilkinson for a save-my-sorry-ass job at the *Wilkinson Gazette*, writing features for what Ray, my editor, always used to call the "Ladies Page," and has since renamed "Night and Day," although there's precious little night life in Wilkinson. Even the students at the college seemed more subdued than they were in my memory.

Ray had promised me that this time, when I wrote for him, I could use my full name, Kathleen Corrigan. He used to bill me as K.M. Corrigan, to hide the fact that he'd hired a college student as his only features writer. But of course, everyone in town knew that back then, especially after the trouble between Lucas and me. Lucas caused me considerable trouble, one way and another.

I thought about Lucas when Ray wrote me—no emails for Ray—saying he needed a features person.

"Someone with a little experience who isn't big-headed about it. Someone who can live on what I can pay. You're not free by any chance?"

He knew I was in trouble. Ten years after we'd last seen each other—because I wasn't much on reunions and hadn't been back, though we exchanged Christmas cards—it was Ray that my friends called when they realized that I couldn't stay any longer in Washington, D.C.

That is, I couldn't stay happy in Washington. I couldn't even stay what my psychiatrist called "even." I'll spare you the Sylvia Plath-isms, because she put it better than anyone else, but after my mother's death, the sadness felled me and I couldn't get up, not after months and months, not after one year stretched to two. I grew so sad, so intransigently sad, that a man who loved me, a kind man who used to make me laugh, reached the end of his patience. After he left, I was hanging on by my fingernails, but I didn't know it. My friends knew it, though. They phoned Ray, among several other people, and they urged me out of D.C., out of an apartment in Van Ness that had never felt like home, out of a cozy but deadening job writing glossy brochures for a tourism marketing group. I went back that autumn, with a suitcase and a secondhand laptop, to the Pennsylvania Blue Ridge that Lucas had never left. Lucas had taken over his father's legal practice, with cases as far as Harrisburg and Philadelphia. He loved the town, and he had always known what he wanted—he knew even when he was a college student. He seemed to me to be one of those fortunate ones whose lives take a clear, unbrambled path. I was so low when I met him again that I'd ceased even resenting that quality in him, except in a mild, dull way.

I'd made an enemy of Lucas when I reviewed him as Mercutio in *Romeo and Juliet.* At Wilkinson College, Lucas had always had the most interesting part in any show. Not always the lead, but the choicest role—the one that could steal the show away from the lead if the right actor played the part.

I'd always given him good reviews, grudgingly, disparaged him as a "pretty boy" to my friends. I knew nothing about theater, but Ray didn't either, so I was free to guess at what made good acting. But even I could tell that Lucas was something out of the ordinary that night. Even when he wasn't speaking, his face alone seemed to hold the audience. There was something about it that great performers' faces have, a mobility even in stillness, a movement of line, a natural delicacy in reacting, so vibrant that speech wasn't essential. It was a face that seemed to know everything but would only tell it to the right person, which may or may not be you. It was also a cocky, Irish American face, with that cockiness that no one nation in the world could have produced on its own. His hair was a soft black and his eyes were the intense blue eyes only dark-haired men have, with the sort of eyelashes that women envy but never get. His movements on stage were light and athletic, power implied rather than demonstrated.

He was brilliant, to put it simply. And beautiful. And I was neither, and never would be, which is why I did a bad thing. At nineteen, I wasn't unattractive, but I was shabby. My friends weren't the actors or school politicians who saw me among them so often, taking earnest notes. My dates came from the philosophy society and physics club. They were intense young men with long hair, who could argue a fine point about William James for hours with passion and audacity but were afraid to kiss you goodnight. When they did, they were bad kissers.

Lucas's crowd ignored me. But Lucas himself had never been mean. Yet that night at the play, sitting next to a dozing young math major named Preston, I was furiously jealous of Lucas. I saw him in the glamour that surrounds any stage and I yearned to be, for one moment, as significant as he was.

That night I wrote in my review, "Lucas Greeves was an eloquent if somewhat traditional Mercutio. If his performance sometimes lacked a twist, a new interpretation of this standard crowd-pleaser of a character, his handsome face would be an asset to any production. A native son, Mr. Greeves has already been accepted to Wilkinson Law School next year. If he can win a jury with the same talents he uses so plausibly on an audience, his future as a litigator will be bright."

Ray ran the review with that paragraph intact. He said only, "You're damning that Greeves kid with faint praise, but from what I've seen of him it won't hurt him any."

Ray is a small, round man with an overwhelming moustache. Though he was happily married with three children by the time I started working for him, he may have remembered the days when he too was disqualified from the glories of youth. Or maybe he was glad to see a little spirit in me, even if it was misdirected.

The *Gazette* printed the review on Thursday morning. On Thursday night, Lucas appeared at my dorm, thrilling a few girls in bathrobes and wet hair. He stood in my doorway and said—rather, declaimed, but I really believe it was his natural way of speaking—"You call yourself a writer? After that review? I never read worse trash. What do you know about acting? Or about Shakespeare?"

I said weakly, "You have a problem?"

"You're not even an English major." He must have checked up on me. Not hard to do at a school with twenty-one hundred students.

"You're upset," I said flatly. I had learned, even at so young an age, that speaking flatly and calmly could deflect or unnerve much criticism. Now when I'm angry, I have trouble showing it—too many years of practice.

'Upset doesn't cover it. I was good. You know I was good. And even a cheesy paper like this one should know better."

I was wearing a black turtleneck that extinguished me completely. All the color in the room was gathered up in Lucas: in his blue eyes with an angry yellow light behind them, in his flushed face, in the bright red of his baseball jacket, one of the many boyish garments he owned that I despised.

"It's the first time I haven't absolutely gushed over you in a show," I said. "Some professional you are."

"And you're some bitch," he'd said, and left.

I learned something important from him that night, and I hadn't forgiven Lucas since for proving me so horribly wrong. I learned that if you are ever given the power of the pen, using it to work out your own grudges and insecurities will bring you low, possibly embarrass you horribly, and not make you feel better in the long run. It may have been because of Lucas that I undertook only harmless writing work after college, promotional stuff designed to please. My mother, who liked to think of herself as "a real lady," thought that this line of work was appropriate and pleasant for a young woman. At twenty-one, you may want to be appropriate and pleasant. At thirty, with your mother gone, it palls a little.

Reports of Lucas's anger followed me around all that spring. He found an unflattering picture of me from the yearbook and had it blown up, then pasted it on a dartboard, and used it viciously during rehearsal breaks. He stopped his subscription to the *Gazette*, and wrote Ray telling him why. This made me the butt of endless jokes at the paper. He kept the one-sided feud going even after I gave him a generous review for overacting his way through *A Streetcar Named Desire* opposite Debbie Wilhelm, a talented blonde Kappa who later became a corporate defense lawyer and whom he dated, rather showily, all through his senior year. They necked in public; they were said to have taken a hotel room over in Chambersburg after the spring formals. Needless to say, I did not attend the spring formals.

But strangely enough, Lucas's anger gave me sudden acceptance. Any notice from him in that self-contained little world, even negative notice, was a validation. The next autumn, when Lucas was a first-year at Wilkinson Law (the same school his father, a state senator, had gone to), my date was proud of my notoriety. When I lost my virginity to the same law school student a few months later, in an entirely forgettable incident, you could have said that Lucas was indirectly responsible. That law school student would never have looked at me if Lucas hadn't transformed me from a hardworking prude to a villainess with a poison pen.

It's funny, too, how some people live on in your memory far out of proportion to the time or place they occupied in your life. Occasionally in Washington, when I'd meet a nice man or sell an article to some trade journal, Lucas's face would float before me. See, I'd tell him, I showed you, didn't I. His face in my mind was like a candid photo taken during an old love affair: you may not look at it often, yet you know exactly where you keep it.

Two months after I came back to Wilkinson, in early September when the humid summer was finally beginning to ease away, I ran into him at the south end of town, one Saturday afternoon at Dancey's Bar and Grill. At that time, I liked bars in the afternoon: their darkness, the cheap food, the way I was left alone. Friends had canceled on plans to visit that weekend, and I was thinking to myself over a glass of red wine: actually, holding that little conversation with my mother that I carried on in spare moments. I had talked to her every other day when she was alive, not out of daughterly obligation but because I enjoyed talking to her, because she was the most fun person I'd ever met or thought I'd ever meet.

My mother had been my opposite: she lit up a room, she *made* every party she went to. Since she'd gone I hadn't really, for an hour at a time, enjoyed myself without conscientiously striving to enjoy myself as a therapy assignment.

My father had died a long time ago, when I was three; my shrink Dr. Browning back in D.C., had thought perhaps I was mourning them both together. This didn't seem accurate to me. My mother seemed to miss my father very little, and I remembered him not at all. Dr. Browning had insisted that I was really grappling with orphanhood, especially as I had only one sister and we were not close. When I reminded him that I wasn't technically an orphan, he said I was resisting expressing my grief. He spoke of Prozac, which I'd vetoed; he talked from time to time wistfully of the great experiences his other patients had on Zoloft. At our last appointment, he'd given the therapist's equivalent of a discouraged shrug of the shoulders and asked me to call him to set up phone appointments from time to time. I hadn't called yet. My sessions with Dr. Browning had made me sad, and at the end there he was beginning to resent my failure to improve. Therapists are only human, after all. I liked Dr. Browning and wished I could have done better, if only to please him.

I didn't see Lucas until he sat down in the booth opposite me.

"The lady reporter," he said. "I heard you were back."

"No one says, 'lady reporter,' anymore," I said.

"It's only a way to capture that Lois Lane quality you've always had."

"How very good to see you," I said flatly.

He hadn't changed much. His hair was kept shorter, and there were a few faint crow's feet at the corners of his eyes. Every lower middle-class kid knows those crow's feet: they come from squinting at the sun when playing tennis. Lucas had been on the tennis team, of course. Nothing clichéd like basketball or football for him. And he didn't have the height for the one or the bulk for the other.

He wore corduroys and a blue- and black-checked lumberjack shirt. His stomach was still flat. I had hoped for an incipient paunch, or at least a slackening around the jaw.

"So how are you doing?" he said. He made some sign to the bartender, who came over a minute later with a Guinness.

"Can't complain." I really couldn't. I had a cheap apartment, my friends came up from D.C. often, I was beginning to stop having those dreams where my mother came alive and I had to tell her that she was really dead, that she couldn't stay. Sometimes in these dreams she cried, and in other dreams she grew angry.

"I heard you took your father's practice," I said. "You like it?"

"Sure."

"What area of law?"

"Mostly personal injury. Med mal. Some pro bono prisoners' rights stuff. A little of everything I like to do."

Rumor had it that he did get a little of everything. Ray's staff loved to gossip. Since I'd come to town I'd heard Lucas linked romantically with young Mrs. Reggie Brasland, of Brasland Furniture, with Mamie Vest, who ran the Betty Zane Hotel, and with Sylvie LaRousse, who taught French literature at the college. Madame LaRousse was stocky and conventional-looking and had a devoted husband who taught classics. She also smelled of camphor. But the town cheerfully convicted her of all sorts of immoralities, because she was French.

"But I'm not an ambulance chaser," he added.

"I'd never heard you were," I said. "Who doesn't want a lawyer when something happens to them? If a hospital takes off the wrong arm or something."

"You married?" he said casually. I thought he was trying to rub it in my face.

"No," I said. "Escaped the noose so far."

"Then you're not engaged, either?" There was no pity in his tone as far as I could see.

"If I were, what I just said would be kind of strange, wouldn't it?"

"How would I know? You were always a bit of a cynic at school."

I said, "You misjudged me. I was only shy."

He gave me a look that would have translated verbally as "Huh!" There were only two other customers at Dancey's, old men watching some cable sports channel showing highlights of the Steelers' training camp. Their comments made it clear that they weren't fans. Lucas and I were alone in the dark intimacy of a date. It could have been nighttime for all the light that reached inside Dancey's.

"OK, I was an awful person in college," I said. "And now that we've gotten that out of the way, what's up with you? You look good."

I was trying to sound like a middle-aged Rotary Club member running into an old buddy, not like a woman who hadn't had sex in nearly a year and a half.

"Right. I haven't changed a bit, right?"

"No, but you look good."

He grimaced.

"You want another one?" he said. "That looks kind of old."

"Sure."

He brought me another glass of red wine and nursed his Guinness. He told some stories about his practice. I had the feeling that he was being careful, that it mattered to him somehow to find some footing, to pretend we'd shared those college years we'd actually lived so separately. From time to time he'd say, "Remember Ed Canivalli? Well he..." and I'd shake my head, and he would stop telling me what had happened to that person. But I laughed at his story of a battle to save the Methodist church—a Victorian monstrosity complete with red and blue stained glass, from developers who wanted to build a townhome community.

"They had everything on their side," he said. "We didn't have a leg to stand on, but the town council just dragged their feet until they got discouraged and went away. I knew we'd win if we just hung in there."

When he said, "I knew we'd win," I could see the boy who had rushed into my room and said, "I was good. You know I was good." I wondered when he'd become so well defended. Things happen to people, of course, between twenty-one and thirty-one. Some of them aren't very nice things. Those types of things keep on happening, until we get old and finally wear out. If we're lucky.

It was this sort of cheerful thinking that had driven my friends to suggest a change of scene, and driven Dr. Browning to agree with them.

He kept studying me as we talked. He seemed to be calibrating a finely tuned instrument in his head.

"I have to be somewhere now," he said at four o'clock. I assumed he had to get ready for a date. I had a date myself, with a professor at the law school, a prematurely creaky forty-year-old who taught Con Law.

"Thanks for the drink," I said.

"Thanks for catching up," he said, as if we were old friends and not old enemies.

After we parted, I took a long walk up to the foothills above the Cumberland Valley. He'd shaken me up a little. He'd begun to move out of the corner of my eye and into my direct vision, and I didn't like it. People are easier to deal with when you've pigeonholed them as a salutary memory.

As that mild fall became a mild winter, I saw more of Lucas than I'd expected. He never asked to see me. He'd simply appear beside me as I was loitering in front of Woolworth's or coming back to the *Gazette* office from an interview.

Wilkinson was an old town. It went back to the Revolution, when the frontier wasn't that far away and the wars with Native Americans were as crucial as the guerilla war against the Redcoats. I thought I knew the town's history inside out. With Lucas I learned it had other secrets.

"Look here," he said once, when we'd met accidentally outside the college library. He led me to the side wall of the building and put my hands on a series of pockmarks in the old limestone.

"What are these?"

"Bullet holes. College kids in some half-assed duel, a month before Fort Sumter. No one got killed. The guys just joined different armies."

"Did they live out the war?"

"One of them did. I think."

It was Lucas who showed me the photographs from the old Indian School, as it was called. The students looked stiff and uncomfortable in their turn-of-the-century clothes. The men's hair was cut short as convicts' and the women wore snoods and choking high collars. The pictures were kept in a filing cabinet in a back room of the town museum, but Lucas had them brought out for me.

"They all look so careful and ill at ease," I said.

"Well," he said, "There was no place for them to be anymore."

Lucas never asked me home for a drink or a meal, to his parents' old house where he lived by himself and supposedly entertained a parade of willing women. It was one of those yellow stone houses with white trim and a small portico that abounded in that part of Pennsylvania. Once in a while, I knew, his parents sent him cards from Florida to tempt him into moving down there. Palm trees and beaches that looked dirty even in Technicolor.

"As if I didn't know Florida has palm trees," Lucas said once when I met him carrying one of these missives back from the post office, accompanied by a tin of his mother's dreadful oatmeal cookies which he promptly foisted on me. "You spend your whole life in a place and then you move somewhere else because the winters get a little cold for you. I don't get it. Although of course they know a lot of people down there. It's a little replica of Harrisburg, their block in Naples. Same people, same lawn ornaments, same lousy Christmas lights."

There were often women with him when I'd see him strolling around on his lunch hour. Women liked him, there was no gainsaying that. Fluttery Mrs. Klupinski at the stationery store where he ordered his letterhead. Thin restless Ellen Stark who ran the library, where Lucas gave a presentation on tort law and access to the courts once a year. Bonnie Weston who tended bar at Dancey's, who'd gotten so heavy that she had to lean on a high stool with everything in reach. Lucas flirted with all of them in his nonspecific, kind way, and they all adored him.

"Women take to you," I said to him one day, after he got me an interview with the high school principal, who disliked Ray for covering a ninth-grade graffiti gang's antics and making the school look bad, but liked Lucas very much.

He didn't say anything.

"They just *like* you, that's all," I said.

"Not as much as everyone may tell you they do, Kathleen," he said.

He took my cold hand briefly and chafed it between his.

"You should wear gloves sometimes," he said, and let my hand drop.

Did I trust him? No. I had learned that it is a rare man who isn't spoiled completely by the constant attentions of women. But something about him helped right my world for me. His youthful assurance might be gone, but his jeweled blue eyes were never despairing that I could see. He was a friend of my own age in a town filled with the very young and the settled old. And I was glad to take part in his impersonal kindness.

I walked and walked that fall, sometimes with Lucas and sometimes without him. The first healthy color of my life crept into my face. I found I had muscles, and could depend on them to carry me some distance.

I met a few more men: the head of the college journalism department, the *Gazette*'s new sports editor (whom Lucas called a poser), a medical student from Harrisburg with whom I was set up by a D.C. friend. None of them made me feel I'd found a companion, but they gave me a small social routine. I felt more anchored to the world than I had been. My body was stronger, and Ray was blue-penciling my copy less and less. I had reclaimed a tacit friendship from an old feud.

The shrink in Washington would have been pleased, but loneliness sometimes sang high and keen under my rib cage just the same. My mother had always made me feel that I was not alone as other people were, and could never be. She hadn't warned me that her death would leave me wandering in the desert, that I would go through decades and decades of my own life without her. Of course she hadn't warned me—my mother had expected to live forever.

Lucas showed up at my apartment one night the week before Thanksgiving. It was only eight o'clock, but it felt later to me. It was one of those nights when I missed the city, missed small crowded restaurants and the chink of glasses and the knowledge that all around me were people. I wanted to go out in the street and hail a fast-passing cab or walk down the block and drop in on a pub singer. To sit two feet from the sax player in some random club in Adams Morgan. When Lucas knocked, I opened the door without even asking who was there. I figured it was my landlady, who often called upon me with small persnickety reminders.

Cold was still clinging to his sweater. He wore no jacket, and his face was flushed.

"Don't you even ask who it is?" he demanded.

"It's safe enough around here," I said.

"It's not exactly safe."

He came in without being asked. He was humming an old song under his breath, an old Irish song called "The Wild Rover." I'd forgotten how good his voice was, even though I'd praised it in the Wilkinson College production of *Little Mary Sunshine*.

His presence embarrassed me. I hadn't done much to make my apartment a home, or even a comfortable stopping-off point. Ray had insisted on bringing me an old, battered, velveteen sofa he and his wife were throwing out.

"Like what you've done with the place," said Lucas, grinning. "Can I sit down?"

He sat in the middle of the sofa. I sat on an old vinyl armchair with an uncertain spring.

"Do you drink coffee?" I said.

"You know I drink coffee."

I spent a long time making the coffee, and poured it into a small cup so he wouldn't be able to linger. I didn't want Lucas in my apartment. Indoors, he seemed too large and too close. Outdoors, I could keep him in perspective. My skin was prickling the way it does in summer when a large bee is flying around you and it won't go away.

"I thought you'd escaped out the back," he said when I finally emerged from the kitchen. "All this time for just a drop of coffee."

He was smiling. He was on to me.

"I'm not what you call domestic," I said.

Then I saw that his shoes were wet. Soaked through, as if he'd walked across several puddles.

"You can take your shoes off," I said.

I crossed the room and twisted the radiator knob. There was a loud banging and a thin jet of steam.

"I won't stay long," he said. "You could sit down here by me, you know."

"No, thank you."

"Then I'll come stand next to you, how about that?"

When he crossed the room and kissed me, I should have upbraided him with a fine virtue. That's how all the women in the Harlequin romances my mother used to read always behaved, and they all did very well for themselves. But I have no sense of strategy. I kissed him back as if I'd thought of nothing else all that fall.

He said, "I should apologize for complicating your evening this way."

His kiss was eloquent and persuasive.

"It depends on what kind of complication you had in mind."

"We're just kissing," Lucas said.

A sad fact: most men don't know how to kiss, even once you've graduated from college. Lucas knew. He kissed the nape of my neck, my earlobe, my eyelids.

"So this is your secret," I said. "You never rush."

"I don't have a secret," he said. "But it would help a lot if you didn't assume I was playing you for a fool every time I talk to you."

"It's just that I don't have a lot of wear and tear left in me," I said.

He led me to the couch and put his arm around me. We sat there, perfectly still. I saw his hand against the shabby blue velveteen. He looked at me intently, as if he were trying to figure out how to explain the workings of a combustion engine to a Bedouin nomad. It was raining a bit, I could hear it now on the windows. Autumn was over, and winter was coming, and winter forced decisions on the lonely and the sad. I did not want the decisions that come from need or desperation. Before my mother died, I'd always felt I didn't need to make such decisions. Now every day I was afraid that I would fall into them, one way or another.

"Kathleen, I keep running into you on purpose. Didn't you notice that?"

"You run into lots of people over the course of a day."

"I took you all over town. I told you my whole life story. Why do you act as if I'm trying to sneak up on you somehow?"

Life sneaks up on you, I wanted to say. Life sneaks up on you and then, when you're not looking, it clobbers you senseless. People you love run out on you just because your mother died and you couldn't get right back up for a while. You can't count on anything, I wanted to warn him. But maybe he knew that by now. He probably knew that.

"Do you know that I can tell what mood you're in from a distance, just by watching you walk?" he said.

"Bully for you," I said. "You're good at reading women's moods."

He said, "How about this? How about this: knowing you again has come so easy to me."

"You didn't know me the first time."

"I read every word you wrote. It killed me that you thought I was just some shallow pretty boy. I know that's what you called me."

"I can't be a girlfriend of the week," I said.

"I didn't sleep with Ellen Stark," he said. "Or Mrs. Brasland."

I watched him and tried to consider calmly.

"You're weighing me in the balance," he said. "You do that with everyone. You study people."

"Is that so bad?"

"No. I like it. I like your clear eyes."

Then he kissed me again, and stood up. He was playing fair. My old enemy, playing fair.

"Just think about a few things," he said.

He left, and I sank back into the warm place we'd made on the sofa and wondered if it made any sense to consider a single word he'd said.

I avoided him until I realized it was needless. He stayed away. Whatever else he was, he wasn't pushy. He sent me one note, at my work address—not even email. That was how conscientious he was, how determined not to seem intrusive. The note said, "Kathleen, come for a walk with me sometime. When you feel like a walk. Lucas." No seducer's tricks about that.

I wondered what it would be like to sleep with him, to watch him forget himself in passion. I thought about the shape of his hands. I thought of how it felt when I was ambling around in town and he appeared beside me—it felt as if the world had just righted itself on its axis by one scant centimeter that no one could feel but me. It was too much to hope, I told myself, that I did that for him as well. Only in movies did the two shipwrecks washed up on the same island manage to be of use to each other. Real life didn't deal in the mutual benefits of lost souls.

It became early December, still too warm to snow. In that part of the Blue Ridge, snow can hold off until January. Temperate air stays trapped in the valleys between mountain ranges, under low-riding dirty-gray clouds.

I hadn't seen Lucas in three weeks. One morning when I left my apartment, there was a white paper bag in front of my door, a plain white gift bag from a drugstore. Inside it was a pair of dark red leather gloves. On the bag was scrawled in pencil, "Remember to wear these. It's getting cold."

Ray liked my work but he didn't like my moodiness. Friday afternoon two weeks before Christmas he snatched a draft about the history of six popular Christmas carols out of my hands and told me I was through for the day.

"Go shopping," he said. "Or take a ride. Get some fresh air. I don't need any pale fainting flowers around here."

He and his wife had asked me for Christmas dinner, but I was going to my sister's in Annapolis. She and her husband had decided to "try" with me. We each seemed to have concluded that someday, it might be nice to know each other. To have each other. She claimed she was doing fine. I claimed I was thriving on country living. We talked once a week, clumsily. Sometimes it felt as if everything I did was clumsy, as if some essential grace I'd always taken for granted had left my body.

But I'd become a good walker. And when Ray gave me time off I didn't hang around. I pulled on my favorite sweater, which lived at the under-heated *Gazette* office. It was long and heavy as a coat, a deep, true, ripe-dark-apple red. I figured my hair would keep my ears warm. I had left Lucas's gloves in a drawer at home. They seemed too lovely to wear. So I pulled my long sweater sleeves over my wrists and walked out of town without much purpose, taking the Spring Valley Road.

When I was almost out of town proper, it began to rain. I didn't mind at first. The mountains hazed into the softest charcoal blue. The town as I left it had the hush of a house when somewhere in it a baby is sleeping.

By the time I reached the old Quaker meeting place, I was feeling the cold rain against my skin. The old meeting house had been painted white once but was bleached silver now, standing straight and simple against the blue of the mountains. There was a small square cemetery behind it. I stood and read the names: Alice Sulley, beloved wife of Jonathan, mother of Mary, Lucy, Alice, and Thomas. Richard Spenser, dead of a fever at nineteen. And one stone, so old it seemed to be growing slantways out of the ground like a tree trunk, marked only, "Jenny Bright." Maybe she'd been a servant, and no one knew her dates. Maybe everyone knew her, and she'd asked for no epitaph. Maybe she was the kind of person who didn't want any fuss. My mother had not been that kind of person, and so my sister and I had planned the kind of funeral we knew she'd have wanted, a funeral as flower-laden and festive and overwrought as a prom night.

"Mom would have loved this," my sister had said as we carried the empty glasses and ashtrays out of my mother's living room. My sister told me that when her time came, she wanted a cremation, with no service. I told her I'd like the same. Morbid, her husband said.

I tried the door of the meeting house. It was locked. I was a little afraid to look in the windows. The sky was getting darker, and it seemed to me I might see them all there still, sitting silent, waiting for the spirit to move them—wasn't that what Quakers did?

I started back home in the rain. Lucas probably knew who had a key to the place. Maybe some sunny day we could come back here and see inside.

Then the clouds opened and the rain came down in huge drenching drops. Spring Valley Road was in actuality not in a valley here, but in the hills proper, and on higher ground than I'd have preferred in a winter thunderstorm. My sweater got heavier and colder, and my hair dripped. I was wrapped in cold wetness, farther from town than I'd thought. I began to cry, because it didn't matter now if I cried, and my tears came down my face and the rainwater squelched between my toes and under my instep.

Then I saw Lucas, twenty yards away, carrying a big black umbrella. Its spindly stem was ridiculous in his farmer's hand. He was frowning, and the black hair was wet against his face, and he was the most beautiful person I'd ever seen. But for once his beauty didn't intimidate me, since rain evens things out. We both looked like drowned rats.

"Are you crazy?" he said. "Ray didn't tell you about these storms?"

"Ray said I needed color."

"Doesn't he ever look out a window?"

I didn't ask him how he'd found me. It didn't seem important.

He let the umbrella drop down, hanging it off his finger by the handle. Then he folded it up and started swinging it like a cane, catching it behind him from time to time. Showing off for me. I wanted to walk forever in his company. The rain began to peter away. The air was damp on my face.

He took us off on a road that was no bigger than a wide bicycle path. I gave one last look at the meeting house, luminous in the dusk and rain. I had heard that Quakers said, when one was in trouble or afraid, "I will hold thee in the light."

I thought of Lucas's face in the light of the stage all those years ago, and of his face a few days later, angry in my doorway. I watched him, now, and it was a quieter face than it had been, but whatever it had that had held me, it held me still. And his presence held me in the light, even now with the light falling all around us.

"Nothing is easy," I said to him.

"No," he agreed. "But you make too much out of that fact."

I held out my hand. We leaned against a tree and kissed until the lightning cracked open the sky once more.

Later, under three quilts, with my sweater drying on the radiator and Lucas's socks under the bed, I was still afraid. Maybe it is in my nature to be afraid now. Maybe fear will always be one of the burdens in the pack I carry on my journey, from here out. Like those old tinkers and peddlers who used to travel through these mountains, I would have to make my peace with unwieldiness, learn to reconcile myself to the dinged spoon or soiled ribbon that I'd never sell and never throw away.

And I was right to be afraid. But Lucas was more right to carry an umbrella after me in a winter storm, and to kiss me under a tree, even on high ground with lightning striking.

Lapsing into sleep, I said to him, "In some ways, you are my last chance."

"There's no such thing," he said—believing that, or pretending to—and kissed the top of my still-damp head as if I were a child.

Kate Blackwell

The Secret Life of Peonies

KATE BLACKWELL moved to Washington, D.C., from North Carolina thirty years ago. A former journalist, she now writes fiction full time and leads writing workshops at the Writer's Center in Bethesda, Maryland. Her short stories have appeared in literary journals and won a number of fiction awards. A collection of her stories, *My First Wedding*, will be published in 2007.

Alexandra arranges six pink shrimp on a white plate, adds a sprig of cilantro, a handful of lemony arugula, a single cherry tomato. Tommy smiles up at her as she sets the plate in front of him. His face is pink, like the shrimp; his hair a coppery red. Then: *clank*, Saturday's mail shoots through the mail slot in the hall. Tommy shoves back his chair with a shriek of wood on tile.

"Where are you going? We're having lunch," Alexandra says.

"Just getting the mail, sweetheart."

Alexandra tenses. She grew up in a home where you did not leave the table until the meal was over, no matter what happened. The ceiling could collapse and Alexandra and her parents would still sit in their reproduction Queen Anne chairs eating fricasseed chicken and plaster. Nor did you read your mail during a meal. Tommy, despite that Princeton degree, was not brought up with these rules.

She arranges her own plate and carries it to the table, sits down, takes a sip of cool yellow wine. The kitchen in this midday light could be a photograph in a magazine. Sunlight warms the Mexican tiles, brings out their rich caramel tones, while silvering the pale wood grain of the table, the granite counter tops. She sees herself in the photograph, a slim woman in white capri pants, face half-hidden because she is looking down. She looks up. She would never allow her house to be photographed for a magazine. They are private people. Still. She looks down at the white plate, the shrimp in their forest of green, that single sphere of red.

Tommy returns, his face now a mottled crimson. He is holding a sheet of paper. A tiny quiver, like sex, forces its way through Alexandra's abdomen. Something has happened. The investment company, she knows, is downsizing; even managers are getting pink slips, though it's unthinkable that Tommy would. He is responsible for huge portfolios; his clients adore him. Anyway, those things don't come in the mail, do they? Maybe it's another wheedling letter from his sister trying to get them to spend a week that summer in her un-air-conditioned house in the Poconos. Something tells Alexandra the letter is not from his sister. Or the company.

She reaches out and takes it, white copy paper, the shiny kind she doubts a financial institution would stock. Ordinary people buy it in bulk at Staples. She reads the single sentence slowly as though she is parsing a foreign language: *You may be interested to know your wife is having an affair with...* A cloud drifts over the man's name. She blinks. Her vision clears. Tommy is looking at her, hunching his shoulders as though he's waiting for a ball to slice toward him over the net, waiting to slice it back.

"Who could have written this garbage?" she says. And sees him straighten. He has recognized her voice: cool, deliberate, very effective with potential donors at the museum. She crumples the paper and throws it on the floor. "What twisted mind—?," then watches as he bends and picks up the letter.

"Tommy, you cannot believe this craziness."

Her voice is less cool now, though not panicked, more the concerned tone a mother might use to calm a child. You aren't afraid of the dark, darling. There's nothing to be afraid of. Why, nothing's *there.*

"No," he says and smooths the paper between his hands. "But we shouldn't ruin the evidence."

"Evidence of what? We should burn this!"

"The guy exists, I presume."

"Mead Latourette?" She forces herself to say the name that has been typed at the end of the sentence. "He owns a gallery. He's on one of our committees. I *know* him—"

She looks down. The light has shifted, leaving the expensive tiles darkly muddy. After all, they *are* mud. She gets up and walks out of the room.

She sits on the terrace holding a cup of coffee. Tommy has gone off to his tennis game—they agreed he should go; the letter is an obscene joke by some loony, they will forget it: this decided after she returned to the kitchen in tears, after he held and soothed her, after they finished the by then slightly too-warm lunch wine. Nausea stirs Alexandra's stomach, where the wine now lies. She clenches her teeth and stares at her roses—pink Queen Elizabeths, red Princess Graces, a peach-tone Cary Grant—and the mixed beds of white and gold daisies, blue cornflowers, lilies in all hues. Women in her family have always been avid gardeners. Alexandra spends hours on weekends taking care of her flowers, while Tommy is busy with tennis, squash, handball, you name it.

Clustered next to the terrace are her favorites, the peonies—she could touch one of the droopy leaves with her foot if she wanted to—their buds swollen fat, waiting for the hot May sun to burst them open. Right now, each bud is swarming with ants, which play some mysterious role in the life of peonies. She read somewhere that the flowers produce a sugary nectar ants like, but what do the peonies get in return? Do those busy black insects enhance the peonies' beauty? Or are they just selfish sybarites? Alexandra believes they help. One year, she carefully dusted all the ants off and the buds stayed closed tight as fists and never bloomed.

She puts the peonies out of her mind and tries to focus on the vicious letter, but her mind is closed tight, like the buds, while in those teeming regions of her inner self, she feels panic, fear, a touch of hysteria. Stay calm, she tells herself. It will be all right. She sets her cup down, cold coffee sloshing into the saucer, anger replacing fear. (She thinks she knows who wrote the letter—the little slut!) They will get through this. There will be a period of tension, a few bad days. Naturally, Tommy feels outraged. He believes the letter writer is someone he knows—the writer used his full name on the envelope: Thomas E. Parrish. She forbore from pointing out that this name is in the phone book.

She remembers Tommy's long white legs in his white tennis shorts as he paced over the Mexican tiles, his porcelain skin sprinkled with pale orange freckles and fine red hairs, so unlike Mead Latourette's smooth beige skin and sturdy limbs. She shivers in the sun. She needs to lie down in her darkened bedroom with a damp cloth on her forehead. She stares at the peony bud near her foot, its skin of moving ants. The lunch wine begins to rise. She leaps up and rushes into the house.

Mead Latourette is an inch or two shorter than Alexandra. His dark hair falls to his collar, his fringe of beard gives his round face a slightly sinister look, ironically, since Mead is the most genial of men. He comes from Alabama, of Cajun descent, and speaks with a laconic cadence which, the first time she heard it, on the terrace of the Washington Hilton, made her whoop with laughter. *You look like somebody I def'nitely ought to know.* She likes to repeat the remark, to tease him. He likes to repeat her whoop. Alexandra, at thirty-eight, tall and coltish, with long auburn hair and a small delicate face (a Filippo Lippi virgin's, Mead says), doesn't look like a woman who makes loud sounds. And she doesn't, often. On the hotel terrace—pre-lunch drinks at a seminar on art bequests—he circled back with two glasses of wine. "For the cool lady with the hot laugh," he said, handing her one. "What say we play hooky?" The invitation, she is still convinced, surprised him, too.

Now Mead says in an appalled whisper on the phone, "Run that by me again, cherie."

Alexandra does, in a flat voice as though she were reading his horoscope: *You may be interested to know—*

"Who the devil—?"

"I thought you might—"

"If I knew I'd kill him."

"Or her," Alexandra says. (Surely he can guess the culprit.)

"Or her," he amends. "How is Tom taking this?"

"I told him it was garbage. He's all right."

Though Tommy is not all right. He lost badly at tennis on Saturday and got sloppy drunk at dinner that night—dinner she did not eat because of the stomachache that came with the lunch wine. On Sunday they hardly spoke. Today is Monday, the first chance she has had to call Mead, safely, from her office at the museum (door tightly shut) to his at his gallery, the Obelisk.

"I take it that you—that Franny—didn't get a letter."

Franny is Mead's wife, a compact blonde with muscular legs. Alexandra has seen her at receptions at the Obelisk. They've even chatted. Franny is an amateur cellist, a health fanatic, also a devoted mother to their two daughters, aged fourteen and eleven. Mead refers to all three as "my girls." "I live a desperately domestic life, cherie," he likes to assure Alexandra. When he's not hobnobbing with artists, she likes to tease, wheeling and dealing in Georgetown and Adams Morgan, coddling and cajoling over Moët and Coors. To her teasing, Mead spreads his hands, those smooth ash-colored fingers, as his eyebrows peak like tents. "Gotta make a living, baby lamb."

The surprising fact, to her, is that she and Mead spend so much of their time together talking about their "other" lives, their spouses, their houses, their weekends. He describes his daughters' soccer games, family bowling trips, his clipping of a very unruly hedge. At the neighborhood barbecues Franny likes to throw, Mead presides over a gas grill. In an apron? Yes, of course, in an apron. "My Cajun chicken is to die for," he brags. "You should try Tommy's swordfish with herbs," Alexandra can't resist replying.

She tells Mead about Tommy's tennis matches—she fell in love watching him play for Princeton, those long legs, that determined jaw, the quick grin in her direction when he won a set. There was a time when she envisioned a life on the circuit, herself in the stands wearing a fabulous hat and sunglasses. Investment banking, however, has its compensations, her new kitchen tiles for one. Also, the sailing they used to do until she made Tommy sell the boat. She couldn't stand the tiny bunks, the constant demands for care that were worse than a child's. "But now you feel guilty," Mead suggests wisely. "Yes," she confesses.

There is also the matter of the real children she and Tommy have decided not to have. "And why do you think you don't want them?"

Mead is concerned. He wouldn't want to be the cause for such a decision. But he has nothing to do with it. It's because she has too many selfish desires: her garden, her house, her job. Her own mother used to tell her she was selfish. *You think of nobody but yourself, Alexandra*—When she came in after curfew, making her father ill from worry; when she refused to continue piano lessons, breaking her mother's heart. Well, all right, she is selfish. She doesn't *want* children. Tommy did at first but now he agrees with her. They are happy as things are. "Then why do you look so sad, cherie?" She begins to cry. Of course, she can never be *sure*. Mead holds her while she sobs. These are the moments she cherishes, not just the sex. If it were just the sex, it would have been over by now. Surely.

They agree that Tommy and Franny will never be hurt by the single hour of pleasure and companionship they enjoy every week—sometimes, actually, more than an hour (lately, closer to two, even three hours, once an entire incredible afternoon), because they will never know. No one will.

Though it appears someone does.

Mead takes a deep breath. "No letter at our house."

"We need to talk."

"Ahhhhh, sweetheart. We're leaving tomorrow for the Gulf."

"I remember," she says coldly. Mead and his girls are going on vacation, somewhere south, near water. They will be away a week.

The pause lengthens. Finally, Mead says in a different voice, "You're right, cherie. Noon at the deli?"

The Lebanese deli off Dupont Circle is where they went that first time they played hooky and stayed for hours, leaning toward each other over little dishes of garlicky hummus and cucumbers and glasses of minty tea, exchanging opinions so thrillingly in sync about Rauschenberg's mixed messages, Frankenthaler's genius, Schnabel's triviality. Afterward, they walked along tree-shaded streets lined with townhouses set in immaculate gardens of impatiens and box, one of which housed the Obelisk, where Mead's assistant, Paige, was holding the fort. He referred to her as "the child," though Alexandra, who has seen Paige many times since, suspects "the child" is closing in on thirty. She has had her suspicions about Paige ever since that first day, when Mead took such pains to avoid walking past the gallery. On another street, he drew Alexandra into the shadow of a holly tree and kissed her so deeply she had to pull away, finally, to breathe.

They still meet at the deli occasionally, in memory of that first time, two years ago. *Two years*, Alexandra marvels.

"Not at the deli," she says now. "At Didier's."

"Ahhhhh, sweetheart—"

Quickly, before he can say more, she hangs up.

All Alexandra knows about Mead's friend Didier is that he is never home for lunch. His apartment is furnished like a hotel suite with white furniture, beige carpets, a huge mirror over the dresser. On the tables are French periodicals, on the walls pale prints of orchids. The single blast of color comes from the plum-colored sheets on the king-sized bed. In this bed, among these purple sheets, they have just made swift sweaty love and now lie entwined, Mead's thick brown legs stretched across Alexandra's slim white ones. She is turned on her side, one arm slung over his chest, her head on his pillowy shoulder. She loves Mead naked. Clothed, he has a professorial air, but in bed he turns boyish. Often he vaults onto the mattress, bouncing with high glee.

The first time she saw him do this, she blurted, "You really like this, don't you?"

"Oh I *do*. I like *you* so much."

Before Mead, Alexandra viewed sex as a matter of high seriousness—akin to going to church, she has realized, with some amusement. The only child of strict Presbyterians, her father a doctor, her mother a housewife whose career was raising a perfect daughter, Alexandra is surprised she isn't frigid. She probably would be if she had not discovered, when she was sixteen, squeezed into the backseat of a smelly Ford with a sweet boy who adored her, that sex was where a perfect daughter could be like anybody else without anyone seeing her—except the boy, of course.

But lovemaking with Mead is so non-serious, so richly antic, so profoundly enjoyable, she feels—has felt from the beginning—there can be nothing dangerous here, nothing hurtful, nothing *wrong*. It's not an affair they are having—Alexandra dislikes the word: it sounds cheap, self-indulgent, *tabloid*; they are having something else, something she admittedly has no word for but would, if asked, describe as healthy, human, even, obscurely, *right*. Now she sniffs the familiar nutty aroma of his skin and traces with her finger the fierce curve of a rib. What would she do without him? This hateful letter cannot mean they will have to stop seeing each other.

"You've been through hell, haven't you?" he says.

"You mean I look like hell?" She withdraws her hand.

"You look beautiful. You *are* beautiful." He is gazing at her sideways, his lips puckered thoughtfully. "Who do you think is onto us?"

"Nobody," she says. "They can't be."

"Haven't you told anyone? A friend?"

"Who would I tell? All my friends are jealous of me as it is."

Mead's eyebrows rise, but it's true; the women she knows are always remarking on her lovely house, her sweet husband, her interesting job. Only the tragedy of no children, as she knows her friends think of it, redeems her in their eyes.

"Really," she says. "I haven't told anyone."

"How about the museum? Anybody mention your long lunches?"

"My director assumes I'm out wooing big bucks. My secretary's grateful for the extra time on the phone with her boyfriend."

She pauses in exasperation. Does he really *not* know who wrote the letter?

"What about one of your old loves?" she says. "What about that artist woman Franny found out about?"

"That was ten years ago. I don't even know where she lives now. Besides, she wouldn't."

"Well, is there any—?"

"As I have told you many times, cherie, whether you believe it or not, I am a monogamist."

"Monogamy" is an odd choice of words, but Alexandra knows what he means. She is not jealous of Franny, but if Mead were making love to another woman not his wife, *that* would be unbearable.

She suspects Mead had a fairly active sex life before he married Franny—someone of his huge attractiveness, his great appreciation of sex, must have had. He has admitted to only one liaison after marriage, an artist, older than he (so is Alexandra, by a year), a talented woman, not terribly successful professionally, but very sensually alive, very—If Alexandra were jealous of anyone, it would be this woman. But it ended disastrously. Franny found out through a careless phone call and all hell broke loose. Her milk dried up—their second daughter was nursing—and their older daughter, then four, woke crying in the night for months. Franny cried. The baby cried. Mead cried. It was a terrible time that showed him how important his family was to him, how he can't bear to hurt them again, which Alexandra understands. She would not want to hurt Tommy either. Still. She thinks of ants and peonies and an almost imperceptible shiver glides over her skin. There is a lesson there if she only knew what it was.

"Could Franny have found out?" she asks now.

"Trust me," Mead says. "I would def'nitely know."

He shifts to his side. Alexandra stretches out on her back. He lifts a strand of her hair and examines it, twisting it carefully around his finger.

"Maybe we should take a small break," he says.

Her breathing slows, fog envelops her brain.

"A break?" she whispers.

"To be on the safe side."

The safe side? What side is that? The side of her next to him feels hot as though he is an electric heater, the kind you buy for those awful little uninsulated houses, the kind that blows up and incinerates you. *Safe?*

"We'll be back a week from Thursday," he says. "I'll call. We'll talk."

She refuses to look at him or to speak.

"Alexandra," he says. "Ahhhh, sweetheart—" Then he rolls away from her over the purple sheets, taking all the heat with him.

That night, Alexandra and Tommy sit at their kitchen table with the letter between them, making a list of possible letter writers. They examine the paper, its size and shape, its flimsiness. It was written on a PC, printed on a DeskJet, not very professionally. Courier font—who uses Courier these days? A woman must have written it, Tommy declares. Alexandra says nothing. She is feeling ill again. Her digestion has not returned to normal since the letter. On the other hand, Tommy says, the language is more like a man's, brief, to the point. She shrugs. Her throat fills. She rushes off to the bathroom. How degrading, she thinks, as she kneels by the toilet. Can this crouching, spewing woman be *she*? She curls up on the floor and closes her eyes.

The next day, she walks past the Obelisk, turns, walks past again. The door is open and Paige flits by, twitching her hips, holding a cigarette in one hand. The "child" is not beautiful, too thin, too pop-eyed, but adoration can be a kind of aphrodisiac and, clearly, Paige adores Mead. Alexandra has watched her at openings, in her dead-black blouse and stamp-sized skirt, circling him like a moth. Paige has the second sight of the besotted. Otherwise, how to account for her childish behavior toward Alexandra, the phone messages for Mead not delivered, the scalding stares when Alexandra and Mead exchange private words at a reception, the wine spilled on Alexandra's shoes a few weeks ago as Paige rushed by. *Oh Mrs. Parrish, I'm so-o-o sorry.* Of course she wrote the letter.

Paige appears again and flicks the cigarette out into the yard. Is it the cigarette that does it? The careless littering? Driven by a rage she never knew she possessed, Alexandra crosses the street and enters the gallery. Paige has arranged herself on a chair in front of a huge painting of a male nude in lumpy red pastiche and is pretending to study a catalogue. Alexandra stations herself before a blue version of the same male.

Finally, there is the squeak of a chair and a shrill, "Oh Mrs. Parrish! Is there something—?"

Alexandra whirls. "Yes?"

"He's not here. He's out of town." Paige sounds terrified. "He's— May I help you?"

Guilt stains her foolish face. Alexandra wants to strike her, to immolate her. She says briskly, "I must have mistaken the day. Tell me, do you have a computer here?"

"No. I mean, it's not working."

"Ah." She stares coolly at Paige. "But you still do letters."

Paige's mouth opens, but Alexandra is already walking out. As she crosses the street, she looks back in time to see "the child" close the gallery door, turning and slamming it shut with her little rump.

That night, again, she and Tommy sit in their kitchen and go over the letter, its texture and tone, the extra spaces between words seen as somehow significant. Tommy is again convinced the perpetrator is a woman. A jealous woman friend of Alexandra's. Or no, more likely a gal at the investment company, someone he's pissed off without realizing it. He mentions a Julie in REITs, a Sharon in corporate bonds, neither of whom could possibly know Mead Latourette. But Tommy appears to have forgotten Mead entirely.

So it's a shock when he says, as he spears a tomato, "Babe, tell me about this Latourette. What's he like?"

The piece of steak she's chewing turns to leather. "Mead?"

Tommy nods encouragingly. "What's the fellow like? You said you know him."

"Oh." She tries to think what Mead is like. "His gallery's so-so successful. He does American Expressionism. It's not all that *in* right now."

"Married?"

"I think so. Yes. I met his wife at a gallery opening once. That was, gosh, two years ago."

Tommy looks at her. She feels her face redden. Her father used to look at her like that. *Alexandra, are you telling me the truth? You did not leave the dance before it ended? You came straight home?* It strikes her that this is not the first time Tommy has reminded her of her father. They finish the meal in silence.

She is sitting at her desk when Mead calls. "All tanned and fat from beignets?" she says in her cool museum voice. He doesn't answer. He asks if she can meet him at the deli, early, so they will have the place to themselves. Of course she can. Eleven-thirty is perfect, cheri.

He is sitting at a table by a window. Though he's been gone only a week, his black hair is longer than she remembers, his skin a richer olive.

She stands for a minute watching his fingers play with a plastic spoon. She crosses the room and sits down opposite him. His hands immediately fold over hers, so hot they scald. She jumps and he takes his hands away.

He says, "What can I get you, my love?"

His Alabama accent is softer, thicker than she remembers. Alexandra feels the prick of a tiny knife near her heart. What will she do if she loses him? While he's getting the coffee, she looks out at the street. Water from an early morning rain lies in pools on the pavement and a soft mist rises from them, giving the street a strange abstract beauty, all varying tones of gray except for a splash of pink where the water reflects a neon sign.

When he sets the cup down in front of her, he touches her shoulder. "It's so *good* to see you."

She nods. He sits, picks up his spoon.

"Tell me, how is Tom?"

"It's taken a toll."

He looks out at the street. "If I'd known this would happen—" he begins, then stops.

"If you'd known, then what?"

"Nothing. I don't know."

She leans across the table toward him. "In a moment of lunacy, I actually wondered if you wrote that letter."

"Good god, Alexandra. Good god," he repeats, as though they are the only words he knows.

"Don't worry. I know it wasn't you."

"You know—?"

"Paige," she says.

"That child? She's my slave."

"Your *what?*"

"I mean she does what I tell her. Paige isn't too swift."

"Paige," Alexandra says, slowly, distinctly, "is in love with you."

"Ahhhh, Alexandra—"

"I've watched her at openings. I've seen the way she looks at you. I know."

"You've got it wrong," Mead says and scowls.

They are quarreling. It's their first time. It is horrible—also thrilling. They sit without speaking. Finally, he says, "Alexandra, I'm afraid—"

He fiddles with the spoon.

She feels a cold mist falling, sinking into every pore.

"Fine," she says. "Go."

He stands up. It seems to her that his face is gray now, like the street. He comes and bends and kisses her cheek. Then he leaves. Through the window she watches him walk away, splashing through the sidewalk puddles. Halfway to the corner, he stops, stares down at his wet shoes and slowly shakes his head, as though reproving his feet for taking him through water.

The next day, she stays at her office until six, then phones the Obelisk. "Mr. Latourette has left for the day," Paige simpers, pretending not to recognize Alexandra. "Is there a message?"

Alexandra replaces the receiver, picks it up again.

"Hello?" Franny says. In the background, one of the daughters is playing the piano. Alexandra recognizes a scale exercise she used to hate.

"Hello? Hello? Who is this?"

Who indeed? A person who makes hang-up calls.

Mead doesn't phone the next week, or the next. It's been a month since the letter clanked into their hall. Meanwhile, she and Tommy have returned to a more or less normal life. They no longer talk about the letter. She doesn't know where the letter is. Tommy must have put it away: *saving the evidence*. Thus, she is completely unprepared when he announces one night as they are eating herbed chicken he has perfectly grilled, "I'm gonna call the fellow."

"Call—?"

"Latourette. Why shouldn't he know about the damned letter, after all we've been through?"

"He does know. I called him." She says this coolly, the words slipping from her mouth as though by magic, like pieces of silver.

"Oh?" A wide-eyed look of surprise, followed by a deep frown of suspicion. "When?"

"A week or so after the letter came. We didn't talk long. There wasn't much to say. He sounded completely shocked."

"That's all he was? Shocked?"

"The point is he obviously knew nothing about it."

"Why didn't you tell me you'd talked to him?"

"Because I'd found out nothing. Tommy," she's suddenly shouting, "*I am not having an affair with Mead Latourette.* Do you want me to put it in writing? Have it notarized?"

He gets up and comes and puts his arms around her. "Don't you want to know who wrote the thing?" he asks, an un-Tommy-like note of doubt creeping into his voice.

She hesitates. Some wayward impulse whispers that she should tell Tommy the truth. Then he will divorce her and she will be alone. Solitude is what she yearns for now.

"OK. I'll clean up," Tommy says and gives her shoulder a little pat, not quite as gentle as it might have been. "Why don't you go out in the garden before it gets dark?"

She stands among her flowers, breathing deeply. The peonies are in full bloom, except for a few buds that haven't opened yet, that are still encrusted with ants. She bends and takes one of the buds in her hand. She wonders what Mead is doing now. Putting his daughters to bed? Helping Franny wash up from dinner? She is not jealous, just miserable. And how unfair that she and Tommy have borne the brunt of all this, that Paige has gone unpunished. What if Franny received a letter, not a vicious one, just a note. *You may be interested to know*— Alexandra feels a pleasurable tingle in her chest. She will mail the letter tomorrow. In a few days, Mead will call to tell her the awful thing that Paige has done. *Again.* She will soothe him. She's been through this, after all. Surely he will call. She looks down and sees that she has brushed all the ants off the peony bud. Now it is clean and virginal and will never bloom.

Mead does not call. The peonies fade, shedding their petals like snow. The roses and lilies have their flagrant season, turn yellow, and die. It is September when Tommy vaults into their kitchen wielding an enormous bunch of cellophane-wrapped tulips, red, purple, white, dozens of tulips, which must have cost the earth; it is not tulip season.

"I've been an asshole," he declares.

She smiles faintly, puts the flowers in the sink, goes to the refrigerator, and takes out a bottle of a good Sancerre, opens the wine, pours.

"Cheers," she says, handing him his glass.

Tommy says, "Let's take this out on the deck."

Her neck prickles. She has told him a thousand times it's not a deck, it's a terrace. But she just turns and goes out.

They sit side by side in wrought-iron chairs.

"You have every right to divorce me," he begins.

She starts at the word *divorce.*

"I went for the whole shit-bag. I couldn't get that letter out of my mind. I started remembering times you'd said you were too tired and I thought, oh hell, you must have been with that guy."

She sighs, drinks. So he did believe the letter. She should have confessed in the beginning, when the letter first came. They would be separated by now. She would be living in an apartment (she envisions one of those new condos near the museum), eating supper by herself, reading a novel at the table while she eats. Oh bliss.

"This gets weird," he says. "I'd look out the window and see you in the garden and imagine you were thinking about this guy. I'd say, 'You're fucking him, aren't you, babe?' I'd say it out loud, real ugly."

He slides off his chair and kneels and lays his head on her lap. She looks down at his pale red hair, as fine as a baby's, so unlike Mead's coarse dark curls.

"There's more. Jesus, how can I tell you this? I met this woman at the club."

"Met who?" she asks.

"She works in the pro shop." His voice sounds congested with misery. "We had a kind of thing this summer. Beers and laughs. OK, some fooling around."

She stares at a coppery curl near his ear. Probably she should be angry, but instead, she feels nothing, just a little relief. Tommy goes on talking.

He's behaved like an idiot. He'll never cheat on her again. But Alexandra is barely listening. She is imagining a scene, the way she's been doing often lately, several times a day in fact, in which she and Mead are walking, hand in hand, in a part of the city she doesn't know. Yellow leaves drift across the sidewalk. She imagines saying to Mead, *You won't believe what Tommy's been up to.*

Tommy is still talking. The letter's history as far as he's concerned. He doesn't give a damn who wrote it, though he's pretty sure it was somebody who got the shaft at the company. They're lucky the s.o.b. didn't storm the office with a loaded gun. *We're getting along better*, she imagines telling Mead. *We're looking for a new boat.*

"Can you forgive me?" Tommy's arms are looped around her waist, his head is raised hopefully.

Alexandra gazes over Tommy's head at the garden, which is messy, almost ugly. Another scene forces its way into her mind: Mead in his kitchen staring white-faced at the piece of paper he holds. *You may be interested to know that your husband is having an affair*— Franny is sobbing, her hands covering her face. The little girls run in and they, too, begin to cry. Mead opens his fingers and lets the paper fall, shiny paper bought at Staples. Alexandra still has the rest of the pack on her desk.

She looks down at her husband, remembering what he has confessed, what he has promised. She believes he is sincere, though it will not surprise her if later he resumes the affair with the girl in the pro shop, or some other girl, and spends more time at the club with his men friends. Theirs will be that kind of marriage now.

All this is your own fault. You are selfish, Alexandra. It is her mother's voice coming from somewhere near the peonies. She hates those flowers now. She will dig them up, get rid of them. How could she have loved them so? How could she?

Hildie S. Block

Snakes

HILDIE S. BLOCK has a master's in writing from Johns Hopkins and lives in Arlington, Virginia. She has taught writing at American and George Washington Universities and leads fiction workshops for the Writer's Center, one of the country's premier independent literary centers. She has over fifty short stories in print including ones that have appeared or are upcoming in *Gargoyle*, *Cortland Review*, *San Francisco Review*, *Literary Mama*, *Motherverse*, *The First Line*, *E2K*, *Strata*, and *bee*. An anthology she co-edited, *Not What I Expected: The Road from Womanhood to Motherhood*, will be published by Paycock Press in fall 2006. Her essays have appeared in *In the Fray*, *Pop Matters*, *Organic Family*, and elsewhere.

The only night I doubted that Claire and Claudia were "just friends" was the second night the snake got out.

The first night the snake got out I was the only person home. Something I think had never happened before, or since. If any of the four others had been home, I think I would have been OK. But I was alone. The lights were all out. It was eerie. The rooms echoed with laughter and post-inhale coughs. It seemed so hollow. After work, I hit my room, changed clothes, and went back into the common areas. Everything was there, just quiet and shadowed.

I headed into the kitchen to do my long overdue pile of dirty dishes. I flicked on the dining room light, then the kitchen light.

Which was when I saw it slither as only a four-foot Ball Python can, across cracking brick-red asbestos tile. It was a ribbon of curves moving gracefully toward the fridge. I phoned Min, who had an iguana as a kid, hoping to be goaded, embarrassed into, you know, picking the damn thing up and putting it away.

I wasn't, after all, "afraid" of snakes. It was a pet. I had held it. Petted it, I guess. Watched it feed. Helped name it, "Sir Pent" (though we were never sure if it was a he or she snake). All that was on my own terms. I didn't mind it slithering around in its glass aquarium on the bookshelf.

Min was no help. We began the descent into hysteria. We were the woman from the Tom and Jerry cartoons who you see from the ankles down jumping on the table.

Eeek! A four-foot snake!

The phone beeped. Thank God for call waiting. It was Claire's soon-to-be ex-husband, a.k.a. the snake's owner. Thank God.

He was in Seattle. That's no help. You can't ask someone to race home three thousand miles on their Kawasaki because you can't pick up a snake.

"Come home. Now." Maybe you can ask. Can't hurt to try.

"You know I can't. I think I'm going to stay on in Olympia."

Hey, I thought he was in Seattle.

"I thought you were in Seattle."

"No, I'm in Olympia. It's near Seattle. You know, Nirvana? Garage bands? Listen, just pick up the snake and put him away."

"OK." I bit my lip and concentrated. I grabbed it by the tail and pulled. Its head was already mostly in, uh, under the fridge. I didn't want to hurt it. Hell, I didn't want to touch it.

"It's under the fridge."

"Oh, he likes it there. It's warm. By the way, do you know anyone who might want him? I seriously might stay out here with Amy."

"It's all the way under the fridge now." I could hear a fan or something hitting it. I winced. Who the hell is Amy?

"He'll come out when he's ready." Duh.

"Now what do I do?"

"Whatever you were going to do before."

"I'm not sure what that was."

"Well, figure it out. Tell Claire I called. Talk to you later."

What I did do was collect the cats, all four of them, and put them in my room. I wasn't sure what a four-foot snake would want for a snack once he finished with the fridge.

I scotch-taped a note on the outside of the front door, "4 ft. snake at large in house. Last seen under fridge. Enter at your own risk. P.S. Cats in my room."

After midnight and after several beers, Rip, returning from shooting pool at Babe's, a grungy former-movie-theater pool hall, found her behind the stove wrapped around the 220-volt cord. After wrestling her loose and putting her to bed, he agreed to take over snake duty while her owner stayed behind somewhere in the Pacific Northwest with some woman named Amy.

That was the first time it got out.

The second time the snake got out, Claire had invited Claudia over. Claire was romantically interested in Claudia, who was already dating someone. Well, not just someone. Claire's most recent ex, Susan, the rugby player. Well, OK. But Claire and Claudia were friends, so who's to say that it's not OK for a friend to come over for lentil pilaf and stay to watch a movie. Even a movie called *Desert Rose.*

I watched the first fifteen minutes of the film with them. I'd seen it a lot because it's the lesbian version of *9½ Weeks*, and it seems like the lesbians I've lived with date a lot. After the first few minutes, I realized it was getting late and I wasn't interested in the film and I didn't want to be a chaperone. So I went to bed.

When I went to sleep it was around eleven, eleven-thirty. When I woke up it was around three. I woke up because Claire and Claudia were in my room and the lights were on. They were looking for something. I think I woke up when Claire lifted my blankets to look in the bed. The bed I was sleeping in. Now it wasn't much of a bed, actually, just a futon on the floor and I slept under a jumble of blankets, but wait a minute…

"What are you guys looking for?"

"Just go back to sleep."

For a second, I considered this a real option. It was, after all, three a.m. I had work in the morning. But there were two lesbians dismantling my room, the lights were on, and I think curiosity got the best of me.

"No, really, what are you guys looking for?"

"You have to promise not to get mad." Claire was firm.

"I think I might be getting mad already."

"OK. OK. We lost the snake. We lost Sir Pent." Claire blew that stripe of blue hair out of her face. One night, I'm going to sneak into *her* room when she's sleeping and cut that thing off. Then she'll have to promise not to get mad.

"We took him out to play and fell asleep and I don't know where he went." I squinted at Claudia as she said this.

"Well, it's not in here."

"Well, we think he is." Oh great. The best part about waking up in the middle of the night to find out there might be a snake in your room, is not finding it.

They didn't find it. Not that night, or the next day. Needless to say, I didn't get a lot of sleep. Every time a strand of hair or a bit of sheet got wrapped around my neck, I woke up.

And when I woke up, I wondered how you fall asleep playing with a snake and all I can see is a nude poster of Nastassja Kinski. You know the one, the one with the snake. So I wondered. Not that it was any of my business.

Rip, the new snake caretaker, found her in my closet two days after she went missing. We all thought it might be in there. Because the cats, if put in front of the open closet door, would leap horizontally, laterally, to get away from the closet. As if there were magnets on the floor and they were polarized.

I came home from work to find Rip on his hands and knees looking in the back of my closet, with only his butt sticking out. My cat, Java, sat patiently by, watching.

Of course, Rip found it. Coiled up in the back of the closet.

"Must be warm in there," was all he said.

Lisa Boylan

Sam Flute

Lisa Boylan has published stories in several journals, including *Gargoyle*, *Chattahoochee Review*, *Main Street Rag*, and *Pangolin Papers*. Her story "Jupiter's Battered Moons" was nominated for a Pushcart Prize. She is a native of Washington, D.C., and lives just outside the city, in Silver Spring, with her husband and three children, Dylan, Liam, and Clare. Her website is http://zeldafitz@blogspot.com.

I work in the underworld of Georgetown University for the Director of Landscaping. I am the invisible woman. I didn't know what to wear my first day, so I wore a blue cowl-neck blouse and a pink silk skirt. I wasn't invisible that day. My mother said, "Dress professionally and the rest will follow!" There's nothing to do for the Director of Landscaping except take calls from his friendly wife and write them neatly on yellow message pads. I am a silk-wearing anomaly from the world of light that exists above this John Deere cage.

I sit in a room with an accountant and a tall pimply work-study kid with a lurking smile. He looks as though he has a stash of explosives in his parents' basement. He and the accountant snicker about me as I sit at the computer and type non sequiturs and take messages. When the accountant speaks, I try to decipher his subtext. I am good at that. It is not like gutting a fish, it is more like filleting it. You have to peel back the flesh of the statement and leave the spindly bones intact so you can remove them. The bones are paranoia. It is better to remove them whole so the fillet lies pure before you.

One day, while working at the university, I got a summons from an illicit shirtless past. A boy with a certain stance and a generous warm smile that indulged. This boy's eyes took in the moment and he bestowed his smile, thoughtfully, on the people he observed. He made allowances, when he liked what he saw. He wrote me out of nowhere, with perfect comma placement, so I drove to the beach to think it over. On the way, the grass was as silent and wheat colored as when he and I had driven down. There was something intrinsically salted, marshy, primal—like an unintended waterway—about our relationship. A little Moses basket of a thing.

His first missive came on a postcard from Tucumcari. He found me, saw my face in every headlight, and wrote me a postcard from the mountain immortalized in a song. I was a fond memory; it had meant something, there was verification, a receipt, an acknowledgment, a deathbed confession. *Dallas Alice, I need a shot at redemption. It's been a long time. Do you remember me? I miss you. Please write.* I wrote him back with carefully chosen, glib, light words, obscuring a variety of inner chasms—loneliness, despair, that sort of thing—and waited for a reply.

I got involved with Sam the summer after I got thrown—gently and sensitively—out of school for locking myself in the handicapped bathroom, immersing myself in hot water, and slicing my veins open with a straight razor. My mother said, "Do you think you were having a breakdown?" No. I just think I have difficulty sustaining my will to live.

Sam saw something in me a lot of men never see. He saw something raw and forbidden, I guess. Because Sam Flute came after me in a most extraordinary way. It was so extraordinary, I didn't even know it was happening.

I can see him now, in relief, his Levi's cords—the color of blueberry Pop-Tart filling—soft, thinly velvetized, no shirt, long hair. That summer was all about sweat, canned beer, tall grass, collusive smiles, and selective sensations. There was a rumpled blue sleeping bag—hot nylon and all wrong for summer—intoxicated fervor, an angry mother (since dead), a conspiratorial brother, giggling younger sisters, wealth, eccentricity, ample liquor cabinets, fat magnolias, and plenty of abandon. Abandon, that's a thorough yielding to natural impulses.

Boys come and go but you never forget the lovers. Which is to say, the real lovers. It's easy not to forget them because they are rare and every once in a while they come along and impress a girl with indelible memories. I think about Marguerite Duras a lot. There's one woman who never forgot a lover. Scream on the Mekong. I couldn't face a lifetime of that scream. I have a strong tidal pull to Sam Flute and a very particular time and place, imbedded in the swampy marshlands of Washington D.C. and the Chesapeake. Rising and ebbing tides are caused by the gravitational attraction of the sun and moon occurring unequally on different parts of the earth.

The mythology of Sam Flute began in eighth grade when he hosted a pool party for our entire class at his house in Georgetown. I remember everyone being a lot cooler and more in touch with their effect than I was. Sam was nice, he greeted me and said he was glad I came. We went on to high school together, but he dropped out in tenth grade. There was trouble; I didn't know the full story. My friend Holly and I noticed him one day before he dropped out. After he left school, he looked up Holly and asked her out. Holly was the only one of us that could garner a date. The suburban Jewish girl who lived in a Tara reproduction and drove her own blue Camero.

For Sam's sixteenth birthday, Holly wanted to do something special for him so she got me to buy him a bottle of Jack Daniel's. In that sad way of geeky girls with no chance of a boyfriend, I delighted in the collusion of the act. It was like a secret martyr mission, hiding the chalice of Jack in my vestments, all for Sam.

The fact that Sam liked whiskey—the down and dirty real stuff, the elixir, firewater—only underscored how much more intense he was than the watered-down boys we were used to. Sam was the Bad Boy who scaled the latticework on Holly's house, penetrated her bedroom—a princess lair replete with canopy bed, eyelet shams, and ruffled curtains—and got her in trouble with her parents. She said, "Sam knows more about our bodies than we do. His father is a *doctor*. He knows things, Alice." We tittered. She said, "He understands me. I told him my mother is a bitch and he said 'It's because she's manic depressive.' Isn't that *amazing* that he would know that?" She hid from her mother at my house, where Sam picked her up. Again, I was an aide-de-camp, a spy, an accomplice. Sam smiled at me. Holly told me he said I was pretty.

One night Holly called me, breathless and urgent, with plans for a covert night mission. She said that Sam asked her to come pick him up at his parents' weekend house on the Chesapeake. Holly told her parents she was spending the night at my house and Holly, Sam's brother Bobby and his friend Anthony and I all drove down across the Bay Bridge to St. Michael's to pick up Sam. He stood outside of the immense white house in profile, an exiled Western outlaw waiting for a midnight reprieve. There was a pool off to the side of the house glowing in the starlit abstract.

When Sam got in the car, I had to squeeze in the backseat with Anthony and Bobby. I was terrified we all wouldn't fit and it would be my fault, involving hip and butt size. Someone will make a comment and I will be exposed as the lardass who is throwing off the symmetry of the sneaky evening.

Bobby nestles into me and says, "Keep me warm." I am flushed by this sudden familiarity, excited that he might be flirting; quickly resolve that this is not the case. We fly back over the bridge—an extravagant journey of two hours in one night just to pick up Sam. He summoned Holly and she came. They have an exciting connection. I am the awkward onlooker, the Cyrano, the Nurse at the balcony of impassioned lovers who are unmindful of my presence until they need my faithful complicity.

I don't see Sam again until I am twenty, when I run into him at a bar in Georgetown. My friend Ainslie remembers him and is thrilled. He buys us drinks. Ainslie is into him. I have advanced from the lumpy onlooker days—taller, thinner, a college girl home for the summer—and yet he still elicits a youthful burn of shyness. He buys me another drink and asks me to dance. Ainslie smiles and asks him to dance.

When we're driving home in Ainslie's car she says, right on M Street, "Sam asked me for your number." She's a little torqued. I clutch my throat. "You didn't *give* it to him, did you?" I roll down the window and tell her I am going to puke. I didn't see this coming; I saw him going for Ainslie, the full-lipped party girl with ice-blue eyes and an iridescent shirt. Ainslie looks fun and wild. Ainslie *is* fun and wild. Sam Flute does not call girls like me. He calls girls like Holly Fender from high school. The bubbly former cheerleader, mistress of the mini-mansion, with symmetrical feathered black hair, a mellifluous smile, and lips seductively encased in a gelatinous sheen of scented lip gloss. Her mother had a Victorian dollhouse in the foyer. Lighted. My father is dead and my mother works for the government.

As it turns out, Sam does call a girl like me. Even without the canopy bed, suburban girl accoutrements, and daddy-bought chariot. I drive my father's beige 1970 VW bug. When Sam calls, my heart wedges semi-permanently in my throat.

"Is this Alice?"

"Yes."

"Hey, how are you doing, Alice? I'd like to take you out."

"No, thank you."

"I'll pick you up on my motorcycle."

"OK."

He comes to pick me up in a red Honda. "I'll have a Harley Davidson one day," he promises. We fly down MacArthur Boulevard and get on the Whitehurst Freeway, past the sulfuric brown Potomac and the shining moon Kleenex box of the Kennedy Center. A scarf my father bought me in India flies off into the night. I watch it waft and fall, landing somewhere on the muddy banks of the river.

We arrive at the Hawk 'n' Dove bar on Capitol Hill, sit in a booth near the front and Sam orders a pitcher, then another. He recounts funny stories about growing up on Capitol Hill, then Georgetown. He tells me how his father called every patch of grass "Dogshit Park." He says if a car passed his father too fast, he would lean out of the window and shout, "Where's the fire?" He laughs when he recounts this. He is affectionate about his father. He says, "My father graduated last in his class at medical school, but he graduated, fused knee and everything. Bad boy motorcycle crash." He winks.

We ride to a park in Georgetown, heavy with the lemony scent of boxwoods. I used to play in this park as a little girl, peeing in the labyrinthine maze of the bushes. My playmate was Anthony, Sam's best friend. He lived in a townhouse across the street from ours and I used to tell him elaborate lies about Martians and vampires. My mother said, "I will always remember that sweet little boy standing at the door asking if Alice could come out and play. He adored you!"

Anthony and another friend Brad are sitting on top of a trellis above the bushes in the park. They are sharing a six-pack of beer and they greet Sam warmly. They say "hi" to me, but Anthony's childhood adoration has clearly diminished. I lean into Sam and whisper, "I don't think I'm the type of girl your friends expect you to be with." He leans back in, squeezes my hand, and says, "You're beautiful, girl."

Sam says, "Do you want to walk around the park or go home?" I want to say, "walk around the park" but I know this will lead to a make-out session I am not quite prepared for. I want a clean break, avoid the pain of being mislabeled, and bypass the scrutiny of the boys. It's OK. Somewhere deep in the frog of my throat I say, "Go home," even though I want to wake up on wet grass with Sam amid the fragrant hedges. He's sweet, mindful of the wayward girl he's got, he's willing to wait. He drops me off at home, walks me to the door and kisses my mouth. He says, "I'll call you."

We meet again at Old Mac's in Georgetown, a dive bar with a deer butt on the wall and a sign above the door that says, "Way Out." In the bathroom, someone has scrawled, into the black semi-gloss paint, "This one here's for Layla." Sam goes to the jukebox and plays "House of the Rising Sun." We order a pitcher of National Bohemian and my back is arched like a nun. I'm afraid I'll break with the pressure. He orders another pitcher of watery suds and my back starts to numb; something is subsiding.

He says, "Walk me home." And I follow him through the chaotic maze of red taillights and double-parked cars on M Street. We turn left at the Byzantine gold dome of Rigg's Bank and head toward the white and green Little Tavern on the corner. I have to get oriented. I am following Sam Flute through Georgetown; I look at his light brown hair lying in a wave down his back. Sam has a slight swagger, a complete masculine confidence centered in his hips, as he walks through the streets he knows so well. I feel like I am in a Tennessee Williams play, following a ghost into something irrevocable.

We take a right and are enveloped in the quiet hush of a Georgetown side street, all ivy and ginkgo trees, with shiny silver remnants of cable-car tracks pushing through the cobblestones, leading nowhere. Sam's house is tall and white with four stories and elaborate black iron handrails. We slip in the side gate, past a wall of paned windows, to the Hockney pool. It's lit up like a perfect aquamarine square, sending off strangled, evanescent water shadows onto the fence.

We sit on the side and I dangle my feet in the water. My jeans have a pink tie-dyed patch. Sam leans over and kisses my cheek. I turn to look at him, he kisses my mouth, and it feels slippery, unstaged, salacious. Not like the preplanned, dry kisses of other boys. He says, "Come with me." He leads me to the basement apartment of his parents' house that he shares with his brother. There's a twin bed along the wall with a blue nylon sleeping bag on it. It's dark and there's a light under the door of his brother's room. The Band is playing on the stereo, accompanied by the sound of muted laughter and beer cans peeling back.

Sam sits me down on the bed. I have that undeniable feeling of an out-of-body experience. Alice has left the building. I'm sitting on the bed, I know we're going somewhere, I'm not ready, I want it and I trust him, but I don't know what to expect. I have a little panic wave—Jimi Hendrix—*are you experienced?* No! I am not up to this challenge. Very little chance of faking the knowledge. A few years behind on the sexual curriculum vitae. We kiss. Knowledge level still accessible. Hand goes for the Danskin. Drunk boy hands get confounded on that one and can't go as far as they would like. He says, "Take it off." That's a new approach. The gauze shirt comes off, then the leotard beneath—the film of my nervous chastity. We're down to a lavender Lily of France sparkle bra. One hand goes around my back and the snaps disengage in a flourish. This is a good sign.

I lay back onto the silky nylon bag and became sort of transformed. Worries and reservations melt into a helplessness brought on by a void of choices. This is preordained, it's happening, he is exercising manifest destiny on the intemperate surfaces of my geography. Suddenly he presses into uncharted territory. Deep intake of air, instinct to push him away, feint attempt, he grabs my hand and keeps on. I am taken aback by the specificity of the offering. There might be a scream on the Mekong after all. Sam moves up and we are fluid, then motionless, on a nylon blue wave lighted by a refracted shard of moonlight.

Next morning, I reapply last night's clothes that look, suspiciously, like last night's clothes. I have a permanent streak of black mascara fused with blue eyeliner under my eyes as we walk the plank into his mother's chaotic half-finished kitchen. His mother sits on a stool and regards me with equanimity. Devout Catholic, hence the five children, parishioner at the stalwart Holy Trinity Church. Loves the son. Calls him "Sammy," which is funny because he is so not a "Sammy." He is a Sam—tobacco, Jack Daniel's, trucks, motorcycles, sex. Beautiful sex. He's obviously accustomed to his mother's indifference toward his lady friends. He wants her to like me, but I am disheveled, postcoital, and undoubtedly regarding Sam with transformed, limpid eyes. I'm pregnant too, but none of us knows that yet.

He calls her "Momsy" and this makes her laugh. She's all business, "Listen Sammy, I want you to..." He tells me later, "Shit. I should have hidden you better. She's not going to like you." I don't care. I am doped with an infusion of wanton nocturnal fluids.

I come home and my own mother doesn't like me either. I cross her on the lawn as she heads off for work. What a proud moment for Mom. Daughter, dragging across the lawn after too many beers, way too much abandon, unkempt, poorly put back together, a slatternly, prodigal girl. She reaches her car, a lemon-yellow Cadillac Seville, turns to me and says, "This better not happen again." Level of remorse: zero. Complete nihilism. "I mean it." Mom drives off to work carrying stylish briefcase. Daughter enters empty house, goes up to blue bedroom, crawls into twin bed and sleeps, replaying best parts of former evening. Many frames.

Sam Flute's summer job is driving a tow truck, responding to AAA calls. He swings by to pick me up and off I go, in the tow truck. He pulls me close to him and puts his arm around my shoulder. He whispers funny romantic weird things that, taken out of context, I would hate but somehow, the way he says them, I love it. Sitting next to him, I am the kind of redneck vision I used to laugh at, "a two-headed driver." I don't pull away.

We go out to distressed motorists and he fixes their flat tires. They always stare at me, the girl, and smile and stare some more. Everyone wants to know how the tow truck driver spends his private time. Or maybe I don't look like the typical tow truck driver girlfriend. I think that's it. Sam smokes Marlboros and doesn't get mad in traffic. He talks a lot, but not about deep things. One time, though, he reveals he has dark periods when it's just him and a bottle of Jack Daniel's. Those are bad times. He turns up the crackly radio when it's a Stones song. *Gimme shelter.*

I have to work too, so I advertise myself as a babysitter and get a job picking up a little boy from day camp, taking him to his house in Bethesda and then waiting for his mother to come home from work. He's a cute little boy; every day when he runs into his cool blue air-conditioned house he grabs his bottom, races down the hall, and says, "I gotta go grunt!" I tell him not to watch TV because it will fry his brain. He says, "I checked with my mom and she says TV will *not* fry my brain." I eat Parmesan Goldfish and turn the bag upside down to conceal how many I have eaten. I think about Sam.

Sam starts coming over to my house after my mother leaves in the morning. He drives the tow truck all night. I leave the door open for him and he comes upstairs and wakes me up with tobacco-laced kisses. He smells like dried sweat. We mess around all day in bed and I am late to pick up Alexander. He's the last little boy sitting on the bench at camp and he looks like he's going to cry. I want to explain to him that I am helpless, I can't come any earlier. His mother, Lise Courtney, an army brat, mentions to me that Alexander is consistently the last kid to be picked up and he doesn't like it. I tell her I'm having car trouble. I apologize. She looks hopeful. I am beginning to recognize a fearful need to stay afloat amid the deep-sea tumult that is causing fissures beneath my delicate emotional crust.

One day at my house Sam says, "I've never met a girl like you before. My friends are mad at me—Brad and Anthony—I'm supposed to be doing stuff with them, but I always want to be with you. This has never happened to me before with a girl. I usually have to cut girls loose after awhile. Not you. Anyway, why do I always have to call you? How come you never call me?" He smiles. That's funny. I can't really explain to him that I am afraid the instant I plug his numbers into the tangled circuit, it will cause an immediate avalanche of failed hopes. I just shrug. He says, "I want you to call me sometime."

He goes into the living room and lies down on the white modern couch in front of the immense picture window overlooking the trees above the Potomac. He takes his ponytail holder off and puts it on the coffee table. His hair, with the sun-baked blonde tips, falls off the side of the couch. He puts out his hand a little and says, "Come here." I stand there looking at him. "Now." I walk, like a freshly minted vampire, toward my summoner. Everything's pretty easy. Clothes slip away—there's no fumbling—snaps, zippers, and buttons unfurl without snags or hitches. It's broad daylight, yet being naked in front of the picture window seems terribly right, called for, intense and warm. We're locked in a haze of sunlight. I turn and look out at my mother's Japanese garden. The house has an insulated, air-conditioned hush with only the sound of a descending plane, following the serpentine curves of the Potomac, resonating overhead.

It's a silent summer since we're indoors all day and in the tow truck in the middle of the night, sleeping, holding each other, and drinking. Sam smiles a lot. It's a fast smile—fast to come on and it lingers. There's nothing behind it, nothing sneaky or subversive, just a perfectly connected emotional radiation from his brain to his soul to his mouth.

We end up at his house in the night when it is unofficially turned back over to the older brothers. The younger sisters are much more cloistered. They go to Catholic school and the mother seems determined that they will turn out differently from her rebellious sons. The boys flip on the pool lights when they're sure their cantankerous father is asleep. "Dad is asleep, Bob, turn on the lights." The girls are in bed, safe in their fourth-floor bedrooms. The lights silently switch on. I love the pool and always want to go in. The boys have the indifference of kids who have grown up with a pool, they could care less, they get in, they don't get in.

"Go ahead," Sam says to me.

"Will you come in?"

"Yeah."

He goes and changes into cutoffs and dives in from the side. His brother disappears. Sam goes underwater and emerges, like a seal in front of me, smiling. He picks me up, weightless in water, and says, "Where have I been all of your life?"

One day I decide I am going to call Sam. His sister Bridget answers. She laughs and says, "Sam's not here!" Gleefully, the way all little sisters do. "He's not here!" It's like a taunt from a fairy-tale gnome. "Can I leave a message?" I know better, but it's worth a try. She says, "He's down at our place in St. Michael's." What am I supposed to do with this information?

"Do you have a number down there?"

"Mooooom, Sammy's *girlfriend* wants the number down at the Bay."

"This is Mrs. Flute, may I ask who's calling?"

Didn't you hear your daughter? This is the tramp you met in the kitchen, the girl who inhabits your house, pool, and son's bed while you're sleeping. I haven't thought of myself as Sam's *girlfriend*.

"Mrs. Flute, hi this is Alice, I was wondering if I could have the number of your house at the Bay. I'd like to talk to Sam."

"All right," she answers, a little frostily, and gives me the number.

I call and the phone rings about ten times. Sam answers. He says, "Where are you?"

"In Washington."

In the background, a purring, sullen, pouty voice demands, "Sam?"

"Alice…" I hang up.

He calls back, "Don't you *ever* hang up on me."

I've never heard him mad before. I hang up, really loud this time. Slam the phone down on the receiver. I am admittedly incorporating some learned movie star-style behavior. Faye Dunaway, absolute, resolute, pissed, unyielding. He calls back, I reach for the receiver, then halt. Let it ring. It rings and rings. And I do not answer, Sam I am. Do not do not do not.

I decide I don't want to look at the phone anymore so I put on shorts, baby oil and take a stack of magazines out into my mother's backyard. I sit on a taupe lawn chair and paint my toenails fire engine red. I sip a toasted almond—amaretto and milk. It's easier to filch rarely used beverages from my mother's liquor cabinet, hence the imaginative combinations. Pretty soon I'm a pretty toasted almond. The air is unusually dry for a Washington summer and I lie in the Japanese garden, enveloped by bamboo and the light trickle of a koi pond trying to bake out the emotional equivalent of a paper cut. I decide that the only way to exact revenge on the entire universe is to become very tan. And drunk. I spend the next five days in the same foggy routine, grateful for the sun in this instance, and for bizarre liquor elixirs that mix well with a variety of household staples.

This is what movie stars do, except it's usually by a pool and not a koi pond. They sit, elegant and greased, beside contained bodies of water with lacquered nails and sweet potables. They lounge, indifferently. On the sixth day, I hear a rustle behind me coming from the path that connects the front yard to the secret garden. It's Sam. I am calm, galvanized. He is shirtless in dark Levi's with a Greek fisherman's cap on. "Can you make me one of those?" He says, gesturing toward the drink. See, here it is, if your parents were diplomats, like mine, you are born with an imbedded compulsion to please, especially as it pertains to providing drinks. I make him one and we sit in the backyard like two ghouls, unaccustomed to daylight and meaningful discourse.

I manage to croak out, "What happened?"

He says, "Holly Fender was in town, remember her? She's still good looking, do you want to see her picture?"

"No thank you."

"It's nothing, it's over. She wanted to see me. I didn't want you to know, so I took her down to the Bay."

Just my luck, I get up the nerve to call a man and he is hidden, ensconced with an old lover, my former best friend, on a spit of land clinging to the Chesapeake.

I say, "I don't want to see you anymore."

What am I saying? It's the movie star talking again. We have to get Faye Dunaway out of here. There is a horrible pause in the proceedings. He wasn't expecting that either. He takes a sip of his toasted hazelnut.

(We've moved on from amaretto to Frangelico.) He stands up, I watch him in slow motion as he walks toward me, puts his sweating drink down on the flagstone, and straddles my lap. My face is buried in his chest, smooth skin flushed like a nectarine. He pulls me into him and we don't say anything for a very long time, in repose, letting the sun and the garden heal it all, silently.

The pregnancy part happens because we're not using birth control at all. I think we don't want barriers to anything. No mixer, no dilution, just mainlined.

One day when Sam doesn't have to drive the tow truck and Alexander's camp is finished, we go on an outing. We are free. We pile into his pickup truck and his sister Bridget comes out to the driveway with a bandana and a lunch bag. She says, "Sam, take me!" My heart sinks, but the feathery girl piles into the pickup cab with us. She shoots me a victorious smile. He slaps her thigh and off we go, mid-morning on a weekday, to the Chesapeake. We drive out of the congested hot summer confusion of Washington and glide across the bridge, against traffic, against the high season, toward the brackish inner coastal refuge. It looks like an antebellum plantation house, an incongruous white mansion set on the water, the same beacon that greeted me the night Holly drove out to collect Sam.

Sam says, "You can go change into your bathing suits upstairs. Bridget, show Alice where to go."

Bridget snorts and takes my hand. "This is the old part of the house, the really old part and there is a secret stairway. Check this out."

We come into the huge kitchen with a stone fireplace and she opens a narrow door and leads me up a steep white staircase to a cloistered bedroom with twin cast-iron beds. "This is me and Annie's room."

I have my suit crammed into my purse. I really don't want to change in front of Sam's little sister. I can hear the dinner conversation now. *She was sunburned, like a lobster! And her thighs...*

"Is there a bathroom up here?"

"It's OK, you can get naked! I know *Sam's* seen you naked."

I mumble something. She singsongs, "We've seen you! In the pool at home!"

Summoning my best grown-up voice I say, "Come on now, Bridget, is there a bathroom here?"

I go into a bathroom with white wainscoting, blue speckled wallpaper, and a warped glass window that overlooks the pale yellow marsh grass and tiny whitecaps on the Bay. When I gaze into the mirror etched with flowers, I am instantly preserved in tintype, my face at that moment, with the smell of the air. I miss that moment and the promise of a beautiful day with no purpose.

We jump into the pool. Bridget climbs all over Sam and when he can extract himself, he swims over to me. This is when I wish we were alone. The Bay is glistening in the distance. Sam loves water. He tells me his mom couldn't get him out of the bathtub when he was little. He says, "There's a picture of me in the bathtub in the first-floor bathroom. Look at it when you go in. I was pretty back then too!"

There are nautical white ropes decoratively surrounding the pool. The grass is dry and crunches as we walk around, our eyes swollen with chlorine, our bodies slick and numbed by sunlight and water. We spend the rest of the day getting in and out of the pool, walking into the house and getting Cokes and beer.

When Bridget goes in, Sam and I try to kiss in the pool, buoyant, but she's never gone for long, eager to come back and interrupt her brother's progress with the interloper. He doesn't mind; he doesn't get irritated with her. He smiles at me, not apologetically, just a smile like this is life, this is unalterable. I take my cue from him and just allow it, suppress the annoyance, accept the chaotic, familial pull of love, jealousy, and possessiveness.

Sam's in cutoffs again. The ease of this breaks my heart—that lifelong assurance of knowing what is what, the absence of worry that comes with a big family, the relaxation with self, making use of the past, something cool, free, frayed, comfortable. Sam and I manage one long kiss under the sun while the Bay audibly sifts its contents in the distance.

Sam's mother appears unexpectedly—stern, all business—to check the house for some renters who are coming in a week. Bridget greets her like a puppy and asks if she can drive home with her.

Sam says, "Mom, you remember Alice?"

"Nice to see you again." I say. She's wearing sensible lace shoes.

"Nice to see you too, dear. Sammy, clean the pool before you go and check the pH level. We've got renters coming! Don't mess up the gravel in the driveway with your pickup either. Bridget! If you're coming with me, get your things together and let's go! Sam, lock the house and turn down the A/C." She shoots me one fleeting glance. Sam has her brown eyes.

When they leave, we sip Budweiser by the pool. As we drive out of St. Michael's, Sam pulls up to a clapboard house with a front porch. He says, "I have some people I want you to meet." We walk in and a group of friends is sitting around—locals that he knows. They greet him warmly. Sam laughs, talks shit with everyone, blends effortlessly with the conversation, the nuances and idioms. It's a kind of universal, hippie, seventies, communal acceptance—a Faberge Organics commercial of wholesome, honey-infused camaraderie.

We leave the house and Sam pulls the pickup onto a wide shoulder in the grass behind the cover of bushes. He puts me on the hood of the truck, right there off the sandy road. The hood is warm and almost soft. His mouth touches me and I listen to the wavelets touching the shore underneath the curve of a half-lit firmament.

Back over the bridge, we stop at McDonald's, the end bracket of the trip. I have a sunburned pinch at the crease of flesh where my bathing suit stopped, my eyes are unaccustomed to fluorescence. The sinking sun encapsulates the arc of the day.

Back in Sam's room, it's as hot as Washington ever gets, humid, suffocating, blinding heat. He doesn't like air conditioning. "It's not natural." This is unimaginable to me. I can't bear it.

"Please Sam."

"It's not natural, you'll get used to it."

We're wrapped around each other on top of the blue nylon bag and I can't stand the sweat, the lack of oxygen. He doesn't care. Soon we are drenched, completely wet, our bodies make a slapping sound I hate, but then it's OK because it doesn't matter anymore. The suction and heat cause the saline rivulets to trickle, transude, and seep. We are bonded again by a licentious disregard, for everything.

I spend the remainder of the summer attached to Sam, following him on summer errands in his pickup. We are in diners at two in the morning, on our own schedule, Washington is completely ours. I sit in his pool house with the water reflecting all over the place and the sounds of Georgetown from all sides. The end of summer smells of decaying magnolia flowers competing with intermittent scents of garbage and exhaust fumes. The brick sidewalks, damp with humidity and moss, buckle above engorged tree roots.

Sam plays the Band all the time. Bobby says, "Don't let him play 'Stage Fright,' he gets the weirdest look on his face when he plays that song. That song, man, it's deep. It's all about isolation and fear and shit, right Sam?"

Sam smiles a little, always indulgent of his little brother, lifts the stylus and puts it gingerly back to the beginning of the song. We smoke pot out of an immense red bong named Rosalita. I feel like we are squatters in Berlin.

It is time for Sam to go back to college. I'm going to stay in Washington, exiled from college for a while, ensconced in my childhood home, trying to find my way. Sam says, "Come to Syracuse with me. You can wait tables and live with me in my group house. You will love my roommates." I can't go with Sam. I'm on a tight schedule with the shrink, after the handicapped bathroom stunt. We spend a final night together, quiet by the pool. I throw up the next morning, a symptom of my as-yet-undiagnosed pregnancy.

Sam's pickup sits double-parked in front of his house, all packed and ready for his return to college. I lean on the open window of his truck, focusing on the fuzzy black substance at the base of the window that protects the glass. This is to keep from crying. I am in the process of loving Sam very much, his incongruities, long hair, fascination with motorcycles, endless banter, summer white smile, the half-finished mansion, and all the secret valuable things he said to me. Mostly, I love his unspoken acceptance.

Sam says, "I'll call you, girl. You'll be up in Syracuse before you know it." But this time Sam doesn't call. I see him when he's home for Christmas a couple of times. One night we walk down to the Potomac and sit on a park bench. I lay my head on his lap and he leans down and kisses me, with the concentric arches of Key Bridge in the background. Another time, I run into Bobby at a party in Adams Morgan. He asks me how I am. I ask him how Sam is. He says, "He's living in Kansas now with a woman named Rose." The words unfold like information on ticker tape, forming one unwanted sentence. I talk to Bobby for a while and I see him watching my eyes and hands as I talk, mostly my hands. He says, "You know, talking to you like this, I can see why my brother loved you so much." Then he breaks into a big smile that illuminates my life for a second. Finally no subtext, just boneless flesh.

I don't hear anything about Sam until his postcard finds its way to my mother's house, all these years later. She forgets to tell me and puts it in my purse when I am visiting. When I get back to my apartment, I pull out my checkbook and the postcard of Tucumcari falls to the floor, like a message in a bottle.

In my letter back to Sam I give him my email address so I can check for his response here at my computer beneath Georgetown University's campus in the Department of Landscaping. One day his address pops up on my screen, unmistakable, samflute@juno.com. He writes,

> *Hey Girl, long time, no see ☹. Regarding your questions about me, men do not "grow up," doncha know? Motorcycles and females are the main game in town. I'm out in California now and I drive a big truck. More importantly, I have a gorgeous purple Harley-Davidson. I had it custom built and rode it across country. I spent some time in Kansas on the way, visiting friends. I lived there for almost 8 years.*
>
> *I miss you and our youth, but I believe we all miss the latter to some extent. I'm positive you are attractive as ever. When we were together, I believe I loved you fiercely. I blame my own foolishness for losing you. Do you remember denting my pickup hood one afternoon on the Chesapeake? My memory says it was*

a naughty two person project! Sorry to tease you, love, it isn't nice.

Thanks for your wonderful letter. I can feel you have a lot of weighty matters on your mind, as always, my serious girl. You please cheer up. I need to hear more from you. I'll be quiet and listen for a while.

I wanted you to know you have always stood alone in my heart, all this time. I miss you, Alice. What would it take to convince you to come out and visit me?

Much love,

Sam

Sitting here in the depths of this university, the words on the screen bleed back into me. I feel like Persephone, regarding irrefutable evidence of what my life was like one summer, above ground. I imagine sitting with Sam beneath crayon-colored light fixtures at truck stops, drinking coffee, with the Pacific pulling itself back and forth, nearby.

Carole Burns

Changing Color

CAROLE BURNS is a fiction writer and journalist who hosts "Off the Page," a series of interviews with writers at washingtonpost.com. A two-time fellow at the MacDowell Colony and the Virginia Center for Creative Arts, she has been published in the *New York Times* and the *Washington Post*, with fiction in *Other Voices*, *Washingtonian*, and other publications. She is the recipient of grants from the DC Commission on the Arts and Humanities and is at work on a novel.

I am sitting in the garden watching my tulips grow. There are ten tall stalks whose flat leaves turn a deeper green each day. I planted them two seasons ago then forgot them until the first leaves pressed through the icy mulch, poked through dried leaves and sticks and grew despite me. I discovered them splayed against the ground, draggled but alive.

Planting them was a small pleasure, then. I knelt on the damp earth, grass sticking to my bare feet, my swollen knees. Leaning over as best I could, my bulging stomach pushed warm against my thighs, I cradled each papery bulb in my hand before laying it carefully in the hole I had dug for it. I placed each one in the dirt, pointy side up. They looked like brown garlic, like lumpy onions. Then I gently pushed the earth over them, leaving them to winter. You kicked. I remember you kicked, right then.

Not all of them came up. Perhaps I crowded them in too small a garden; perhaps I knocked one on its side. But I root for them all; I try to take care of them all.

One is especially tall and strong, her leaves wider and greener than the others, her stem thick yet resilient. She was the first to lift her heavy leaves toward the sun, the first to bud. Though none of them have flowered, she is already the queen tulip, reigning at the center of her bowing ladies, feeding off their beauty and generosity. I am appalled by her, and enthralled.

I spend an inordinate amount of time sitting alone by my tulips. My neighbors are beginning to wonder. I start to bring out a chair with me, a book. I turn a page occasionally so they think I'm reading. But I cannot. I soak in the late spring sun; I take off my sandals and burrow my toes in the grass, in the dirt. I watch my tulips. I want to see them flower, to see their orange or red petals blossom. I want to witness their moment of grandeur, their triumphant debut.

"She's so beautiful," he said.

I held you in my arms. You were ugly and old-looking, wrinkled and supernaturally red. All tummy, you had skinny arms and legs, bent like a crab's, that wriggled around you. You smiled and stopped, smiled and stopped, your muscles not strong enough to form a grin. But your gaze was steady, tiny blue eyes that wouldn't let go. They squeezed my heart.

"Isn't she?" I said. I could barely breathe.

Elizabeth. A long name for such a small entity. We wrapped it around you like a blanket. We had planned on shortening it to something cute and modern—Bethie, Lizzie, Zee. But we never could. If anything, your name ended up longer. "Elizabethie," we said, tucking the extra syllable around you.

Your cries and whimpers and squeals filled up the house. Your slightest sound sent us running. Even when you were napping, we listened. On the monitor, your gurgles sounded alien, a radio broadcast of static-laced slurps, tiny sighs, and delicate coughs. Sometimes you giggled in your sleep. Sometimes you woke up screaming; there seemed to be no pause between sound sleep and pure terror.

"And what did our princess do today?" he asked. Still in his suit, he bent over your crib, catching his tie before it dangled in your face. You smiled for him, moved your arms about in a circle, as if you were swimming. You gurgled like a mourning dove. Performed. You were happier than you had been all day. "Eat a little? Nap a little? Poop a little?" he asked.

"Exercised her lungs," I said. "A lot."

"Oh, are you making sure your lungs are big and strong?" He smiled at you, nodded his head encouragingly. He seemed enormous next to you, as bulky and awkward as King Kong. "You make sure you do that during the day, for Mommy." He wagged a finger. "But not at night! There's more oxygen during the day."

"Gee, thanks," I said. I walked over and wrapped both my arms around one of his. It was meaty and muscular beneath his starched blue shirt. His free arm reached toward you. He placed his thick finger in your skinny, wriggling hand and you squeezed. I watched him watching you, watched him tickle your double chin with his thumb. "I wish you would tickle my chin," I whispered.

"Oh, does Mommy want her chin tickled?" he cooed in the same voice.

~

"She's a difficult one," the nurse said cheerily.

You were whimpering as I put you to my breast, as I put my breast to you. You wanted no part of it, you thought. At a few hours old you already seemed to know what you wanted. I placed my nipple near your mouth but didn't put it in—I wanted you to come to me. For a moment I felt your tiny lip on my breast, wet and warm, and then you jerked your head away as if on purpose. More new cries. Everything a first.

The nurse stuck her raw, chafed finger between us, turned your head and pushed my breast so my nipple filled your mouth. I almost pulled it out—it looked like my breast could smother you. But then you sucked, so hard it hurt; I knew we'd done it right. "Can't be shy," the nurse said. I felt reprimanded.

Sometimes I still needed to force it into your mouth—you often fought the breast. I'd let you fuss first. Difficult. I wondered if you'd always be difficult. But then you'd suck, pain and relief at once. Who would think you could suck so hard, my nipple pulled long and taut, like the umbilical cord we had to cut.

❧

You slept on your belly, your limbs curled in around you. So quiet, so peaceful. I was going to look only, watch only. But I didn't see your back trembling, your blanket shifting; I didn't see any sleepy spasms in your fingers. You weren't supposed to be on your stomach. Had you rolled over already? I leaned into your crib, trying to place my cheek near your lips, to feel your hot angel-breaths. I felt nothing. I leaned my large face closer: still nothing. I was about to panic when you sneezed, woke, cried. I patted your back to soothe you, but you wouldn't quiet down. You screamed. I picked you up. Aaron poked his head in the nursery, a towel hugging his waist. "What did you wake her for?" he asked. "Why do you make it hard for yourself?"

❧

My tulips are beginning to reveal the secret of their color. Their brilliance is peeping out beneath the enclosing bud, which for so long was dark and protective, sheltering their vibrancy and life.

In just a day they are fully in bloom. I marvel at the speed of their opening, the medley of color. Three tulips are deep fuchsia, gorgeous and sad as promise. Two are a tropical Miami orange, with a deep summer shine. Several are striped two colors—pink and white, yellow and orange.

Yet something about them looks weak-kneed and limp. At least compared to my centerpiece. Although plain yellow, she has the largest blossom, the sturdiest petals. If I had to name her I would choose Jane, or Sue. There is nothing elaborate about her, yet her fragile power affects me. Plain Jane. Sensible Sue.

Aaron walks by me sitting in the grass. I listen to his heavy footsteps passing me, for the hundredth time, it seems. He's early—the first time he's home before dark in weeks. Or maybe the days are getting longer. The sun sends weak light in our direction.

"What are you doing?" he asks. We never ask "how" anymore, just "what."

"Nothing." I don't open my eyes, don't move.

"I bought some bread for dinner," he says. "And wine."

Though the sun is dipping dangerously close to the hills I feel warmth like candlelight. I remember the round of a wineglass cupped in one hand, his fingers cupped in my other, as we sit cramped in our small kitchen. But the light flickers. We haven't eaten dinner together in weeks.

I hear him clinking dishes in the kitchen, setting the table for two. "Honey, come inside." He uses his authoritative voice, the one he must have been saving for you.

"I'm not hungry," I say.

"Keep me company," he says, changing tactics. I pretend not to hear him. "Hon. C'mon!"

I shake my head so slowly I can feel my muscles creak in my neck. When I open my eyes to peek at him he is gone.

❧

I needed to put on your coat for a walk. You'd been crying and fussing and I decided we both needed air. Round and round the park we'd go, several sets of mother-and-carriage. Some talked to each other but I always said an overly polite hello so they wouldn't bother me. I had a disdain for stay-at-home moms, although I had become one myself.

You weren't in the mood for anything that day. You raised your eyebrows, puckering your forehead as I put on my sneakers. "You're going to get premature wrinkles," I told you. "You shouldn't have such an expressive face." You looked at me blankly then, wondrous, all creases suddenly disappearing, and I laughed. "Silly."

As I approached with your coat you scrunched up your nose and scowled. I gently took one of your arms and you squirmed. You let out quick breaths that I recognized as the prelude to a tantrum. You began screeching as I succeeded in getting arm number two into the lavender windbreaker. "Damnit!" I screamed, banging my palm on the counter next to you, startling you, for a moment, into silence.

You screamed even more loudly, started shrieking as my palm began to smart. I zipped your coat up to your chin, slowly, trying not to lose my temper. "Shit!" I hissed again, irrationality building within me then dipping back down. I watched you calmly. Your brow was doubly wrinkled;

your nose twitched. "Why do I have to do all the bad things?" I asked. "Put on your coat. Change your diaper. You won't hate Mommy for it, will you?" You were hysterical now, your face purple red. "Is that a yes or a no?" I asked, then answered for you. "Yes, Mommy, I won't hate you."

By the time he came home you had fussed, nursed, napped. It could take you an hour to wake up, groggy and grumpy as a forty-year-old. Then, for him, you were all grunts and grins.

"She's been crying all day again."

"You're kidding." He lifted you higher, bounced you until you seemed as light as a doll. "Are you giving Mommy trouble? Elizabethie? Or is Mommy pinching you again?" You squealed and squeaked. Then his adult voice, mock-accusing. "Once she starts talking," he told me, "you're going to have to stop pinching."

⁂

I have decided to cut down my tulips. Beauty is worth nothing. Their sweet faces bob in the breeze, nodding, agreeing. I kneel on the grass with the scissors, grasp them in my hand. My knees graze the dirt of the garden. I will cut the healthiest flower first. The scissors squeak open. Their metal touches the thick stem of my yellow star.

I cannot cut. The scissors squeak open but I cannot move to sever the green stem. It is too strong. It holds too much life.

I think of the fresh milky-green sap, the life-blood, inside the stems. I put down the scissors. I fill up an old plastic garden pitcher and water them instead.

⁂

The house was silent and dark. We lay still as if the slightest noise would wake you, as if the monitor were reversed. You were in your room but we whispered like stowaways, not wanting to get caught. We were talking about you, of course. After crying all day, you had been sleeping an hour, and we hoped for several more.

Finally, we hushed, prepared for sleep ourselves. He patted my fanny. His fingers grazed my bare thighs. I reached for him and we were suddenly alone. "You," he said. "I remember you." I don't know how long it lasted but soon I was bearing the weight of him. He had just maneuvered inside me when I heard you, waking. A complaining old invalid, you were insistent, persistent, your whine pathetic and helpless. It seemed like you knew what we were doing, and disapproved.

"Shit," I said. He laughed, was suddenly hysterically laughing, barely breathing as he rolled off me. "Shut up," I said, sitting on the edge of the bed, bare feet searching for slippers. His guffaws increased, but he eked out a few words.

"I can get her."

"I'm so freaking tired," I said.

⸙

I would sleep out here if I could. I would sleep in my bed of tulips like a girl lost in a fairy tale. But something prevents me; a nagging sense of appropriateness filters through my madness. So I wait shivering in the cool May night, damp with dew, until he has gone upstairs. I wander inside then, turn off the lights as if I'm going to bed, and stray through the darkened rooms as if my house were a museum. Except there are no pictures to look at, just blank walls subtly lit by the moon and the domes of streetlamps, her apostles. I rest occasionally in a couch or chair, curl onto the floor by the chair where I rocked you, the wood hard against my bones. This way, I never experience the shock of waking up—the shock of memory after thinking everything is normal.

I am roused by a gentle shaking of my shoulder, a warm hand on my arm and on my hip. He leans down, whispers. "I'll carry you upstairs," he says.

I stiffen, jerk away. I lean sleepily on my arm. "No—don't. You'll drop me."

"Come upstairs," he says.

I shudder, suddenly cold. "I'm not tired," I say.

⸙

I was wearing a purple silk dress with a red sash, preparing for our first outing alone since we became a threesome—our (his and mine) anniversary. I click-clacked to the bright lights of the bathroom, makeup bag in hand. You were in your bouncy seat—bungie jumping, we called it. I strode past Aaron to the bedroom for my eyeliner, and noticed you watching me. I sidestepped in front of you; you followed me the only way you could—with your eyes. They shined light hazel, flecked with green some days, yellow others, so large they made you look skinny, though you were a bouncing cherub, in the ninety-fifth percentile. Your gaze fell about waist-level—my red sash.

I shuffled to the left; I shimmied to the right. Your eyes were wide and alert, as if you knew you would see only so much, as if you knew that you had to pay attention. I tap-danced in a wide circle around Aaron, my arms flailing back and forth like Gene Kelly's. Both pair of eyes, now, bright and adoring, followed me closely. You squealed with delight.

I scanned the babysitter for bloodshot eyes or burned-out hair or the faint afterwhiff of pot. But she seemed more efficient than I did, asking where the diapers were and the time of your last feeding, details I'd forgotten to tell her. Everything about her was tidy and calm: her pale folded hands, her tucked-in ironed T-shirt, flowers embroidered on her breast pocket.

We guiltily slunk out the door. I felt naked leaving you behind. At dinner, I fingered the red silk beneath my white linen napkin. I was reluctant to hold his hand; it meant letting go of the sash. It meant letting go of you.

Black is fashionable any time, necessary only a few. Convenient, actually. I had several dresses to choose from: long and flowered, long and plain, short and flowered, short and sexy. I fingered another dress, bright purple silk, red silk sash. Inappropriate but it's what I wanted to wear. Then I could know you'd be watching me.

I chose the long, plain dress instead, sober and fittingly tragic, then took the red sash and wrapped it around my neck. The end of it trailed down my back.

We were trying to get to sleep early—adult time for reading or renting a movie, another habit we seemed to be giving up. Instead, I listened to the silence. "Do you think we should check on her?" I asked.

"You'll wake her up."

Not a gurgle. Not a sigh.

"She's never this quiet."

"That's good, isn't it?" he asked, sensibly. He turned to hold me, to warm away my worries. He wrapped one hand under my breasts; he slipped the other beneath the elastic of my cotton underpants. The silence was drowned out by his hardening, the slow, increasing caresses of his hands then lips. We didn't get to sleep early, but, eventually, we slept, and peacefully.

৵

He discovered you. "How's my princess today?" he sang as I filled the coffeepot with fresh water. "How's my sleepyhead?" He opened your shimmering white blinds. I took the coffee out of the freezer, measured out the frozen grounds. "Elizabeth?" His tone was unusual. Something attracted my attention. I heard, "Elizabeth—Oh my god!"

I ran to your door but I felt like I was not moving at all, as if the room, your crib, the light from your window, were moving around me. He was holding you to his shoulder, patting your back, as if you needed burping, then rocking you with his arm. Your entire body fit into the crook of his elbow. I went to hold you, to take you, but something told me to think. "I'll call 911," I said, my voice sounding outside me. I found myself in the kitchen listening blankly to the dial tone. I didn't remember what to do. Then I hit three buttons, heard them say, "Mrs. Josephs?"

I was excessively polite. I said, Please and Thank you. I said, Please come. My baby isn't breathing. Please hurry. Please.

He was kneeling on the floor then, curled over you, as if in an extravagant bow. "Let me see her," I said. I wanted to find a minor problem, a minor glitch. Like I could switch the batteries around; like I could fiddle with the plug. "Let me see her." Slowly he stood up, stretched out his arms, holding you, extending you to me like an offering.

I learned the meaning then of stone cold. I cradled you in my arms. I pushed you underneath my breasts. It was always warm there, even warmer since you. I wanted to warm you; I wanted you to be warm. When the medics arrived I refused to give you up.

My eyes were dry until the night of the funeral. Wind pierced my eyes; no tears soothed them. I watched you, my still infant; nothing closed my eyes. Until we were trying to sleep and I could hear only silence.

After I was crying for ten minutes, after I began heaving and gasping, he held me. He placed his hand under my breast; he slipped a finger beneath my underpants. "Don't," he said. "I don't—" Don't think don't feel don't know what happened don't cry. By habit he grew hard, but we pretended not to notice. Don't. When I woke, I was lying on the very edge of the bed.

⁂

Overnight, Elizabeth, a transformation. I find my Yellow Sue, my Plain Jane, is changing into a tiger, a jungle lily. A Suzanna, a Janette. Black stripes now charge up her petals. I miss her simplicity, but I am in awe of her brilliant sophistication.

The next day she has changed again, her yellow deepening into a velvet orange, sweetened by a tinge of pink. Yesterday's brazenness turns into today's beautiful regret. She is my flower, after all.

⁂

I don't turn to look at him but I listen. Aaron's steps don't pause, though the sun is hours from its end; his steps scrape busily by me, thin dress soles whistling against the cement walk. The afternoon is extra quiet now; even the tulips have stopped their chatter. A breeze picks up for a moment and maybe that is why I don't hear him stepping off the porch. "How is my princess today?" he asks. I look up and he's standing with your quilt, rolled up and stashed under his arm, as if he's taking it a long way.

"Where are you going?" I ask.

"Picnic," he says, oblique. He loosens his arm, catches the quilt with both hands, and throws it into the wind. Its sturdy cotton takes up the sky for a moment, clouds become patches of yellow flowers and blue dogs, which land so softly on the grass the blades barely bend. It is the first time the quilt is used; you never graduated from your receiving blankets, soft as your skin.

He has my attention now. He steps quickly down our walk, turns the corner. I hear the car door open and shut, and see him return, three grocery bags dangling by his legs. He eases them onto the quilt, goes into the house and comes out with plates, silverware, wineglasses, corkscrew. He sits sideways on the quilt, pours two glasses of wine. "C'mon," he says. "Sit with me." He brings out cheese spread, crackers, tiny grapes the size of dewdrops, shrimp salad, and bread.

I leave the comfort of the beach chair for the quilt, carefully cross my legs so I am Indian-style, back as straight as I can make it. I clasp the glass he offers.

"Look," I say. "She turned."

He gazes at the tulips curtsying at the border of the quilt.

"Is that the yellow one?" he asks.

I nod, as if we've been discussing the tulips all along, as if I knew he'd been watching them too.

"That's amazing," he says. "I didn't know they changed colors."

"Me neither," I say.

"You know," he says, "in the morning, they're closed up." He holds his glass up to the sun, cups the curve of it in his hand like a tulip. "Like you." Shadows flash through the golden wine.

"Am I going to change color?" I ask.

We sit on this patchwork of white and blue, green and yellow, linked by thread so thin it's invisible, laden with holes made by a prickling needle which stitches together as it pokes, opening circles then filling them.

"Three months," he says. "Three months today."

"Is that all?" I ask, after a moment.

The fresh light of spring is deepening to summer as I sit in my garden, not wanting to leave the sun, not wanting the sun to leave. These are the things I wanted to teach you: Tulips. Grass. Red. Yellow. The sun sets, the moon is full. I am here.

Jennifer Cutting

Thursday Morning, 9:00 a.m.

JENNIFER CUTTING happily combines careers as a songwriter, bandleader, ethnomusicologist, and record producer. Her poems have been published in literary journals including the *Aquarian* and *Gargoyle*, and her lyrics have won such prestigious awards as American Songwriter Magazine's "Song of the Year" and the Mid-Atlantic Song Contest. Her CD *OCEAN: Songs for the Night Sea Journey* swept the 2004 Washington Area Music Awards, winning her Songwriter of the Year, Album of the Year, Musician of the Year, New Artist of the Year, and Best Contemporary Folk Recording. She has her own studio in Takoma Park, Maryland, where tofu grows on trees, and even the house pets are bisexual.

Thursday morning, 9:00 a.m. He took his usual route through the city that day, part of the purposeful press of black-and-white bodies swarming toward their honeycomb tombs. At the edge of his workaday tunnel vision, the commotion caught his eye. It was a woman, struggling with insect determination to free herself from a pile of cellophane packing material. Now curious, he moved closer. The woman was shedding. Several layers of her had fallen away already, accumulating in a brittle pile behind her, dull transparent husks that eerily retained the outlines of her original shape. Still attached at the heel, they clung obstinately like an old scab to that last point of connection with the living tissue.

None of this was noticed by the passersby, whose faces were set in stony compliance with the unspoken Law of Commuting. He knew what he had to do. Brandishing the Swiss army knife he kept faithfully tucked away in his briefcase for God-knows-what...squirming slightly as he drew closer to her glistening moistness...he knelt and cut quickly until she was free. The woman stepped away with a new lightness, thinking *finally* she had wrestled her high heel from that pesky grate, unaware of the metamorphosis that had just occurred.

Ramola D

The Smell of Tulips

RAMOLA D's fiction, poetry, and essays have appeared or are forthcoming in *Green Mountains Review*, *Prairie Schooner*, *Small Spiral Notebook*, *Literal Latte*, *So to Speak*, *Agni*, *Indiana Review*, *Northwest Review*, the *Asian Pacific American Journal*, and *Indian Express*. A story received an honorable mention in the 2003 Zoetrope Short Story Contest. She teaches creative writing at George Washington University and is finalizing two collections of short fiction and a novel, while also working on poetry projects. She conducts interviews with bicultural fiction writers, some of which have appeared in AWP's *Writer's Chronicle*. She holds an MFA (poetry) from George Mason University, and a BS in physics and an MBA from the University of Madras, India. Her collection of poems, *Invisible Season*, won the Washington Writers' Publishing House prize in 1998. She received a National Endowment for the Arts fellowship in poetry in 2005.

At five p.m. one Wednesday evening, Pravin stood, rigid, on the top outside step of the Washington Dance India Institute's studio, looking in at his wife Mira, trying not to feel irritated that she wouldn't turn, look at him. She floated, arms raised, in her magnolia-pink sari in front of her students, demonstrating Kuchipudi dance gestures with her hands. Skin flushed pink, sweat glazing the moon of her forehead, as if she'd been dancing all afternoon.

Crocodile, he'd heard her say already, as he came up the stone path to the side of this lovely performing arts center in this cherry-tree brimming suburb of Northwest DC. *Bird sitting still. Bird flying. Look, wings flapping!* It made him remember the first time he'd met her, at her parents' house in Madras, with his parents beside him. Her voice the first thing he heard. Outside the front window, shaded by tall yellow-and-red speckled crotons, a small ecstasy of longing. *I want to dance,* she was saying, in a rush of little-girl whirling, *I want to dance!* She was laughing. Her voice smooth as brandy, sweet burn of cognac swirled in a glass you held up to appreciate in mellow, yellow lamplight. And there was so much to appreciate in Mira Krishna. Her satiny shining hair, almost-Punjabi peaches-and-cream skin, exquisite dancer's gait, that especially, sinuous slide of satiny thigh and hip through always stunned, admiring air. Pravin appreciated the barely withheld gasps when Mira walked into rooms, at his side. Her long-lashed dancer's eyes etched in charcoal blue eyeliner, lips lush pouts of Revlon raspberry red, her exquisite Agra jewelry lighting up her throat and earlobes, intricate filigrees of silver, deep burning hearts of topaz and garnet and emerald. Her saris jewel colors too, in georgette and silk. Even her jeans as unique, soft as brushed velvet. She was both beautiful and elegant. Well-endowed and well-appointed. Trophy wife. His Indian beauty. And a dancer. What a catch.

People came right out and said it to him. He affected distance, cool and all-accepting, as if this were simply his due, as if all Indian women were this astonishingly beautiful. "Indian women," he'd murmur, and leave it at that. He'd schooled himself to be self-deprecating. He'd spent years shaping this quality in himself. From very young, there was a certain something he'd wanted to be seen as, cool, cerebral, remote, it was how his father was, and some of his uncles, and his most deliberate professors in business school, the image of success, he learned, he'd trained himself into it. High on ideas, low on words. A self-confessed *visionary,* like the other non-techie managers at his IT consultancy, who didn't have a specialty to warrant the appellate "technical" but had *visions* of things. They understood him. Him saying a little meant a lot. They understood this.

They weren't to know he'd chosen her for her looks. Or her talent. He had specified these, in his criteria for the marriage. The bride must be fair, he'd always known, and independently talented. He'd meant, she must have an interest in building a singular, separate but domestic life, apart from him. (He'd imagined home decor, laminated maple leaves in the fall, glazed baby squash in straw baskets at the door, wreaths of pine on the bannisters at Christmas. He had lived just long enough in the States to consider these quintessentially, almost agelessly, American.) He'd wanted a dancer. An Indian classical dancer, schooled especially in that ancient South Indian art, Bharatanatyam. My wife is a dancer, he'd always wanted to say, with a slight, urban smile. Permitting the weight of ancient history to enter the room on his arm. He smiled when his American colleagues remarked on the ancience of the art, how Bharatanatyam perhaps was older than anything in America. He did not dispute or elaborate. He had learned to smile, to say simply: My wife is trained classically.

At which reminding thought Pravin coughed, a gentle, vocal hint. But his dancer wife was absorbed in flowers now and could not hear him. *Flower opens,* she said, delightedly to the room full of rustling seven- and eight- and nine-year-olds. *Jasmine or rose. Champa flower. Sweet-smelling, so sweet.* He noticed faintly, approvingly, with the back of his mind, that she did not say redbud, or cherry, or daffodil, all of which were blooming outside, in the middle of this Washington spring. (It was a feat to remain in touch, mentally and emotionally, with one's own culture when one was living in the West, tens of thousands of miles away, it was surely commendable.) She closed her eyes, moved open-cup fingers in front of her nose, pink pallu trembling as she inhaled. *Long stem of flowers opening*—she opened and closed her cupped fingers along her arm. She was absorbed and could not see or hear him. Seemingly lost in herself—he recognized the signs. For days, no, months he'd felt this absorption in her, growing like a secret flower-bed, full of closed-in scents and slow, heated obsession. For months he'd felt his own resentment at it bruise and graze like hive-stricken skin. A flowering of his own, rough tonguing of annoyance, a springing of tiny, sting-tipped hairs on a rose stem. He felt it now, unwanted irritation rasp along the outside of his arm. He wanted her just to turn, look at him. But she wouldn't.

It was one little pony-tailed girl, pointing to another, whispering, See, man at the door, that seemed to wake her to his presence. She didn't stop talking and gesturing, she turned, smiling, to Pravin for a moment, then moved her eyes away, Come children, let's go over our *hasta mudras* before we close. *Path-ah-ka* said the children obediently. *Tri-path-ah-ka.* Holding up their palms, variously moving their fingers in the ancient Natya Shastra gestures for the hand. Sounding for all the world like they were learning Sanskrit in India, in an ancient temple. But Pravin felt mollified. She was closing. He looked affably around the room. Three white American girls, one Chinese American, two African American, the rest Indian. Children of expats like him. Eager to inculcate the consciousness of the ancient culture in their children, make sure things like the dancing and the veena-playing and the sitar were not lost, but carried down, through the generations. You couldn't just talk about your ancient culture after all. You had to be able to show it off. It was at times like these he felt superior, viscerally Indian. He would never confess it out loud, to a single American he worked with or knew socially, but he felt secretly, despite what he knew of the pre-Columbian history of the Americas, that what America didn't have was a sense of tradition carried down through the ages (wasn't America essentially young, and full of the folly of youth?), and it was tradition that was folded deep into the meaning of this place, this moment. The Indian dance institute in the middle of America's capital. The Indian woman, teaching dance to the next generation. *His* wife. *His* children.

Well, the latter not exactly his, right now. Not yet. But soon, one day. Very soon, in fact, given his plan. Pravin stepped back to the patio and lit a cigarette. He hadn't expected to think such a thought, at this precise moment, but perhaps it wasn't that unexpected. All things are fate, he thought, if you took the *shudh* and proper Hindu view. He was thinking these larger thoughts, about civilizations and history and the formerly unrecognized art of Bharatanatyam being passed down, fluidly, to the next generation, precisely because he had been consulting his calendar and had realized it was time, now, to start their own quest for lineal continuance. It was time. The universe was saying this to him. Strengthening his resolve, rooting for him, willing him to go onward.

He knew exactly how he was going to broach the subject to Mira. Reopen it, that is. They had been married two years and had always intended to have children later and now it was time. Candlelight, a glass of Sicilian Cabernet, just before the National Philharmonic concert at the Kennedy Center. He would be gentle, teasing, affectionate. Only faintly, allusively sexual. That language of skin on skin, the passion that still flared between them, that could come later. He might run his index finger down her arm, maybe, or tuck a tendril of silky hair behind her ear. She was wearing a sari.

He might slide his fingers delicately over her exposed hip, touch the in-slope, vortex of her navel. It might start to get heated. But he would pull away, smile, say, let's go make the baby at home, darling, what do you say?

She would laugh, in that crinkly nose, lip-puckering way she had, she would lean forward—

At this moment a melee of children broke out of the studio, chattering. Mira pushed through a cluster of girls frozen at the door and said, frowning, I had no idea you were coming to see me.

The itch of discomfort he'd begun to feel lately in her presence returned. I told you I was coming to pick you up, he said. The concert, remember?

What concert?

Mozart's Piano Concerto in F Major, with Andrei Buganov and the National Philharmonic—it's tonight, at the Kennedy Center.

O god. She sounded as if she were discovering a stomach cramp in her lower abdomen.

He felt a small, petulant coldness enter his voice. I thought you might enjoy it.

Yes, yes, she said, as if resigned. Yes, you do like classical music. She was rummaging in her purse, as if for her car keys. But what will I do with my car, if I come with you?

I'll drop you off tomorrow, he said. You can leave your car here.

I suppose. She stopped searching in her bag. But she looked bereft.

We already talked about this. He realized that tone, of impatience, had crept back into his voice.

I forgot.

She sat primly in the seat beside him as he drove through shoals of evening traffic on MacArthur Boulevard, then M Street, heading for his favorite Italian restaurant in Georgetown. Then she sighed. I get so tired after teaching all afternoon, she said. It's not even like we're dancing a lot, these kids are just learning. But just talking makes you tired. She pulled out her makeup case and began fluffing up her hair, sliding eye shadow sticks over her lids. Always make up your eyes if you're falling asleep, she said. Cardinal rule of cosmetics. Look wide awake through artifice.

If he hadn't been trying to cut off an SUV (outsized Expedition, too big for DC roads), another SUV (mid-sized, Explorer, the kind he might want for his children), and a red convertible (almost perfect for a bachelor, but he wasn't one anymore) changing lanes just then, he might have responded with a small, stroking compliment (you know you never need makeup, darling), but as it was, he could only grunt.

They had barely settled into their table when she excused herself to go to the Ladies' Room. Freshen up, she murmured, although she had been doing that nonstop in the car. She sailed away, leaving the whole room to watch, mesmerized, the hourglass curve of her open hip and the rose-pink shimmering of her sari as she moved.

Later she ate as if starved, twirling parsley-spattered spaghetti round her silver fork in haphazard frenzy, cutting the ends off with her knife, or biting them off mid-air with her white shiny teeth, so yellow butter dripped down her chin and hot fresh bits of tomato and artichoke flecked her lips. The sensuousness of this spectacle drove through his body as solidly as sun wedging through ice. He wanted to lean, eat the food off her lips, kiss, at least touch, slide his fingers into her mouth. But she was as quick with her napkin as her greed, she flicked and wiped and pressed the shimmers of chive and garlic away, he flinched, almost, to see the red lips so casually abraded, so flattened and pursed away.

She wanted to talk about the children, the mothers, the dances she liked and disliked, the steps she wanted to invent, for their Christmas concert, months away. He listened, poured her more Cabernet, sipped remotely at his own glass and measured the slow rise of his unease as the wine slipped lower between them. The children, he murmured at one point, imagining segue. But, yes, she responded excitedly, I want them to do it by themselves, come up with a whole dance of their own. Wouldn't that be fabulous?

He frowned, could not answer. These children were not his children. There was no reason to act like they were hers. He would bring her back to Georgetown, he thought, just before they crossed the river, after the concert. They'd stop for liqueurs—deep, smoky, sweet, something with anisette perhaps, or blackberry—in large round brandy snifters. They'd gaze into the liquid translucence, then sip, let the fire slide down their throats and all over their bodies. He'd broach the subject then.

But he hadn't bargained for the effect of the concert on his already exhausted wife. Sometime after the interval he noticed she was fast asleep, head lolled down on her shoulder, purse slipping down the slippy nylon pleats of her sari to the red-carpeted auditorium floor, while a whole orchestra of violins slanted their melancholy up to the crystal chandeliers. The after-dinner liqueur had to be shelved. They drove across the river on Key Bridge in silence. Mira slept, and Pravin took in the flicker of window lights on the tall buildings in Rosslyn. To his left, he could see Roosevelt Bridge, a dazzle of lights on dark water, and his day's intentions churned far beneath, as he drove. He strove to collect himself. Always be positive, he told himself, recalling his MBA lessons. Bounce back after a breath. Never let yourself be stopped, by any kind of obstacle whatsoever. It was, after all, just one day. The first day of his intention in action. Tomorrow, he told himself, tiredly, would still be the right time.

But the morning, unfortunately, augured badly. He caught a glimpse of her as he stood in front of the dining room mirror, nervously adjusting his cuff links. The coffee maker on the sideboard still. No smell of fresh-roasted Kona beans in the air. Beyond, the curtains were drawn and the sliding doors slid open. Across the grass, by the pale, drooping arms of the flowering cherry which had persuaded them to buy this lovely old house in McLean, despite its exorbitant price, she stood in her lavender satin pajamas, pouring birdseed from an old coffee can into the blue cottage-shaped bird feeder. Beyond stood the mimosa, also reminiscent of home, which had also persuaded him, its feathery green leaf buds shivering slightly. A breeze blew through the exposed wire screen and Pravin went over and pulled the glass doors shut. He was cold, it was too early, he wanted his coffee.

She looked across, waved. But she went back to her bird-feeding. Her arms bare in their sleeveless top, as if she didn't feel the morning coolness in the air. It was clear she was in no hurry to come in, make the coffee, like she did every morning.

Pravin left through the front door. The lush sweet smell of the purple hyacinths they'd planted by the front washed him in dizzy fragrance. Long orange light touched the stubbly new grass. Lime-green leaves sprouted from the Norway maple in front, and from the red oak across their quiet McLean street. He inhaled, and a thousand smells, of sap, magnolia, hyacinth, spread damply into his lungs. He felt how alive he was, how hungry he was. He drove, trying to decide between cranberry orange muffins and banana loaf, for his coffee stop at Starbucks. Luckily there *was* a Starbucks, fairly close. He'd discovered it a few weeks ago, in the dead of winter, when Mira had forgotten to wake, make him coffee. She had a later schedule than his, she didn't have to leave until ten. But she always made coffee. Or rather, she had used to. It was only lately that she had started to slip.

For over a year, he ruminated, they'd had the perfect marriage, the kind he had always wanted. Roles, he had said to her the day after the full formal ceremony of their first, brokered meeting at her parents' house, when they were more relaxed, on their own, at an ice cream parlor. I believe roles make life smooth, make life work. What do you think? And she had said, obliquely, yet wide-eyed, lit up, as if she wanted to flirt, I believe it's important not to alter anyone's core beliefs, don't you think? And she had smiled, and they had both let the question sit, like melting ice cream, between them, and he had weighed the soft womanliness of it, the slight evasiveness of it, and found it good. She wasn't protesting. She was young, impressionable, pliable. She was a good Brahmin girl, trained in house-making. I like things in the house neat, he said next. And she concurred, smiling. No other way to live, she said. I pursue perfection, he said. I am a perfectionist. But I know that, she said, smiling more sweetly. You found me. They dissolved into mutual appreciation thereafter. He felt they'd worked through that fine clingy gauze of tension that had sprung up early between them. A tension that was understandable, he thought, given the contrived way they had met. But they could move on now, to other conversations, considerations. Music, art, dance. Culture. All equally important.

Dancing is our most ancient art, he told her. You know I have always wanted a dancer for my wife.

Yes, she said, smiling, as if he amused her. Yes, I heard that.

What does it make you feel? He watched her.

She shrugged. *Wanted,* she said, extravagantly, with a little flourish of her hands and a smile. But I am a *dancer. I want to be wanted*.

What do you mean? Something about the immediacy of her answer, as if it were long known to her, long thought of, pulled at him, made him uneasy.

I want to dance! It's what I want to do! He heard again the raw, boyish eagerness in her voice he'd first heard, outside the window, the day before, the childlike chanting.

Perhaps it should have served as danger flag then, first sign. But the perfection of her jasmine skin, doe's eyes, swan limbs, her elegant dancer's fingers moved him deeply. Looking, he could imagine a world experienced through her—green grass, hiking in the Shenandoah, smell of damp earth on rain, all of it, mist, snow, steam from a rose-soaked bath, light from white candles, a whirling of bubbles in champagne moving through her, sensuously, into his being. An uprush of emotion seized him, just looking at her perfectly put-together face. She was everything he had wanted. Someone to turn a side of him to the world, articulate for him his fine aesthetic sensibility, his unspoken sensitivity, his talent for perfection. He would marry her.

But a few things remained to settle. My life is in the United States now, he said, carefully. I have my consultancy there.

I know, she said. You're a green-card holder. It's what I wanted.

He was taken aback, but only slightly. The seeming forwardness of the remark struck him. But this was an arranged situation, he reminded himself. It should not be unusual to imagine that she too could have expectations. So he said nothing, merely raised an eyebrow. Who doesn't want to go live in the U.S., she said, in explanation. (Even to him, faintly suspicious, probing—it was after all 1985, everyone he knew thought the U.S. the ultimate destination—this felt credible.)

I want to travel, after we are married, he said. Every year, to a different country. Take cruises maybe, to Alaska, Greece, the South Pacific.

She smiled serenely. Who doesn't want to travel, she said.

They cruised to the Mediterranean (Greece, Turkey, Italy, Spain, Portugal, Morocco, Algeria) for their honeymoon. One year after they were married, she traveled with her Indian dance troupe to Australia. She was gone for three months, dancing across the continent. When she came back she was five pounds lighter but as beautiful. In less than six months, she had started teaching dance, Kuchipudi and Bharatanatyam at this dance institute in Washington. And everything had started unraveling.

Not noticeably, no. Such things happen slightly, without warning. A missed meal, a vase growing black fungus in the water, among the dead aster stems, a cracked plate set before him, a fine network of cracks in the white face of once-pristine china. So he stared down at it, not registering just then, what any of it signified. Once he saw a trailing spider-thread of web, gray and mist-like, on the ceiling in the hallway, beside the front light. He came home to an unlocked door, the velvety purple African violet he'd bought her last Christmas dry and curled without water. The dishwasher filled and not run. Coffee cups unwashed in the sink. The fluffy blue bathroom rugs, meant never to be tumbled dry, lifted from the dryer in balls and clumps of fur, sprayed like cotton fluff all over the basement.

It told him something. Something had lifted, something slight and necessary, from the calm mantle of bliss between the front and back doors, that he'd taken for granted after the first year of their living together. There was a slight air of uncertainty now to the house, like it might tip over into the future, undusted, unmopped, slipped clean of its cover of familial warmth, unhoused. The uncertainty crept over and covered her. Nights when they were home together she was lost in research, or sewing a dance costume, or planning her classes. Too busy with teaching now. Too busy with dance. It was as if she had closed herself in, like a mimosa leaf. All the tiny openings in her once sprayed out in series, branch upon branch, in daylight, now closing inward and flattened to his gaze so what he saw was the silver backside of her attention, a slight shimmer, deep sleepiness, as if it were permanent twilight now, violet approach of dusk.

For a month or so, with the back of his mind, he felt an urgency root and move in him. A fine thread of anxiety knotted and pulled, the fear that she might step, further and further into herself, out from the bright circle of his need. And his need swelled and blew about him, palpable and seen. He knew he needed to do something to bring her back, to the house, the home, the life between them.

Surely, it was time.

In the evening he stopped by at the florist's next to the Starbucks and was persuaded to buy a sizeable bunch of warm red tulips, the bright dizzy red of their marriage sari. Hers, yes, but hadn't he always thought of it as theirs? In India, he felt, what a woman wore expressed what everyone wanted. The tradition of the culture always carried into the present on a woman's back, on the slide of a silk *choli* across shoulder bones, or the glint of a silver anklet on delicate ankle bones, or *mehendi* scrawling its patterns of leaves and waves on painted toes. So the brilliant brocade of the marriage sari she wore had always been his. And the smell that rose to him as he raised the bouquet to his nostrils, faint sweetness of cut pineapple, faint crushing of cinnamon, faint smoke of vanilla rising from a baking cake in the oven, all spelled for him the memory of the woman who stood, more surely, for the essence of what he understood was his culture, his memory: his mother. He looked deep into the satin heart of the tulip, with its black stamens and bright yellow spuds of pollen and breathed, and stood once more in his mother's kitchen, with the hot smell of *sambar* cooking at lunch, or *payasam* or cake at tea, or fried bitter gourd or cauliflower at night. He could almost smell the plain butter cake she baked for birthdays, rich with vanilla and nuts, that she layered and filled with cream. He felt, once again, the cosmos close in on him, as strongly as if a series of spiral galaxies had suddenly opened before his eyes. No, not the one with the roses, he told the woman helping him. This one, the red tulips.

He wanted to surprise her. He held the tulips behind his back as he walked up the path to the front door.

It was dusk. The birds were singing their evening songs. He saw the mockingbird that lived in the sweet lilac fly up onto the roof of their house. He imagined how Mira would come to the door, deep sultriness of her voice, delicacy of her movements, shape of her body. Moving like a dancer. A wave of forgiving affection swirled through him on the thought. He knew that everything about her was shaped by her dancing. He remembered what she'd told him about the time, long ago, when she had first started dancing, at five or six. My soles cracked, she said. The skin peeled and swelled and blistered, I danced so much. The dance school had a cement courtyard. It was flat and even, but when you danced you could feel the small grainy imperfections in the floor. I danced more than all the other girls in the dance school, even the older ones. I wanted to learn everything, all at once! I wanted to know dance, inside and out, the body of dance. For years my feet peeled and cracked, before they became hard, developed a skin to match the skin of the concrete.

Now she used foot creams obsessively, essential oils and foot soaks, all variously scented in lavender and jasmine and rose. It was her nightly ritual, before she slept. She sat on her side of the bed, half-lotused, smoothing and massaging. The skin of her soles still not soft, like her hands, but smooth now, firm and confident. A dancer's feet, a mature dancer. No longer a child in training. A woman dancer.

Warmth flooded him, considering that.

He knocked, waited, but she did not open the door. Dusk clung bluely to the air around him. He imagined her upstairs, in the shower, on the phone. He leaned in, listened for footsteps. Silence tossed. After five minutes, he let himself in. The hallway was dark. He switched on lights, paused to smell the softly heated air. The smell of the ginger-peach candle on the hallway table, unlit, came to him, sweet and pungent. No smells of dinner cooking. It was then he remembered he had not seen her car parked outside. She wasn't home yet.

He stood for a second in the dining room, gazing at the smooth shining surface of the table. The emptiness of the house closing in on him. Outside, he could hear the mockingbird begin its endless round of bird imitations. Robins, titmouses, Carolina wrens. As if it were perpetually in apprenticeship to other birds, other masters of song, perpetually in learning.

He opened cabinets, looking for a vase. He went into the kitchen, found the glass vase shaped like a giant conch shell—a wedding gift. He slid the cellophane off, cut the ends of the stems, emptied the small packet of flower preserver into the vase. He half-filled the vase with water, slid the tulips in. He cleared the debris away.

He took the vase to the dining room, to the table, put the tulips down. He stood, uncertain. Then he went over and pulled the curtains aside. For a long time he stood by the glass doors, looking into the clumping spread of dusk. The raw clammy feeling spidering its way through him causing an old memory to rise. As a child, at six, he had thrown a tantrum on the veranda of their house in Madras one evening, with relatives looking on, because his mother had told him she was going out shopping now with her sister and would not take him with her. His mother had always been by his side. She met his every need, anticipated his wants, knew to read his mind. He was an only son, fourth in a family of four, the long-awaited boy—first boy, only boy. He was used to being listened to, to being treated differently from the three girls. He was used to never being denied or thwarted. He wanted her to stay when he wanted her to stay. It was tea time, he wanted her to assemble his snacks and milk for tea. But she was not going to, she said. Someone else would, soon, maybe the servant-lady, or his father. Not she. So he kicked every relative in sight with his sharp little shoes (his mother's whole family had come for lunch that day), and he screamed and threw books and papers from the hall into the garden. His father picked him up, kicking and shouting, and took him inside. Tears of balked intent and rage streaked down his face.

This was around the time his father began to teach him restraint. Grown men remove themselves from emotion, his father, the general manager of a textile mill, told him. Whatever the emotion, you grow a skin over it. Learn what your role in life is, as a boy. His father started to spend more time with him, taking him to the factory, introducing him to the workers, letting him sit in on disputes with workers, managers, government inspectors. He took him to Crocodile Park one Sunday and showed him, in the twist and lash of the scaly creatures threshing with each other in a muddy pool what he meant by skin: a powerful sheath, deflective, protective, even lethal. At home, Pravin followed his father around the house, watching and learning. Even on the days when he was silent with his mother, his father let him privately into his confidence, so he began to see his mother then through his father's eyes as well as his own: less, inevitably, as a woman, soft, who used tears as a weapon. *For men there are ways to get your way without tears and other useless emotion.* There are other ways to express your displeasure than screaming. And over the years Pravin learned those ways, learned from his father how to get what you want through raising your voice in threat or walking away, not speaking, bottling it up and spilling it out in petulance, or coldness, or irritation. Through building a skin over your real feelings, to deflect and hold in, both, a cool, urbane skin, like metal.

But he never forgot that day his mother first turned from him, or how he felt—the rawness of it, furious, but worse, despairing. With a keening sharpness to the feeling, as if a hole with teeth were gouging its way downward into his guts and he could do nothing to stop it.

It was the feeling that tore silently, screamless, through him now. He did not know why Mira was so late, why there was no dinner being made yet, although it was nearly seven. He did not know how, when he was finally making an effort to set aside the pressures of his work life and make space, mentally, for a change in their family, she could be so removed and distant that she was neither receptive to his thinking nor capable of intuiting it. She was barely in his presence, he thought. She had neither called tonight nor left a message. It was as if she had a life apart from him, he didn't know it anymore.

Outside, a life of its own was going on. The yard seemed alive with wings and cries. Birds flew in and out of the cherry tree, taking turns at the bird feeder she had filled in the morning.

When she came home, at nine, he was eating a heated-up frozen dinner of black bean enchiladas, the newspaper propped open on the table. She seemed surprised to see him.

You're home early!

He sipped from his glass of Heineken and strove to calm himself. I was here at six-thirty.

That's really early for you! She stood in the doorway in a black jacket over a brilliant peacock-blue sari, soft slippery georgette, patterned all over with blue daisies picked out in satin embroidery. Her purse slipping, clutching a sheaf of papers. Her eyes all lit up with dark blue eye shadow, face radiant, as if she'd run all the way home. Usually, you're never home before nine.

This was true. He did not know how to answer without injuring himself. For the past year and a half, he had stayed late at the office every day, as if this were his religion. Or taken clients out to dinner before he came home, pecking at his food at both places. He had built a strong client base, forged *robust* client relations. His focus was essential to the success of his firm. Without this kind of sacrifice, they would never have acquired the strong foundation he had envisioned. He had gone over this with Mira earlier, many times, each time she protested. Which she had, for months, before she stopped protesting. He could not explain now that things had changed.

Where have you been, he said instead.

It's a good thing you're eating, she said, ignoring that easily, putting her papers down, taking her jacket off. I've already eaten.

Oh? Where did you go? He felt confused. With whom, was what he wanted to say. Is this a habit of yours? Do you make dinner late, just for me? Are you always home late, or is this an exception? But he did not know how to open this conversation without sounding powerless and overlooked and ignorant.

She herself was not withholding. Oh close by, you know that Italian place at Dupont that has the fireplace—we went over there after work, it was Amrita's birthday. She seemed buoyant, alive, as if it were the beginning of the day, not the end.

She saw the tulips at the same moment as the phone rang. How lovely! She pulled the vase to her, bent close, the red tulips fanning out extravagantly above her peacock-blue *pallu*. Hmmm, these have no smell. But they're gorgeous. She picked up the phone. Hello? Oh—hi Adrian!

Pravin put his fork down and stared at her. Smell it properly, he wanted to say. It took him a minute to register it was his CPA on the phone. British, buoyant Adrian Stone. He scraped the last of the black beans and corn off his Styrofoam dish and downed the last of his beer, preparing for the phone. But she was in no hurry to hand it over. She went to the window, talking to Adrian. She had lowered her voice so he couldn't hear. But she turned every now and then to look at him. Her face seemed to glow. She laughed a few times. It did not annoy him so much as abrade him. Not merely the fact that she was chatting cordially with *his* business colleague, but that she was, effectively, ignoring him. Pravin sat still, looking fixedly at the tulips, which seemed to burn where they sat, hot cups of flame, and waited.

At lunch the next day he ran into her on K Street, at 17th. He had just crossed over with a group of his colleagues and a new client they were taking to lunch. He saw her as they crossed the road. She was with someone. It was the first thing he noticed. She was not alone. She was laughing, a hand on Adrian's arm, her long black hair swinging free on her shoulders. He registered the image with a strange shock of recognition. A kind of shifting inside him as he looked, as if tectonic plates inside him had slid, one under another. That was Mira. She was with Adrian Stone, his CPA. She looked up as they walked toward her, she stopped and talked to his colleagues. Adrian patted him casually on the back. I've had the pleasure of lunching with your lovely wife, he said. We just had lunch together, she said. Calmly, as if it were an ordinary occurrence. They had run into each other at Chapters, the bookstore—yes, what a coincidence, Pravin agreed, keeping his voice just as calm. Adrian looked fit and casual in his blue denim shirt and sports jacket. Mira looked like a Benetton model in cream slacks and a reddish brown sweater intricately patterned with cream circles. Her eyes made up in gold and brown eye shadow, lips glossy in brick red. They were both smiling and restless.

I have to go check in with Amrita, she said.

Isn't it your day off? The words creaked out of him with difficulty.

Oh, yes, but you know how overworked we both are, she helps me out, I should help her. Besides, I haven't danced today, I must. Mira smiled and turned to Adrian. Ready, Adrian? Adrian offered to drive me to my car, I parked a mile away, she said.

Oh. He could not offer to drive her himself, since Robert Bowman, his Commerce client, was standing one foot from him, looking pointedly at his watch. I have to get going, he said. See you at home, then.

Bye! They waved cheerily and walked away.

You have a beautiful wife, said Robert, as they walked into Bombay.

Thank you, he said mechanically, she is a classical Indian dancer.

He made other mechanical responses as they were seated, ordered drinks, then sipped their drinks. It was second nature now, to him, to present the calm façade they had grown to expect while his mind ticked in multiple directions at once. He looked down at his iced tea, at the cubes of ice jostling against the candy-cane straw, the brandy-colored tea, and remembered that the office party at his house, a few months earlier, was where Adrian had met Mira.

What did it all mean? He stood in his office after lunch and considered. He remembered the trail of tea lights in votive frosted holders she had laid up their front path and into the house, the sound of Bert Kaempfurt's trumpet from the album *Dancing in Wonderland* trailing up the steps, soft welcome to their guests. She had made easily a dozen unique, interesting vegetarian dishes. She was eager to prove to his meat-eating office that vegetarian cuisine could be delicious and complete. The smell of roasted spices, green chilies, and fried garlic clung to the air, even as you stepped in.

She was dressed in a long navy and turquoise skirt, a white polo-neck sweater. Her hair swept up into a sleek black knot. Long silver filigree earrings with sapphire-blue glass accents touched her shoulders. She stood by the sideboard in the dining room, poured wine, smiled and talked to everyone. He remembered Adrian staring at her when he walked in, as if she were slightly unreal. Aren't you going to introduce me, Adrian had said, without taking his eyes from her. When he did, Adrian kissed the back of her hand, as if he were French from his single trip to France the previous year, and Pravin was invisible. Mira, losing her sophistication in one sweep, blushed and dissolved into nervous giggling. Adrian was tall, fit, blonde, a skier with a taut physique. Pravin, who had never been athletic, and only walked for exercise, had never felt less than any man—he carried in himself the knowledge of having been first in class, after all, in every subject, all through school, college, his B.Sc. in Math, his MBA—but right then he felt like wilted spinach beside the athletic Adrian.

He got Adrian a drink, then stepped into the living room to mingle with his colleagues and their families. When it was time for dinner he returned to the dining room and saw they were both seated by the table, avidly talking and laughing. Adrian cooks, Mira said when he entered. I'm trying to get him to cook for us. He didn't remember what he said just then. He didn't cook. It wasn't Indian for a man to cook. No, it wasn't manly for an Indian man to cook. He strove to ignore the creeping discomfort he felt, each time he ran across an American man who cooked. Or British. Worse, prided himself on it.

He remembered only how she looked, looking at Adrian, her hair sweaty and damp near her forehead, skin shiny. The look in her eyes. Dazzled. Lit. As if something had sparked fireworks inside her, whistling rockets and platinum fountains and trains of sparklers, and she could no longer see the room, the walls, the table, just him.

But she was not married to him.

Pravin stepped away from his window overlooking L Street and sat down at his desk and stared at his computer screen instead. He thought of his friends at work, of their children. Dave had two adorable toddlers, three and two, golden-haired, blue-eyed little Nordics, like himself. Joanne had just recently had her baby, a brown, soft nugget of a child, a perpetual bounce to his limbs. Nita, his sister, was still nursing her newborn—pink-brown, barely a foot long, a bundle of eyes and mouth.

Surely, it was time.

He picked up his coat, left the office. It was about three when he reached her studio. The sunlight of noon had been replaced by a layer of cloud, behind which the light pulsed a silver gray. The color of the air here, under the trees, was a curious pause between lime green and gray, the color of impending rain. He could almost smell it. He walked up the path, feeling a lightness to his bones, as if they were dissolving into the air and the sweet wet earth, everything bursting and blooming and growing around him. He felt rawly, vividly alive. Wrapped in a weather of the senses, drawn deep into himself and out, edgily in clarity, in control.

He heard her voice as he came toward the open door, caught a glimpse of her moving, gesturing. (Reddish brown and cream, the glimpse.) But this, the incongruity of her attire, the untraditionality of it, made him pause. She was still in the slacks and sweater. Teaching dance—classical Kuchipudi dance—to the next generation of Indian American dancers in jeans and a sweater. He ceased his forward movement. She was moving her fingers like a bird flying, a wing lifted. Her body was pounding a rhythm on the floor. *Goodbye*, she was saying to her class, *God be with you, farewell.* And *goodbye,* her class echoed, *farewell, goodbye, farewell.* Her voice the rich sure contralto he loved.

He wanted to step forward, make himself noticed. But she seemed to be in the middle of her class. He stood before the steps, undecided. He put a hand on the wall and the textured surface of it cracked beneath his hands, came off. Small, a flake of creamy plaster. He stared for a moment, uncomprehending, looked up.

The wall was swollen and cracked, as if water had long seeped and spread under it. He stared at it, hearing the rhythmic thud of feet on the wooden floor inside, as the children danced. First they danced forward, then they danced back, pounding the same patterned beat.

Something was singing behind him, maybe a bird, or a memory. Words he did not understand covered and smote him. They were notes, sharp, discrete packets of notes punching holes into the lime-green air, songs stolen from birds—cardinals, wrens, titmouses. A mockingbird, singing.

He stared at the wall. A child's warm foot floated up before him and he rubbed the sole, feeling the peel and blistering. Feeling how countries were drawn on the surface, as if on a map, whole coastlines and oceans in the cracks and the swells, islands breaking loose from plaster. Feeling how skin was only skin and could flake away from a wall, exposing whatever was beneath. He was not in the open mouth of the door and she could not see him. He had stepped back, so he too could no longer see her. He was pulled up, down, outside himself as the music rolled. His body inert, all sense of direction suddenly closed inside his limbs. He crumbled the plaster flake in his hands. Not sure, anymore, how to step, in what direction.

J. H. Diehl and Susan Coll

from *Brain Fever*

J.H. Diehl is the author of the children's book *Loon Chase.* A fifth-generation Washingtonian, she has been parking at the Bradley Center since toys along the old back wall of Bruce Variety cost a dime. Susan Coll's third novel, tentatively titled *Acceptance,* will be published in March 2007.

Chapter 1: Bethesda, Maryland 1999

"Madame, you are stealing my parking space!" shrilled an elegantly accented female voice. Three quick honks punctuated her impatience. Flustered, Miranda fumbled with the parking brake and struggled to unlock her door. She was still getting used to the various gizmos of her new minivan. Fluency with its digital locking system was one thing: the van seemed to require an adjustment of her self-image to fit a lifestyle that warranted a vehicle the size of a school bus; suggestive of a mom who toted hockey teams around the county, or who stashed bags of perfectly pumped soccer balls and huge refreshment coolers in the rear cargo compartment. It was a demographic that didn't include her husband's large-breasted, garbage-encrusted sculptures, she thought, glimpsing the plaster human body parts crammed behind Zoë's booster seat.

She decided to ignore the angry woman's verdict. Her very big van was going to sit where she had finally managed to squeeze it, between two much smaller vans parked at the outer edges of their respective yellow-lined spaces at the Bradley Center on Arlington Road. At ninety-eight wretchedly humid degrees it was far too hot for confrontation of any sort. It was almost too hot to breathe, let alone run errands. She'd been living abroad the previous few summers and had forgotten how bad August in Washington could be. In her absence the air seemed to have taken on new properties. It was no longer the odorless invisible gas she had learned about in elementary school science class; it had become somehow *tangible*, like latex.

The door opened only halfway before it bumped the side of the van in the next space. She squeezed through the narrow opening between the cars and rummaged under the dirty laundry in her arms to find her hand, holding the new key chain, so she could be sure to touch the right button to lock the door. Was someone still shouting? A couple of Rick's shirts fell to the pavement. Miranda scrambled them back into her arms, ready to press through the dense heat to the sanctuary of the dry cleaners. Yes, it was the same voice, yelling further allegations about the stolen parking space, and accompanied by another, jarring minor chord from the horn. People walking across the chaotic parking lot stopped in their tracks to watch, setting off a chain reaction of screeching brakes and additional horns and the seemingly spontaneous ignition of a high-pitched car alarm. Miranda looked at the yellow Mercedes convertible with diplomatic license plates that was now positioned perpendicular to the van, blocking any possibility of an exit. Behind the wheel sat a tiny woman—a woman so petite that it was hard to imagine her as the catalyst of so much noise.

Despite the humiliating circumstances, Miranda couldn't help but smile at the coincidence. The coincidence being not that the belligerent woman was wrapped in a silk sari the same shade of yellow as her car, but that she appeared to be from India. Miranda had only just returned from India herself, after living for four years in New Delhi. Now she was prepared to rethink this encounter, to view it as somehow fortuitous.

"I'm so sorry," she offered, approaching the Mercedes, pausing to pick up a pair of Rick's paint-splattered trousers, which had fallen too. "Have I done something wrong?"

The woman did not reply, as if to suggest that the question was absurd. Instead, she raised her arm, the flesh of which was barely visible beneath a heap of gold bangles, and pointed her index finger at the minivan.

"I didn't see you," Miranda offered. "I certainly didn't mean to take your space, but you seemed to come out of nowhere. Are you from India?" she asked, hoping to steer the conversation onto friendlier ground.

"Yes," the woman said imperiously. "And in India we do not steal parking spaces. I will wait for you to be moving."

"I wouldn't do that... I mean, it's so big, you know. It's just a giant relief to get it parked." Miranda gave a deflated nod back at her van. "I have a few errands. I need to stop at the pharmacy—my ayah has allergies. We've just brought her back with us. She's finding Washington terrible for allergies, so I said I'd get her some Benadryl or something. And the dry cleaner, of course," she said, gesturing with the laundry. "I need a couple of things at the hardware store, too... I may be half an hour or so." She glanced at her watch.

"Are you absolutely daft?" asked the woman.

"Excuse me?" Miranda was stunned. No one had spoken to her this rudely since she had fought with her brother as a kid. OK, there had been a misunderstanding, now why didn't the woman just move along? Miranda examined the small, angry face, set so stubbornly, and found herself wondering how this person even managed to drive while wearing so many heavy gold ornaments. Numerous ingeniously wrought necklaces weighed from her neck.

"You bloody Americans think you are so superior. I was here first. I was waiting for the parking space, I had my blinker on, even, when you came along in your giant red...your giant red truck thing and stole my spot. I will try to be reasonable with you. If you move your truck now, I will not press charges."

"Press charges?" Miranda screamed. She had actually been contemplating relinquishing her parking space just to be nice, to be bigger than the situation, to be the sort of person who was not so petty as to be undone by these sorts of idiotic incidents. But this last remark irked her wildly. "Press charges?" she repeated, incredulous. Granted, she had been living out of the country for a long time and many subtle things had changed, but she wasn't sure that taking someone's parking spot had risen to the level of a prosecutable crime.

"And just for the record, for when you press your goddamned charges, it's not a truck, it's a minivan," she snapped. "A Limited Edition Suburban Field Cruiser to be precise."

Anticipating a possibly amusing brawl, a small group of people had clustered on the sidewalk in front of the row of shops. An elderly woman leaning over a walker gawked from the entrance to the drugstore. Customers at the beauty parlor peered through the window; one, with her hair on full alert, imprisoned by dozens of silver foil wraps sticking in various directions, even walked out of the salon to see what the fuss was all about. Humiliated, Miranda turned and walked toward Bradley Cleaners, deciding that any further conversation with this mad woman could only be counterproductive.

Rapid, breathy toots escaped from the horn. This time Miranda forbade herself to look back, even as they turned into a continuous wail.

"You'll be sorry," the Indian woman screamed to anyone who could hear. "My husband and I are here in an official capacity! I will be telling your government. You will be hearing from us!"

"This damn heat brings out every nut in town," sympathized the clerk at the cleaners. It was so cool inside the sparse shop that Miranda wished she'd brought a more complicated order, requiring her to linger.

"Thanks," she responded in a singsong she hadn't quite intended. "No starch on the shirts please. And the pants have gesso on them again."

These days, she was trying hard to be cheerful, to not dwell on negative things like the weather—or the pathetic state of her house, or the confusing state of her marriage, not to mention the alarming bank statement that had just arrived, or the forthcoming lunch with her new boss. Even so, she couldn't help but observe that it was actually hotter in Washington than it had been in Delhi for most of the summer. The fact that the air conditioner in the house had been broken until this morning did not help to ease what was already proving to be a very difficult transition.

She had mistakenly believed that the hard part—uprooting her husband and two young children and moving to a foreign land—was behind her; that returning to Washington, to her own house in a familiar neighborhood, would be easy. But ever since the plane set down at Dulles Airport, she had been feeling as though she'd blown some sort of mental fuse. Her latest theory to explain this sense of dislocation was that perhaps the advent of jet airplanes had created a world not meant to be. A world in which people were expected to make seamless transitions from landscapes of dusty cow-clogged roads dotted with begging children, to paved streets and affluent suburban driveways topped by basketball hoops.

She'd failed to anticipate a number of things about returning home. For instance, the house: Had the family of four to whom they rented it been members of a satanic cult? Towel racks had been ripped from the walls; several floorboards were missing; six windowpanes were cracked. The walls in all the bedrooms had been painted black.

She and Rick had purchased it six years ago when they moved to Washington after she landed her job with a small put prestigious hotel chain, the Henry Group. They had both been reluctant to leave New York, and Miranda had just learned she was pregnant. Nevertheless, the tiny but quaint three-bedroom colonial in the leafy Maryland suburbs seemed like a perfect place to start a family. It was a bit of a stretch; Miranda was still paying off student loans from her master's in hotel administration, and Rick, who was from Poland, couldn't expect to earn much from his adopted profession as a house painter—particularly as he wished to devote increasing amounts of his time to sculpting.

They managed to meet their mortgage payments those first two years, but just barely. This explained why, when Miranda was offered an overseas posting, they eagerly accepted, though neither of them particularly desired to live in India. A Henry Group executive, encouraging Miranda to take the job, tried showing off his sensitivity to economic globalization issues, and to their transatlantic marriage, by describing India as being "like Poland, but with fruit." Rick winced at the comparison, since he had struggled for years during the Cold War to obtain a visa to the U.S. and had stood on long queues in Warsaw for Cuban oranges and bananas, only rarely available in Communist Poland.

Going abroad meant generous tax breaks, a company-subsidized lifestyle and just generally ducking out of the American rat race for a while to save some money. And they had, in fact, saved money. They had also managed to spend all of it, in less than three weeks, on home repairs and a red minivan and summer camp for the girls, plus a hefty security deposit on the lease for Rick's studio.

The house seemed smaller now than when they had left, though Miranda couldn't find a way to blame that on the tenants. Perhaps she had been spoiled by her more spacious lodgings in India. The children, of course, were also that much bigger. And now there was an additional body, since they had convinced Mary, their ayah, to come with them to look after the children when Miranda returned to work in September.

Personally, she had been ambivalent about bringing Mary. She and Rick had struck a deal, of sorts, back when she had accepted her unusually demanding job. He'd given her an inspired pep talk about what a brilliant opportunity it was for her career. He insisted that he viewed being a stay-at-home father in India as a privilege. But over time she had begun to see Rick's pep talks more as sales pitches. A pattern of bait and switch was slowly becoming apparent. Yes, he was still, technically, the stay-at-home parent. But how much did he really stay at home? Now that his sculpting career had begun to inch forward, he felt the need to devote himself to it full time, he said. He couldn't be truly creative without a bit of child-care relief and a room of his own in the form of a studio. Miranda tried to express her support, but in truth, she would have liked to stay home with the children and work on her own quashed artistic aspirations, a fantasy she tried hard not to entertain now that they had a mortgage.

There was also Mary herself to worry about. In India she'd been a trusted, though supposedly occasional, babysitter. Miranda traveled so much for her job that in truth she had spent almost no time with Mary until now. The ayah's habitual diffidence in front of Miranda was annoying. Rick had hired her, and she was used to talking to and receiving her instructions from him.

Life in Washington was probably going to be rough for Mary. She didn't drive, owned only saris and sandals, and spoke limited English. She had never been outside of Delhi, let alone India, and had not been thrilled about coming. She agreed to stay a year, but only after they promised to take her to Disney World and buy souvenirs for all of her family members. The arrangements had come together at the last minute. Rick—who was one of those people who usually pulled through in a crisis—somehow managed to get her a passport and visa in time and secured her a seat on the same flight as theirs to Washington.

At Mary's first sight of the basement guest bedroom where she was to live, the expression on her face suggested she found it vastly inferior to her quarters in the windowless, single-car garage she shared with thirteen other people in India. Miranda tried to cajole Mary into believing she was actually lucky—the bedroom in the unfinished basement was at least *cool.* The only cool room in the house, until that morning anyway, when Miranda had written a four-thousand-dollar check for a new air conditioner and a new furnace, both of which had been replaced four years ago before they moved away. How had the renters managed to wreck the entire system? The satanic cult theory continued to hold as the most plausible explanation.

The transition home also threatened to be tougher on the children than anticipated. Miranda had assumed it would be easy to find a day camp or some other equivalent form of amusement for Hannah and Zoë. It turned out that in Washington one was required to make summer plans in February. She called seventeen local day camps in Maryland and in DC, and five in Virginia, until she found one with two openings. The name sounded a bit off-putting: "Life Cycle Studies of Cold-Blooded Vertebrate Animals and Crustacean Arthropods." But the woman on the phone at the Montgomery County Recreation Department insisted that it was, indeed, not a typographical error but a day camp, with activities geared toward five- to eight-year-old children who demonstrated an acute interest in sea life and were considering careers in marine biology. Miranda tried to put a cheerful spin on the situation, and told the girls that they were lucky to be going to a special "fish camp," especially when other, less brilliant children had to make do attending boring old day camps where they only did things like swim and play tennis and make lanyards out of gimp. She was thankful to have found a camp of any sort, since even a temporary membership at the local pool had a wait list of approximately two years. There didn't appear to be a single child riding a tricycle or manning a lemonade stand or otherwise spending the summer sitting idle. School would be starting in just a few weeks, she told Hannah and Zoë, and they'd make lots of lovely new friends in kindergarten and second grade.

Waiting in line at the pharmacy with a packet of allergy tablets in her hand, Miranda picked up a copy of the *Washington Post* and glanced at the headlines, wondering whether she would ever be able to reengage in things like the Orioles, who appeared to be in the midst of a losing streak. Did she care who won the school board race in DC? Did she even know who was running? And where was Loudon County, anyway, and was it really essential that she participate in the debate over whether to approve an Inter-County Highway Connector?

On the bottom right-hand corner a more intriguing headline caught her eye: "Transportation Nightmare Predicted as Concert-Goers Flock to India's Holy City."

Below the headline was a picture of an auto rickshaw wallah, a cigarette dangling from his smiling lips, posed beside his cab full of young Western tourists, with the Ganges River in the background. The gist of the article was that a hundred thousand people were expected to be transiting through the Delhi and Bombay Airports en route to the largest music festival ever to be held on the Indian subcontinent. Three-time Grammy Award-winning German rock star Kaspar Kaspar had organized a gala that was to include thirty other well-known musical groups, gathered to raise money to combat mosquito-borne disease.

In addition to the not wholly unexpected logjam at the airports, a train derailment earlier that week had virtually paralyzed the entire rail system, and two highly publicized bus plunges in Nepal—admittedly another country, but one nearby—had scared people away from the busses. Beneficiaries of this situation, the taxi drivers and rickshaw wallahs, were charging customers more than ten times the normal rate.

Now here was a story Miranda knew something about. Some of her hotels had been booked for weeks for Kaspar Kaspar's concert, especially the Henry Hotel at Varanasi, where the festival was to take place. She saw what the trouble was: the Indian Tourist Board had projected only ten thousand for this event in its advance notice to the hotel industry.

No wonder it was a story. She felt grateful to the newspaper for writing about what still, to her, constituted local news, and made a mental note to renew her subscription.

Another one of the changes that had occurred during her four-year absence from Washington appeared to be the introduction of color to the paper, and it seemed to her they hadn't quite perfected the art. The blue of the sky in the photo seemed fine, if a bit bright, but the color of the Ganges was almost purple. Not the sort of purple that might be mistaken for the dark blue of a river, but a sort of bright purple, a lavenderish shade.

"Do you want to pay for that or not?" said the man behind her.

She turned and saw a long line had formed behind her at the register. "Oh, I'm very sorry," she apologized, pulling a ten-dollar bill from her wallet and handing it to the clerk, who was himself distractedly studying his lottery tickets.

"Do you want the paper, too?" he asked.

"Yes, please."

"That's $16.95."

"*Sixteen ninety-five*?" asked Miranda. "Really? For allergy pills and a newspaper? Wow. Sorry." She pulled another ten-dollar bill from her wallet. It was all beginning to feel like play money, anyway.

Balancing the many packages she had accumulated on her dash through the strip mall, Miranda patted the pocket of her summer dress and managed to retrieve the keys without dropping anything. She was about to open the door when she heard the voice again.

"Twenty-five minutes and thirty seconds," the Mercedes's driver said, staring at her watch and recording the time in a note pad. The car hadn't moved, and was still blocking Miranda's exit.

"Look," she said helplessly. "What do you want from me? I've apologized already. It's only a parking space. Can't we just forget about it?"

"I want your name," said the woman.

"This is ridiculous. I'm not giving you my name. We didn't have an accident, and I didn't do anything wrong. I need to get going. I have to pick my kids up from camp. You can have my space now, if you'll let me out."

"Give me your name and I'll let you out."

"If you really want my name, I'm sure you can figure it out from my license plate."

"Of course I can, so why are you giving me so much trouble? Just tell me your name and I'll let you go. I've called my husband on my mobile phone and told him that I'm being harassed by you. He agrees that I should get your details."

"Oh for Christ's sake," said Miranda. "Miranda. Miranda Smith. All right? Are you happy?" She chided herself for giving in, but she did not want to prolong this encounter.

"Yes, I'm delighted," responded the woman sarcastically, turning on her ignition and putting her car into reverse. She moved it back ever so slightly, leaving Miranda little room for error.

Miranda backed out slowly, still unsteady with the dimensions of the van. She saw the little yellow Mercedes in her rearview mirror, and thought briefly about accelerating hard and crushing it like a bug. But she did the mature thing and simply drove away, slamming on her brakes at the exit of the parking lot just in time to avoid hitting another car. The episode with this nasty woman had rattled her. As she turned onto Bradley Boulevard, she must have been mentally back in India, for she pointed straight into oncoming traffic, on the wrong side of the road. She swerved the van into the right lane; it moved like a giant blowfish, all body, no tail. She caught the wheel, and herself, just in time.

CMDupré

Cream, Pink, Ruby Red

CMDUPRÉ has completed "Fifteen Strange Tales of Illumination" and the collection called "Sacrifice." She generally writes on two inductive levels or with an interwoven triadic theme. James Maddox's critical writing explains the development of fiction as a search for words in an "ocean of the unnamable," forcing the author into a prismatic, rotating acquaintance with incipience and stark insight. Dupré has taught philosophy and literature, and art theory. She is also a painter who pries out interconnections between the arts and real world where human workings are diabolically assessed or refreshed, but she considers crafted language of the short story form especially able in its thrusts, inherent dissection, and creative reverberations.

The city streets were breathtaking: refining all the filmmaking techniques that embellish night effects—even, especially, without any aid of color—refining the mood, refining the virtual *mise en scene.* Glassy wet, high-contrast trickery, unlikely shapes, false conjectures flatly slithered one after another in silent succession under her moving car. So it was that after three solid hours of gallery hopping, facing a dozen complacent alpha-white walls and dull sanctifying hush, soft huddles of susurration, the city's streets were a livelier foil to her thoughts. Bold cuts of energy acted as ground. She found her way with ease, having done it many times and with a stroke of luck slid into an open space around the corner from Murph's DC. Having tucked herself in with an excess of back-and-forth attempts—confessing on occasion, severally guilt-racked, that she was indeed genetically impaired in the area of spatial acuities—she finally completed an orderly pattern of gray-car, white-car, black, gray, white, down the block. This repetitive formation was not only satisfying but in all likelihood, on this night of wavering street signs versus rigidly stenciled parking spots, a good omen. Her bag was locked tight under her arm even though she saw no one lurking near the intersection that even remotely broadcast waves of brazen menace. The streetlights were all bright tension, blinking nervously. Within a dozen yards she approached the outer door labeled M's DC and was grabbed from behind. A raspy voice at the back of her head: *this is it lady: no fucking farther and no sudden moves.* Then he breathed heavily into the secret cave of Marianne Labaque's ear, a grave-like sound worse than words. Her legs rubberized, folding to the rough pavement. This appropriate reflex angered him as if she were fighting back. He jerked her upright. I am prone to this, she thought in a pulse beat, letting out a faint, thin cry of exasperation skimming over a hugely untapped fountain of fear.

⁓

Twisting and turning she fought her way out of a deep sleep and the comforting touches from bisecting dream parts. She pirouetted clumsily in those funny infantile preconscious lurches, fighting out of sheets and flannel blankets. Always waking in a near-perfect parody of a newborn's struggle into the world and by instinct finding it so revolting, so early, to catapult her sensitive self onto the matrix of a debauched civilization. Nonetheless, she'd planned this rarity in detail herself: breakfast for them both, a gesture as fanciful as it was unnatural. Her husband never expected domestic roles to govern events except of course for his attention to large bushes and the heavy command of fences, cabinets, casements, roofing. She delicately maneuvered burned-out light bulbs while often perchance losing the chair, hanging from the fixtures themselves with a dread of being labeled a suicide. She was not like that. No emotive drama, *non, non, s'il vous plaît*, no drawing a circle of attention around her selfness. Or even her defeat. So he expected to go his own way, Marianne hers. Any meal they had together however, in putative accord, rested with her: otherwise it reeked of red meat, exorbitant heat, tainted by a hodgepodge of perilous coils. This morning, as on most Fridays, he'd be home till nine-thirty, ten. She found the determination to face this uninhabitable, uncharitable hour simply in order to establish some modicum of sit-down-togetherness however manufactured this appeared, for numerous unresearched good reasons. Most not tabulated adequately and certainly not rehearsed as they should be. He'd leave in a blink for the gym, an eight-mile run on a ten-mile trail, the Greenway Depot, in that order. The window of time for her verbal interjections would last an hour, perhaps less if her comments grew too narrow meaning haggard, hinting, or specific. She sighed. Usually the interjections didn't amount to much more than lean descriptions of occurrences, which she found actually quite interesting. She'd recite a string of comments in her stylistic monotone, a characteristic she developed to avoid superlatives. He did like gossip. His eyes would light on certain items, little details. Marianne hated gossip as a rule so she'd define each source carefully, adding detached comments "So-and-so said, but just yesterday so-and-so said the opposite; so-and-so said it's more than likely born of misunderstanding; or jealousy, though it's probably not the case, not actually. But if you weigh one thing against another..." and so on.

She was hungry anyway she found. She skipped dinner yesterday because of a slingshot schedule aimed at finishing a canvas, or, she felt with some wariness it could, by many standards, be complete until falling under a fresh critical eye; sitting on the committee for new art club members; putting frames on three definitively done canvases; painstakingly aiming her Minolta at each new painting, recording her own work history but, even more pressing, finding that reassessing slant that comes from another less compromising medium, the photographic print.

In the long pink T-shirt she'd slept in, she leaned over the sink watching the minuscule hummingbird. She mused awhile about its pattern of non-flight held in space, its slippage up and down, its rotating lilliputian efforts to be face-on to the feeder. The table behind her was arranged aesthetically and, if he never seemed to notice, she at least basked in its minor beauties—old lace from Aunt Tiffany, copper teapot, blue and white Portuguese container of yellow daisies and white narcissi—wreathed now by a fragrant haze of hot sausage, warming bread, eggs over light topped with hollandaise. The sausages were turkey not beef or pork so in a way made their amends for the insouciant retrogression of hollandaise. But still, she would see him complain, inwardly, by the flex of a cheek muscle, the lift of an eyebrow, yet still managing a few forkfuls chewed slowly, with a kind of regulated objection. A gulp of orange juice, an apologetic glance toward his plate, a second glance toward his watch, third, the door. Limited arena for engagement, properly speaking, she thought. *Bon Dieu.*

The hummingbird had eyes like small black pebbles that never turned, never seemed to focus, never blinked a hint of confusion. They were simply hard black dots on either side of the face. The bird's coloring was exuberant and Marianne wondered if this should always, usually does, make up for lack of expression.

He came smoothly into the breakfast room with a manual, carefully aligning it with his fork. "You're up early. Smells good."

"Wasn't sure you'd be up for this."

"Always," he said, lining up his perfect teeth. "Always room." He patted his flat belly. "What's going on?"

"Nothing special. Thought we'd talk." They passed serving plates back and forth.

"About?"

"Nothing special. Odds and ends."

"Everything's OK I hope." In that brief moment his face opened in mock concern then shut down, a protective glaze over his pupils.

"Oh yes. Well." She put her fingers to her mouth as she coughed. She could see the hummingbird from here, its gyrations up and down, its minor adjustments in perfecting a vertical path, wings invisibly pumping, faster than the laziness of a human eye. A lot of tedium for such a small creature. Yesterday she was as busy as that, as invisible as that, zooming in on her paintings, working the images, the color. Looking for an entry, finding it, obscuring it. Willing the thing to life, to attain a sense from contradictions meeting in a clash and forming something new, never before seen. Never experienced, she thought. A jumble of colors, fine hairlike lines trembling across disparate objects, circling them or riding through them, a plastering of inchoate phrases—clichés, blistering curses, bits of poetry, aphorisms—blearily over and waftily under the surfaces. Over the last two years or so she'd begun to work like this, in a flurry of subject matter, unrelated things that came together in a puzzle-like way and made a special kind of sense. For her. Let's be specific. Not immediately obvious, ever. *Mais discontinuité, et désincarnation.*

She put her fingers under Aunt Tiff's lace to feel its strength and fragility, to examine the color which was a bleached sort of white, a white with the body of age, of antiquity almost. The flesh color behind it became distorted to purple. She pulled her hand away: it looked normal. Odd, this juxtaposition.

"And what will you do today?" A question never asked. Her schedule was written on the calendar always tacked to the fridge. His was by rote, generally understood. "Anything special?"

"No. But I'll go round to some galleries tonight, see what's going on." The calendar said *galleries 6–9.* She knew this also, that she'd be out late beyond gallery closings, abetting a sweetly sensate night-time cadence; bits and pieces on a concordant plane, faces, strains of music, salutations, words, gestures, the glow from Chardonnay, laying out a harmonious ground for rhapsodic dreams.

"Mmm." He patted his lips with pink rosettes over navy blue, hand-hemmed by Marianne. She patted her lips, pale puckered buds over languid green. "So," he said in preamble to rising, leaving. "What else?"

She realized he was curious. And she'd wanted to talk but hadn't found the keynote that would open onto clausal relevance: the tone. The problem of any use of space was connected to tone, she thought. She'd be out tonight, she'd said. She didn't mention with whom. Whether meeting someone or alone. Exactly where. He'd be out as well. She was not curious. She wouldn't allow herself. There were many cautious boundaries. She coughed and it sounded prim, even to her. She'd eaten too much as usual and felt fat. Once out of bed she could feel her body expand and soften. The skin under her eyes would sag no matter how much she'd slept. Maybe such lengthy depths of sleep was the problem. She tilted her head back. Her hand on her stomach, she coughed again. "Well, considering our routine," she said, thinking it was fine, so ordered, so nonconfrontational, so well established. What do I want to do, put a glitch in it? She said "Shall we continue along this way?"

"What way?" he asked and she could admit, foremost to herself, that it'd become so ordinary that it didn't seem in the least extraordinary. That they knew one another only through a tinted exterior. Despite sex, body on body, the sheen of cream, pink, ruby red. The hummingbird had to eat about a hundred times its body weight in one day. Unimaginable chore, she thought.

The last canvas might be harried, too confused with marks and squiggles and dabs, lines and dots. Where does it go? To what end does it lead?

Incredible, this opposition in her work; a frenzy so unlike the dreams that bathed her in comfort, celebrated her compactness, her health and beauty. Those traits were witnessed and confirmed by the breath and fingers of ghostly visitors.

She stood and leaned against his shoulder, patted his cheek with the back of her hand. More in an earnest forgiveness or a catholicized indulgence than intimate touch. Nothing nearing passion these days; her touch was more of a neat, circumspect release. And her husband also took this as a sign of dismissal which was basically analogous to the intent, and made his lithe exit through the door. Marianne sat pondering the path of the hummingbird as well as her own obsessive use of space that, when thought about at any length, was a matter that became irrelevant, almost nonexistent. There was no real space or background material in her paintings. This was fact. Everything got used up with the activity of her brush, the profusely nervous punctuation of its rise and fall, its spidery netting and continuous building movements. Layer upon layer of swirls that built up over the figures, animal, human, and the roadways, bridges, cookie-like houses, smokestacks, haystacks, lopsided poles, and degenerating tree trunks. Once long ago she'd painted a group portrait of her family, Aunt Tiffany in the center, Mom, Dad, the others, some still children. It was one of her first canvases and already her stamp was pressed over it with the distracting swirls and the filling of each and every area, every corner, setting the thing—that is, setting all these people, their immediate areas and all the painted objects—into an unnatural but marvelously disheveled whirl. At some level, of course, this is how she saw them, at cross-purposes and at a flatly intense level of interconnection, impeccably fortuitous motions.

She worked out a motif that was both alarming and peculiarly well founded.

Today she decided to take notes of the stages of her work, not by writing which would require too much of her work time and wearisome effort, but with the Minolta. She'd paint for an hour, record it, another hour, and so on. By this method she might understand the mystery, exactly how she progressed, how much the underlying colors controlled the rest of the work, how she became embroiled with gothic, unending detail while losing all sense of quiet space or airy contemplative portions, losing what allowed the hollows an achievement on their own. She might begin to understand her control or its lack, and whether or not her almost automatic pattern that became in every case her concept did, actually, represent the authenticity of her work. Was there anything about this process that could change and by changing be better?

A professor had once told his entire class of painters that change was the hallmark of an artist and that artist's work. Without it there was no growth. This was the primary nettle in her creativity. It wasn't difficult to acknowledge that her work was above all else intimate and subjective. In that one sense similar to her dreams that nourished themselves, satisfied their own inner workings as well as her inner, psychic sustenance, and projected in an entire history of repetition: she could argue that it was enough. More than enough. And no two paintings would ever be the same. She spent several hours alternating between the paint and the camera. The tripod was fixed, a hook stuck in the wall. Each print would show the painting centrally, shot at exactly the same proportions, the exact same size, the detailed stages of development exacting enough to layer them or set them side by side like timed exposures.

What she discovered, after about five days, was an interesting schematic of events. She laid the prints out on a clear tabletop. There were three or four prints for each day and eighteen all told.

⁓

"Can you take a break?" Carly asked. "I'm starved." It took Marianne several seconds to recognize the words and to recognize the other painter. Carly was wearing coveralls garnished with the siennas, burnt umbers, and golds that were her signature, but it appeared as if she were babysitting a naked four-year-old with ghastly explosions of diarrhea. But the odor was one they both reveled in, of oil pigment, wax, and copal medium among other additives just as potent, including turps and varnishes. So far no one complained of these smells coming into their restaurants, mingling with the succulent fragrances of yogurt sauces, simmering garlic, sautéing veggies. "Put your brushes down Marianne. Let's celebrate. I won the Artist-of-the-Year which means a goodly sum and a solo show."

Ah, Marianne thought. She's connecting with the audience and she's appreciated.

"Mmmm," she said. "You're bringing it all together, that's wonderful."

Carly's eyes sparkled with a hint of something devilish, perhaps daemonic. "I've got the formula," she said, using a fingertip to wipe away a spot of turquoise on Marianne's nose. The brushes went back into the fattest jar, once holding gefilte fish, and she rubbed her hands down her apron, untying it, throwing it over her easel.

After their rice bowls and chopsticks were settled on the table they lifted and clinked their little pots of hot sake. "So," in unison. "It's good." It was good for Carly. But what about *moi, la pauvre petite* Marianne, she thought, smiling at Carly. As the sake went down golden and flanging she gave in, as she occasionally did, to quiet seething, under her prosaic domestic banners, flapping in winds from the wide Western plains—democracy, meritocracy, equality, the Golden Rule and all other forms of tenuous reward—that cut their chancy swaths through trust and desire.

"Tell me then about your formula."

⁓

With little resistance the man strong-armed her back into the bushes next to the building, pinning her face down against broken glass, gravel, the ungiving city-hard ground. She felt as if any normal reserves of strength had been punctured like a series of translucent balloons, her breath and substance leaking away in systemic disclaimer. She heard clumsy unmanaged sounds emitted toward her unprotected featureless, colorless, eyeless, expressionless back, sounds that seemed more a hardened incompetence than a deft plan to harm or steal. She felt a cascade of angry dominion from a stranger who was also an enemy. She had fallen onto someone's battleground.

~

The gallery rounds had been pretty much par for course, the usual, with the walls blanketed by the particular stylistic features of the day. One genre was the newfound core of abstract-conceptualism that translated everything in the world to large fields of over-painted under-populated spaces, two or three wide bands of muted and blinded color, or a massively swollen organic shape, or the strangling strings and tendons of charcoal-colored drips over thumb-printed white, like a stained barrier. Pieces that'd displaced sculpture as it had been known floated in the gallery spaces with disparate ribbons of transparent plastic, accepting an unaccountable intrusion of glass vials each holding a dull black marble or a yellow tile. Everything she saw seemed to be melded into place yet the whole affect as she moved from gallery to gallery was one of concentrated but imbued, untranslatable movement. All the placid stillnesses and spatial *déférent* weights engendered the interloping of other minds, even another's remonstrance, not to mention subtle warnings, asides, of apocalypse.

Anything figured was disfigured. Paintings of *abbatoirs* and basement hallways and ramps leading into black squares and isolation. This was her world but it wasn't her world. There was a division.

It was for divining this division that she made these rounds, to continue her game of solitaire, her game of accountancy in which she could place all the cards in lines according to suit: hearts, spades, diamonds, clubs. Weighing her dreams against these deficiencies that marked the rule of resemblance, even sameness: and that also seemed to celebrate themselves.

Or mount themselves on a height. Seemed not to care if they were strictly triumphantly relegated or called themselves suicides. She had no distaste for them per se, but rather a cool understanding like a backhanded pat on one's stoically satisfied husband's cheek.

Carly's formula was something different from all these gallery productions since it was based not on observance of a world-gone-mad but upon her immediate needs.

"Just a matter of figuring out what the average person wants. There's lots of leverage in that and as a tool it's always been around. Always marketable." She pulled in her lips and looked at the ceiling.

"You don't play the game of hierarchies, of 'important' art. You just concentrate on making 'good' art."

"Well, yeah, I suppose. I know the bulk of what's going on. I take bits and pieces, the best bits and pieces, and incorporate."

"And you keep them small. Salable."

"I need to make a living. That's what it's about. For me. The way to do it is simple."

"Let me guess," said Marianne, scooping up the last of her shrimp-fried rice. "You don't deal in catastrophic truths."

"I mix it very carefully, with a goodly portion of fantasy. Wonderment. It's representative in its thinking and its making: not so much a dire prediction. Just a bit of whoops and uh-oh."

Marianne thought of showing Carly the series of photographs, talking out the procedure that was linked with color application and, also, by its own unwritten law eschewing an even tone and, of course, empty space. How, if she began with a dark sketching-in movement, sketching translocation of metamorphic images, large, small, interconnecting, then the artwork's development—beginning as drawing quite similar to cartoons—forced all other color and color values to bounce in cacophony against its lead. Since it was true that she always started with a dark color by drawing with a wet brush—dark ultramarine blue, burnt umber or raw umber, blue black, maroon, payne's gray, oh, love a darkling gray—she surmised its integrity leaving her little choice but to allow its ringmaster's carnival instincts, to follow its energizing narrative, disarticulating lines, a story that unfolded helter-skelter under the attached, affiliated, and fond motions of her hand and brush. Not only the total therefore broken explosion of color, but broken description; not merely description, but links that meandered all around the canvas connecting everything and leaving no one thing to dominate such a sensational big-top performance.

She could tell Carly that this was so because there's no particular accent, no singular accountability. Maybe that's because I never start with a field, she thought, or with a ramifying well-mixed color base: a fleshy mixture of lightened cadmium or the mud of pale ochred gray. Any of these 'clearances' could introduce a major theme.

If she could manage to lighten and blend instead of chop; incorporate space as unmitigated featureless space—what would happen? If she could manage a kind of logic formed in the dumb warmth of an established solicitous pool, instead of revolving happenstances in a series of accidents, how would that change her art and her life or even her ornate over-worn dependencies?

Why would she want to go into all that with words and defenses, especially now and with Carly safe, on a roll?

❧

He tore the tote bag from under her body that felt so heavy now, muttering ridiculous almost laughable guttural epithets *fucking whore* and *pig slag* now somewhat removed from her ear and the hollow of her neck. The individual clacks of items spilled round her head. Clattering, pinging, rolling. She heard the thump of an olive-green leather key pouch, flickering fall of bank cards, her laminated driver's license, the revealing ticks of a hurtling stack of prints: the explorative photos. At that point she began to lift up on her hands with an unchecked anger from the indignity of being crushed, of eating dirt, of hearing her parts disassemble. She cursed back, explosive, incensed.

When he cut her she could feel the back of her neck and shoulder open with a kind of certainty or guarantee, without noticeable pain. It was color that she felt. A redness, certainly; also the pink of the wound, the pink offering itself to the clear rush of air and then to the grit that surrounded her. The grit that rode on the surface of the streaming ruby red. The cream of her skin slashed apart, opened so very wide at last; she began to feel an ache spread in a circle around it like an aura, almost a luminescence that freed something alien. There was a tumult of impressions when he dropped her, when she rolled, when the streetlights and the halos of rain began to whirl and her vision started to constrict into a roll of negatives, a lighted rolling pin in the mutating shades of cream, pink, red. The scant line of his shirt back ebbed away like a chalk mark, rescripted colors of the stoplight flashed dioptrically on and off, rewritten curses now more oblique as if decanted from the origin: then louder; now shouting; directing and demanding; all these imminent kaleidoscopic forms. Changes: the changes would save her, wouldn't they, with time enough? Changed palette, light. Dark, stretching out and giving over. These odd enfolded sights and sounds would revolve almost endlessly round her dim sense till they slowed for the answers she always sought in the spaces she couldn't find, and the subjectivity she had known and seemed to cherish would free her into the hard rhythmic rapping on the world's door, rapping of the world on her door. *Délimite l'esclavage.* I'll gather enough strength for this, she thought.

Patricia Elam

Young Boyz Drinkin a Forty out the Bag

PATRICIA ELAM is a freelance writer who lives in Washington, D.C., with her three children. A graduate of Northeastern University School of Law and the University of Maryland's graduate creative writing program, she has written for the *Washington Post*, *Essence* magazine, National Public Radio, and other publications. Patricia has won an O. Henry Award and a Surdna Foundation fellowship and has been nominated for a Hurston-Wright Legacy Award. Her novel *Breathing Room* was published in 2001 by Pocket Books, a division of Simon and Schuster. She has taught writing at Goucher College, the University of Maryland, and the Writer's Center; currently, she chairs the creative writing department at Duke Ellington School of the Arts.

1.

They waitin for Brotherman in front of the liquor store on North Capitol Street. They all wearin baggy jeans lowdown on they butts without no belt. If you get up close you can see they drawers cause they cool like that. Dude they call Puff, he so fat, you can see the crack in his butt when he bendin over to tie his tennis shoes. They be telling him that shit is nasty but he swear girls think it sexy. All that boy be thinking about is pussy, uzis, jeeps and more pussy.

The twins, Shalimar and Shannon, sportin bald heads. They say they shave each other head. Their shit shinin like they waxed it. Shalimar talkin about some girl ask him to use a rubber when he was gettin ready to smash her.

–I don't play that shit, say Tonio.

–Me neither, say Drey. –Only time you need one of them things is if you with a freak.

–Yeah, that shit don't even feel right, say Puff. –Don't feel natural. Everybody laugh then.

–What you talking bout, man? What you know bout what feel natural? You know you ain't never felt the real thing. You better stop that lyin. Tonio push Puff shoulder hard.

Then Brotherman come out the liquor store. He always be smilin big like he hit the daily lotto or something. He carryin a brown bag tuck under his arm and he smoking a cigarette. He not scared of getting cancer or nothing, many packs that boy smoke a day. He only nineteen and his teeth yellow as corn cept for that gold one he put in there sometimes. Brotherman real black, too. Navy blue black, fire escape black. With slanty, Korean ass eyes. Weird combination, ain't it? But bitches love it. They love them some Brotherman. He can pull bitches you wouldn't believe. Light skin ones, specially. Long hair down they back. Wavy hair on they pussy. He can get all that shit without even tryin. Some girl try to kill herself over him last year. When she got pregnant he stop messin with her and she swallow all her grandmama heart medicine. She didn't die though. When she came back to school everybody kept tellin her how stupid she was. Brotherman got arrested for beatin her ass after that but she drop the charges. To Brotherman getting pussy is easy as drinkin out the water fountain.

2.

Everybody walk over to the park near the projects. Brotherman take a long taste of the forty while it still in the bag, lettin some of it drip down his chin. –Man, that shit good, he say, shiverin his body like a snake. –I can feel that shit in my toes. He laugh and pass the forty to Tonio.

Brotherman born cool. Tonio try to act like Brotherman. Tonio sit on the top part of the bench and drink the forty too fast. Start chokin and shit. Shalimar take the forty from Tonio. –Give me that, man. You wastin the shit.

Everybody just waitin they turn. Twins leanin against the tree and Puff sittin on the bench with his jeans all caught up in his crouch cause his thighs pressin together, big as two cities. Drey talkin about how his mama found his 9mm last night.

Brotherman givin his usual lesson bout life. –I keep tryin to tell y'all hardheads you can't trust nobody but yoself. Not nowadays. This war out here, brothers. Ain't nobody lookin out for you but you. That how you gotta think. You got to always think ahead of shit and be ready. The forty all gone? Brotherman look at Puff who guzzlin the rest of the forty like it a damn Arizona.

Brotherman he good for makin you think about shit. That for damn sure. Even if you don't like what he say you gotta give him credit for makin you think.

3.

It a nice mood out. Everybody loungin, floatin a little from the forty. Smooth, slow-ridin feelin, kind that make you close your eyes on your problems.

It startin to get dark, the sky the color of nickels and dimes that been layin around in your pocket for awhile. Park lights used to come on bout this time but somebody knocked them out few months ago and they ain't never fixed them. They always sayin they gonna fix stuff up around here but it a lie. Them swings look like they been here since the cave kids, got splinters and shit comin out them. Glass all in the sandbox. Girl name Pansey—her baby got stitches from playin that damn sandbox. And just last week some kids found a man out there in the grass with his head blown off by a AK-47. Now that ain't no shit for a little kid to see. You know it ain't.

4.

Puff wipin his mouth with his shirt, cheeks saggin down like a bulldog. –Hey, he say. –Let's go over to the Rec. See if any bitches over there.

–Damn man.

–I told you that all that boy be thinkin bout, say Shannon.

5.

Drey and Puff only been to school once this month. Twins bout to graduate from junior high and try to act like they don't be studyin. But they pops is a fireman and he don't be bullshittin. He make sure them boys go to school.

Tonio he might as well drop out—he ain't been in school all year. No tellin what grade he in. He sixteen though. Tonio mama came to school with him one time cause he flunkin out of everything even PE. First, he just grinnin with his no tooth self. His mama bout thirty, look like she twenty. She got them high pushed up titties and she had this purple blouse on you could see through better than a shower curtain. You could see her bra (it purple too) and she ain't finish buttonin the blouse so you could see them ice cream cone titties just itchin to bust out. Somebody start whistlin and carryin on and then somebody say, –Shut up, that his mama. But Tonio mama smile kind of sexy-like and act like she like it so everybody start whistlin again. Tonio face change, look like he want to pull out his .38 and pump somebody. His mama make him chill out though. The other bitches hangin around the school yard twist they face up and start talkin bout his mama ain't all that. But, for real, she all that and they know it.

6.

Everybody keep tellin Shannon to leave them stuck-up bitches alone. But he say he like it better when it harder to get. If you tell em you buy em some shoes or some pampers for they baby, they don't play that. You got to be talkin bout I love you and I want to be with you and only you and all that bull. Anyway, now Shannon got hisself a big ass problem. One of them stuck-up hoes say Shannon got her pregnant and she gonna take him to court. He ask the girl how she know he the father. Girl real piss then. She say he gonna pay out his ass.

7.

Goin to Brotherman apartment like goin to a vacation joint. He got palm trees in there, fake birds singin out a cages and neon lights bouncin off the walls. Feel like Atlantic City for real. He got a leather couch and matching loveseat from Marlo. The CDs be turned up so loud when you come out you still be yellin.

He let the youngins hang out there after school; sometime he be sendin them on errands and he be payin them crazy bank. He give them food and sodas but he don't let nobody bring no bitches in there cept him. He say too much shit goin down, bitches ain't ready. He say wasn't for pussy wouldn't even need bitches.

–Brotherman, let me be in bidness with you, man. You got it made, Tonio always beggin.

–Naw, you ain't ready. You gotta go to school to work for me. I need me educated partners. Little brothers who can strategize. I got a lot more I want to get. He spread his hands wide around the room, like eagle wings. –This shit I got in here. This ain't nothin.

–What you talkin bout, Brotherman? You got everything. You got a Lexus, bitches all over town, three cell phones. You got everything, man. Puff look at Brotherman, wait for an explanation.

–I want more than this, Brotherman say. –Ain't you never heard about dreamin big? I got a dream today, like Brother Martin used to say. You all hip to Brother Martin, right? Well Brother Martin was a punk. No heart. Now Malcolm X. That a righteous brother. That mutherfucker had heart. That what I'm talkin about, That dude wasn't scared of nothin. Like me. I'm a get what I want. By any means necessary all the time. Remember that. Brotherman through talkin, stand there strokin his face. Face smooth and black as a bowling ball.

Brotherman love watchin videos on his big tv screen. He either watchin *Goodfellas* or *Scarface* (them his favorites, he seen them joints bout 100 times each). If you be talkin to him he won't even answer you till them joints over. –That mutherfucker Scarface, that mutherfucker was a bad mutherfucker, he always say. Brotherman know damn near all the lines in the movie and his lips be movin the whole time he watchin. The parts when everybody shootin and shit, Brotherman be right up on top of the tv with his mouth open like it the first time he seen it.

–Brotherman, you ever kill anybody? Shalimar ask him one time.

Brotherman eyes got wide first then settle back down but shine like piece of broke glass in the sun. –Man, first time I pump somebody, I had the shakes real bad, everybody thought I couldn't do it. Mutherfuckers teasin me and shit so I had to do it. When I finally did it, it was easy. Wasn't nothin. But then I kept thinkin bout that boy head I hit, kept thinkin bout the hole I put in it. After a while though I started realizin how perfect the hole was, how round and clean it was and how the blood busted out of there like it couldn't wait. In other words, little brother, I saw the beauty of it. That when I knew I was a man.

8.

They at the Rec, shootin hoop. Cept Tonio had to go meet his probation officer. Shalimar do a pretty dunk, twirlin in the air and shit, tryin to be Barkley. When he come down he tap Shannon. –Why don't you tell em? See if anybody got any knowledge.

Shannon lookin sad, he still shootin and reboundin, though. He a little shorter than Shalimar, but chunky, biceps like 50 Cent and shit. Him and Shalimar got the same face though; like somebody trace one to get the other.

Game over. Everybody grab they T-shirts, wipe sweat and dirt off they faces like it hard work. –Hey, Drey, Shannon say. –You know how much abortions cost?

–Naw, man. Both bitches I knocked up wanted to have the kids. One born a month fore the other over Barry Farms. Don't know nothin about no abortion. Why you wanna know?

–Cause my pops told me and Shalimar don't never bring home no babies. And he ain't kiddin. Now this girl sayin I got her pregnant. You know my pops. He gonna whup my ass. Me and Shalimar gotta go to college and shit, play football. He big dreamin about us makin them kind of moves. We ain't sposed to be makin babies. If my pops find out bout this shit, he gonna try to kill me. He probably will kill me.

Shalimar steady noddin his head. Everybody know bout they pops. How he got a big-time fireman job, made hisself into somebody, move out the projects and into a house. He a big beefy man with round arms that hang off him like they belong to somebody else. All the kids scared of him. But he a hero to the grownups cause he walked into a burning house a few years back and brought out two babies that was trapped.

He got his right ear burnt off behind that. He don't take no mess from nobody, specially his boys. He whup Shannon so bad one time he couldn't go to school for a week cause his back all bruised up and sore. Twins pops don't want them hangin out with the brothers who still live in the projects but them boys is hard-headed.

They mama rough, too. She work downtown and always be tellin dudes they need to go to the library and read books and shit. Her pointy face get tight and mean when she say it. If she walk pass you hangin out front of the liquor store or somethin, she go, –You all need to be at the library. You all need to be tryin to learn somethin for a change. Then she walk away. Everybody laugh when she gone cause she be thinkin her boys in the library and for real they be hangin out tryin to act like gangstas.

9.

–Why don't you tell the bitch to go to one of them clinics? Say Puff. –They do them abortion things there and they cheaper than the doctor office. My sister best friend had one there last year cause she already had three damn kids.

–That the thing, man, Shalimar say. –Now she don't want no abortion. He lookin at Shannon.

Shannon noddin. –She just wanna take me to court. She say I might as well forget going to college. I be damn if I'm a let her mess up my future.

–That's what I hate about bitches. They always tryin to pull some rank just cause of they pussy. Drey shakin his head. –Why don't you get some other bitch to beat her ass? Kick her in the stomach and shit. Make her have a miscarriage.

Shannon sweatin bullets. –Naw, man. That too much trouble. I gotta figure out something quick, man. She ain't playin. She actin real mean and shit. She be callin me up sayin, I got the court papers right her, and shit like that.

–She might jest be bluffin, man, Puff say.

–Naw, say Shalimar. –I see her. She one of them fine bitches, too fine for her own good. He dribblin the ball hard down the street, like it the bitch messin with Shannon.

–Blackmail her ass, say Drey.

–Damn, man, that what she doin to me. Pops gonna tear my ass up. I can't let her do it. He rememberin all the whuppins he got.

–Man, I'm a get me a virgin bitch next time. Don't know nothin about nothin, say Puff.

–Where from? Outaspace. Ain't no virgins in D.C. Shannon, man, you do got a big problem. You know who you need to talk to? You need to talk to Brotherman, say Drey.

–That what I told him, Shalimar say.

–Brotherman gonna say I'm a punk or I'm stupid. You know he always talkin about us spendin too much time on the pussy.

–Yeah but he gonna know what to do. Brotherman been through a lot of shit with bitches hisself.

–Yeah. You right. I better go see Brotherman.

10.

Brotherman outside talkin on his cell phone when Shalimar and Shannon come by. They tryin to be patient, suckin on Now and Laters and shootin the wrappers into the street. Lots of little kids runnin by cause the ice cream truck at the corner. Some kid with a runny nose go up to Brotherman Lexus and Brotherman give him a dollar. It summertime officially. You can always tell cause of the ice cream truck and the beggin kids.

Brotherman call twins over wavin his arm out the car window. He got on dark shades and Solbiato joggin suit. They get in the backseat—car smell like cologne. He got Game vibin on the CD player. –What up, y'all? I gotta make some moves so talk fast. Brotherman leg stretched out cross the front seat.

–We wanna ask you somethin, Shalimar start out talkin.

–Let me talk, man, Shannon say. –It my thing.

–Well go ahead then.

–What is you all? Dumb and Dumber and shit? Brotherman pickin at his gold tooth in the rearview mirror. Then he light up a cigarette.

–Brotherman, I got a problem with a girl, I mean, a bitch. I need some advice.

Brotherman look at Shannon over the top of his shades and listen to him talk. Shannon talk fast like he in a race.

–One of them stuck-up hoes you got a hard head for, right? Brotherman suck his teeth just enough to make Shannon feel low.

Shannon look down at the carpet. The car sparklin clean, no paper, no cigarette butts or beer bottles, like most of the cars he been in.

–Didn't I tell you all to stay away from them bitches? They ain't nothin but trouble. They look good on the outside but on the inside they spoilt, just like rotten fruit. What you want me to say, little brother? You want me to wave some magic wand over your head and say your old man ain't gonna beat your ass like he should? Huh? You want me to make it go way with the snap of my finger? Well that ain't the way life works.

–I know what you sayin, Brotherman, Shannon squirmin. –But I can't let this girl take me to court. And I ain't got no job.

–How much do she want?

–She don't want money. She gonna keep the baby. She just wanna mess my life up. She talkin about she gonna make me pay every month till the baby turn eighteen.

–Twenty-one in D.C., little brother, Brotherman say.

Shalimar dyin to say somethin. –And the girl all right but she ain't all that.

She might a had somethin you couldn't see. Somethin you had to feel, right, my brother? Brotherman easin up on Shannon a little, wink at him quick-like.

–Yea, first she didn't want to gimme none but I made her change her mind. Only did it twice, though.

Brotherman take his cigarette out his mouth and crush it in the ashtray. –Well, shit it probably ain't even yours then. Don't let it faze you, man.

–She say it mine, she say she ain't did it with nobody else this year. Brotherman, this girl—she pressin me, she out for blood.

–Well. That what she gonna get then. Brotherman lookin through his CD case for what he want to hear. Put on some L'il Wayne.

Twins lookin confused for real. –What you mean? Say Shannon. –What you gonna do?

Brotherman don't say nothin for a minute. Just look at them with half a smile. Brotherman got a easy way of talkin to folk. Sometime almost sound like one of them counselors at school. –My brother, my brother. It ain't what I'm gonna do. It what you gonna do. Brotherman smile full now, showing all his teeth. Then he take his hand from out his lap, slow-motion-like, and put his thumb up and index finger straight out. –Pow, he say.

11.

Shannon start to talk when the lights out in they bedroom. –Don't know if I can do nothin like that, man. I mean she a pain in the A and shit but I guess I think bout she got my baby in her. If I do her, that mean the baby gotta go too.

–It ain't a real baby yet, man, Shalimar say. –It just some slime right now, like a jelly fish. Member we seen them pictures in the science book? Even Brotherman say this the only thing left to do. Girl tryin to short-change your life.

Shannon don't say nothin, just starin into dark space, feelin like he in a big black box. He can't sleep. Same shit keep wakin him up, got him tossin and turnin.

12.

Shalimar spendin a lot of time tryin to chill Shannon out. Tryin to make him see only one way out the mess. Brotherman way. Bitch call again and they pops pick up. He wanna know why some girl callin Shannon all the time. Pops ain't stupid. He know she not callin to find out what the homework is. He say, –Y'all better be usin them rubber willies if you out there tryin to act like a man Ain't no such thing as a mistake, y'hear?

–That ho sweatin you, man. You gotta do somethin. She gettin on my nerves now, say Shalimar.

–This ain't nothin to make no fast decision about. I can't think straight no more. Maybe I just ain't got that gangsta heart.

–Look, you ain't had no blood test. You don't even know if it yours, like Brotherman say. And if she woulda had the abortion like she s'pose to the baby be gone anyway.

–Right. You right.

13.

Twins go over Brotherman place. He buzz em in. He watchin *Scarface*, got his uzi out, laying cross his lap. He rubbin his hand over it like it a baby. His other hand holdin a cigarette. Movie almost over so they gotta wait. After it go off, he show them his whole collection, tellin them which one good for what and schoolin them bout barrels and clips and automatics. Brotherman all right. He treat them good. They pops don't let them touch his.

Shannon's sweatin and carryin on even tho Brotherman got central air. Brotherman like, –Yo, little man, take some deep breaths or somethin. You gettin ready to grow up right before your own eyes. Find out what it mean to be a man. Lot of responsibility come with that. Know what I'm sayin?

Shalimar eyes wide. He lookin at the one with the black handle. He keep pickin it up, turnin it around. He pick up the bullets too, roll them between his fingers.

Brotherman make a couple of phone calls. Then he say, –Be ready to go this weekend, little man?

–I don't know, man, I ain't ready, Shannon say.

–I'm a do it for him, Shalimar say.

–Y'all sure? Brotherman look at both.

–What? Say Shannon.

–Yeah. I'm your brother, ain't I? I got your back.

14.

Brotherman pick them up on Florida Avenue in a Escalade with tinted windows.

–Where you get that? Shannon say, mouth open.

–Don't be askin me no questions bout what I do or how I do it, understand? If I want you to know I'll tell you. You got enough to worry about so just be glad you got somebody smart as me to get you out of this bullshit. Brotherman tell Shalimar to sit up front. Shannon get in the back givin directions where the girl street at. –Oh, she a real fancy bitch, Brotherman say, lookin at the rowhouses and the fake gardens. Girl little sister outside on a skateboard. She tell them girl ain't home, went to PG Plaza.

They get on East-West Highway, go to the mall. Brotherman drive through the parking lot couple of times lookin around the place, makin sure he know all the ways to get out. Then he park, show them where he gonna wait. He smokin cigarettes one right after the other. –Make sure she don't see you, he say. They get out, walk around, lookin in stores they think she be in, Bakers and Up Against the Wall and shit. Shannon see her near Lady Footlocker, but he don't say nothin. Then Shalimar see her. –There the bitch go, over there with her girlfriend. They laughin, mouths open, poppin gum. Her girlfriend pushin a little kid in a stroller. She swingin her braids and her Coach bag thinkin she all that.

–She don't look pregnant, say Shalimar.

–She only three month, say Shannon, turnin his cap around on his head.

They go back outside, get in the Escalade. Brotherman move it closer to the stores.

–We spot her whichever way she come out. They didn't see y'all, right?

–Naw, man.

15.

They waitin. Brotherman got headphones on cause Escalade ain't got no radio. Brotherman head movin like his neck a spring. Shannon feel like he ain't peed all year. –Man, I gotta find me a tree or somethin, he say.

–Can't you hold it? Shalimar say. –Damn.

–Naw, man, I gotta go real bad.

Shannon lookin around for a spot. Shalimar, too, while he holding the 9mm on his lap, under his jacket.

Shannon look down at his hands. They wet and shiny between the creases. He wipe them on the seat. He tap Shalimar on the shoulder and whisper, –Ain't you scared, man?

Shalimar shake his head but he don't look at Shannon. –Stop worryin. It ain't gonna be nothin. Gonna be over just like that. Then everything be all right again.

–I'm a go pee behind that van, say Shannon, pointin. He get out the Escalade slow, look for the girls.

–Where he goin? Brotherman move the headphones, look at Shalimar.

–Goin to pee.

–Now? Damn.

Shannon jump down from the Escalade, put his hand on his chest, try to get the pounding to slow down. He look over near the mall entrance, don't see nobody. He run over where the van at, lookin side to side. He look around again, see the girls this time. They eatin ice cream. They step off the sidewalk, bouncin the little kid round in the stroller. Shannon runnin through cars tryin to get back to the Escalade.

Girls walkin near the Escalade. Shalimar say, –That the bitch. One with the braids. Where Shannon at? Damn.

–Can't wait, man. Brotherman lean cross Shalimar out the window, yell out, –Yo, Miss African Twist. Ready, go! He say to Shalimar.

Escalade movin in slow motion. Shannon see it and start runnin. –Don't. No. I changed my mind, Shannon yellin, cryin. He hear sound like rockets, firecrackers bustin up the sky. –NO. Stop. He see the one with the stroller runnin, screamin. Escalade turnin, comin to him. Now he see the girl twisted up on the ground. –No. Get up. We didn't mean it. We was just playin. He lookin at her, hear Shalimar callin him. He grab onto the Escalade tryin to open the door. Somethin sting goin through his leg, makin it hot, makin it burn. He turn, look down—blood—look up. Security guard in black and red runnin, shootin. Then Shannon pee his pants.

–Get in, punk mutherfucker! Brotherman yellin. Get in! Shit. Shannon climb in holdin his leg while the Escalade rollin. Tires screech. Guard still shootin outside the window. Shalimar call for his mama and the Lord Jesus while his head fall down between his knees.

16.

Girl paralyze from neck down. Doctors in P.G. hospital ain't take the bullet out cause they worry bout the baby. Shannon in there, too, cause he got a hole in his leg. When he get out, he goin to Upper Marlboro jail till his court date. Probably won't get to go to his own brother funeral.

17.

Nobody ain't seen Brotherman since he left the twins in the Escalade and ran through traffic cross East-West Highway. Drey, Puff and Tonio found somebody else to cop them a forty and then they poured some on the ground for Shalimar. –This for the brother who ain't here, they said like they seen in the movies.

18.

Shannon try to figure out how come he can't see his life no more. He lookin but he don't see no sun, no rain, no clouds, no flowers, no little kids. He try to go forward but can't take no steps with his mind. Bars in the way all the time. But if he close his eyes real tight and make fists out his hands sometime he can also see hisself and Shalimar back on the corner drinkin a forty with the boys. Picture only last for a minute though.

Herta Burbach Feely

Perfection

HERTA BURBACH FEELY is a writer and activist. In 2006, the DC Commission on the Arts and Humanities awarded her an Artist Fellowship in Literature. She received an MA from the Johns Hopkins Writing Program and was invited to the Squaw Valley Community of Writers in 2003 and 2004. A previous grant from the DC Commission on the Arts and Humanities allowed her to travel to Peru and inspired her novel, "The Trials of Serra Blue." She also has stories appearing in the *Hurricane Review* and the *Potomac Review*. She has worked for numerous causes, including solar energy, human rights, and children's health and safety. She lives in D.C. with her husband, two sons, two cats, and a dog.

People had said it so often that Susan finally came to believe it herself. Her hands were the most perfect part of her anatomy. Of course her friends hadn't said it exactly that way, but that's what they'd meant. Now she glanced at her hands. Her nails needed a good polishing. She needed it. About to step inside Nail Spa, her neighborhood manicure salon—though it was more shop than salon—she heard her cell phone release its Mozart Sonata chime. Should she answer? She didn't much feel like it. When she saw that the caller was her daughter, she snapped the phone open.

"Hi, honey, where are you?" she said automatically.

"Just heading to Subway for a bite, and then, uh..."

"And then?" Susan detected a note of reluctance in her daughter's voice. Perhaps she was imagining it. So hard to tell these days. "Then what, Emma?" she said, a little more sharply than she'd intended.

"Don't say no, OK, Mommy? Because it's not like you think. We're going to this thrift shop—"

The words *Mommy* and *thrift shop* put her on alert. "Thrift shop? Again? Where?"

"Over, uh, in Southeast."

That was a good thing about Emma, she rarely lied. At least not yet. And she could still tell her what to do. Most of the time. "No, Em, you're not going to a thrift store in Southeast. That's crazy. There are plenty of secondhand shops and other shops you love in Georgetown. I'm OK with that. Anyway, you know you have to be home by six to baby-sit your brother."

"But Ma-awwm—"

"I'm serious."

"All right, bye." Click.

Susan stared at the phone. Should she call her back? With little more than two hours to go, how much trouble could Emma get into?

⁂

Susan gazed, almost lovingly, at the assorted shades of polish. She didn't know why, but an hour getting her nails and toes polished always soothed and relaxed her. Whenever she left the shop, armored with perfect nails, she felt a sense of completeness. Fixed. Ready for the complexities of the world.

"You have appointment?" the male receptionist asked. He was Vietnamese, just like the petite, dark-haired women in the shop who lacquered nails and toes, who offered upper lip and eyebrow waxes, who sang their language across the room in a constant string of syllables that all sounded vaguely similar yet foreign, and seemed to be formed at the back of the throat or somewhere in the nasal passage. He eyed her, awaiting a response.

"Yes," she said. Normally she bestowed a smile on this man, whose name she didn't know because he never wore a badge like the others, but today a thought flashed through her mind. He treats these girls like his harem. If he'd been in Vietnam during the war, they would have been his prostitutes.

"Missus…?"

She frowned at him, though she hated frowning. It caused all sorts of ugly little lines. "Mrs. Winslow," she said. "Here I am. I'm listed as Susan." She aimed her perfect finger at the appointment book and released a hollow little laugh. "Three forty-five," she said and glanced at her watch, on the dot, "with Thuy (twee)."

She made a point of using Thuy's real name. On the walls hung all the cosmetology licenses, which featured the women's Vietnamese names—Quynh, Anh, Trang—while on their badges the names were unabashedly American. Like Tina (as in Thuy's case), Lisa, Linda, Crissy, and Tammy. As she searched the room to make sure Thuy wasn't otherwise occupied, she finally spotted her toward the back of the long, narrow room, just finishing up with another client. They exchanged a small wave, Thuy indicating she would be right with her.

Susan turned her thoughts back to nail polish. Her eyes scanned the shelves, briefly resting on the row of colors girls wore these days—turquoise, metallic blue, lime green, violet, yellow. For a fraction of a second, she considered painting her nails in one of these exotic, youthful shades, then she remembered she'd forgotten to ask Emma who she was with. She knew her coterie of friends, or at least she used to. Lately Emma had begun hanging out with a new crowd, one she didn't know, and one she kept hoping she'd abandon for her former group. At least they came from good families. Some of these new girls wore deep purple, or was it black? Ugh. She shook her head as if to focus on the task at hand.

She lifted a bottle into the light. What color was she in the mood for? Cherry Bomb? Too bright. Arabica? Maybe, though the name conjured up all the wrong things. Fleur de Lis? Too pale. Key Largo? The name itself lifted her mood. It reminded her of a trip they'd taken when Emma was ten and could still be easily persuaded and manipulated, never mind that she'd adored her mother. She sighed. At last, she settled on a hue that smacked of sunset. Tequila Sunrise. She laughed lightly, thinking she could use a drink. Again, the thought of calling her daughter crossed her mind. She wanted to make sure. Sure of what? She didn't know exactly. If she called Emma with a hesitant voice, or in a slightly probing, prying way, the girl would only lacerate her with an impertinent reply. And really she hated being distrustful. All the books said trust was essential.

"Hello, Soosann?" Thuy's lilting, deferential voice called out to her. "You pick a collah?"

Susan stowed her earlier thoughts, grabbed the tiny bottle, and waltzed over to Thuy, ready to be transported, ready for Thuy's special form of magic.

↝

Susan extended her hands to Thuy almost as a supplicant would to a priest. For a while, she studied the concentrated movements of Thuy's hands, then the top of her head with its neatly parted hair, until her eyes moved beyond Thuy.

Raised up on a tall platform a television flickered with silent staticky and shaky images. The shop didn't have cable, and the antenna wasn't strong enough to deliver a clear signal. Sometimes this annoyed her. Sometimes too she wanted to listen to the drone of the TV while Thuy worked on her hands, manipulating her fingers with the cool splash of polish remover, the quiet snip snip of cuticle scissors, the gentle massage of moisturizing creams her hands and nails cried out for. But the shop owner rarely turned the volume up. The best she could hope for were subtitles. The *Dr. Phil* show was nearing its end, local news on next. Cut to commercial.

The place buzzed with activity. Every workstation occupied. Too crowded, Susan thought. What did she expect? It was Friday afternoon. The ululating ring, if you could call it a ring, of someone's cell phone went off. Several women reached for theirs, held them to their ears or glanced at them, then returned them to their various perches, ready to respond should they choose to. The teenager whose phone had rung answered loudly. Too loudly. Then she laughed, irritatingly so.

This answering of phones anywhere and everywhere had become a nuisance, a ridiculous habit. Of course, she did it too. Nonetheless, she was all for banning the things inside public establishments. Did everyone need to be on call *all* the time?

The girl's voice dropped to a whisper. The room grew quieter too, or was it her imagination? Susan listened more intently. Someone else's secret, especially a teenager's—and a teenager who wasn't her own—now that was worth an eavesdrop. "You think you can get it?" the girl asked.

"I have money. I'll pay you back." Drugs flitted into Susan's mind. She assessed the girl more closely. Were those circles under her eyes? Briefly, her thoughts were drawn back to Emma, then to the TV.

Dr. Phil sat there with two girls, in their mid-teens, and two sets of adults who appeared to be their parents. Susan watched Dr. Phil's lips and read the delayed subtitles. "So, young ladies, from now on you're going to be honest with your parents?" She could hear his trademark inflections in her head. "Because what you were doing almost got you killed?" The girls nodded dumbly. "And you know that's not what you want?" Nod, nod. "And, in the future, you're going to be careful? You're not going to do that *ever* again?" They continued nodding, though not very convincingly. "Right?" he demanded.

Their little smiles made Susan doubt their genuineness. What had they been discussing? She wished she knew. She really ought to get to know Emma's new friends. She realized she'd been avoiding the whole thing. Who were their parents anyway? She thought she knew most of the parents at Emma's school, one of the elite private schools in Northwest D.C. One of Susan's friends had mentioned recently that two new girls in their daughters' class were actually from an orphanage. Did orphanages even exist? No one ever spoke of such places anymore. Everything was about foster homes and their abuses. Were these new students Emma's friends? What sort of influence might they be? And that music Emma listened to! Using words like 'ho for whore, and fug and all sorts of foul, misogynistic language. She had to start paying more attention; she'd talk to Emma about these lyrics. And about her friends. There was always so much to do.

Thuy, whose soft, gentle features belied the strength in her hands, was massaging Susan's arms, her palms, moving down to her fingertips. Susan closed her eyes and relaxed her shoulders. Sometimes she pretended it was her own daughter who handled her so lovingly. She released a long exhalation of air.

"You have long week?" Thuy asked in a low voice.

Susan merely nodded. Work at her law firm had escalated to the point that she sometimes wondered if she shouldn't cut back. Friday was the only day she allowed herself some "down" time. When she got home, she planned to pour herself a glass of Chardonnay and read the paper. She'd sit in her clean house, assuming the cleaning lady had come, and sip the wine, or maybe she'd have a Tequila Sunrise, though God knew she didn't know how to mix one, and she'd read until Emma arrived.

Emma. She'd given her daughter a no-nonsense name. Not something cute like Ashley or Tiffany, or ethnic like Caitlyn or Sasha, or pretentious like Nicole, or a last name that served as a first, like Taylor. No, she'd named her Emma, hoping for a strong and independent, yet honest and kind girl, a solid head-on-her-shoulders type who could withstand peer pressure and the vagaries of today's world.

A local news commentator's head appeared on the TV. He wore an earnest, worried expression as he spoke. His mouth moved rapidly, though for some reason subtitles now failed to crawl across the bottom portion of the screen. It was anybody's guess what he was saying. Anything could have happened. Anything from those exploding sewer lids in Georgetown, to a drive-by shooting, to a kidnapping in broad daylight. Another act of terrorism. For God's sake, a nuclear disaster might be under way! Why don't they turn the volume up? Momentarily, she wondered why her head was filled with such toxic thoughts. Then the image on the screen flipped to a neighborhood, a low-income one, clearly in one of the other quadrants of the city, not Northwest where she lived. Then at the bottom it said, Southeast. Before she could focus on it further, the announcer's face returned, and she saw him mouth the words, "breaking news story," and that they'd be back in a minute.

Shaking the small bottle, Thuy asked, "This one? You like?" She mangled the words Tequila Sunrise. They just couldn't be said at the back of the throat.

Susan nodded absent mindedly. For some reason, she wanted Thuy to hurry up. She began tapping her foot as Thuy applied the base coat. Expertly manipulating the brush, Thuy moved rapidly from one finger to the next, from pinky to thumb. Then, while Thuy lacquered the nails on her left hand, Susan held the wet nails up to the miniature fan to dry, inhaling the familiar scent of polish. For a moment, she allowed her eyes to linger on the most beautiful part of her anatomy. Her fingers were long, lean, shapely. Emma had inherited her father's short, slightly chubby fingers, his unimaginative hands. It was the only feature of her daughter's Susan found unattractive.

The teenager had stopped speaking into her cell. She seemed distraught. In repose, this girl had a pouty lower lip, and an angry slant to her eyebrows. She wasn't very pretty. What does that matter? Susan chided herself. She's someone's daughter. She'd rarely bothered to wonder what other adults thought of Emma. She'd always taken for granted that Emma was wonderful, smart, reliable. She considered this as Thuy brushed the color of sunset onto her nails.

Actually, she'd thought that until last year, when Emma had begun bringing home piles of used clothing. Piles of smelly men's pants, coats, and shirts, women's dresses, and even old petticoats and tattered jeans. God only knew where she found these things. Had she been going to Southeast shops all this time?

One day—when was it?—Emma told her she wanted to design clothes. With her stubby, nail-bitten fingers, she began ripping these hideous clothes apart, then sewed the dark swatches of fabric, layering them into skirts and assembling them into misshapen jackets. At first, Susan had been opposed. She wanted to steer her daughter toward sensible professions. But Emma, suddenly passionate, determined, headstrong, had worn her down. Besides, Susan wanted to appear supportive. It was bound to be a phase she'd outgrow.

Then Emma began wearing her ragamuffin designs to school. That's when Susan had approached the headmistress and suggested a dress code, but the woman had given her little more than a sympathetic smile. Now Susan rarely entered Emma's room, she couldn't stand the smell, unless her suspicions were aroused. Anyway, she'd never found anything. Though she wondered, had she really looked?

Susan glanced back at the TV. The commercial was just coming to an end. The same neighborhood as had been featured earlier reappeared, along with police cars, lights blinking furiously, and a crowd of people who'd gathered behind the reporter at the scene, mike in her slender hand. Now that was a profession Susan endorsed. The reporter was saying something, her mouth moved exaggeratedly. Without subtitles, Susan could only guess at the content. Her eyes drifted to the cluster of people surrounding the woman, mostly African Americans, though whites were among them, a few Latinos.

At once, a girl standing with a policeman caught Susan's eye. A white girl! She could swear she was wearing a jacket that looked like one of Emma's concoctions. Susan jumped out of her chair, squeezed her way between manicure stations, moving toward the TV set, shouting for the volume to be turned up. As she drew near, the camera angle shifted and the girl disappeared. Susan gazed emptily at the reporter. The anchorman returned and said, "Thank you."

Susan turned away. Everyone in Nail Spa was staring at her. Embarrassed, Susan shook her head and in a low voice said, "I thought, I just thought the girl looked…" she stopped, her eyes scanning the clientele, who awaited the rest of her sentence. Groping for a word, she added, "Familiar."

Thuy wore an indecipherable expression as Susan sat down. "You OK?" she asked.

"I guess." Hidden beneath the manicure table, Susan's leg bounced up and down in short spastic motions.

Thuy painted the rest of her nails in silence, then gathered Susan's things and escorted her to the reception area where women sat for five to ten minutes, allowing their nails to dry. "You sit here, least five minutes. OK?"

Susan nodded dumbly.

Barely three minutes passed before Susan delicately guided her arm beneath the strap of her purse, and, with her fingertips, lifted her keys and cell phone, carrying one in each hand.

As she rushed out the door, Susan nicked one of her perfectly polished fingernails.

Robin Ferrier

Harry Potter and Maple Syrup

ROBIN FERRIER holds an MA in writing from Johns Hopkins University. Although this is her first published work, she has had a play performed as part of the Source Theatre Company's 10-Minute Play Competition, and her story was selected as a finalist in the 2005 Washington Write-a-Story Day. She lives in Rockville, Maryland, with her husband and her German shorthaired pointer.

She met him at Screen on the Green. He stood out from the crowd, from everyone eating and talking, from everyone throwing Frisbees and footballs. He stood out because he wore a brightly colored felt hat that looked like a parrot. And he wore that hat while throwing a Frisbee with her new friend Becky. As the evening wore on, as he sung along with that week's movie, the musical *An American in Paris*, she found herself charmed by his happy-go-lucky personality. Not charmed in a this-is-a-man-I-have-to-date or have-to-have way, charmed in a someone-fun-to-hang-out-with way. After all, only a gay man would wear a parrot hat in public.

She talked with him more the next weekend when Becky invited people over for a game night. He loved charades, and whenever it came time to choose teams, he made sure they were teammates. The fact that he spent much of the evening focused on her, asking her questions and trying—successfully—to make her laugh, didn't escape her. But she didn't know what to do with that bit of information.

Their paths crossed again at a party the next week, then at a karaoke bar. He sang—songs from musicals, no less, songs like "Summer Loving" from *Grease*, which Becky sang with him—for much of the time. He tried to drag her on stage with him for "People Will Say We're in Love" from the musical *Oklahoma!*, but she declined. He sang anyway, singing to her, embarrassing her. That night, he joked about people thinking he was gay. Then he invited her to go see *Moulin Rouge* at the Arlington Cinema 'n' Drafthouse.

"And you wonder why people think you're gay?" she asked.

He ignored her response. "Will you go with me?"

She said yes, though she wasn't sure why. He was nothing like the men she dated.

~

He didn't take her home after the movie.

"Have you ever seen the monuments at night?" he asked.

She shook her head.

"You've lived here your whole life, and you've never seen the monuments at night."

She shrugged. "I'm the worst type of Washingtonian. The one who never takes advantage of the city."

"Well then, that has to change. Are you up for it?"

She said OK to the field trip, though she wasn't sure why. She had fun with him, enjoyed talking with him, but she didn't wonder what it was like to kiss him. She always knew a date was headed in the wrong direction when she didn't spend at least some time imagining what it would be like to kiss the guy.

He steered the car onto Route 50.

"In high school I was never allowed in the city," she said.

"And you've been out of high school how long now?"

She didn't answer. The question didn't really require one.

"Though I did come down once." She stared out the window at the Potomac River as they crossed the Roosevelt Bridge. She stared at the Washington Monument shining white in the distance, a lighthouse for the sad souls of the District.

"For Clinton's inauguration," she continued. "We took the Metro. I told my parents I was ice skating and watching a movie and going to dinner with friends. They believed me. I never told them the truth." She paused. "They hated Clinton."

They found a parking spot on Constitution Avenue. He opened the door for her, then took her hand and guided her toward the monuments. She let him keep her hand, though it felt awkward. He led her past the Vietnam Memorial, and she let her hand trail along the names of the dead. She had never visited the memorial, had never seen it in person.

"It's better during the day," he said as he continued walking. "The Lincoln Memorial, though, that's the night monument."

They walked up the steps of the Lincoln Memorial, finally settling down near the top.

"It's beautiful," she said, looking out toward the Washington Monument. "So peaceful."

Before long he hopped up and began singing "Your Song" from *Moulin Rouge*. He danced around her, up and down the steps, and she followed him with her eyes, watching him try to charm her. He finished the song down on his knees at her feet. She smiled and looked down at her hands. He hopped up, then pulled her to her feet, racing down the stairs with her trailing and stumbling behind.

"You need to walk along the Reflecting Pool," he said when he paused at the bottom of the steps.

They strolled softly between the pool and a line of trees, stopping to sit on one of the benches to enjoy the view. No man had ever set up such a romantic evening for her. No man had ever taken the time to try and woo her in this way.

"I've never seen the city so quiet."

"Sing for me," he said.

She told him she couldn't sing, and he pleaded, so she agreed on the condition he sing with her. Together, they sang a few lines from "Your Song." He told her he loved her voice, and she knew he was either lying or delirious. She had a horrible singing voice, a singing voice not even her mother could love.

After a few moments of quiet, he started singing again. He grabbed her hands, pulling her to her feet to dance with him. He twirled her around the trees and dipped her like she was Ginger Rogers to his Fred Astaire, and she felt like she belonged in some old black-and-white musical. And then, when she least expected it, he abruptly stopped dancing and singing and leaned down to kiss her.

It was a nice kiss, though nothing like the kisses she received from the other men she dated.

❧

He sent her emails, calling her a princess, weaving tales of her kingdom, each email another chapter in the life he created for her. He starred as a knight in these tales, a knight that admired her from afar. His emails fascinated her. He fascinated her, how easily he expressed his feelings, how effortless it seemed when he flattered her. She was used to men who dealt out their feelings in increments, like precious clues to the ultimate puzzle of how they felt about her, like they feared that if she solved that puzzle and knew what they were feeling, somehow they would self-destruct.

❧

They played mini golf on their second date, a double date with Becky and her boyfriend. He wasn't very good, yet he didn't seem to care that he couldn't make par. She loved that about him, that he could laugh at his own shortcomings. She was used to men who wanted to win, who got angry when they missed an easy putt. But he didn't care about winning. He cared about having fun, about enjoying himself.

She began to see his assets more clearly, and to overlook the things about him, like his tendency to break out in show tunes at the oddest moments. She began to understand why she had said yes to that first date, even if he was nothing like the men she usually dated. She wondered if his being different was the key to her happiness. She never thought of herself as the type to choose the "wrong" man, but this experience made her question her past decisions.

They talked on the phone most every night, right before she went to bed. They talked about their families and shared stories of growing up.

"My uncle makes real maple syrup in Vermont," he told her. "I used to love going up there to visit. I loved helping him collect the syrup from the trees. Someday I'll take you up there and we'll do it together. We'll make maple syrup together and bring it home and use it on our pancakes and every time we use it we'll remember how much fun we had collecting the syrup. My uncle would love you. He'd tell me how beautiful you are. He'd tell me not to mess this up, that you were a keeper. And he's not easily impressed."

They talked about movies and books. He loved romantic movies and the *Harry Potter* series. He couldn't believe she'd only read the first *Harry Potter* book.

"I wasn't that impressed," she told him. "I had heard so much about them. I expected more."

"The second was even better than the first."

"I'll take your word for it," she said, before hanging up the phone and going to sleep.

❧

They'd gone on one more date—dinner and the movie *Legally Blonde*—before the wedding invitation arose.

"I can bring a guest," he said. "And you'd know people. Becky will be there. Will you come?"

She almost said yes. Then she thought about what a weekend trip might mean, about having to negotiate sleeping arrangements and being introduced as, well, as what? His date? His girlfriend? She wasn't sure she wanted to move the relationship to that level yet. To the level of "girlfriend," which denoted exclusivity—not that she was seeing other people—which denoted a level of seriousness she wasn't sure she felt.

"I can't go," she finally said. "I have a softball game."

"You can miss one game."

"I can't. They won't have enough girls to play if I don't show."

"Please." He gave her his sad eyes, laid his head in her lap. "How am I supposed to go a whole weekend without my princess? Who will I dance with? Who will I sing to?"

She smiled at him. "You'll dance with Becky. You'll sing to the bride and groom. And I'll drive you to the train station."

He pouted, but she didn't give in. And a week later, on a Friday morning, she dropped him at Union Station before heading in to work.

"I'll be back on Monday morning," he said. "Dinner Monday night?"

"Sure. I'll even cook for you."

He smiled. "Lucky me." Then he leaned over and kissed her. "I still wish you'd come. It's not too late."

"I'm not going."

"Fine."

He got out of the car. She watched him walk toward the entrance. Just outside the front door, he stopped and turned toward her. He got down on his knees, kissed one palm, and blew her the kiss. Then he hopped up, and went inside to catch his train.

⁓

Hidden in among the bills and the catalogues that arrived in the mail that Friday she found an envelope with handwriting she didn't recognize. She opened the envelope and pulled out the card. The front had a cartoon basset hound with droopy eyes, droopy ears, a sad face. "Missing you already…" it read. She opened the card, "…and I've barely left." She smiled. He must have sent it two or three days ago for it to arrive today. Just like him. When he called that night, she thanked him for the card and he sang to her—"Your Song," his favorite song these days—before hanging up.

Two more "missing you" cards arrived in Saturday's mail. *This is overkill*, she thought, even if three cards did match his personality. She knew he lived in extremes. In singing and dancing whenever the mood hit. In big gestures. He did nothing halfway. Who was she to complain that he lived life in a way other people only dreamed of? In a way characteristic of movies and television? Every girl wanted the "I love you" over the airport loudspeaker preventing her from taking that flight that would signify the end to a relationship not meant to end. Every girl wanted the hockey game wedding proposal, the room filled with hundreds of candles and rose petals, the stuff you read about in books and watched on screen, right? Who didn't love John Cusack lifting the boom box over his head in *Say Anything* or the acrophobic Richard Gere climbing the fire escape in *Pretty Woman*? That's who he was, she reminded herself. He was the classic romantic hero, making grand proclamations of his love, though the word love scared her seeing as she'd only known him a month.

And just because she wasn't sure how to deal with the romantic hero, having never dated one before now, didn't mean she should fault him for being what girls claimed they wanted.

But still, when he called that night, she didn't answer the phone. And on Sunday, she took her phone off the hook.

The fourth card showed up in the office mail on Monday. Her co-workers declared her lucky, asked her to tell them more about this Romeo she'd never mentioned. But she didn't tell them anything. She didn't know what to tell them.

"He sings to me," she imagined saying. "He sings in public. All the time." They'd tell her how romantic that was.

"He writes stories that feature me as a princess." Even that would get some admiration, envy.

She'd continue: "He enjoys movies like *Moulin Rouge* and wears a big, brightly colored parrot hat when he goes to Screen on the Green." Perhaps not making him a manly man, but still not something with which they would likely find fault.

"He sent me four cards when he went away for a weekend."

No, she couldn't tell them about him. So she just walked away. She kept him a secret.

He called when he got back into town. He had taken an early train home. He wanted to take her to lunch, but she told him she couldn't, that she had work to do. He wanted to pick her up from work, but she had driven the 0.2 miles to work that day even though the grocery store was on her way home from work and she normally walked there. He conceded and asked what time he should come over for dinner. She told him seven o'clock. A half hour later, he emailed her another installment in the story of her kingdom. Then he emailed her a poem he'd written for her on the train ride home. She didn't reply to either email.

At the end of the day, she stuffed the card in her bag and headed to the grocery store. She bought lettuce, green and red peppers, cucumbers, and tomatoes. She bought salad dressing and croutons. She bought skinless, boneless chicken breasts and raspberry jam and red pepper flakes. She bought potatoes and onions and flour. She bought raspberry sorbet and coconut cookies and Cool Whip.

She went home and made dessert while looking at four cards he had sent that she had propped up on the dining room table.

She shredded potatoes and diced onions and thought about the emailed poems and stories.

She cut up peppers and cucumbers and wedged tomatoes while remembering him singing to her on their first date. She'd always hated dating boys who wouldn't dance. He danced. And twirled. And sang. To her. She always thought dating someone who sang to her would be romantic.

She prepared the chicken while picturing him throwing the Frisbee in his parrot hat. She slid the chicken in the oven and set the timer. Then she waited for him to arrive.

She waited for the knock that came right on time. She answered the door, and he leaned down to kiss her. She turned so he kissed her cheek instead of her lips.

"Dinner smells amazing," he said.

"We need to talk," she said.

He laid his bookbag on the floor. "No."

"No?"

"No." He pulled a bottle of red wine out of his bag. "We're going to have a nice dinner. We're going to pretend like everything's OK."

"But—"

"You owe me that."

She didn't know how to respond.

"Wineglasses?"

She retrieved two glasses and handed them to him as the timer went off. He poured the wine as she fried the potato mixture she'd made, laying each potato patty out on paper towels to drain off excess oil. When she'd fried all the potatoes, she loaded them into a big bowl that he carried to the table. He moved the four cards from the table to her bookcase.

"How was the wedding?" she asked.

"Great."

She pulled the chicken out of the oven and put a chicken breast on each plate, then carried the plates to the table. They sat down for dinner.

"Did you have fun?"

"Yes."

"Did you sing at the reception?"

"Uh-huh."

"'Your Song'?"

"No. That's your song."

She took a bite of the chicken and chewed in silence. She sipped the wine, then took a bite of her potatoes.

"The chicken's good," he said.

"Thanks." Silence. Awkward silence. "I got your cards."

"I saw."

She stared at her plate as they ate in silence, and when they were both done, she cleared the table. He stood up to help, but she told him to sit, that she would take care of it. She piled the dirty dishes in the sink, then returned to the dining room, hovering in the doorway.

"We need to talk," she said again.

"You don't need to say anything."

He leaned over and pulled a new copy of the second *Harry Potter* book out of his bag. He held it out for her.

"What's that?"

"A parting gift," he said.

She shook her head no, so he laid the book on the table.

"The second is better than the first," he said. "I had planned on reading it to you, a chapter at a time, over the phone each night before you went to bed. Read it. You'll like it."

He reached into the bag again and pulled out a huge jug of maple syrup. He put it on the table next to the book. He stared at it.

Finally he spoke. “My uncle’s maple syrup.”

He zipped his bookbag, got up, and headed toward the front door.

“Wait—”

He turned around. But she didn’t know what to say. She pulled the raspberry sorbet dessert out of the freezer. “Take some dessert?”

He shook his head no. “It was the fourth card, wasn’t it?”

“Yes.” She paused. “And maybe the third.”

“The second?” he asked.

She shrugged.

“The first?”

“No.” She shook her head. “The first one was OK. It was nice.”

He nodded, then unlocked her door and walked out, leaving the door open behind him. From the doorway she watched him walk slowly to the row of elevators. She almost expected him to break out in some sad song, some song of goodbye. Instead, she could just catch a trace of him humming “Your Song.”

She stepped back into her apartment. She closed the door and locked it. She put the maple syrup in the refrigerator and curled up in the corner of her sofa, the *Harry Potter* book in her lap, but she didn’t read. Instead, she thought about him, about his singing, about how he gave her Washington at night, about his big gestures, about his heart-on-the-sleeve personality and *Moulin Rouge* and the stories of her kingdom. She knew eventually she’d delete the poems and the stories from her email inbox. That she’d go through her sent mail also, deleting her messages to him. She always erased all traces of past relationships at some indefinite point down the road, often when a new guy started to make his way onto the scene and she no longer needed the comfort of what had been.

But mostly she thought about how he was different from the other men she’d dated, about how he’d left her with *Harry Potter* and maple syrup. She wished she knew what it meant, but she didn’t. Maybe some day, she would.

Sara Fisher

Earthen Vessels

SARA FISHER grew up in the Washington area and remains a Washingtonian by extension, although she now lives in Leonardtown, Maryland. She holds an MFA in writing, has received an Individual Artist's Grant from the DC Commission on the Arts and Humanities, and works at Georgetown University.

Word gets around, you know. I learned about her the same way you'd discover things like a new brand of hair color or a decent mechanic or another way to cook salmon—from the girls in the sauna. Since I'd recently sloughed off a husband and begun flirting with literary agents, I was looking in an offhand way for someone to keep up a level of cleanliness in my house while I worked on the novel that Ross, the aforementioned husband, saw no reason I should bother to write. Never mind the details of Ross's leaving; all anyone needs to know is that I sent him packing. For the rest, although I've got precious little to show for any lit-gent's help, I can vouch for the fact that St. Lucy Madarang came highly recommended.

"I've got her two days a week," said Madge. "She really does a pretty decent job."

Ellen's towel slipped as she jiggled the sauna thermostat. "Is that OK with you all? Where do these people come from anyway? They just sort of appear like those little sugar ants that show up in my kitchen every spring."

"You got those, too? God, they're a pain." Carol rolled her head. "This St. Lucy person is in my neighborhood, too. Nobody ever says anything against her. Pretty strange name if you ask me."

I leaned back against the wood paneling. I was feeling way too rubbery to say to Carol that no one had asked her, but I probably wouldn't have made that kind of crack anyway. Saunas will do that to you. There's something about being in a small steamy place on a regular basis with women you wouldn't recognize if they had street clothes on.

"Calendar," I mumbled. I was just about to say that in some cultures parents call the baby after whoever's name is on the calendar the day they're born. Learned that from a journal. Grandparents'. The ones who got religion, left their offspring, and went off to the Philippines to save pagan babies. Just about to say that when a wedge of cool air hit my arm. Jane slipped through the door into the sauna. "Calendar," I said. "I got a nice one at the museum. Sale bin. It's all watercolors."

Ellen slid over. "Watercolors are nice," she said.

Nobody disliked Jane. She managed to make time for some kind of exercise once a week, as we all did, whether it was a few laps or a shift on the treadmill. Then she came to the sauna afterwards to sweat and socialize. But Jane was a family chick. Kids. Church suppers. Husband. A husband, in fact, who worked for Immigration. She yammered about all of it; we never asked for details. Some things we just didn't talk about when she was there. Like the Ten Commandments. Like condoms. Like women from elsewhere who clean neighborhood houses.

"Hi, y'all," said Jane. "I love watercolors. Have you seen that wonderful Winslow Homer that's a house in the Bahamas with palm trees blowing? We have a print of that in our dining room. Anybody read the latest Patrick O'Brien novel?"

I'm sure there wasn't a sea lover among us, but since I expected all of them to read my novel some day, I couldn't think of bad-mouthing someone else's. Carol said something benign about kids. That was all Jane needed. She was still talking about hers when we left the sauna for the shower. As the others padded down the tiles to the locker room, I whispered to Madge to have St. Lucy Madarang come to my house on Tuesday morning. I would have supplies and would pay in cash.

Tuesday came, and I had a vague feeling I ought to clean up before she got there, but I stifled it. I brought in the newspaper and kicked out the cat. I had barely closed the storm door again when a middle-aged woman in a white peaked cap, navy wool cape, and far-too-sensible shoes appeared on the porch. She was a solid woman with olive skin and dark eyes that I only caught a glimpse of. She clasped her hands in front of herself. "I am St. Lucy Madarang."

I didn't get the sense she was the sort of person who could be ushered, so I just opened the door and let her in. English was apparently not her first language, but she didn't seem to question what she heard or the surroundings she found herself in. Then again, nothing about her surprised me either. I'd met a lot like her through the grandparents' journal. Perhaps she'd even been one of those pagan babies ransomed by Methodists. It did occur to me, though, that I wasn't yet ready to call her either "St. Lucy" or "Miss Madarang"; so I showed her brushes and cleansers underneath the kitchen sink and left the house to her. All except the space I'd turned into my workroom. Full of notes and folders and drafts. And that journal. I left the house to St. Lucy Madarang and closed myself in.

Back in the days when I was absolutely sure I could produce a prize-winner of a book, I never wrote a thing. Now I don't think about that anymore and I find it much easier to get carried away pouring out something that will one day actually be an artifact. I spend time writing, of course, but it's funny how ideas will knit themselves together even when I'm not poised over a piece of paper. I can be standing in the shower, and the word I needed hours ago will suddenly come. If I wore suspenders I'd snap 'em in pleasure. Who wants to waste time cleaning when life can be like that?

I came out of my workroom after about four hours to get coffee and check on St. Lucy Madarang. She was standing where I had left her, cape on, cap on her head, and no sign of being put out. In the least. I could see, though, that the pile of the carpet was streaked with those comforting vacuum cleaner marks, while the stainless steel in the kitchen had not a speck on it. No sign of bagel crumbs in the sink. Not a single mote anywhere in the house, and not a thing out of place.

"Next Tuesday, then?" I said. I added a couple of dollars to what the gals in the sauna said she usually got. She nodded slightly, took the money, and disappeared. I'd gotten a clean house; she'd gotten the money she'd worked for.

"Another satisfied customer; you all were right." I sank to the space on the bench I usually took. Madge and Carol each slumped into a corner; Ellen sat near the sauna door as usual. We were all done in from a heavy-duty racquetball game together, but, as always, managed to find our spaces with a minimum of choreography.

"Aside from the fact that we're always right," said Carol, "what in particular have we been right about this time?" She sighed as if she were exhaling smoke that had finally gotten to her after a long time in the stem of a cigarette holder.

"That St. Lucy Madarang person," I said. "House is spotless." No need to be oblique. Jane hadn't arrived yet. She was probably ferrying her kids to a recital or something.

"I told you," Madge said. "And not only does she do a good job, but you'll find your house will stay clean longer with no man around to muck it up." That was the kind of comment we wouldn't make in front of Jane. Nothing about immigrants, and nothing about men.

I glanced toward the door. "Funny thing is, I wouldn't keep it that clean for a man, but as far as I'm concerned, she can come every week to my place. I'd rather think up plot twists than worry about dust bunnies any day."

"So. Tell us about a plot twist or two," Ellen said.

Sharing plot twists is sort of like letting myself be mugged; after it happens, the goods are gone. I used to tell Ross about ideas I had for stories. Not only did he pooh-pooh the idea of his wife writing stories, but once I had told *about* them, I didn't have any stories left to tell. I had, though, figured what things I could share with the girls in the sauna. They never seemed to tire of hearing about that ceramic bowl where I kept my ideas on scraps of paper and how it happened to get from my missionary grandparents to the desk in my workroom. I was on the point of saying something more of the same when the door opened.

"Oh, hi, everybody," Jane said. "Guess I'm late again. Chris's soccer game went into overtime, and then I had to wait for a turn on the StairMaster." Her skin was flushed from exercise, but her hair was damp only at the temples.

"S'OK," said Ellen. "We were just talking about ancestors." She patted the bench beside her. Jane slid onto it.

"Oh, I love genealogy!" she said. "I took a course once on how to track down all that information. Libraries, county seats, graveyards, everything. I never got back too far, but I've always enjoyed it. Anybody else find any good stuff?" Jane pushed a lock of hair behind her ear.

Carol scraped her back on the sauna's paneling. "Just love a good scratch, don't you?" she said. "Somewhere back a couple of generations I've got somebody who was a brewer in West Virginia. Got here by signing on to be ballast on a ship. We found a book of notes and recipes in his handwriting." She looked toward me with her eyes half-shut. "You, Sandra?"

The sauna was too small to look at her and not have it be noticed. I dropped my towel just so I could pick it up. "Nothing to speak of," I said casually. "Who else is ready for a shower?"

Nothing much I cared to speak of, although I had plenty to write about. St. Lucy Madarang kept cobwebs at bay for me so I could work on it. I mean, if you had material like that, would you spend time worrying if doilies were straight on the back of your armchair or there were a cup in your sink?

That journal. That's what I had. Part of my grandparents' journal, one they had kept while they were missionaries. Methodists. In the Philippines, of all places. I had no idea why they'd left farm and family to go to another part of the world where they had to eat starch and live on a dirt floor—well, it escapes *me* anyway—but it could be if your life boils down to barbed wire, burgers, and Old Style, maybe it's easier to get religion. Even if it isn't, I could use that as a reason. Mama never talked about them, that's for sure.

Other than that, all I had was that pottery bowl I managed to get hold of, something they sent back for one reason or another. It's squat and open, has animal heads on three sides. Of course, that part of the world makes me think of baskets (they would have been easier to ship, in any case), so a pottery something must have been special. Maybe it held ritual grain offerings. Maybe incense. Maybe blood from a human sacrifice. You never know what folks might have held to before somebody convinced them to become Methodists. At any rate, whatever it used to hold, I kept it on my desk and used it to catch ideas. If I happened to think of something, I'd scratch it on a piece of paper and toss it into the bowl. I loved to see ideas mount up, almost as if the bowl itself called them out of me. I could feel a book coming on surer than sneezes in spring.

I worked at the odd hour among all the other things I kept busy at, including exercise with the girls and time in the sauna, but always took the whole morning on Tuesdays to write. As far as I was concerned, having St. Lucy Madarang around was like being able to count on Rumplestiltskin to get done all the chores that were just too much to put my head to. She always came on time and showed up in the same cape and peaked cap. Four hours later everything was spotless, she took her cash, and disappeared. I never even saw her roll up her sleeves. If I believed in such stuff, I'd say that St. Lucy was a blessing. She was in any case no less than a boon.

One afternoon I was just pulling myself out of a good relaxing session in the bathtub when I caught the glint of something on the floor almost out of sight behind one of the tub's claw feet. I picked it up. No way was it anything I had lost. It was a small oval medallion with a sort of laurel wreath on one side and a bust of some long-haired girl with a plate in her hand on the other. On the plate she had what looked like two eyeballs. It had to have been some trinket St. Lucy had dropped. Yeah, I could have returned it to her, or at least have left it dropped, but I was not about to get into encouraging grotesque stuff like medals of chicks with eyes on platters no matter how much I wanted her to stay. I wrapped the thing in a tissue and put it in a pants pocket to throw away at the gym. She'd forget about it, and I wouldn't even bother to think about it again.

Only I did end up thinking about it again. Two evenings later as I was squinting at myself in the mirror trying to find the hole in my lobe for my earring, I noticed what looked, well, sort of, like a vague stain on the dresser scarf. Except it wasn't. I touched the place and found that something had been slid underneath. I found a plastic card with a picture, in the most flagrant colors you could imagine, of a woman with her eyes rolled up, holding a flaming, bleeding heart-sort of thing. Something else that sure wasn't mine. And it didn't just drop there by accident.

The only person who'd crossed the threshold lately besides me was St. Lucy Madarang. She had work to do, and the house was spotless. For a while, I kept an eye on the spoons, the sugar, the toilet paper. I mean, after all, if I were in a strange country and the only thing I could do to keep myself together was to clean houses for other women, I'd collect a few necessities here and there. Not only did nothing disappear, but she left things besides. On purpose.

I suppose it would have done me good just to go out that evening the way I'd planned, but I was in no mood. I sat in my room to work on my novel about two young people who escape the Midwest by becoming Methodist missionaries to the Philippines and trying to save godless pagans who rip the hearts out of people, but nothing would come. I stared at the animal bowl; I stared at each of the scraps of ideas that I'd thrown into it. The next sentence was always just out of reach, while some thought of St. Lucy Madarang, her cheap little medal, and her stupid ugly picture sprawled right in front of all my thoughts and kept poking a stick at my consciousness. No work to show for that session at my desk, and precious little sleep to show for the night spent there either.

Promptly at eight a.m., St. Lucy Madarang knocked on the door. I'd forgotten it was Tuesday; she would be there to clean the house. All I could think of was that I didn't want to see her, didn't even want to think of her. I nodded slightly and stepped aside.

"I'll go for a little while to the sauna this morning," I said before I realized it. I'd had my writing session, and it had been like rubbing myself on a saguaro. I needed to lean back and steam my brain. With any luck I'd meet Madge or one of the others and have a chance to ask about this St. Lucy person and her apparent weirdness. With no luck, I'd meet Jane, but even that would be preferable to sitting home watching that woman with the long sleeves and the peaked cap bustle around my house and wondering, wondering. I grabbed a sweater from the back of the chair in my office and headed for the door.

But I arrived at the gym to find a hand-lettered sign on the sauna saying it would be closed for a week while they ordered and installed a new heater core. I slammed the door of the Audi and roared around the corner the two blocks to Stand Your Grounds. Hated the Audi (although in a divorce you grab all the goods you can get). At least I could mope over a good cup of coffee.

And the coffee at Stand Your Grounds really is good. All their stuff is Fair Trade coffee, which I believe in. Plus, they have a "bottomless mug" policy, so I can go in there, read the *New Yorker*, and drink refills all afternoon. I was just gathering up the last bits of a piece of raspberry crumble and sipping at my second mugful when someone tapped me on the shoulder. I barely recognized Carol, perfectly coiffed and wearing a melon-colored knit shirt.

"Sauna's closed," I said, and made a brusque gesture in the direction of the gym.

"So we both know," said Carol. "Join you?" But her question had just about no hang time before she was sliding into the booth opposite me. She opened two packets of turbinado sugar and let them run slowly into her Dark Roast.

"Guess who I saw last Sunday morning at that big intersection where Monroe crosses Jefferson Boulevard," she said.

I couldn't have cared if it had been the Prince of Wales, so that's what I said. "The Prince of Wales."

"Well, I intend to be serious even if you're not," Carol said. "I saw a couple of women in white dresses and peaked hats. They had pamphlets and plastic buckets with a cross and a dollar sign painted on, and they were going from car to car at the intersection. And one of them was our St. Lucy Madarang."

I pulled my mug in close and raised one eyebrow. "And?"

She leaned toward me. "I didn't dare look at either of them head on, but I could tell that what they were passing out were tracts. You can bet your crumble they weren't collecting for the Moose Lodge."

"Holy sh…!" A lump of coffee caught in my throat. "Who do they think they are blocking traffic, pushing their crazy ideas, and scamming people?"

"Some folks just don't know their place," said Carol.

I drained my mug and left her pleating empty sugar packets into tiny fans.

I got home and headed toward the office to ditch my sweater. There were no cleaning sounds in the house; everything was strangely quiet. At the time I didn't pay much attention. I had wanted, needed, a sauna, and I couldn't have it.

The office door was ajar, as I'd left it. I could see books with papers straining at their bindings lying around as they always were. I reached for the doorknob to drape my sweater over it. Then I saw her in the middle of my workroom.

St. Lucy Madarang stood poised in the middle of the room looking just as she did every week when she appeared on my porch—overly sensible shoes, navy blue cape, peaked hat. Her hands were clasped in front of her. There at her feet were the shards of my animal bowl, and scraps of paper strewn everywhere. For the first time since I had met her I could see into her eyes. They looked straight at me, and if they could have talked they would have said, "Yes, go ahead. Hit me. I'm ready."

Shaking your fist or gathering shards—what good does either do, really? I glanced quickly at the remains of my bowl and looked at her again. She was ready to be struck, but I wasn't ready to throw a punch.

"I'll have some friends to lunch on Thursday if you could set the table for that, please. Not too formal. I know the woman you work for and I'll make arrangements; I'd like you to be here to help me serve." I couldn't call her by name, any name. "There will be five of us." Gym or no gym, I'd host a gathering of the gals from the sauna. And be sure, for once, to invite Jane.

Lee Fleming

Dancing for Angels

LEE FLEMING has been writing, editing, and teaching fiction and nonfiction in the Washington area for more than two decades. She currently is the "Fixes" columnist for the *Washington Post* Home section, and a speechwriter specializing in financial policy and cultural trends. Fleming has been recognized for her essays, criticism, and fiction, receiving the Larry Neal Writer's Award, a Ucross Foundation fellowship/residency in creative writing, AAUW's award for excellence in local reporting, a Mid-Atlantic States critic's residency fellowship, and two DC Commission on the Arts and Humanities' fellowships. Her essays and short stories have appeared in small press magazines and anthologies. Her first novel, *Someone Special*, was published by Ballentine Books; she is currently working on a second. Her three cats are her severest literary critics.

The glass of the big window was divided by cold dark metal that made crosses between the panes. On late afternoons, when the sun finally swung around the corner of the building opposite, the light streamed in, swimming with dust motes. If she narrowed her eyes until her lashes made a blurry curtain, the dust particles started to look like tiny floating dancers.

The sun rays came to rest on the carpet in rectangles that grew broader as they stretched into the room, away from the wall with the window. Whenever Nancy, the babysitter, ran upstairs to her own apartment to answer the phone—they could hear it ring through the ceiling; they could hear Nancy fighting and crying with her boyfriend, too—she would play indoor hopscotch, switching from one foot to the other diagonally down four rectangles, then back again to the small end of the sun squares.

Beulah, who watched her when Nancy didn't, said this wasn't real hopscotch—for real hopscotch you needed a sidewalk, chalk, numbers in the squares, and pebbles to mark your place—and she should give it another name. But she didn't know what else to call it. It *felt* like hopscotch, but was filled with peril. If she stepped on one of the shadow crosses, her mother would never come home, her father would never walk through the door as the sun faded and night claimed the room. She hopped from one rectangle to another balancing on the points of her shoes, like the ballerinas who danced in black and white on TV. She lifted her arms to make a circle, fingers almost meeting above her head. "I am the princess, my daddy is the king, my mommy is the queen, and my brothers are the princes," she singsonged down and back, down and back again.

"Lily! Stop that right now!" Nancy was back, and angry. "Don't let your poor father hear you saying that. Do you understand me?" She grabbed at her arm and shook it. "Don't ever say that again."

"Why not? I always say it. Daddy doesn't mind."

"Well, he will now." Nancy's eyes were grim. "So don't do it. You hear me?" She gave her arm another shake for emphasis.

"Why? Why?" Nancy's face was white with two spots of red glowing on her cheeks, her lips were pressed together, hard, her eyebrows drawn together like they wanted to touch ends over her nose. She looked at Lily the way her mother did when she caught her playing with the bottles stored under the sink. Angry and about to burst with it.

"I don't want you here," she started to wail, "I don't want you, I want my daddy, where's my daddy?"

Nancy dropped her arm and stood back, looking down on her. "You poor kid. Don't cry. I didn't mean to hurt you." Lily kept crying, though, making high, thin, hiccuppy noises until she was hiccupping for real, big loud whoops that shook her body.

"Oh God." Nancy retreated to the gloom of the kitchen and came back holding open a brown paper bag. "Here," she forced its open mouth around Lily's and clamped it shut with one hand while stroking her hair with the other. "Breathe, honey, just breathe. Close your eyes, calm down, calm down. Big breaths now. *That's* right."

She began to feel blurry, like the top layer of her skin was dissolving away. Her hair seemed separate from her head, like some sleek animal stirring under Nancy's hand. When she'd had appendicitis, the nurse had dripped ether through a cone to make her go to sleep. This floating up through layers to a place just outside her body was a little like that. No, she thought, it was more like being in a warm bath in the big tub at her grandmother's house, eyes closed, while Noni's fingertips rubbed her temples to bring on sleep.

The hiccups stopped; Nancy took away the bag. "Better," she smiled and spoke in the bright tone grown-ups used when they wanted her to think everything was all right. But Nancy's smile was not real—just a stretch of the lips. Lily could see the worry in her eyes and she knew she had put it there. She suddenly felt powerful.

"When is my daddy coming home?" she demanded, stamping her foot like she'd seen Shirley Temple do in the old movies that played on TV in the afternoons that Beulah watched her.

"Come here." Nancy took her hand and walked her over to the window, then moved a chair against the wall so she could stand on it and look out with her. I am almost as tall as Nancy, she thought as they stood there side by side, hand in hand again, inches from the cold glass. This was what it was like to be big. Chair-less, only the upper half of her head cleared the sill. She had to stand on tiptoe, braced against the wall, to bring her chin above it. But when she moved the chair herself and stood on it, her mother punished her. "Don't do that, Lily," she said, "you could fall and hurt yourself," and she would lift her off and smack her on the hand.

The front of the building across the way was in shadow, the streetlights had come on although the cars parked nose to tail along the curb and the single big tree at the end of the broken sidewalk were still gray blue in the leftover light of day. "Your father should be here soon," Nancy said, glancing at her watch. There was a knock at the door. Nancy looked over her shoulder, as if she could see the front door through the living room wall. "Here, Lily," she said, taking her hands and laying them palms down on the sill. "Use these for balance if you need to. Lean in and try not to move. And don't rock the chair. I'll be right back."

Was it her daddy? No. She recognized Mrs. MacEnroe's voice, accompanied by the rich tomato-sauce smell of another hot casserole. Since her mother had been gone, Mrs. MacEnroe and Mrs. Steigler had been bringing them food almost every day. These were not the kinds of foods her mother made—slices of meat precise on the plate, peas to one side of the meat, rice or mashed potato to the other, everything clean, nothing touching, never any sauce. Mrs. Steigler's food was covered in bread crumbs, "fried," Daddy said. Mrs. MacEnroe's food was all mushed up, layers of meat and chewy macaroni and sauce with bits of tomato in it. Italian food, her father told her. Mrs. MacEnroe was Italian. "Eat up Lily, you'll feel better," Daddy said. But that wasn't true because he ate up but it didn't make him smile.

She twisted her head toward the sounds beyond the wall. Suddenly Mrs. MacEnroe and Nancy appeared together under the archway into the hall.

"How's my Lily? How's my Mrs. Busy today?" She didn't know when or why Mrs. MacEnroe had started calling her this. She didn't think she had ever done it before her mother went away.

"Lily!" Nancy was giving her a look that said she should answer.

"OK, I guess," she ducked her head back around to look out the window again. The lights and darks of the scene behind her were reflected on the window. She pretended it was the murky crystal of a wicked witch, with Nancy's and Mrs. MacEnroe's silhouettes swimming deep inside. At night, her father told her stories and wizards, and horses whose legs stretched to carry the wizards and brave children over rivers and mountains, past the moon, past the stars, to save their village from bad people like wicked kings and evil witches who looked into bowls of water or mirrors or big glass balls to see the future, to see where the good people were and to stop them from rescuing the world.

"Poor child," Mrs. MacEnroe was saying to Nancy. "Do you think she understands?"

"I know Dan told her something," Nancy answered. They were whispering, but their words had edges that sent them hissing at her from across the room. "But at five, I doubt it means anything to her."

"Has she asked about her mother? Or the twins?"

"Not really."

"No? I'm surprised. She was always talking about them before it happened."

Against the night, in the windowpane to the right of her head, she saw their two figures darkly reflected. They seemed to be staring at her back. She hunched her shoulders against their eyes. She was wearing her favorite pale pink sweater with roses up by each shoulder; as she stretched her shoulders toward her ears, the roses rose, too, clustering by the pale reflection of her jaw.

In the middle of the blackness before her, a car door opened, shedding light. "Daddy," she cried. "Daddy's home."

"Lily, don't," Nancy began, but she had already clambered down off the chair and was running toward them, past them and through the arch, to wait inches from the front door.

Outside the sound of a key clicking into the lock. The door swung open, with her father framed in the doorway, the hall light behind turning him into a dark mountain, gray hat pulled low over his eyes, gray overcoat buttoned high against the cold and draping around his body. "Daddy! Daddy!" She flung herself forward and grabbed his knee through the thick material. "Lily." He reached down and ruffled her hair. "How's my girl?" She couldn't speak, afraid to break the magic of his return with the wrong words.

"Nancy, Rita." His leg was moving forward, breaking from her clutching fingers. "Here, Lily, let me take my coat off." She backed off as he shrugged off the overcoat and dropped it on a chair. "Was she good?" he asked Nancy. "Did she give you any trouble?"

"Always, to both." Nancy smiled, this time a real smile that spread from her lips to her eyes. Mrs. MacEnroe was smiling, too. Women always smiled at her father, even now when he looked tired and a little sad.

"Well, thank you again. I'll see you..." he paused.

"Day after tomorrow," Nancy supplied. "I'll be here. And in the meantime, if you need anything, you know where I am." She moved into the hall, her body still turned toward Lily's father.

"Well, I'd better be getting back to Jack," Mrs. MacEnroe said, moving out as well but turned back, too, like Nancy. "I left you some rigatoni and sausage, Dan. Enjoy!" She wiggled her fingers at Lily's father, who said thank you and smiled with his teeth not his eyes, then shut the door.

"Rigatoni." He shook his head. "More rigatoni. Are you hungry?" She stood in front of him, hands clasped, trying to gauge his mood. "No, huh?" She shook her head.

"Me neither. But we should eat. Come on. You sit down and I'll bring out the food."

She liked eating with her father. He didn't make her sit at the small table and chair that her uncle had made. He let her sit at the grown-ups' table with him, on a real chair, on top of a stack of *Life* magazines. "Your booster seat, madam," he joked each time he lifted her up onto it. Mrs. MacEnroe's food was still steaming when he brought out the two pale green plates like the ones they had in the restaurants they stopped in when they went to visit the grandparents. He had piled them high with rigatoni, firm tiny tunnels burrowing through the ooze of meat and tomato and cheese.

She used her spoon like the steam shovel that had stood at the end of the street all through the summer, scooping away at a bank of red dirt shot through with roots and topped with trees. Celia's grandfather had taken them down to watch, holding their hands so they could not get near the yellow maw of the machine. "This is where they'll put in more apartments," he told them, as they watched the big rough steel teeth cut in the earth and pull out skunk cabbage and laurel bushes.

She imitated its motion with the rigatoni: down, forward, up, into the mouth, and back down again for a new load.

They ate in silence until after her father had started working on his second helping, putting one out for her as well. "Lily." He cleared his throat. "Mommy's coming home soon."

She couldn't think of anything to say, just nodded. "You've missed Mommy, haven't you?" Another nod.

"Well, we have to be very nice to Mommy when she's home again," Daddy continued. "You've got to be the best girl you can be." He stopped and looked over her head. She wanted to turn to see what had so deeply caught his attention, but at the same time was afraid to take her eyes off him. He was being so quiet, a serious Daddy. She didn't know how to respond. What would a grown-up do? So she kept her eyes on his face. He cleared this throat again. "Mommy was very sad when she lost the twins. Your brothers. I told you about that, do you remember?"

How could she forget the long time of waiting, of watching her mother and father coming together in a happiness that seemed to shut her out. They were waiting for the twins. Her grandparents were waiting for the twins. The neighbors all came by and smiled and wished them luck and made jokes. The neighbors were also waiting for the twins. "Your brothers, or maybe your sisters. Or maybe one of each," her father teased Lily. "You'd like that, wouldn't you? One of each."

"You mean *you'd* like it, Dan," her mother laughed, and they kissed and laughed again.

Lily didn't know what she felt. She supposed it would be good to have someone else to play with besides Celia MacEnroe and Mikey Steigler. A baby brother or a baby sister. Two of both. Or one of each. She would be their Big Sister and they would love each other. It would be like the families on TV.

But already everything was changing. It had been barely June, the day after her kindergarten graduation, when her mother and father first told her about the twins. All through the summer her parents talked about the babies with an excitement that they used to show about her. The triumph of her first day in first grade had been muted by coming home to find her mother painting the room next to her parents' bedroom—the room that had been hers—a yellow like ripe lemons for the twins.

"Where will I sleep?" she asked.

"You're a big girl now," her mother said. "We're going to put you in Noni's room. You'll like that, won't you? We'll go to the store and you can pick out wallpaper and new curtains and it will be your special space."

Noni's was the tiny room at the end of the hall, as far away from her parents' bedroom as any place in the apartment. Her grandmothers stayed there when they visited, Noni, her mother's mother, and Nana, her father's. "I don't want to be in Noni's room," she complained. "I hate it. It's too far away and it's dark and if I cry you won't hear me. I won't go there." Her mother was sitting back on her heels, looking at Lily as if she were a stranger. She thought of the wicked witches in her father's stories, of her friend Celia's brother who had just told them about Dracula the human bat who drained your blood and left you for dead.

At the end of the hall they could get to her, no one would know. "I'm scared. Please, Mommy, I'm scared."

"Where is all this coming from?" her mother asked. Lily could tell she was annoyed. Her face had lost its early gaiety; her brows were drawn together and the blue in her eyes had turned blue gray; it looked like ice.

"I don't want Noni's room, I want my room!"

"Lily, don't be difficult. I'm hot and I'm tired and I don't have much patience for little girls who are complaining about something they should be grateful to get."

"I don't want it," she persisted. "I won't sleep there. You can't make me."

"All right, be as stubborn as you want to. But you are sleeping in that room, starting tonight." Her mother stabbed her paintbrush into the tray of yellow paint and slapped it onto the wall. Tiny yellow dots flew from the bristles, speckling the old pink paint of what had been Lily's room. She turned and ran from her mother.

That night and the next two, she dragged her blanket and pillow down the hall and slept on her parents' threshold, wrapped so tightly, so completely, inside the blanket that nothing showed—not head, not hands, not feet.

"Lily, how can you breathe like that?" her father worried as he unwrapped her one morning. On the fourth day, he came home with a panda bear nearly as tall as she was, to be her company at night. She called him Penny. "Don't you worry," her father said. "Penny is a special panda. He's here to protect you. If anything happens, he'll tell me and I'll come right away. I promise."

"But how will you know? What if you're asleep?" she cried, thinking of Dracula, blood dripping from his fangs, appearing at her door. She couldn't tell her father, he wouldn't understand, he would call her a baby. But she was haunted by the tale.

"We'll trade thoughts," he said. "Even if I'm asleep, his thoughts will wake me up. I'll know." Reassured, she fell asleep wrapped around the black-and-white bear with black-and-white target circles for eyes.

"Thank God for that damn bear," she heard her mother tell her father while they were putting away dishes in the kitchen while she put together outfits for her dolls in the living room. "It did the trick. I didn't know what we were going to do about her sleeping in the hall every night. But you were right."

"She just needs something of her own to hold onto," her father said. "When I was a kid I was afraid of the dark, too. It's a phase."

"I was never afraid of the dark," her mother said.

"You were a warrior woman, an Amazon," her father said. By the tone of his voice, Lily could tell he was teasing. "You were braver than the braves. Me, I was brave as long as I had my old rabbit Jemima to protect me."

"A rabbit!" her mother exclaimed. They laughed. She heard scuffling sounds and a plate dropped and shattered. "Daniel!" her mother cried out, but she did not sound angry.

The line was drawn. Her parents had the twins; she had Penny.

That fall, she started tap dancing. Beulah came by the school on Tuesdays and Thursdays to take her downtown to the Masonic Temple building where the classes were held. Beulah had told her about the Masons, pointing to the weather-softened insignia nailed over the main door. Lily was confused. Temples were supposed to be big, and beautiful, like the one in the Bible stories Noni read to her. But this was just a big Victorian house a block away from Main Street. Its clapboard had faded to a pinkish brown. The trim, a darker brown, was peeling. "It's just an old house," she told Beulah. "That's what you know," the old woman narrowed her eyes. "There's things happen here at night," she continued, ominously. Lily stopped dead. "What things?" She thought of Dracula, bloody fanged, appearing at the top of the linoleum-clad stairs. "What things?" "Never you mind. Come on now, we'll be late." Beulah jerked on Lily's arm to start her moving up the steps to the second floor studio. After that, Lily kept a watch for Masons, whom she imagined would be wearing capes and accompanied by bats. But no one except tap dance students and their mothers ever appeared in the dusty halls.

"You don't want to go to ballet school?" her mother had asked when she announced she wanted to learn to tap. "Are you sure?" She sounded disappointed. But Lily loved the sound the metal taps made on the staircase to their apartment. She loved the way Shirley Temple broke into song and danced down the stairs in the movies that ran on the afternoon TV. Rat-a-tat-tat! Rat-a-tat-tat! Who wouldn't want to make that joyful noise?

As her mother's belly grew bigger, Lily imagined that the space between her and her mother also was stretching and swelling, and that the air in that space was gray and thick, forming an invisible barrier that she could not step through.

"She doesn't even like me anymore," she told her mother's mother; Noni had stopped by for a short visit on her way to Lily's aunt, who lived in another city to the north.

"Don't be silly," Noni told her. "Your mother loves you. Nothing has changed that. She's just going into herself to get ready, that's all. Every woman does this, Lily. You'll see. When the twins come, everything will be the same as it was. Only better."

So Lily began her own preparations. She made up stories about the adventures they would have—the twins, herself, and Penny. She cradled her dolls and bossed them around and called them not by their given names but by the names she had heard her parents say: Daniel, Louisa, Evelyn, James.

"You're a funny kid," her father said when he heard her doing this.

"I'm practicing," she told him. "I'm going to be a big sister."

"That's a lot of work," he agreed. "It's a good thing you're starting on it now."

She worked on her tap dancing, and she worked on being a good sister, until the day her mother left in a snowstorm for the hospital.

"Don't worry, Lily," her mother said, giving her a hug as Mrs. MacEnroe hovered at the door, waving her car keys in the air. "When I come back, you'll be a big sister for real. Won't that be wonderful?" She kissed her, picked up the small bag that had been standing by the door for weeks now, and stepped out into the hall. Nancy moved forward to shut the door behind her.

"Don't you worry about your mother," she said. "Rita used to be a nurse, so even with the snow, everything will be OK. They'll get to the hospital OK."

So her mother was going to the hospital, the same place where she, Lily, had gone when her appendix burst. "Will I have to visit her?" she asked, suddenly fearful. The hospital had not been a friendly place. She had been scared, during the day when the nurses came and went, washing all the children in the big room, combing their hair back, pulling on it so tightly to catch it all up into rubber bands that she had cried. "Don't be a baby," that nurse had said. "Look at that little girl in the corner. She's got cancer, she might die, and *she* doesn't cry."

After that she had been afraid at night, too, unable to sleep in case the girl in the corner, surrounded by stuffed animals and balloons and cards on ribbons, would climb over the bars of the bed and come across to Lily's bed, to give her whatever it was that might make her die.

"Oh you'll want to see your new brothers or sisters, won't you," Nancy said. But did she? She wanted to dance for them, to dress them up like dolls, to tell them stories using Penny as her hero. But go to the hospital...

Nancy stayed in their apartment that night, and in the morning Mrs. McEnroe appeared. And that was the start of the whispering and all the "poor childs." Now she was here with her father, the one person around whom she had always felt safe. And he was so quiet. So sad.

"When is Mommy coming home?"

"Next week. We think."

"Good." She ducked her head over the new pile of rigatoni, transformed by her spoon into a volcano with a crater at its center, tomato bits picked out and piled around the rim of white macaroni. She wanted to pose the question but again was afraid to say the wrong thing.

"Daddy..."

"What, Lily?"

"I made a dance for Mommy and the twins."

"Yes." His tone was not promising.

"Daddy, would you like to see it?"

"Not now, Lily." His voice was weary, as if each word had to be pushed out of his mouth to fall into the air, into her ear. "Not now."

Her mother did not come home the next day. Not the next week, not even the next month. When she finally appeared one morning while Lily was driving a yellow plastic shovel into the tightly curled design of the gray-green living room rug, nothing about her was right. Lily felt the wrongness, pushing down on the shovel end until it buckled and then cracked. This pale woman in a silvery gray bathrobe edged with turquoise piping that made her skin look silvery gray too was her mother, but not. Her eyes were tired, her mouth drooped at the corner, her wrists were thin—so thin that the gold bangle she always wore, the one with leaves and fruit and flowers worked in tiny lines, like a circular garden, was falling off her hand. She was pushing it back on as she came across the floor to Lily, who did not look up again after the first sighting, but just kept shoveling.

"Oh Lily, aren't you going to give me a kiss?" her mother asked, bending down, but still a yard or two away.

"Lily, get up and kiss your mother," Noni commanded from somewhere behind her. Lily said nothing, tracing circles on the rug with the shattered shovel.

"Lily, what's the matter?" her mother cried in a voice sharpened by distress. "Don't you remember me?"

The child nodded, still intent on the carpet pattern, the little pilings where her shovel had pulled at the rug to separate the texture design from the plain wool backing. "Then why won't you kiss me?"

Instead, Lily turned and crawled to her grandmother's knees, a little way behind her. Burying her head in the hem of the dark blue skirt, she started to wail.

"What's wrong, what has happened," she heard her mother start to cry too.

"Now then, Lily, stop that," Noni was pushing her away to go to her daughter, standing gray and bereft in the home she had not entered in almost a quarter-year. "I need to help your mother. You be a good girl, stay there."

"Mom, she didn't even know me," her mother was crying as Noni led her away, back into the recesses of the apartment where the bedrooms lay.

"There, there, of course she does. She's just shy, you're a little bit of a stranger, that's all..."

Some time passed, and her grandmother was back in the room.

"Lily. Lily, look at me." She looked up, shovel clutched in her hand. "Lily, that was very wrong. Your mother loves you. She was looking forward to seeing you. And you weren't very nice, were you?" The child hung her head. "No, you weren't. But you want to make it up to your mother, don't you?" She nodded. "So go into the bedroom and kiss her now and tell her you missed her."

"I don't want to," Lily mumbled.

"What did you say," her grandmother's tone was sharp.

"Don't..."

"Are you afraid, Lily?" Afraid was so much less than the confusion she was feeling; it seemed simpler to agree.

"Yes."

"There's nothing to be afraid of. Come, give me your hand." She led her back to her parents' room, where the curtains were drawn against the feeble afternoon light of early April. Her mother was propped up by a big green pillow, edged in turquoise that matched the color of her shiny, quilted bed jacket. Turquoise and green, her mother's favorite colors, in this dim light only bleached her skin and dulled her black hair, cropped short like Lily's but once long and lustrous like the tiara-topped locks of Lily's princess doll.

"Amanda, Lily's come to see you. She was just a bit scared, that's all. Here, Lily, let's help you up onto the bed." And with that, her grandmother flew her through the air to land against her mother's side.

"I'm sorry, Mommy," she pressed her face against the bed jacket's ruffled trim. "I'm sorry."

"Oh Lily, Mommy's sorry too," her mother said, as both began to cry.

Noni was staying with them "just until your mother's stronger," she kept saying. Lily noticed that Mrs. Spiegel and Mrs. McEnroe no longer presented themselves at the apartment door with fragrant offerings. Noni's food was very different: thin slices of ham with pineapple and sweet red cherries. Green jello with grapes at the bottom. Chicken, rolled in bread crumbs and beaten egg, then fried. Liver with thin onions and bacon.

"Can we have rig-a-toni?" Lily asked one afternoon as her grandmother began to dredge yet another purplish-brown piece of liver in flour and pepper. The flour mix flew off the plate into her nose, reducing her to tears. "Please, can we have RIG-A-TONI?"

"No," her grandmother said firmly, offering her a tissue to blow into. "It was very nice of your mother's friends to bring you food while she was gone. But that is not what I cook. That is not what we eat."

"Why not?"

"Because," Noni said, and that was the end of it.

Nancy didn't come anymore, either. Noni was there to dress her and walk her to school. She was there to walk her home, too. And Noni shared her secret, the dance she was practicing for her mother, for the school assembly. "That will be a lovely surprise for her," Noni said. "A dance just for her. That will cheer her up, to see you look so pretty and like a princess up there on the stage."

It was Noni, not Beulah, who took Lily to her dance classes now. Mrs. Kendall, the teacher, wore her hair in the same bun style as Noni. They were the same age and after class would talk about events, places, and people that meant nothing to Lily. It was Noni who suggested that Lily set her dance to a song she and Mrs. Kendall had danced to when they were young.

"Alexander's Ragtime Band, it would be perfect," said Noni. The two women suddenly burst into song: "Come on and hear, come on and hear!" they sang together, voices girlish again. "It's the best band in the land!" They grabbed each other by the waist and still singing, skipped and trotted around the room until they'd finished the song. "Oh yes," exclaimed Mrs. Kendall, laughing while trying to catch her breath, "we'll use that. Oh definitely. Won't that be fun, Lily?"

Her mother had promised to come to the school program, her daddy, too. "The child is working so hard," she had overheard Noni saying to her daughter. "You must come. You owe it to her to make an effort. Daniel, too."

Whatever her mother had mumbled back, Lily missed. But Noni had said, "Good," so Lily knew her mother would be there. Noni would make it happen. Like she was making the costume happen.

"Can't we just buy her something?" her father asked one night in the kitchen, where he and Noni were sitting at the table after dinner—Noni with a cup of steaming tea, her father with a glass filled with an amber liquid that made Noni frown whenever she saw it in his hand. Lily was sitting on the floor in the doorway between the kitchen and the living room, walking Penny through a story that was playing out in her head, although unspoken around the grown-ups.

"No, after all this, she needs something special, Daniel. And you must come. You're hardly home before she goes to bed, these days. She needs her father. And her mother."

"So what kind of costume are we talking about?"

"Oh, I think it's best left a surprise. But I do have some ideas. I'll take Lily along to the fabric store on Saturday. We'll make it into a treat. You and Amanda can be together. Do something together..." Her grandmother's voice trailed off. The room was very still, even the refrigerator's grinding had stopped.

Her father drew a deep breath. "Sure," he said, taking a long drink from his glass. "Sure, whatever you say, Mrs. Fox." He turned to Lily. "What are you doing down there, Silly-Milly?"

"I'm not Silly-Milly, I'm Lily," she responded.

"Of course you are. And that's Penny the Brave Crusader," he scooped her and the bear up, carrying them away from Noni into the living room. "Penny the Panda, like Roland at the pass of Roncesvalles..."

"The what?" she giggled, "the pass of rigatoni?"

"Why not?" her father cried, "why not? Penny the Brave at the Pass of Rigatoni." Noni appeared in the doorway.

"It's time for bed, Lily."

"No," she clung to her father. "I want to stay with Daddy."

"You'll see your daddy tomorrow." Noni stepped up and lifted her out from her father's arms. She looked imploringly over her shoulder as Noni pulled her close.

"Your grandmother has spoken. Bedtime." He made a deep bow and handed her the stuffed panda. "Don't forget your champion."

She and Noni had spent the next morning at the fabric store, where her grandmother moved with assurance between the aisles of colored cloth hanging like flags from the top of their bolts. "Not this, not this…" Lily trailed behind her; Noni seemed sure of what she was looking for. Lily felt very small. The search seemed very long.

"Why am I here?" she whined as her grandmother considered then rejected a length of sheer pink fabric that to Lily's eyes was the stuff of princesses and fairies. "You don't care what I want!"

"Of course I do." Noni's voice was calm but her eyes held a warning. "I know you want to look your best and look like a lovely dancer, a big girl, and that's what we're going to find and make for you—a big-girl dancer's dress."

"I want the pink!"

"That pink won't make a good dress," Noni answered, drily, "unless you plan to show the world your underpants, too." Coming out of nowhere, the remark stopped the spiral of frustration and fatigue into which she had begun to sink. *Her underpants.* The ones she wore that day were covered in rabbits and flowers.

"I don't want them to see my underpants," she said.

"I thought not." A few more aisles, and Lily asked, "what *will* I wear under my dress, then?"

"Underpants, of course. Nice ones, with ruffles. So it won't matter if they're seen. But of course, no one will see them unless you pirouette. Unless you twirl."

Lily considered. "I twirl."

"Not a lot, you don't. And if we make the skirt long enough, everything will be fine. You'll look just like Shirley Temple, Lily, when she's got a party dress on."

In the movies Lily had seen, Shirley Temple was always enveloped in crinoline layers that lifted her skirt to waist level. What movie had her grandmother watched, to envision Shirley Temple in such modest dresses? In the end, her grandmother chose a different pink, like satin, crinkly. "It will drape beautifully," she said, holding it against Lily's side to gauge the success of the color. "Yes, I think this is the one."

At the apartment door, Lily hugged the brown paper parcel tied with string hiding the glories of her costume-to-be as Noni fumbled for her key. The door suddenly swung back.

"Oh, it's you," her mother said, stepping back, frowning a little. "I thought it might be Dan."

"Isn't he here, then?"

"No, he went out about two hours ago, something about work..." Her mother paused, dropping her head. "I thought he'd be home before you two made it back."

"Look, Mommy, look," Lily pulled at the string, trying to distract her mother and grandmother from a tension that made the air seem gray and cold. "Look what Noni got me!"

"Lily, why don't you take that back into Noni's room and unwrap it very carefully for me," her grandmother said. "Don't drop anything—no zipper, no thread on the floor, now."

"But I want..."

"Lily!" Both women spoke her name at once, a command in chorus that could not be ignored. Depressed, she trailed off, dragging the package along behind her by a lose length of string. No one noticed.

"I am going to dance a great dance," she confided to Penny, beneath whose watchful eye she unwrapped the parcel on the cot that was her bed while Noni stayed. 'You wait and see. I am going to dance the most beautiful, the most wonderful dance, that will make everyone happy." She pulled the bear toward her, across the pile of cloth and notions. "You can't be in it, Penny." She wrapped the panda in her arms, swaying in place with her silent partner. "But you'll know, because everyone will talk about it and they'll all be so happy. So happy..." She leaned back into the limp pillow across whose case Wendy and Tinker Bell and Peter Pan flew, and pulled Penny across her face, his fur-roughened tummy drying the tears that burned her eyes and refused to stop.

"Are you all ready, now—are you, are you—Listen to me!" Miss Davis commanded the uneven line of first-graders caught between the folds of the heavy curtain, where it ran into the darkened wings of the stage. They came to attention. "Now you know what to do. Wait for the music, remember to count...and SMILE!"

The curtain swept back toward them with a solemn soughing noise, letting pools of colored light spill onto the bare wood stage. The first strains of "Toyland" were heard from the auditorium's speakers. "Go, go now!" Miss Davis whispered, pushing each hand-in-hand couple out into the light, to space themselves uncertainly across the stage. Lily's partner squeezed her fingers so tightly it hurt; she shook the palm clenched around hers, trying to break his grip. "Stop it, Liam!" she hissed under her breath; like a startled rabbit, he stopped dead, staring at her. She tried to push him, pull him forward with her. "I can't," he breathed. "You have to," she demanded, digging a fingernail into his soft palm. In a flash he came alive again, his feet moved with hers toward their place, in time to open their mouths and start swaying with the rest of the chorus: "*Toyland, Toyland, dear little girl and boy land...*"

The auditorium was a great black cave that as she stared into its depths began to sort itself into recognizable shapes—rectangular doors edged with faint light at the very back of the hall. Rows of bell-like shapes that resolved into heads of hair and hats, their crowns faintly reflecting the gold-pink lights. Somewhere in the rows were her father, her grandmother, her mother. Her stomach twisted, anticipating the moment when the music would stop, the other children shuffle off, and she, Lily, would stand alone before this crowd. And she would triumph.

Now. Liam dropped her hand, they were flowing past her to the wings, the lights fell to nothing. Miss Davis came out from the wing, bearing a microphone on a stand, which she positioned downstage as a spotlight picked her out in the darkness. "Now we will have a tap dance from

Lily…" she heard the teacher begin; the rest was lost in the upswelling of energy that made every limb tingle. She could feel her blood gathering, ready to carry her away when her music started. But first…

"Lily, will you please tell us the name of your dance," Miss Davis was saying. Beckoning her closer to the microphone.

She moved carefully, taps muted, to where Miss Davis stood, lowering the mike so Lily could be heard. "Thank you." Her breath suddenly caught in her throat as faces in the front rows revealed mouths, noses, eyes. No words came.

"Yes, dear," Miss Davis was smiling, but the hand on Lily's shoulder was digging into it like a talon, urging her on.

"My dance is called…'The Angel Dance,'" her voice, released, boomed through the microphone.

"No, Lily, no," Miss Davis was hiss-whispering above her. "It's 'Alexander's Ragtime Band.' *Tell* them."

"It's called 'The Angel Dance,'" she said more confidently, twisting her shoulder from under the teacher's hand. "I made it specially for my brothers. They were twins but they died. So they're angels now."

She looked up at the shadowed rafters, willing the twins to appear, to see their big sister celebrate them. For an instant she thought she saw a gleam of gold—a harp? A wing? "I'm dancing for angels," she finished and stepped back.

Miss Davis, sighing heavily, whisked the microphone off into the shadows. A murmur ran through the hall as Lily retook her place at center stage, poised to start. For what seemed like forever the air was filled with the rough scraping sound of a needle seeking the music in the groove. *Scratch, scratch, scratch,* it went, *scratch scratch.*

She waited, eyes shut, blood already pulsing to the beat that was to come. The bright refrain started: "*Come on and hear! Come on and hear! Alexander's Ragtime Band.*" She thought of the twins, her brothers, far up in heaven among great white fluffy clouds; they would be wearing wings. The record rolled on: *"Come on and hear! Come on and hear! It's the best band in the land*!" In the audience a woman's thin wail gave way to ragged sobbing. Lily began.

Colleen Franklin

Piece of Cake

COLLEEN FRANKLIN recently received her MA from the Johns Hopkins University Writing Program. She lives in Urbana, Maryland, with her husband and their parrot, Oscar.

Cake. Chocolate cake. That's all I can think about. These stupid pantyhose are strangling my ass, and I know Kevin's waiting downstairs and I should hurry-the-fuck-up as he says, but while I check my seventy-five-dollar up-do hairstyle and smooth down this ugly lavender bridesmaid dress for the hundredth time, I know that I'm going to be in the same room as that chocolate wedding cake in just two hours.

"Julie," Kevin says, "Hurry the fuck up." I can tell he's standing at the bottom of the steps and his mouth is full—stuffed I'm sure, with the last piece of chicken from lunch. He has no idea how hard it's been for me. I've lost twenty-five pounds but it's taken three years. Dad keeps reminding me about his diabetes, how I can't—I just can't—end up like him taking insulin shots on schedule, the regimen of a new, forced lifestyle. He'll squeeze a little bulge of pale skin, glance up at me to make sure I'm watching, and inject slowly. It annoys the hell out of me, but I think he gets more and more pleasure at my discomfort each time.

Kevin pounds the bedroom door and my glass Siamese cat drops to the floor, breaking in two.

"What the hell are you doing in there? We're gonna be late," he says.

I tell him to hold on, that I'm almost ready, though I've been ready for twenty-five minutes now. In the mirror I watch myself, trying to get lost in my own eyes while I take another deep breath. Calm down, you can do this. It's easy, piece of cake.

How am I going to resist that cake? I can see sweet swirls of frosting, layers of dark spongy cake, chocolate shavings lightly sprinkled on top of the three-tiered monument of pure dessert heaven. Why can't people serve wedding fruit for dessert? Maybe it will have raspberry filling—that's fruit.

I bend to pick up the cat's bottom half by the brown tail. I open the door, thrusting my headless cat in his face.

"You broke my cat."

His head shakes, his eyes pinch up, and he plucks the cat from my hands. "I'll get you another one. Let's go."

⁓

I've known Kevin for almost a year now, three months longer than my cousin Virginia has known Mike, her fiancé. My relatives think it's bizarre that I'm not engaged yet, being two years older than Skinny Ginny (my pet name for Ginny, who now insists that because she's a mature twenty-three-year-old and about to become Mrs. Cauley, I call her Virginia). My mother asks often, "Any marriage talk lately, any hint of a ring?" Even Virginia prods, "So when are we going to see a diamond on *your* finger?" The funny thing is Kevin and I aren't serious about being too romantically involved. Right now, it's a major achievement that we've been friends this long without killing each other. Though I have fun with Kevin, our on-again, off-again dating works best for me at this point in my life. While my friends are all married or engaged, I'm still wandering around in Dateland. It's fine by me since our arguments about everything from politics to the color of a shirt make me a little hesitant to want to be messily involved. And besides, I refuse to walk down that aisle as a size ten.

Today though, I have no choice but to walk down the aisle in this unflattering, too-tight taffeta dress. Thankfully we don't have to wear those long gloves or else I'd be Miss Piggy's twin. We line up for the procession, Ginny—I mean Virginia—and Uncle Steve last in line and almost giddy, giving each other tearful winks. I glance behind me. In her sleeveless silk gown, she stands confident, ready, and radiant with a warm, pink blaze settling in her cheeks. I don't see her thin arms or bony legs but rather a graceful woman. My cousin, beautiful and thin, has always been my opposite.

⁓

I was never so painfully aware of our differences in appearance until our vacation to Wildwood, New Jersey, in the summer of 1993. I was excited to get away to the beach front motel and generally liked hanging with my twelve-year-old cousin. At fourteen, I was already too heavy and looked much bigger next to petite Skinny Ginny. She had a similarly light complexion as me, but her skin was clear while mine popped out zits on a regular basis. My hair almost always snarled, especially around the beach. I'd use lemon juice to lighten my sandy hair as Ginny had suggested (she knew a lot more about fashion and beauty). Ginny's hair, a deep chocolate brown, shone and easily fixed into a ponytail while mine just frizzed.

For the first time, Ginny and I were allowed to walk the boardwalk alone that summer. We met Matt, a tall, dark cutie who'd just finished his freshman year in high school and lived only a few blocks from the beach. He came up to us while we were at the foosball table and just started gabbing like it was the easiest thing in the world. I liked him almost immediately because he had no fear; he was shameless in making jokes, and unlike me, he was so comfortable in his skin. I could tell right away he was interested in my cousin by the way he kept watching her, hardly noticing me.

"You guys don't look like cousins," he said after Ginny explained how she and I knew each other. With every word, I felt myself shrinking into the noise of the games. Ginny talked easily to him, flirting with big smiles and little knowing glances.

I couldn't take it. After a while, I told her I was going back to the motel, knowing she'd have to come because we weren't allowed to split up. Before we left, Matt took Ginny's number and the two of them ended up kissing on the beach later that week while I sat on the steps behind them watching, eating chocolate bar after chocolate bar. My mother would have been appalled, not at the fact that my twelve-year-old cousin was making out in public with a strange guy, but that I was stuffing my face with the very thing she had admonished me to stay away from lest I get diabetes like my father, or worse, ruin my chances of getting married.

The wedding music grew louder, a signal to start forward in our individual, spaced-out paces. My legs feel weak and sluggish suddenly. It occurs to me that I may never be the one in white to walk down an aisle to a hunky fiancé. Mike, poised before the altar in his black tux, looks like a model; masculine and stylish and all the right proportions. I glance around for Kevin, hoping that if I see him maybe I can get down the aisle a bit easier. Even before I get more than a few steps into the church, my hands get sticky around the white and purple lilac bouquet. All eyes are on me, but I don't recognize anyone. People turn to each other and whisper softly, making a low hum throughout the church. I work to keep my ass, cupped snuggly against the dress, from swinging too far in either direction. It's about five hundred degrees in this church.

I can't get to the front of the church fast enough. I feel like I'm going to fall flat on my face. Moisture between my legs from the friction of walking builds up in the netting of the pantyhose. My armpits burn with a dampness that I know will spot this fabric quickly. I try to focus on making my way to the front, closer to the moment we get out of here to start the reception, closer to that chocolate cake. I see my parents towards the front along the left side pews. My father, chin down, eyes up, smiles at me while my mother gives me a fast, energetic little buzz of a wave. They look polished and sharp and I'm not sure I came from their genes.

Finally we're all lined up, and Virginia and Uncle Steve make their way through the standing observers. Now that all eyes are taken off me and are on her, I'm free to relax and my body temperature goes down a notch. I look attentive with the obligatory smile stretched across my face, but I can only think about the moment I put my mouth on that moist, chocolate cake.

I started hiding my chocolate after overhearing my mother give my father a loud, long lecture on how he should know better than to eat and give me sweets. She'd already begun to get on my case about watching my weight and exercising more and standing up straight and taking better care of my skin. But I couldn't help that I loved chocolate. I'd become absolutely addicted. I'd sneak Hershey and Nestlé bars into my room and then, in the middle of the night, softly peel open their wrappings and indulge. After a crappy day at school, heaven awaited at night in the darkness of my room.

These days, I still look forward to binging out on chocolate shakes, ice cream, cake, fudge, cookies (praise those semi-sweet chip chunks), hot chocolate, and candy. It doesn't matter where I am or what I should be focusing on, for instance, an important meeting at work; I still fantasize about sitting down and unraveling with my chocolate. My coffee is always filled with mocha. My candles in my townhouse are fudge flavored to give just the right aroma to my living room. I ponder which treat I will pop in my mouth—white, dark, semi-sweet, bittersweet—and which brand: Godiva, Lindt, Hershey, Nestlé. Some people relax by doing yoga or getting a massage or reading a good book, but for me it's tasting the luxurious smoothness and richness that only chocolate provides. No one knows about my little habit, but I'm sure I'd be close to excommunicated from my family if they knew.

⁂

The reception hall is dark except for the glow from the hurricane lamp centerpieces. I'm thankful for the dim lighting. The shadows may work to reduce my size. I spot it right away. It's gorgeous; separated on a white linen-covered table, set apart like royalty. It's three-tiered just like Virginia had said, with white-chocolate-covered strawberries circled around the bottom of each tier.

"Are you OK?" Kevin says, placing a warm hand on my shoulder. I jump in my seat, not having seen him approach from behind. His breath smells heavily of alcohol. He must have been drinking himself into comfort, as he's a bit shy around strangers. I feel guilty that I've dragged him here as my date while we've had to sit apart.

I stumble for words. It occurs to me that I have just eaten the salad and main dish without really knowing (I think it was some sort of chicken dish because of the aftertaste in my mouth). In my chocolate fantasy daze, I've complied with small talk to the two girls on either side of me without really knowing what the hell I was saying.

"What are you doing, Julie?"

I realize that the entire head table is out on the dance floor. Who knows how long I've been sitting here alone. What can I do? I give him a stupid smile and try to clear my head. He stands and leads me by the hand out to the dance floor, closer to the cake. I feel my heart rate speed up knowing my parents are in the crowd somewhere, that my mother could be watching me and swoop down to call me out in a split second if I were to try and eat a slice. I don't know if I can resist but I'm terrified of her making a scene.

We're shaking down to Bob Seger's "Old Time Rock and Roll," and my Aunt Karen bumps me on the dance floor.

"Have you lost weight, Julie?" She eyes me up and down, leans closer, and says again, louder, "Looks like you lost some weight."

Of course my mother's sister points this out. I have overheard them multiple times talking on the phone about my fluctuating weight. My increasing and decreasing blub has always been a favorite topic between them. What could my mother ever say about Skinny Ginny? It would have been nice if just once she could have stood up for me and said, "Well at least my daughter's bones aren't sticking out."

I glance at Kevin. Of course he's heard; his eyebrows are raised and he looks as though he's holding back a smile. He's known about my struggle to lose weight but has no clue how infatuated with chocolate I am. I'm sure he's proud of me or something stupid like that but I want that damn chocolate more than ever now. I manage a thanks to my aunt and casually work my way towards the wedding cake, Kevin dancing drunkenly around me.

"That must make you feel pretty good, huh?" he says.

"I guess." He has no clue how embarrassing it is to always have your body discussed by your family. How they make it their business to discuss ways to get you a boyfriend so that you can one day have a beautiful wedding like this.

"You look good, Julie, you know? If I haven't told you before."

He must want to start dating again. Before I can say anything, he turns abruptly, nearly knocking a guy down.

"I gotta take a piss," he says over his shoulder. The music changes and some Celine Dion song starts. Couples pack the dance floor and my cousin wraps her arms around her new husband. My parents make their way out there too, engrossed in each other as if they were alone.

And before I know it, I'm standing so close to it that the edge of my butt is up on the lip of the table. I can feel its presence behind me, tempting me, calling my name. God, help me. I lean back slightly, slipping my hand on the table as if for support. Just an innocent girl taking a dancing break near the wedding cake. My finger slides, bumps a strawberry and I roll it carefully aside. And then into the icing. Innocent, all innocence. I plunge deeper and feel the coolness of the cake.

I spot Kevin coming out of the men's room across the dance floor. He stumbles a bit, scanning the room for me. I don't have much time.

I pull my hand from the cake slowly, ever so slowly. My mother's still occupied with my father on the dance floor. Kevin's approaching fast now, having located my position. He's walking, not so straight, straight through the dance floor. I bring my finger up and clamp down quickly on my chocolate-coated finger with my mouth. I close my eyes. Possibly this is the best chocolate cake I've ever tasted.

I hear a shout, flick open my eyes to the noise to see Kevin make a classic drunken trip over my mother's silver-sandaled foot. The commotion of missteps, arms flailing wildly, and he's stumbling forward towards me, towards the cake. Wide eyes, turned heads. The force of his weight plowing into me. My balance thrown and we both go down, bits of chocolate flying, dotting the air, coated strawberries rolling down my dress onto the dance floor. The cake crashing to soften the fall, my body smushing into the cool frosting and spongy cake, chocolate in my hair and on my skin. Kevin on top of me wiggling, coating me more with the chocolate. Screams then from my cousin, arms and hands shoved down to help us up.

I'm in pure bliss.

Amy Fries

Eating My Heart

AMY FRIES is an editor at the Virginia-based publishing house Capital Books and a freelance writer whose articles have been published in many consumer, literary, and trade publications. In addition, she has taught composition and literature at George Mason University. She received an MA in writing from Johns Hopkins University. Her novel, "Harmony Beach," is currently being represented by the Elaine Markson Literary Agency.

MORNING

"Howdy partner. Howdy co-parent," I say to my ex-husband as he arrives at our house to pick up the kids—four-year-old Jason and two-year-old Abigail. Can you believe he left me when the kids were that little? When Abigail was just fifteen months old? I had just finished weaning her off her bedtime breastfeeding the month before. He waited until after Christmas to tell me he was having an affair. He said he wasn't in love with this woman; he just wanted to see other people.

"See other people?" Couldn't he have told me that before two kids? He tells me he needs the intensity. Says he still loves me—but in a plain love kind of way—and of course he loves the kids, especially the kids. He keeps saying that. "I'm still my children's father. The divorce doesn't mean I don't love them, that I don't want them."

The obvious implication is that he doesn't want me.

"Our love just isn't intense enough," he says. "I need that intensity. I crave that intensity."

I try to tell him about honeymoon love and how that doesn't last forever. That if he hangs in there our love will mature, bring its own rewards. But he wants intensity. I translate that inwardly to mean he needs intense orgasms. The kind that only new, bright, hot love can bring.

So here we are. He glares at me when I say facetiously, "Howdy co-parent." That's what we're supposed to be now. That's what the therapist said, and the divorce lawyer, and the mediator, and the judge.

"I'm committed to a relationship with you, just not a marriage," Ristan keeps saying to me.

That's his name, Ristan, and he likes intensity. I knew that when I married him. That's probably why I fell in love with him. Love him still. Intense energy is an attraction in itself. And yet I dream about killing him, annihilating him. The way he's annihilated me. Poison would be good. Oh no, the bitter ex-wife, you say. But I'm digressing. I'm telling you, not showing you. You want to see what I'm doing now. Or maybe you don't. I don't know. I don't know anything anymore.

OK, so I'm at the kitchen sink washing the syrup off dishes when he walks through the front door. I make pancakes for the kids each morning from scratch. They love them, and I have to pretend to be happy. I don't want to damage their delicate psyches with my own damaged one. "How 'bout some pancakes this morning!" I say when they crawl out of bed, sleepy eyed in their oversized T-shirts. They're so beautiful, it's heartbreaking. I have to part with them now every Thursday and every other weekend. Not much you say, but would you want to hand over your babies to someone else? Someone and his new girlfriend?

Don't think, I tell myself. Thought is death.

"Where you been?" Jason asked when he climbed out of bed this morning. He's worried. Four years old and he knows. Kids always know. Even Abigail at her itty-bitty age looks at me and knows.

"Running," I said. I've been running on the treadmill for two solid hours—at six miles per hour. Up since four. Up most of the night to tell the truth. I run until I leave salt marks on the heart monitor bar, until a salt ring forms around my lips.

Now Ristan is walking them out the door. He's smiling and happy. Why not? He's got the life he wants. I can see his mother in the car. Can you believe it? His mother. Ristan has never taken care of the kids on his own, not for more than an hour or two. So his mother is with him when his girlfriend isn't. Thirty-three years old and hanging out with Mom.

But Ristan really isn't pathetic in any traditional sense. He's a professional athlete. He runs in triathlons all over the world, most notably the Iron Man. You may have heard of him. He's semi-famous, if you follow those kinds of things.

Abigail is stumbling along behind him in these little white huarache sandals I bought her, looking all curly-headed and Bambi-eyed. She glances back at me. Something about the way she holds the ratty stuffed gray poodle to her chest makes me swoon with adrenalin. Jason is already running for the car because Grandma is waving with one hand and holding up a present with the other. Bribing already. And he falls for it. So young. So easily deceived, influenced, taken away from me.

Ristan stops, turns, looks at me. It's hot already, a record-hot summer all around. The bright Colorado sun melting us all away. "When are you going to quit being mad?" he says.

"When you fucking die," I say with great pleasure, eyes sparkling, treasuring each word, loving the way the F spits off my lips. Empowering me in ways too pathetic to even contemplate. At least the kids are out of earshot. I'm not that bad. Not that far gone. Ever since the split, I've taken to swearing like the love-sick, hopelessly immature teenager I've become. It's such a stress reliever. You might want to try it some time. I hope I don't get addicted to it. I'm afraid some day I'll slip when I drop off Jason at preschool and say, "Have a nice fucking day, honey."

Ristan smiles. Sad and weary. The one who leaves always gets to be generous and superior. "You look beautiful," he says. That's all he cares about really. All he notices. The only reason he ever really loved me. I *am* beautiful, but don't think I'm conceited, because it's the last thing I care about now. OK, I do have strawberry-blonde hair à la Nicole Kidman, slate-blue eyes, and flawlessly creamy skin. I only tell you this because I want you to know that I don't care about that. A lot of good it did me. He still left. Though I must say I'm way better looking than his new girlfriend with her dyed hair and wafer-thin lips. But that didn't matter. I wasn't fresh. Ristan needs fresh. Now I'm thin, too thin, and getting thinner. My friends think I'm anorexic. I look like a piece of beef jerky, when before my cup runneth over. I was lush, luscious, milk and honey, baby.

I guess I'm just staring at him, speechless. Because he says again, "You're beautiful, you know that, don't you?"

"You're ugly," I say. And I realize at that moment that he is. He's got about zero percent body fat and his face is skeletal. A death mask. All teeth and jutting jawbone.

His face falls. I've hurt him. He is so weak and vain at heart. There will never be enough people in the world to love and worship him. His daddy left him when he was little. Signed the adoption papers that gave him away to a stepdad who beat him and preached to him at the same time. His born-again mother's been married four times. Her latest divorced husband was a pedophile—not convicted, just busted by her when she found his stash of *Barely Legal* porn. She used to talk to me about "graciously submitting to my husband." Last week, I said to her, "You submitted to a pedophile, you idiot." Then I whispered that I'd murder her in her sleep if she ever spewed that sexist trash to my children. Or did I just fantasize that? I don't know what I say out loud anymore. My tongue hurts from talking to myself. Either way she looked scared.

In a way, she is the one thing Ristan and I agree on. He's never liked her procession of bad husbands, and when he found out about Jerry the pervert, he banned her from ever bringing one of those losers near our children again. He has a fierce temper. Cross him and you are on his shit list for life. We're a bit alike that way. Once we were watching some show about parents who forgave their child's killer. We looked at each other astonished. We would never forgive anyone who hurt our children. We're on the same page with that. We'd be looking for some serious revenge.

So when Ristan put Momma and her born-again bullshit in her place, I almost forgave him at that moment. For a split second, the seething anger and hatred were gone. "Submit to your son," I almost said to her out of spite. But I didn't. I don't believe in submitting to anything anymore. Except my own bottomless anger.

He walks away from me after the "ugly" remark. At some point soon his patience is going to run out. He is not a patient man. He is a badger in the face of insults. He only puts up with me because he has to—to get his "quality" time with the kids. He only puts up with me because he feels guilty for dumping me. He thinks I'm pathetic. He pities me.

The kids glance at me once from the car. I see their faces all wavy like a mirage through the window. Then they look away. Then they're gone. I'm alone.

Afternoon

I'm working in my study. No, I'm sitting in front of the computer Googling my ex-husband and his new girlfriend. A bunch of watercolors are sprawled on the floor. Old ones. I have them there just for effect, in case someone walks in on me. I'm an artist. Or I pretend to be one. I'm supposed to be painting right now. Creating. But I'm staring instead, staring at a picture of Cheyenne Wilson, Ristan's new girlfriend, holding Abigail at the finish of a triathlon.

I've been Googling them for hours. I do it every day when Jason is at school and Abigail is napping. I do it all night, which is why I'm so sleep-deprived. You'd be surprised at the amount of information there is on them online. I told you he's semi-famous, and there's a whole weird triathlon subculture out there that follows his every move. Fans even comment on our divorce. "At least she got his money" is the general consensus.

There's a lot of info on Cheyenne too. She's ten years older than him but blonde and beautiful and buff. You may have heard of her; she's co-founder of a multimillion-dollar adventure travel and clothing company, and co-founder of a women's art co-op with chapters in nine countries, including Tanzania. The latter she just does as a hobby. Her way "to give back." I once had a showing of my work at a delicatessen in Durango. Someone bought a painting for a hundred and fifty dollars. Ristan sent me two hundred dollars' worth of roses to celebrate.

I am rocking back and forth now in front of the computer screen, fearing my head will explode. I've done it. Googled until I've found what can hurt me the most—the picture of Cheyenne with Abigail.

Abigail is not smiling in the picture, I note with a tangled mixture of satisfaction and fear. She looks unsure. Nervous. Yet there's Ristan and Cheyenne looking so, so happy.

The other night I had a dream I was sitting in front of a dinner plate, a knife and fork in my hand, staring down at my heart. I am literally eating my heart out.

Someone must pay for all this pain.

Evening

Ristan brings the kids back after dinner. He gets up very early to work out, so they don't sleep over. A small blessing, which I take like water in the desert every time.

He lingers. And I—having already consumed two glasses of wine—let him. Though I hate myself for this. Hate that I still want him around, need his attention, desire him in some way. I let him help me put the kids to bed. Abigail is a limp noodle as we wipe her face and hands, swish a toothbrush in her mouth under the guise of brushing. She's asleep by the time I lift her into her crib.

Jason is jumping up and down on his bed. He's caught a devious second wind, which I pray will not last. We are in his room. Ristan in jeans, a white shirt, and flip-flops; me in an ice-blue, plunging-neckline, spaghetti-strap top, white pants, and bare feet. And then Jason starts with the questions we always dread. "Are you going to move back into Mommy's house?" he asks Ristan.

"We've talked about that, sport," Ristan says. "We're living separately now. But we're still your mother and father. We still love you and your sister exactly like we did before, forever and ever. That will never change no matter where Mommy and Daddy live, OK?"

Jason doesn't like that answer. He only understands NOW. He understands too much. He turns his head and bites his bottom lip, and in that moment he looks just like his dad. But he has my personality. He can't let go.

"Do you love Mommy?" he asks as Ristan pulls the covers up to his chin.

Now I'm the one who turns away. He doesn't ask if I still love Daddy. Even a child can see that. There's a sharp intake of air as Ristan steels himself for the lie.

"Of course I love Mommy. Like you love Abigail."

"I don't like her," Jason replies.

"Yes, you do," Ristan insists, and Jason laughs to show it's all a joke, to make us banter with him a second longer, to make us stick around. But we don't. Because no matter how much we love Jason, there comes a time to call it a night. Comes a time when we must walk out the door, turn off the light, and take care of ourselves, leaving Jason alone with his nightlight and questions. An early life lesson. One we're apparently never done learning.

When we get downstairs, Ristan says, "Can I have a glass of that wine you've been drinking?" Then he adds as if to soften the accusation, "Your lips are really red."

I get out the cheap wineglasses because that's all I use now—they fit in the dishwasher. The ones he likes, the ones that go "bing" when you tap on the crystal, are just too difficult. Difficult to hold with their thin, thin stems and top-heavy weight. Difficult to lose—all that money when they break. I'm getting more practical, I note with a small sigh of satisfaction.

He glances into the family room, which is littered with toys. He turns away with a grimace as if he's just smelled something bad. Ristan has always been neat. Now that he's gone, I don't have to be. We—the kids and I—don't have to be.

I follow him into the living room. He carries the bottle of Merlot by the neck and holds it down low by his knees, as if he's dragging something along. The glasses he carries carelessly yet expertly by the stems. He kicks off his flip-flops when he reaches the Oriental rug. The couches in this room are white silk and deep. They're a dangerous companion for wine. This room, I do not let the kids into. I don't even sit in here. It's like a portal to another place. Ristan's favorite room. He used to play his guitar in here. I laugh to myself at the image. Ristan is so corny really. It's as if he's absorbed every image of cool. Sometimes I wonder if he's even real.

Yet when he pours the wine and offers me a glass, I take it. Damn, if I'm not still falling for all this. My heart racing like some stupid little girl's. This guy has screwed me over, dumped me and the kids, despite his self-promoting, public proclamations of devoted daddyhood and his every-other-weekend visitations. He is no longer a day-in-day-out dad because he never wanted to be one. We cramped his style. He couldn't hack it. Ristan, the endurance champ, couldn't endure.

We drink the wine and make small talk. Both of us have one elbow on the back of the couch. We face each other in a parody of casual, intimate conversation, pretending to be oh, so civilized. Two co-parents sharing a drink after putting the kids to bed. Our sides pressing into the soft pillows. Our legs slightly parted. My right knee angled toward his left knee, a mere inch apart.

I take another sip. "I miss you," he says out of the blue. "I miss your hair. I miss your smell. I miss your body."

I know why he's doing this. It's because I said he was ugly and now he wants validation that he's not. He wants to bring me down again so he can be back on top. He wants to prove that he is the one who is loved more. That he is the one in control.

He puts down his wineglass on the coffee table. Then takes mine and puts it down as well. He puts his hand on my inner thigh and begins slowly moving it up and down, watching his fingers as if mesmerized, as if this will lead to the palace of wisdom. And those are the words that I have longed to hear for so long. *I miss you.* Because, God help me, I've missed him.

I was twenty-two when I met him, twenty-four when I married him. He swept me up in his hurricane of energy. Took me around the world for races. There I was—cheering at the finish line, photos in *Triathlete World.* It wasn't the residual fame that hooked me. OK, maybe that was part of it. Ristan is the type of person who when he shines his light on you, you glow; and when he takes it away, you're alone in the dark again. For whatever reasons—bad, shallow, and otherwise—I loved him. He has the guts to live a life of his own creation, the same guts that enabled him to cut me out of his life so completely. Now I don't know who I am without him. I must re-create myself.

"You're getting awfully thin," he says. "It's the running. It doesn't suit you. I liked you better with your soft layer of subcutaneous fat and your luscious breasts." He caresses my right breast, now wilted from breastfeeding, and laughs. I understand the joke. I'm in on it. You had to be there. You see, it took us a while to conceive, but the doctor told me not to worry. Said a woman built like me with a nice "soft layer of subcutaneous fat" shouldn't have too much trouble. "It's the skinny ones you have to worry about," he said. We joked about it ever since—this soft layer of subcutaneous fat—which no longer exists. I ran it all away.

I'm so sick of all this. Sick of thinking. I just want to stop feeling bad. "I miss you," he is saying again. He leans in and kisses me, all soft tongue and wet lips, and I kiss him back. We are so good at this. Back on familiar terrain. We've gone from zero to fifty in a minute. And I've been alone for so long. I am drunk, and these are the lips I've wanted. I put my hand on his face and run my hand through his hair. He is a womanizer, world-class. I looked the other way, and still, it wasn't enough. He needed free rein. Now he wants me again now that I'm no longer the "wife," but someone else, a new challenge to conquer.

I lean back, away from him. "Thank you," I say.

"For what?"

"The opportunity to reject you."

He gives a little smirky laugh. His lips still wet from our kiss. His face flushed, as I'm sure mine is. I can feel it burning. I am burning.

Maybe it was the photo of Cheyenne holding Abigail. Seeing your husband in another woman's arms is hurt; seeing your child in another woman's arms is war.

"What did you think?" I say. "That we'd go from husband and wife, to co-parents, to fuck buddies? That's one too many demotions for me."

Then I pick up my wineglass and spill what's left all over the beautiful white couch. The couch Ristan picked out. It doesn't fit anymore. Tomorrow I will take the kids and buy new furniture. Let them pick it out. Maybe I'll put in padding and a jungle gym.

He looks at me sadly and shakes his head. "You need help, you know that? I hope you're not acting like this in front of the kids. You're drinking. God knows what you do with yourself all day long."

"Shut the fuck up," I say, still hopelessly inarticulate. Though the words don't have the edge anymore, as if I don't need their fiery reassurance.

He shakes his head again. "You know the judge said we're not supposed to dis one another in front of the kids, but I know you say bad things about me because they act weird sometimes. Maybe I'll tell the judge about all this bullshit you're pulling, about your nightly wine binges."

"Go ahead. You get the kids, then what? You can't even have them overnight because they interfere with your run."

He stands up, all righteous. "I left you because I don't love you. But for the millionth time that doesn't mean I don't love the kids. You just have to get over it, face the fact that I don't love you anymore. I'm sorry, but I don't."

"Who was just trying to fuck who?" I say and stand up with him. "And what would your precious Cheyenne have to say about that?" I follow him to make sure he gets out the door, for the satisfaction of turning the lock behind him. Then I lean against it for a long, long time, way too distressed, heart pounding, aroused, with nothing to look forward to except myself and my hand under the covers. Yet, I think, I hope, that maybe I did right. Summoned a sliver of self-respect.

Finally, I turn around and at the end of the tunneled light flowing up the stairs is Jason, sitting at the top, half-obscured in the dark. I look up at him, and he looks down toward me. I don't know what to say, how much he's seen. I wait for his pronouncement, his judgment. But all he says is, "Will you come read me a story?"

And I say, "Yes, I will." Because I am the one who's here, who chooses to be here. The one with the strength to endure the intensity of love.

Dorothy Hickson

Cashing In

Dorothy Hickson's short stories and poems have appeared in *Word-Wrights!* and other magazines, several anthologies including *Alice Redux*, and her own erstwhile zine *dodo*. She is currently seeking an agent for a lighthearted noir feminist SF novel, has started writing something completely different, and would be hiking the Appalachian Trail right now if she hadn't broken her ankle.

> "Your intention was to become superhuman, skin thick as steel, unflinching in the face of adversity, out of the grasping reach of others… And no, it doesn't work. But it seemed like a good idea at the time."
>
> —*Marya Hornbacher*

AnaBeth copied quotes and song lyrics into her notebook, and practically the whole text of Marya's *Wasted*, like she was making a secret copy. In case she was caught with the first one. A journal of recovery, it was mostly about the descent before the healing, and she pored over it the way amateur mountaineers read and reread the accounts by men whose lines broke, whose partners froze to death, who had to crawl for miles in the snow on frostbitten stumps. The hiker nods, says *I* would have taken a cell phone, *I* wouldn't have ended up having to cut off my own limbs. You study the disaster tales so you can climb that summit yourself without falling into that crevasse.

Just that morning some evangelicals had come to Daniel's house to talk about his immortal soul. He said, "Take it and get out." When they wavered, he slammed the door. And he'd been late for school—he'd shown up with a fleck of shaving cream on his obviously unshaven face, like he'd started and then stopped.

Now she wanted to ask the store clerk if there was any kind of energy finder, some way to tell whether Daniel and his soul were still together in the same place. Because if he did all that cutting and the car thing while he had his soul, maybe he was right and the Jehovahs should just take it.

Her head hurt, and she had an acidy pain near her heart. She leaned against the brick wall and looked in her purse for a Tums. AnaCrys said a Tums was six calories. Beth held the chalky circle in her mouth without chewing. Then she chewed, counting to twenty. Her acid heart retreated.

Between the sidewalk and the street, the township had planted pansies. They huddled in pot-shaped clumps, but they were beautiful: purple and yellow rimmed in mascara black.

The magic shop had the same kind of sign as the others—even the McMurder on the corner was trying to blend into the planned décor. The signs were all cocoa-brown Arial on beige. On the left was Nicole's Sweet Shoppe; on the right was the fat women's store. Nicole's had a counter in the window so ice-cream-eaters could look out. Beth did not look in. The dress shop had a window full of business-ugly dresses with big lace collars.

She hadn't eaten since dinner last night, except for two Tums and a cup of unsweetened tea. She had to eat dinner because they were watching. Two bites of macaroni and cheese, seven bites of salad, and while they weren't looking she put the bread in her pocket to throw away later in her room. She tried to purge but it was hours later, they'd all watched a TV movie together and it wouldn't come up. The bread was crumbly and horrible in her pocket. She brushed all the crumbs out into the trash and threw the jacket in the laundry.

Today was cold. All she had on was a big sweatshirt over her turtleneck and jeans. The pansies shivered in the wind. She looked back at the shop in the middle.

The Arial sign said "Crystals and Conundra." The shop window was crammed with candle holders, little mirrors shaped like suns and moons, gargoyle statues, wizard dolls, wind chimes, a chess set made out of tiny castles, and all sizes of geodes and crystals. Every time the door opened, she smelled soap and spices. They never had decided whether you could gain calories from really good smells.

The door didn't open very often. None of these shops were doing much business, except Burger Death. It was too chilly out for ice cream and the large ladies seemed to be managing elsewhere.

She thought about running up and down those concrete stairs to the other parking lot by the real mall—run up and down them ten or twelve or fifteen times and have her breath all caught by the time Mom came to pick her up. But she was so tired.

Mom had said she was thinner. She told her it was from doing Pilates. Mom said, "Just don't go overboard with it," and she forced herself to laugh and said, "I don't really think you can."

But then when she was trying on the hated blue shirt, the one that was too tight around her fat triceps, Mom said, "A little baby fat is natural at your age." Baby fat, as if she wasn't fifteen.

She exercised harder after the baby fat line, and after the thinner/Pilates/overboard. She could be influenced only in one direction: thinner.

Daniel was getting thin even though he was trying to put on muscle. He ran, and swam, and got thinner. He had some weights at home, but when he was home he just played Sega. And cut.

A charm to keep Daniel safe—maybe his soul hadn't gone too far away. A transparent thing that barely moved a fraction of an inch if you pushed all day.

He would curl up the left side of his mouth if he thought she believed in it, but if she gave him the charm without any explanations, he'd wear it.

She owed 3Januce an email. The site was going up: the index page and the intro were almost ready to post. It needed to be perfect and so pretty that everyone would bookmark it right away. She was queasy at the idea of her words going into all those other people's machines. Not that Crys and Januce weren't careful, not like anyone could tell it was hers, but just the fact of all those eyes. Like having your top fall down at the beach.

So many things she wanted to take back… last night at 3:52 a.m. she'd added lines to the endless list. The note-passing thing with Shar. The blue dress. She'd had the best comeback line but not until it was too late. And that time at the dance. Your only hope was to be invisible. And she was a fat whale. Her stomach rolled up in folds when she leaned over. Her thighs were slabs of white fat.

The website was called This Order. It was a joke with Januce—they couldn't have an eating disorder because they each had a very specific eating *order*. Januce arranged everything by color and ate it in color order. Beth didn't have a color order but she had sequences to follow and not all of them were easy to explain. They had both, separately, trapped at their separate dinner tables, remembered that conversation at the exact same moment and thought "Eating This Order" and laughed or smiled right at the dinner table. And could not explain.

Before she went in, she reached up under her sweatshirt and took hold of both her hipbones. She held their hardness and dug her fingers in.

Heat and cinnamon, lavender, vanilla—too many perfumes fighting each other. There was a whole rack of Fae cards right behind the door. Faeries, elves, naiads, the Green Man, and others she didn't know. She felt shaky all of a sudden. Her left eye hurt. She wished she could be a faerie, incorporeal, get out of this fat bag of meat.

A sticker on the door had a line drawing of an angel inside a red circle and slash. She thought of the website Ana's Angels. So the first thing she said to the woman behind the counter was "What does that sign mean, no angels?"

"That's right—no angels here!" the sales lady said cheerily. "Angels imply a particularly bureaucratic form of Christianity and I don't subscribe to that."

The sales lady was beautiful. She had the perfect willowy shape, and her collarbones showed above the neckline of her batik dress. And the shop was cluttered in a good way: something to look at everywhere, things piled on top of and behind each other. Pendants and necklaces hanging in tangled clusters. But nothing was dusty. "You must spend like your whole time dusting!" Realizing that might sound rude, she added, "I mean it's so clean."

"Yah, we wouldn't want the Wicca Board closing us down."

"I guess they could probably just turn the whole store into a frog or something." The sales lady laughed and pointed to a stack of red and white plastic signs. *BROOMSTICK PARKING ONLY—ALL OTHERS WILL BE TOAD.*

"So what can I help you with today? Jewelry, henna tattoos, something for the dorm room?"

She savored that before admitting, "I'm in high school. Actually I'm a freshman?"

"We all have to start somewhere."

Beth paused in front of a cone-shaped wizard hat, midnight blue with gold stars and moons—"Is that the Conundra?"

"That is for wanna-be wizards, of which this exurb has an astounding quantity."

"I guess everyone wants to be something." She hoped the clerk didn't ask her what she wanted to be. There was a ceramic picture frame on the counter that held the words Talia Dumphries, prop. "Are you Talia? This is your store, right? I mean like you own it?"

"I do that. My real name is Natalie, but it has such a muggly sound, *Nat*-lee."

Beth laughed. "I'm Beth? But my friends sometimes call me, Beff." It was only Daniel who called her that, and they had both forgotten why.

Talia's shop had a whole shelf of beautiful embroidered pillows. They were deep purple and blue velvet with tiny mirrors on the borders: night sky and night stars. The pastel blue and lavender of the site began to seem weak. Maybe they could redo it in jewel-tones, amethyst, emerald, and indigo.

She chose a pillow for her desk chair. Talia put it in a big shopping bag with handles and tucked a piece of paper over it like she was making a doll's bed. A faerie's bed.

Mom would see it and sneer: "Why'd you buy a *pillow*?" "Cuz all of yours—" she wouldn't end the sentence—"*suck*." She wanted it to sit on, because her tailbone bumped against the desk chair, and she secretly liked it when that happened but it was making a bruise, and in her own room she wanted everything to be soft and lovely. At school she sat on her coat or tied a sweater around her waist. At home she would have this velvet pillow with the little mirrors and embroidery.

As Talia bent over the shopping bag, she tucked a wisp of hair behind her right ear. The ear was laced with eight or nine small silver rings all the way up the rim. And one through the little bump at the front. Beth imagined putting a Q-tip through that one accidentally.

"Can I get you anything else?" It sounded like a standard form question, but it gave her the courage to ask.

"Would you maybe have like a charm?"

Talia looked up. Her face was kind.

"Like for protection. For a friend of mine." Beth pressed her cheek against one hard shoulder. "A boy." In case it mattered to the spell.

Talia did not say, "A boyfriend?" And did not pry into the nature of the trouble. Only after she selected one of the tiniest dreamcatchers from their cobwebby wall display, attached a loop of green twine to the top of it, and opened a box filled with glittering beads, did she ask, "Enemies from within or without?"

Beth took a breath. "Both, I guess."

"Law trouble, heart trouble?"

"Kind of like, soul trouble."

A short nod. Talia found the right bead and threaded it into the web. It *was* the right stone—it was a deep golden/molasses swirl, almost wood grain, and it gleamed with tiny flecks of green like Daniel's eyes.

"Traditionally this part would be rawhide and not hemp," Talia said. "But I'm a vegan." AnaBeth took possession of "vegan" as her own charm against the forces of dinner and pizza and popcorn. She shoplifted the word up her sleeve for future butter-drenched excuses, permission to restrict.

"Anyway, we aren't exactly using every part of the buffalo, here in the strip mall. Hemp is the closest part of nature we ever touch anymore."

Beth nodded. Imagined a buffalo walking through the parking lot. Huge and shaggy, stepping on the pansies.

Then the phone rang, and Talia said, "Mind if I just grab that?" She ducked behind a sheer dark-blue curtain, into her office.

Beth looked at the overstuffed book racks. A heavy volume on the second shelf with gold lettering, the something codex. She wondered if it was even in English, but it was: cramped black print that ran almost to the edges of the pages, slightly ragged edges that looked like they'd been cut with a bread knife.

> —a blood component, in simultaneity with the chanting,
> enhances the spell's potency—

A blood component. Daniel wouldn't need any help on that part.

"Sorry about that," Talia said. Beth slid the book back into its slot. Talia hadn't noticed, and was already back to rummaging through the plastic tackle box of beads and tiny stones. She attached a silken tassel to the bottom of the charm, a forest green deeper and shinier than the green of the hemp twine. "It's supposed to have a feather," Talia said, touching the little tassel. "The bad energies get caught in the web and this is where the good energies float down." She rang it up and gave Beth her change. "Need a box? I can gift-wrap."

Beth shook her head. Holding the charm by its loop of twine, she eased it into the pocket of her hoodie. "That's it then? There aren't any words to say or whatever?"

"Words... Traditionally, not so... oh, wait, there's the Three Questions." Talia grabbed a little note pad that had alternating lavender and pink pages. She flipped over the top page, pink with a phone number on it, and wrote on a blank lavender page. "It's like the way you wish on a wishbone? You have to be holding it. Ask him these."

She had the prettiest whispery handwriting—it was printing but so curvy and fine that it looked like cursive. It was like faerie writing.

Now that money and magics had changed hands, Beth felt a strange formality come upon things. "Thank you," she said.

"Come back and visit," Talia said with a half smile.

Beth looked at the angel sticker again as she left the store. Her shoulder blades wanted to unfold and be wings.

It was Fuckit time. Mom didn't have her phone on, but when Beth wasn't here waiting for her, she'd check it. "Mom I have to go over to

Daniel's so I'll just get dinner there and walk home right after dinner OK? So I'll see you later. Right after dinner. Bye Mom."

Daniel was an only child with his run of the moon. He could have had a live kangaroo in his big basement room and everyone would've been fine with that. His mom had turned his old room into a guest room, and they moved all the sewing and games and boxes to one end of the basement so he had his own space.

Beth called him after the hideous dinners and they talked about the awfulness of everything. He was always up late. He sometimes used to have his mouth full while they were on the phone—eating SpaghettiO's right out of the can, or double-chocolate Pop-Tarts for dinner—but not in a long time. Maybe he was holding hands with Ana too.

At the corner, she started to feel floaty. Her ears clouded over, so the traffic became muffled, bee-like. But she stood very still with her knees locked and took long slow breaths, and it went away. She stood very tall and flattened her empty stomach to her spine.

You couldn't live on air. One had to eat enough to subsist. Except AnaCrys had written, "enough to subside," and Beth looked it up. She imagined subsiding like a wave subsides, getting smaller and smaller. Eat enough to subside.

The air smelled like exhaust. Crossing the bridge over the main artery, she was a razor blade. A tatty flag had been pinned to the fence and left for dead. It must have been there since 9/12. The reds were all rusty and the whites were all gray.

Daniel in his room was making perfect blood-bead-trails along his forearm. Forearm: a leg has shin and calf, but an arm fails to differentiate between the tough, faintly hairy back of the forearm and the paler, softer skin where the veins hide. He was not gouging, not aiming for that bluish snake. Symmetry counted. The first cut was at the thumb side, almost on the bone, where arm-shin segues into arm-calf. Then each cut must be straight, parallel, even, right next to the previous cut, a UPC code of blood. If the wriggling blue vein chose to lie beneath one of the perfect even lines, then maybe it would get nicked. He was not aiming for it. He was following the rules.

The life of the mind. He saw it in red neon lines, like your arm was the Earth's crust, your blood was magma. The life of the mind, but there is no mind and no life without the weak, spindly, aching failure of the body.

The life of the mind, but he wakes up with his penis in his fist. He's been holding it in his sleep. For dear life. Dear: expensive, costly, extravagant.

He and Beth had sat together scratching white lines like chalk marks on their dry skin. That was years ago; she probably wouldn't remember. He got better at it and deeper, and the white marks on his legs now were scars. It was a girl thing to do (he'd been told) and that made it gay. He was careful to keep covered. At the beach he wore board shorts that flapped below his knees.

He wanted that purity of flame, the life of the mind. Somewhere ahead, he would spend whole nights scribbling inventing creating burning. He ignored his bodily needs and kept writing till the sun was high and his imaginary roommate begged him to eat something.

Here in the present he noticed every tick of the minute hand. He inspected his skin, twitched off the dry scabs, scratched carefully. It was always time for another drink or cigarette or Kleenex. The mind was the dull slave of the body—its devoted caretaker—its mom.

He kept switching disks in his five-CD changer so the music would never stop playing. He had the sound cranked up on the video game so he could hear it over the music, but now the game was paused.

People are blood inside a sheet of skin. Lines in the skin. Not a puncture wound to deflate and disrupt. Only the lines.

And the girl—Amelia. Tiny, perfect, popular. She was so outgoing she talked to everyone *including* him, which was worse than if she excluded him, because at least then she'd be noticing. He wasn't even an outsider; he was one of the eighteen kids in her math class.

She was so blonde, her face had those tiny whitish sideburn hairs, like on little kids.

She was so little, but her breasts were full and soft. Probably soft. He imagined the touch of her lips. She would taste sweet. She would let him touch her, and he would smell her on his fingers. She would put her mouth around it.

He held himself in new ways, experimented with textures. He took the cashmere scarf Beth had forgotten. Then he threw it in the garbage so she couldn't ask for it back. It might have had drops on it, stiffness memories. Secret secretions.

Now his hand drifted, again, below the waistband of his jeans, but he stalled—he would do it after this game—and it was during the rest of the game that Beth came and scratched on the sliding-glass door. She never knocked; she scratched at the door like a cat. He hit the pause again.

"Hey man, 'zis OK?" she whispered as he let her in.

"'Course. Hey." He answered her in a normal voice.

"I didn't mess up your game?"

"No, I paused it. C'mon." She sat on the bed while he played the rest of the level, and he did better than ever because Beth was watching, so he saved the game to come back to later. "So you went shopping?"

She showed him the pillow. The charm and the words were in her pocket.

"Pretty," he said. His hand traced a path between the tiny mirrors, staying on the unembroidered softness of velvet. He used his fingertips, then the heel of his palm. The other side of the pillow was plain purple satin. "You want to go for a walk?"

"OK," she said.

It was almost night in the yard, and the sky had changed from gray to that blue that is more intense than anything.

Daniel wore his nylon jacket, but it scraped against his forearm as he pulled it on.

"You have blood on your hand," she told him.

"Your voice sounds like your mom's voice."

"Fine. Well do you want to get a Band-Aid or something?"

"Hold on." They were beside the back porch, and there were some gardening tools under the steps. He reached into a bucket and came up with a cloth.

"Oh my god, that towel is filthy. You'll probably get infected."

"I will get gangrene and die," he said, and Beth laughed. She covered her mouth and looked away, as if it was a private act, like burping.

They walked toward the line of trees that separated his yard from the neighbors'. "So, what's wrong with being dead? Why do people care. Anyway if they believe in heaven, they should be happy."

"No, because if they believe in heaven, they believe in hell, and that's where you go if you commit suicide."

"But not if it's an accident. Or crime victims. Really the greatest thing you could do would be sacrifice yourself to hell, by killing all these innocent people and sending them to heaven."

"Ew. That is so fucked up. I'm glad you're not a Christian."

"Even if I was, I wouldn't want to go to hell to save everyone else. We're talking eternal torment."

"Lake of fire."

"Lake of fire," he repeated.

They were almost to the trees. "Hey, turn around," said Daniel. There was the moon, rising between the houses.

"It's almost full."

"I think it's going to be full on Thursday."

A trickle of his blood—black in the moonlight—ran down from the towel. She took out the charm and squeezed it between their hands. It was only a little blood. Maybe it was enough.

"Don't ask. It's a thing. Just hold it. Hold my hand."

She unfolded the page with one hand and tried to read it in the moonlight. The lacy writing was too small, but she remembered what it said. She held his hand tightly as she asked him the Three Questions.

M.H. Johnson

Opus 22

M.H. Johnson is a fiction and nonfiction writer, a graduate of Johns Hopkins University MA program in fiction, and an alumna of the Heritage Workshop at George Mason University. Her short story "The Middle Stretch" appears in the Winter/Spring 2006 edition of the *Baltimore Review*, and her short-short "As Is" is forthcoming in *Gargoyle*. Some of you know her as Holly Sanders. Old/new name, new life, all good.

Grace is on hold. She stands in the kitchen, phone pinned between her right ear and shoulder, holding her daughter slumped on her left hip. Monday morning at the pediatrician's. She should've known better than to call when they first opened. Every parent has been waiting for the weekend to be over to decide if her kid is sick enough for an appointment. She's usually the last one to drag Olivia to the doctor's, but this time it's different. Olivia seems much older and smaller than her four years, as though some fundamental thing in her were receding.

It's probably nothing, she tells herself. Children get fevers so often.

Pressing her lips against the heat radiating from the damp skin of Olivia's forehead, Grace rocks to the ancient rhythm of mothers of sick children. She sighs. All she wants is an appointment. She listens into the phone, reaching out for the nurse to come on, but instead finds…music. Not just any music. Her music. When Grace hears it she realizes it's been playing in her ear the whole time.

Dvořák. Yes. Two bars and she flinches with recognition. *Serenade for Strings in E Major*, Opus 22. The fourth movement, the "Larghetto." For a moment, Grace is no longer in the kitchen, she is in another place—a place she misses, a kind of secret home. Her left hand twitches against her daughter's slender calf, straining to remember the fingering. She closes her eyes, and lets herself wander into what feels like a cathedral of sound. Grace remembers—

"This is the triage nurse. Is this Ms. Burnett?"

"Yes. Olivia has had a high fever for over forty-eight hours now—"

"How high?"

She doesn't even have a thermometer in the apartment. All those fussy mothers with shiny eyes excitedly repeating the numbers at the playground: "He got to 103.8!" As though it were an SAT score. Besides, a doctor friend once told her a kid's fever really doesn't matter until they start convulsing.

"I don't know the exact number, but she's been prophesying and waving her arms in the air—doesn't that usually mean over 103?" Grace expects laughter and gets none.

"Have you been giving her any Tylenol or Motrin?"

Olivia's breathing is raspy and regular. Grace has moved to the sofa where Olivia can rest her head in her lap. A trickle of the sinister-smelling orange medicine trails from the corner of her mouth, as her mother runs her hand through the girl's sweat-darkened bangs.

"Yes, Tylenol every four hours. But it only brings her out of it for short periods."

"Olivia is four, right?" Grace hears pages in a chart flipping. "Any other symptoms?"

"A little cough last week. And achiness, the fever, I assume. She's been complaining about her joints. But nothing major."

"Bring her in this morning. Better safe than sorry. I'll transfer you back to the appointment desk. Hold, please."

The *Serenade* returns. Grace feels it lift her, like all great symphonies, making her insignificant and uniquely important at the same time. Like looking at the stars. But there is melancholy in it, a taste of bitters in those strings. It's so often called Dvořák's most joyful piece, written after he won his first music prize—large enough to allow him to compose full time. One of the lucky few, Grace thinks ruefully. He composed hundreds of pieces, his *New World* arriving much later in life, as Opus 95. This, despite all the hardships he faced, the deaths of his children. So many failures, his own and others. This minor key feels like foreboding to her —knowing what she does of Dvořák's life—but then the major theme returns. Or perhaps the melancholy is simply what Czech joy tastes like in an American mouth.

"Ms. Burnett? We have you down for a ten-thirty with Dr. Nichols."

Grace never liked wearing her coat to school, and now that she was in fourth grade *and* it was officially spring, she was definitely not going to put it on. "No!"

"I don't care what the calendar says," her mother told her. "This is Indianapolis, not Miami. It's still too cold!"

"I am not wearing my coat!"

Grace's mother sighed. "After nine years of experience, I shouldn't go to the trouble of arguing," she said. "A sweater. All right? Wear a sweater, Grace."

She tossed it over Grace's shoulder as the girl headed out the door.

Grace ran, wadding the sweater into a ball and hugging it, her lunch box, and bookbag to her chest. Three houses down, out of sight, she shoved her arms through the sleeves, and pulled on her ash-blonde pigtails to tighten them. In a corner of her mind where her mother couldn't hear her, she wished for her coat. And her tights. Her knees felt raw in the air, and the scab on the left one itched. She tugged on her skirt, vainly trying to cover her long, bony legs.

She started running again, then stopped, breathless, her nose sniffling, in front of the Garrisons' house on the corner. She hopped up and down on both feet, trying to stay warm until the bus came.

The Garrisons' yard was covered in hoarfrost, the dead, brown necks of last year's black-eyed Susans and cone flowers staring stupidly over the top of the low picket fence. Grace smelled bacon coming from their kitchen. From Margaret's room upstairs came a warm, golden light, a sort of glow parting the early morning gray, as though some fairy lit the space. Margaret Garrison was a sophomore in high school.

Through the half-open window Grace heard a sound she didn't recognize. It was something like a voice, but too spindly to be human. It started in quietly, a high, pure tone; then, louder and deeper, as though joined by other voices. Fairy voices. The music slid down her spine, lifting her out of her saddle oxfords. She took a step closer to the fence. She could see her breath huffing from her open mouth, but she couldn't see anyone in the room. Then a chirp, like a bird with its tail caught, came out of the window. The sound stopped as Margaret stepped back. Grace saw in silhouette the girl's shoulders slumped, the bow in her right hand, the instrument in her left. Slowly, Margaret lifted first her head, then the bow, and began again. The fairy voices came back.

Grace had never heard anything quite like it. She shivered, but not from cold—now she felt warm, somehow. She knew what she wanted. She wanted to make music like that, music that made you feel large and small at the same time, music that made you feel like you were home inside.

It was Beethoven's *Spring Sonata*, Grace decided much later, that she heard that day coming from Margaret's bedroom—and on the next day and the next, on through to June, until the last day of school when she got up the courage to ask Margaret to show her her violin.

~

Dr. Nichols's face scrunches up exactly the way Grace's mother's used to when she hit a clunker. She even pulls her head in a little, tortoise-wise, like her.

"No cough, no phlegm..." The doctor is scoping Olivia's ear. Olivia is slumped on the examining table, her ash-blonde hair swirled in soft, sweaty curls. Her hands are limp at her sides, her palms twisted up, flung down like a doll's. Grace wishes she would whine and flail when the doctor touches her, as usual. The doctor looks at the nurse's notes. "Joint achiness? Where? Get down and walk for me, Olivia honey, will you?"

She watches as Olivia walks across the room, her left leg limping slightly. The doctor's frown focuses itself into her pursed lips as she writes furiously on her pad.

"I want her to get a blood test, to rule out an infection." She opens the door and calls to the nurse. "Laurie, can you take Ms. Burnett and Olivia down the hall to the lab?" The doctor turns back to Grace. "It shouldn't take more than an hour to get the results. I'll see you back here then."

The bloodwork is horrible. The tech can't find Olivia's veins—this is a pediatrician's office, for pity's sake, Grace almost says—why can't you find her veins? Instead, she speaks soothingly to her daughter and holds down first one arm, then the other. Olivia wails with incomprehension, her eyes rolling wildly at her mother as she helps these people do this to her. Even her Blankie doesn't help calm her. Finally, they have enough blood collected, and Grace goes back to the waiting room where they started this morning. She sits with Olivia in her lap, humming Brahms to her, the same piece she hoped would lull her to sleep at four a.m. as she played by the half-light coming from the bathroom.

Olivia sniffles. "I want to go home, Mommy."

"I know, pumpkin. Soon." Grace presses her cheek against the furnace heat of the top of her daughter's head. She stifles a fleeting urge to call her mother. No need. "We'll have cocoa when we get home. Would you like that, Livvy?"

They are back in the examination room. Grace hears Dr. Nichols speaking rapidly, explaining the results of the blood test.

"She has an unusually high sed rate—ninety-two. A normal sediment rate in blood is somewhere around twenty-five," she says. "By itself it doesn't mean much. It's an indicator, a pointer to the source of a problem."

"So, what does this high...sed rate mean? Is it a reaction to a virus, or something?"

"It could be viral, or a blood infection, or a problem with her bones. We aren't sure. But that limp has me worried. I think you should see an orthopedic surgeon. We took the liberty of getting you an appointment at the university hospital with Dr. Shannon. It's in an hour. Do you know how to get there?"

~

She fell in love first with his wrists.

He was standing to deliver the solo from the Mozart Horn Concerto No. 3. Grace was first chair that night. She had seen him around the university, but hadn't heard him play until this rehearsal. He was slender, a small waist and reddish hair thinned by the stage lights. Grace imagined freckles across his nose. As his breath came singing through the horn, she saw Mr. Gringold in the first row of the empty auditorium lean his head to Ms. Nash and whisper a comment. Ms. Nash nodded sagely.

Grace watched his fingers on the stops, nimble and lithe. The notes rounded through the auditorium, inviting in the spring evening standing just outside the doors. The sound seemed so much larger than he. It gave his body a gravity, a solidity it lacked on its own. But not his wrists. There was something sturdy and completely reliable in his wrists and the musculature leading to them in his forearms. Farmer's wrists, Grace thought. Only a suggestion of the power beneath. They remained immobile, firm and steady, while his fingers flew and his cheeks flared and his translucent eyelashes blinked frantically, as though trying to keep up with the music that had taken over the rest of his body. Somehow the breathless clarity of his sound was pinioned there in his forearms. A frail, freckled farm boy, with a gift for the French horn, whose only resemblance to his stocky family lived in his muscular, beautiful wrists.

Afterward, they walked back to the dorms together through the clouds made by their breath. The campus glowed gray and pink in the chilly final glaze of sunset.

"I've heard you play," Jon said. She was almost as tall as he was. They walked carrying their instrument cases so they wouldn't bang into each other, Grace's violin in her left hand, Jon's horn in his right. She had seen him pack it, how gently he laid it in its case. Mr. Gringold said you could tell a lot about a musician by how he handled his instrument. "Last week, at the recital. I just—I've never heard Brahms like that."

"Thanks."

"No really—it was, it was very moving." He slowed his gait, lopsided by the weight of his horn, and looked at her as he said this. Grace felt a warm shiver down her back. She let it blossom inside her.

"I've been working on that piece a long time," she said with a satisfied sigh. "Mr. Gringold says if I could bring the same inspiration to my other work, I could really go someplace. But you—well, after today, there's no doubt. You're definitely one of the lucky few."

"Oh, I don't know about that." Jon's chin dipped down. Was he blushing? Grace thought he looked even more like a farm boy than ever. She sneaked a look at his wrists sticking out of his coat. There they were. She shivered again.

"Are you cold?" Jon asked. He looked distressed. She thought he might be ready to build a fire right there on the quad.

"No, just, it's the air. I'm fine." Grace straightened up slightly, quickening her pace. "We were talking about you, what you'll do when you get your big break."

"I'll be happy just to play."

Grace rolled her eyes. "We'll all be happy to play—but how many people are sitting on the other side of the lights, and who you're on stage with—doesn't that mean something to you?"

"Of course it does. But I guess that isn't what I think about when I'm up there."

Grace snorted. The thing was, she could tell he meant it. She shook her head. "Well, all I know is if I end up teaching high school band I'll commit suicide." If my mother doesn't kill me first, she thought.

They were outside her dorm. Grace turned to face him. Somehow, in the split second after they stopped, Jon had come apart: he stood with all his weight on one foot, his case tipping him off balance; one corner of his coat collar had flipped up crazily; his hair had rebelled and was sticking out on the left side, as though trying to escape his head. His eyes pleaded with her as he bit his lip furiously. She tried not to smile.

"Want to come up?" she asked.

❧

The university hospital is in a part of town Grace isn't familiar with. She doesn't want to be late for the orthopedic surgeon, and she's afraid she'll miss the entrance, so she does. Cars behind her honk and pull around as she squints and drives too slowly. Olivia lets out a whine as Grace finally pulls through the parking lot gate a half block past the emergency entrance. God, will she have enough cash to get out of the lot? She scrounges for change in the ashtray, cracker crumbs and wadded chewing gum wrappers sticking under her fingernails. Then she digs in her purse, where with a sigh of relief she finds a free-floating five in the bottom. She carries Olivia, stuffed into her snowsuit and sweating, across the lot, dodging the blackened rinds of unmelted snow as she goes, then back again to retrieve the forgotten Blankie from the car seat.

They sit in Dr. Shannon's examining room, staring at a hip ball and socket and a model of the human foot. Predictably, Olivia is better, not deathly pale as before, not delirious, just sitting there on Grace's lap. Olivia reaches to play with the foot. Grace pushes it away. Look sick! she wants to say. But when Dr. Shannon comes in the room and Grace says, "Elevated Sed Rate of Ninety-Two," she can see she has his full attention.

Dr. Shannon has a transparent halo of strawberry-blonde hair and a leprechaun's bushy eyebrows, which rise as he tilts his head. "Ninety-two? You're sure?" He looks as though he were listening to the rounded tones of a Mozart horn concerto. There is some clarity, an idea forming. He smiles.

He shifts his attention to Olivia. "Hi there," he says, looking into her face, half-hidden in her mother's shoulder. "You don't feel too good, do you?" He stares at her chart while pushing the model foot closer to Olivia, who pounces on it. Grace says nothing and the doctor keeps reading.

"This could be a number of things, including a nasty virus. You say she hasn't had any wounds, cuts, or anything of that sort recently?"

"No, nothing like that."

"Olivia, honey, does your knee hurt? Can you show me where?" Dr. Shannon asks. Olivia points to just below her left knee. "No bruising. No punctures," he says, examining her leg like something from the produce aisle.

The doctor starts talking about a possible diagnosis. Grace hears "infection," and "inflammation," but there are other, bigger words that do not stay with her. Her chance at using those years of high school Latin evaporates as she blinks stupidly at the doctor, as though he were speaking in light waves, or discrete particles meant to impart meaning, but which only bounce against her ears and slide out. Technical terms in music comfort her, give her a sense of expertise and control; here, they only confuse.

"We need x-rays," Dr. Shannon says.

⁂

They were standing in the parking lot, the cicadas screaming in the trees. She hadn't meant to say any of it, but especially not just as he was about to get in the car to go to the airport.

The driver's door was open. He'd already closed the trunk. They'd said it was going to get to a high of 90 degrees, but it felt like 101. Or maybe that's the way it feels when you're pregnant. But not at only six weeks, probably.

"You'll become a prima donna. All arrogance and brilliance. You'll be able to get away with anything, just because people want to hear you play." Worse, now she was crying.

"Grace, I know this is hard." Jon reached out to touch her arm.

"I just know what's going to happen to you. It always does."

Jon stroked her face, a half smile curling on his. "You could come with me."

"What? Follow you around the world, doing your laundry, keeping your calendar for you? No thank you." Grace smeared tears across her face and shoved her wrists into her damp armpits. He didn't know about the baby. She couldn't tell him. If she did, she knew he would stay. And she knew she couldn't go with him, not like this. She had to think, think it out. But he wouldn't offer again. This was it. They had already discussed her going along twenty times since his job offer had come through. "Dammit!" Grace said.

"Then play. Just play, for God's sake, Grace. Don't just stay here and feel sorry for yourself. Don't cheat yourself, your talent—"

"Feel sorry for myself? That's what you think?"

"You had one bad recital, two months ago. We've all had bad performances. Remember when I—"

"It's not just the recital. It's more than that. I know I can't make the cut. I have to face facts." Grace swallowed. This was not about the baby. Her throat was parched. It was too hot to argue like this. "I can't afford to fool myself about that."

Jon put down his horn. It was the last thing to go into the packed car. A slight wind brushed through the big oak overlooking the parking lot, rustling its half-crisped leaves, causing the air around them to move in imitation of a breeze. Jon took both her hands in his. She looked longingly at their hands together.

"Grace, I have a lifetime of mistakes ahead of me. It's crazy to think I've got it any easier than you. If I'm *really* lucky, I'll be humiliating myself in front of large audiences, nightly."

"If that were true you wouldn't be leaving for London right now." Jon dropped her hands. Grace had stopped crying. Now she was angry. "Look, I can't kid myself. Something has changed. As a kid, I had something, I was different. Now, I don't know, something is gone. And I'd hate myself if I ended up some middling player for some mediocre community symphony."

"Then practice, play harder and more than ever." Jon laughed. "Grace, you need to make more mistakes, not less."

"I don't know. I don't think it's going to matter. I can't kid myself about my so-called talent."

Jon shook his head and picked up his horn. "I can't argue with you when you're like this." He put his hand against her cheek. "I'll call when I get in." Then he put his case in the car, climbed in behind the wheel, and drove away.

೨

Dr. Shannon tells Grace very gently that, based on his review of the x-rays, we need to get Olivia checked into the hospital. He says it that way: "*We* need to get Olivia into the hospital." But not just for tests, not for an unending search for a mysterious childhood bone disease, but for one thing, only one of the possible multisyllabic somethings. Osteomyelitis. Grace's Latin makes a brief reappearance, enough at least to wrap her mouth around this one. Osteo is bone. A bone infection.

"It's highly unusual, like lightning striking. Usually it's due to a puncture wound. It's not unheard of, in children her age, for an infection to work its way into the interior of her upper tibia—" Dr. Shannon taps Olivia just below her knee, "—but caught early, there should be no after effects."

Grace holds her breath and asks about all the things she thinks could go wrong: No lasting damage? No limp? No tendency to infection? Or possible recurrence?

"If we treat it properly and thoroughly, now, we can make it go away. Completely."

Antibiotics. It means hospital time, more x-rays, a bone scan to confirm, but an end to the mystery, a way back to normal.

Hospital parking, four levels down, two miles from the lobby. Paperwork. Admitting. Calls to the neighbor, feed the cat? New message on the answering machine, calls to the high school to cancel practice. Find the room. Roommate is a seven-year-old boy with two broken legs and fourteen relatives. A doctor walks the floor, a little boy just eighteen months old slung on his hip. The child has pink burns the color of pain on his face and hands. "He's only quiet when he's held," the doctor tells Grace. She looks sadly at all the hospital beds masquerading as cribs.

The IV pole hovering above Olivia with its jellyfish bag of fluids holds no interest for her, but she likes the big bed that moves up and down on a push button, and the prospect of unlimited television delights her. The nurses are kind, to her and to Grace; the food is terrible; and the chair by the bed impossible to sleep in, all as expected. Grace is glad there is no music here.

For three days, she does what all the other parents do, their harrowed faces over cups of bad hospital coffee—she goes back and forth directly to her child's room without lingering to see the other sad little bodies and faces. The parents all have exactly the energy required to take care of their own, no more.

She feels as though she has been burrowing into the earth, holding her destination in her mind like a lantern before her. The destination, though, oddly, is behind, back to health, a place that feels oddly distant but which existed only four or five days before. She knows the only way through this is with the same single-mindedness of purpose she used when practicing a passage again and again, until it felt engraved in her body tissue.

↠

Budapest. Prague. Vienna. Lucerne. Grace showed the postmarks to Olivia as they came in. "This is where Daddy played last month," she'd say, as the baby shoved the envelope in her mouth. She always made sure she took the checks out first. "He'll come to visit, soon," she told Olivia. It was never soon enough. First, every three months, then every six. Jon talked about getting a teaching position at Bloomington. "But your career is just taking off now," Grace said. "We miss you, but we're fine. Really. Your folks come down every few weeks to see the baby."

"But I miss you both so much—" he said.

"Jon, this is your time. Take it."

She meant it, mostly. She did hate working at the high school teaching music. She never played publicly, only for herself or Olivia, and sometimes for Jon. He promised someday she would travel with him, go to all the places he'd seen. Still there were times, late at night, when her mother's bitter words seemed true: "He got the career and you got the kid." One look at Olivia and she knew she'd made the right choice. But as Jon's success grew, it got harder and harder for him to come home, and Grace got better and better at not expecting him.

↠

Dr. Shannon is making his rounds. A cadre of interns flanks him as he stands at the foot of Olivia's bed, reviewing her chart. "Excellent progress," he says, and snaps the chart's jacket shut. "The bone scan showed only a slight infection. With the home course of treatment, it should be completely cleared up in eight or ten weeks."

"When can we go home?"

"As soon as they put in the pic line," the doctor says. "Hasn't someone covered this with you already? You need to give her daily doses of the antibiotics directly into her bloodstream. The IV in her wrist would never last for the full eight weeks. So we insert a tube in a vein in her arm, here," he gestures to the inside of his elbow. Grace notices he has gone back to saying *we*. "It travels up into her arm. We take it out when the treatment is complete. She can play, she can bathe, and she'll get the use of her hand back again."

"Do you have to put her under to do it?"

"Of course. There's no other way. We need her to be perfectly still, especially a child with veins this small. But it only takes about twenty minutes. We do it all the time."

Grace nods. What choice does she have?

The flock of white coats exits and goes on to the next room. Olivia looks up at Grace and smiles. "It'll be OK, Mommy."

*

Grace is outside the procedure room, standing in a small waiting area populated by exhausted parents, children dragging their IV poles, everyone trying to look less miserable than they feel. A man sleeps, his feet in a chair, his head bobbing against his chest as his own snores fitfully wake him. The paths worn in the industrial orange carpet reverberate softly with the remembered shuffle of a thousand pacing feet. The magazines are shredded by constant fruitless flipping. Grace notices there are no clocks in the room. Until now, she has been good at maintaining enough distance from herself to keep moving to the next phase, the next cure.

She reminds herself she is not afraid of medicine.

A few minutes before, they wheeled Olivia's entire bed into the treatment room, down the hall from her room. Olivia didn't even notice them switch connections on her IV. Grace held her hand as a new clear liquid, falsely innocent, poured through the tube into her veins. Olivia's head rested in the crook of her mother's arm, where once her entire body fit. She seemed so, so small. In seconds, what is Olivia silently receded, leaving her suspended, a cameo creamy and perfect and still. Grace held her hand until they made her leave.

Sitting in the waiting room, she sees herself signing the release paperwork, sign, initial, sign again, just as she had on reams of forms since they arrived at the hospital. She'd read quickly through the legal jargon, her eyes skipping wearily over the familiar threats and promises. Then she'd stopped. This phrase was new, not on the other papers she'd signed. "Risk of possible cardiopulmonary arrest." The anaesthesia. Everything else they'd gotten through, and the anaesthesia could be the worst threat. The words bared their teeth at her unapologetically.

Look, she'd told herself, it's on the same page with dry mouth, drowsiness, nausea. Like allergy medicine. Grace cut herself a deal, sucked in her breath, and signed anyway. But the threat was there, the incisors visible, immobile, waiting.

Grace looks at her watch. It's been thirty minutes. They said twenty.

She closes her eyes and tries to prepare herself, just in case. She imagines them saying, "We're sorry, your daughter—" a carefully formed expression on their faces, the one used for breaking bad news, "—there was nothing we could do," they say. She cannot imagine what she will say, or feel—her heart carpet-bombed, her complete deforestation. But no imagined fire could burn as hot. Beside, it's too late. She signed the paper. Possible cardiopulmonary arrest. Why didn't she say no? How could she ever trust them with Olivia, even the slightest chance? She has made another terrible mistake, one that will haunt her forever, burn her to the ground.

"You OK? I mean… can I get you something?"

Grace lifts her face from where it has been buried in her hands, her shoulders shaking silently. She looks at the man who has broken the silence. He sits four chairs away, a heavyset fellow with a worried frown furrowing wild eyebrows into a peak. He reminds her a bit of Mr. Gringold from the conservatory: youthful face, ready smile, only a few deep lines in his forehead to give away his age. He looks kind.

"It's been three days," Grace hears herself say. "It's just starting to get to me. I mean, I thought she was fine, and now this, this procedure."

"Your daughter?"

"Yes."

"She in there?" He points to treatment room number 3. Grace nods.

"Mine is in number 4, next door," he says.

The ass sounds glad to meet a neighbor, Grace thinks as she rubs her temples.

He frowns again. "Do you have someone you can call?" the man asks.

"No," she says, too quickly. She wipes her face and sits up. "So, what is yours in for?"

The man takes a breath. Grace isn't sure he'll let her deflect the conversation this easily, but after a moment's consideration, he begins. "Nothing major. Just an LP." He catches himself. "A lumbar puncture. Troy—my son—has acute lymphatic leukemia." He says it so fast Grace only hears "leukemia." "He's in remission—he's fine, really, but has to come in and get tested now and again to make sure everything is OK."

"And the test is—a lumbar..." Grace tries to imagine what is happening in the room next to Olivia, and decides not to.

"A lumbar puncture. They need to test fluid in his spinal column, make sure he's clear of leukemic cells, lurking around his central nervous system." The man nods. His tone is that of a mechanic explaining why cars need oil changes. "It's not that big a deal. He's fine. I mean, he's got a ninety percent chance of being fine."

"So he'll be OK?"

"Oh, yeah. Now, thirty-odd years ago he would've been dead. Ninety-five percent chance of that. These days they know where to look, how to get those suckers. This is his eighth year with it, and so far," the man raps his knuckles on the plastic arm of the chair, "he's been clear."

"How old is Troy?" Grace asks.

"Ten."

Grace exhales.

"I guess we're one of the lucky few," the man says, rocking forward as he examines his shoes. "What about you?"

❧

The proscenium arch yawned over Grace's head, studded with lights like gleaming molars all pointing at her. She couldn't see the jury, but she thought she saw their breath rising out of the blackness surrounding the stage's perimeter, the empty auditorium unheated in this chill Bloomington evening. The only sound in the dense quiet was the click of her eyelashes, and then, the echoing cough of her accompanist, as he cleared his throat to signal his readiness to begin.

She had prepared several pieces, including the *Spring Sonata*, but the jury had asked her to play another Beethoven piece from her selection: the *Kreutzer*. It was difficult, a little showy perhaps, but she'd chosen it in part for the challenge. If she was going to get the recommendations she needed to get into a decent-sized symphony, she had to distinguish herself tonight. She took a breath of the cool air, and began.

The first and second movements went well, that confident place in her roaring along in control, the music lifting her off her feet. She was with the stars—not standing below looking up, but surrounded by them. Grace felt her shoulders tighten slightly as she approached the third movement, the finale. Here the violin and piano chase each other in six-eight time, leggy and quick like a greyhound bounding after a hare. The timing is crucial. The passage could sound ragged and forced, or she could easily stumble out of synch with the piano, if the tempo was allowed to falter in the slightest.

This movement had plagued her, her errors worsening as the recital date loomed closer; it seemed as if each time Grace corrected one error, she tripped over a new one. She had redoubled her practice time, determined to conquer this piece. The work paid off. She had it cold, twelve times without error the day before the recital, sixteen times the day before that. Never, never soaring; but proficiency, accuracy, some small mastery was hers.

There, under the lights, Grace sought that moment again. By the sixth bar she began to think she could do it. She told herself to relax, and tried to think of Jon, whom she knew stood just on the other side of the auditorium doors. The space between her shoulder blades loosened, and she exhaled lightly.

It was a mistake. The calm radiating from her interior was quickly transformed into some chilly inadequacy leaching down her arms to her fingertips. She watched her fingers with a strange detachment as they fumbled, stumbling not only at the same critical points she had conquered weeks before, but with new, creative variations in error she couldn't comprehend. All the heat and intensity of each stage light burned into her without mercy. Quicksand. A member of the jury exhaled. She imagined the seats filled with all her instructors since the beginning, Dr. Mueller, Ms. Porter, on through to Mr. Gringold who really was sitting there; all of them sadly shaking their heads.

Grace stopped. The piano tumbled to a halt then, too, the last note ringing unresolved in the air. She saw it all at that moment: the mediocre recommendations this would mean, her certain rejection from any major symphonies, her life teaching music to children, her mother's face. Her mother's face, her mother's voice, contemptuous of her failure.

She was immobilized. Start again, from the beginning? Impossible. She was two-thirds through the piece. Besides, she knew with absolute certainty that she would make the same mistakes in the same place again. The jury waited. The silence rose with the motes of dust in the lights; then, from the darkness on the other side of the stage came the voice of Mr. Gringold, gentle and commanding. "Finish, Grace. You must finish."

❧

"We're sorry you had to wait," the doctor in treatment room number 3 says. "We couldn't get the pic line into Olivia. We tried both sides, which is why it took so much longer. Those lab techs must've blown both her veins drawing blood. We'd like to try again tomorrow—"

"No," Grace says. Olivia is struggling with consciousness as she comes out of her deep chemical haze. The inside of both her elbows has a small bruise and a Flintstones Band-Aid across it. Grace holds her hand in hers, pale and precious as snow about to fall.

"Ms. Burnett, we need a way for you to get those antibiotics into Olivia. Now, we can give her veins a couple of days to heal, or we can go in through the carotid artery in her neck—"

"No." Grace looks at the doctor. Her mother would call her a nice young woman. They seem to be getting younger with every procedure Olivia has.

"We'll need to speak to Dr. Shannon," the nice young doctor begins.

"I've spoken to Olivia's father, and we won't release you to go in through the carotid artery," Grace says. Her turn to use the power of *we*. "We think we should try giving the home antibiotics through her IV, and if it starts to degrade, we can move it, or consider putting in the pic line then."

"I'm sure Dr. Shannon would appreciate a chance to speak to Olivia's father," the doctor says. So, Grace thinks, I am now a Problem Parent. You won't have an easier time of it with Jon, she thought.

"That's fine. He'll be here tomorrow. He's flying in from London tonight. I'll call Dr. Shannon's office and get an appointment, if it makes you more comfortable. But we'd like to go home tonight."

All she had to do was ask Jon to come. It was that simple. She might not need him for the whole eight weeks, but she needed him now, and he was coming. The thought overwhelmed her. And instead of having the expected sense of weakness and neediness, there was a kind of quiet gratitude and strength that felt oddly familiar—great and small, at the same time.

"I don't know about the IV. They're temporary. It'll mean coming back in, getting it changed, maybe every few days," the doctor says.

"We'll see how it goes," Grace replies. Suddenly she is very tired. "We've been pretty lucky so far. Maybe it'll hold."

☙

For the first time in many years, as she drives Olivia home from the hospital that night, Grace thinks about the way that college recital actually ended. The *New World Symphony* is playing on the car stereo as she thinks back to that evening, a time before she could imagine Olivia or anything beyond that moment.

Standing in the Indiana chill of the unheated auditorium, Grace heard Mr. Gringold's words ring in her ears. "Finish, Grace. You must finish." Some part of her she didn't know existed responded, almost automatically. She raised her bow, heavy as though lined with lead. She watched it place itself across the strings, and, closing her eyes for a moment, found her place. Then she started over, and played flawlessly to the end.

Alma M. Katsu

Pipefitters Union

ALMA M. KATSU writes fiction and lives in Reston, Virginia. She is working on a novel.

Hey, come here, I wanna show you something—the trouble with Randall started that simply. After one week with Randall, I knew he could be getting ready to show me anything: a decapitated head that he toted around in a shopping bag, a dead mouse floating in a beer bottle, webbed toes.

Turned out Randall wanted to show me a photo of his wife, naked. Such a thing was not unheard of in our line of work, construction. A surprising number of guys carried around pictures of their wives with no clothes on. A guy you barely knew would hold out a crumpled Polaroid for you to appreciate. It seemed funny to me, that there were men who got satisfaction out of this act, affirming—what? That they were generous, good-natured? *Look at what I get to go home to.* Usually the women weren't that much of a treat to look at. Maybe these guys were looking for condolences.

Randall picked the Polaroid out of his shirt pocket and slid it to me like a card dealer, without taking a look at it first. I held it close, embarrassed for the wife even though I didn't know her, trying to spare her nude body from casual onlookers. I suppose I should've been thinking about sparing her from *me*.

She was gorgeous. Couldn't hardly be eighteen, in that photo. It went to figure that of all the insane sons of bitches I have worked with on construction sites, Randall would be the one to score a knockout wife. He wanted me to wonder how a crazy-ass trailer park boy like him ended up with a Hollywood-looking wife.

Randall was an institution among the pipefitters at the site, I learned that right off the bat. I suppose that's why I got paired with him. Randall was the only one without a helper—Randall's helpers always moved on. That's what one of the Hispanic day-jobbers told me, that first day. Sometimes Randall's helpers wouldn't last a week.

There were other reasons they paired us up. I was at a low point in my life. I had just arrived in town, where I knew exactly one guy—the brother of an old high school friend—and it was his couch I was sleeping on. I had my reasons for leaving the last town, and they weren't so different from my reasons for leaving the town before that. And they weren't so different from what makes most men leave their domestic situations: they'll tell you it's her fault, but it usually starts with the drinking and the fighting and trouble with police and goes, well, downhill from there. All shit travels downhill; that's what we say in the pipefitters' trade.

The job boss probably took one look at me—unwashed, slightly hung over from last night's drinking binge, not in the least presentable—and figured we were a good match. Or that Randall would freak me out less than he'd freak out anyone else.

Usually, a pipefitter and his helper become close, at least while you're at work, because you have to work as a team, like a pitcher and catcher. You become close in some way, even if that way is mutual hate and loathing. Usually you become friends, fall into each other's rhythms. Talkers and listeners. One is a nonstop talker, the other never says a word. Or one goads the other to take stupid risks. Or one is brooding, the other sinks into his silence. Otherwise, that's where the mutual hate part comes in, because you are stuck with each other, for eight hours a day, on the top of two ladders, deltoids burning from holding up the two ends of pipe. Usually the boss will swap out partners before it comes to going at each other with a length of metal. Suicide pacts are not unheard of.

I was pretty nervous at first, and it wasn't just on account of Randall. I was weirded out by the site we were working on, a new stop on the subway system. I hate working underground. Working in, say, an underground garage is bad enough but even more I hate working in big, subterranean spaces, like a subway station. We had to lay some pipe with the duct workers in the lower section, where the trains came in, and we had to put in a sprinkler system in the upper levels. That wasn't so bad, on the upper level, because the ceilings were almost normal height. But that lower platform, it was like going down into Carlsbad Caverns to work. I felt like I was marching into Hell, every morning.

Randall definitely was a redneck. I had that figured out by the end of our first day together. He lived out in a rural area, an hour's drive away. It wasn't uncommon for these guys in live in trailers set out in the woods on cement blocks, or in hunting shacks way off on some ridge. During the week, a group of the guys might stay at a cheap hotel, or flop at somebody's apartment. Not a quitting time went by that Randall didn't make the commute; he didn't like to be away from home. After he showed me that picture of his wife, I could see why.

At that point, we hadn't socialized much. Randall's oddness made me nervous. Like every other pipefitter and helper, we ate lunch together, sometimes went to a bar for a beer (and no, we weren't supposed to but of course, everybody did it once in a while.) Anyway, we didn't socialize because Randall never wanted to go out for a drink after work, he was anxious to get on the road for the reason I already explained.

Then one day, Randall asked me if I wanted to come to his house for dinner the next night. I would get to meet his honey. Of course, he wouldn't drive me back to town that same evening, so I'd either have to spend the night or hitchhike back on my own, but since all that was waiting for me was a couch and a blanket and a now-surly reluctant roommate, it wasn't a difficult choice to make.

I had a hard time concentrating the next day, and almost burned my thumb soldering on more than one occasion. On the long drive out to Randall's home I felt like I'd made a mistake and got fidgety, that is, until we stopped to get some beers. I couldn't remember the last time I'd been to an area so unpopulated. There were fields and woods just about everywhere you looked. Every house we passed was small and run down; no better than the city, really, except that there was grass and trees to look at instead of another junky building just like the one you were standing in. At least the beers were cheap.

Randall asked me to wait in the truck while he went into the house by himself. It struck me as kind of odd, like maybe he hadn't cleared my visit with his wife first, but knowing Randall it didn't seem likely that he needed to ask for permission. I figured he'd explain it to me later, and decided to relax about it, and popped a beer. His house was no better than his truck, had the same beat-up look, minus the rust. Seemed no bigger than a garage. But who was I to talk? I hadn't had an apartment of my own in over a year.

I'd gotten halfway through the beer when the door opened, and Randall leaned out to call me over. Standing behind him, just visible through the screen, was his girl, the one in the picture, except with clothes on. I saw right away that a photo is an inferior thing, compared to a woman's body. What was flat and blurry and kind of abstract, like a map, was suddenly hilly and curvy, rounded and peaked, and right in front of me. Dressed in cutoff shorts and a sleeveless shirt knotted at her waist, she looked like a country girl right out of *Lil' Abner*. I got a woody just looking at her, even with Randall standing beside her (and there was no question of who would be the loser in a fight between the two of us, and that's saying something, considering I'm neither scrawny nor weak.)

Randall introduced me to Gina. She could barely look at me, and seemed to want to run away to the kitchen. Then Randall told me not to expect her to say anything to me because she was mute. Of course I asked if she was deaf too, and he said no, she could hear OK but she hadn't spoken the entire time he'd known her. At that point she broke away from us. Randall and I went to the living room, drank our beers and watched the news—for the sports—and all we knew of her presence in the house was the tinny sound of pots being lifted and put down.

You learn things about people in their homes that you would never, ever learn about them out in the world, not on the job, not watching them in a diner or walking down the street. For one thing, I hadn't figured on Randall being a toker, but as soon as we sat down in his living room—him on an old recliner, me on a spindle-armed sofa like the one my aunt got from Amvets—Randall reached under his chair and pulled out an old cigar box, and sure enough he had enough pot in there for a couple of doobies. It was good stuff, or maybe it just seemed that way because I hadn't smoked in a while. I wondered how he found such good pot out in the sticks or if he bought it off one of those guys who hung around the construction site.

By the time Gina came to bring us into the dining room, we were snorting and laughing at just about everything; it had gotten to the stage, you know, when you start laughing just because the other one *looks* at you. I was so relaxed, in fact, that I was no longer creeped out by Randall, and could eat and even look at his wife under Randall's crazy stare. Gina was a good cook, as you can imagine, stay-at-home wife with few other duties besides cooking. She made the kind of food guys like Randall go for—pork chops and applesauce, potatoes cut in circles and fried crispy in bacon grease. She didn't eat much herself, but kept an eye on Randall's plate, offering to refill it if it got too empty.

I expected something weird to happen that might, and it started right after dinner. Randall asked if I wanted to watch the ball game, and I said sure, even though I don't care much for baseball. Before the end of the second inning Randall called Gina over and made her sit on his lap. Pretty soon, I noticed, by the blue glow of the TV screen, that he had worked his hands under her shirt. He was playing with her breasts while he watched the game. She just sat there like a statue, not watching the television, not exactly *not* watching it, either. She wasn't looking at Randall and she sure wasn't looking at me. After a while, he undid the fly on her shorts and slipped his hand inside; I could see the waistband of her panties ride up on the back of his hand, barely peeking from behind the open zipper. I could see his hand moving under the denim.

I'll be honest with you; I was of two minds, as I sat kitty-corner to this live peep show. On one hand, I was mad at Randall for what he was doing, making me as horny as hell, and embarrassing his wife. I could tell she wasn't part of this, because she didn't act like she was turned on. The way she acted, you could tell it was entirely his idea. I wanted to jump up and punch him, but I already told you how an encounter between us would turn out. Also, if I did manage to get the better of him, what was I going to do? Knock him out and take off in his truck?

I had no illusions that he wouldn't track me down, and no doubts that there wasn't a hunting rifle somewhere in the house.

Then there was the other hand, and it was in Gina's panties with Randall. I was as turned on as I could be, partly because I hadn't gotten laid in a while (no money, no place to bring a girl—figure the odds, huh?) but partly because it was like a wet dream come to life. Was he going to offer me his wife? Was he one of these guys who wanted to see his wife ride another dude? Like every other guy in America, the only place I heard about that happening was in readers' letters in porno magazines and even I know those are made up by hard-up losers with overactive imaginations and fixations on their neighbors' wives.

Randall made her stand up. He undressed her right in front of me, taking off her shirt (bra-less underneath), her shorts, and her panties. She was as luscious as I thought she would be, big jutting breasts, an ass as round as a globe. Randall, still in the recliner, inched his pants down and had her climb on top of him, straddling him like a jockey who doesn't know how he ended up on the back of this horse. She sat facing away from me, so I could stare at her buttocks stretched wide to accommodate him. Her hair tumbled down the length of her back. His hands reached up in the direction of her breasts, and I could see a sliver of his face past the arm of the recliner. He was exactly where I would give anything to be.

I stayed until he climaxed, and he yelped a little as he shot his load. I excused myself then, stumbling past them to find the bathroom. I got off in about two strokes, standing over the toilet, trying not to think how I was reduced to masturbating in this psycho's john. It wasn't until I washed my hands and was about to turn out the light that I noticed that there was something funny about the bathroom. While it was cramped and cluttered, like any solitary bathroom in a household would be, it had almost no girly stuff lying around. No tampons, no curlers. No makeup.

When I got back to the parlor, I saw they had left. The door to the bedroom was closed, so I stretched out on that miserable couch and tried to fall asleep.

We had to leave really early—in the pitch black—in order to make the drive and be at work in time. Randall followed the same procedure as when we'd arrived, but in reverse. He asked me to go wait in the truck, and a good ten minutes passed before he came out. He started up the truck and we drove in silence almost the whole way. I kept waiting for him to say something, to explain last night, but he didn't. Finally, when we were about five minutes from the job site, I turned to him and blurted out, *what the fuck was that about*? The crazy motherfucker grinned so wide that he showed his teeth, but he didn't say a word.

The rest of the week went by almost what I would call normally. I could tell Randall wanted to say something; he spoke less than usual, but his expressions were something else, like every face you might find in a lunatic bin. And me, there were plenty of things I wanted to say, but was afraid to. I was afraid that if I spoke, I would ask questions that were personal and going to take us in a direction I wasn't sure I wanted to go. Then again, who was I fooling, because after the events of that night, we were ripping off in that very direction already—like driving the wrong way down a one-way street at night with no headlights.

Friday, at the end of our shift, Randall offered to give me a ride home. By now I was so nervous around him, I want to tell him I'd take a pass, but I was afraid of offending him. We got into his truck, but he didn't start it up. He just sat there, hanging his arms from the top of the steering wheel, chewing gum with an open mouth. He had this air of foreboding, like he was going to take out a gun and shoot me. I had watched him fuck his wife, hadn't I? What could possibly come after that?

No gun. He asked me if I wanted to come up to his house. That night. I don't recall even saying yes, but nodding and shaking all over, like Randall had caught me doing something dirty. He sure as hell had caught me *thinking* something dirty.

I'll cut to what you want to hear, and get it out of the way: he let me screw his wife that night. I remember having two thoughts during the ten minutes of actual screwing that took place: what the hell was I doing having sex with a crazy man's wife, and why had Randall picked me? Maybe that was all I really wanted to know. What had Randall thought when he met me? Did he look at me and see himself? The truth was I was nowhere as destructive and outright wiggy as he was. He may've been fooled that first week but Randall had to see by now that I was not in his league. Randall was in the majors, in terms of fucked-up-ness; I was a bat boy. So I couldn't pay bills on time or keep a friend longer than six months without owing him money or wrecking his car (or his sofa or his love relationship). What was I trying to do, hanging with him, prove that I was just as fucked up as Randall by doing his wife? I slept that night on the couch where I'd done the shameful deed, an old army blanket thrown over my dirty work clothes, my work boots stinking from under the coffee table—or rather, I tried to sleep as I wondered what was going on between Randall and Gina on the other side of the door.

I had just about decided to try to hitchhike back to the city—it was the weekend after all, I couldn't expect to stay with them for two more days (and hitching was sure to be an all-day effort for a man in my condition: filthy, unshaven, and looking as guilty as hell)—when Randall came out of the bedroom, and asked if I knew anything about carpentry. Turned out he was planning to remodel the kitchen, and was putting together some new cabinets. He asked if I wanted to stay the weekend, help with the carpentry. Eat some good food, get high, watch the ball game. He said those words, *ball game*, rolling his eyes like there was any way I wouldn't get his point. I said OK, not sure how else to respond. It was an attractive offer, in a strange kind of way.

That's how we spent Saturday. He kept all his stuff—wood, tools, sawhorses—in a shed. We worked in the yard, in the sunshine, and after those weeks underground, I gotta tell you, it felt good. Gina stayed in the house pretty much the whole time, except to bring out beers. She had on a thin sundress which, when backlit, seemed to be transparent. Every time I saw her, I ached for what I knew was coming that night.

First we had this motherfucker of a cabinet to work on, though. When Randall measured it out, I thought he had to have made a mistake. It was gigantic. I didn't think it would even fit in that kitchen. Randall explained that it was going to be some kind of broom closet, would go almost up to the ceiling. I just shrugged; it seemed ugly as hell, but it was his kitchen.

When we ended for the day, we just draped it with a tarp and left it on sawhorses in the yard. I swear it looked like a big coffin. It gave me the creeps.

That night was pretty much just as I expected: meatloaf, tequila shots with beer chasers, a doobie the size of a woman's pinkie finger. The baseball game droned, softly, in the background, while I watched Randall screw his wife on the couch. When it was my turn, I kept my eyes on the TV—bottom of the seventh; swing batter batter swing!—just to keep from erupting too quickly. At some point, Randall wandered to the kitchen for another beer, and I stole a glance down at Gina. She had her face closed to me—closed, like I was not even there. Her arms were rigid, at her side, her fists clenched. I was about to apologize to her, when Randall came back into the room.

Sunday passed about the same way. We worked on the cabinet until two o'clock, when Randall said we should carry it down to the basement, where he would do the sanding and staining in the evenings when he got home from work. I took the front end, walking backwards, and he took the back, to steer. I thought I'd lose my temper for sure, trying to wedge that big motherfucker through the door and into the house. I wondered if Randall had measured any of the openings in his own house, for crissakes. I mean, that's the one thing pipefitters have to do well, *measure*, to make all the connections and fittings work right. Was he too stoned to give a damn on his own place? I hoped, to myself, that once Randall saw what a big ugly monstrosity it was, inside that small room, he'd realize that he'd made a mistake and he'd give it up. I even dropped some hints, as we gingerly moved it through doorways and around corners, but he didn't take the bait.

I had just about come to the end of my patience, carrying that thing backwards down a set of stairs, into the basement (which, I will point out, is another subterranean space). Sweating and swearing under my breath, it was about all I could do to put my end down on the cement floor. Wiping my forehead, I straightened up and noticed, right away, that there was a second one of these big-ass cabinets in the basement. They were a big-ass ugly matched set.

Only they weren't. I walked up to the other one, kicked it with my toe. This box was older, had that look of being chewed around the edges. Instead of a door pull on its hinged lid, there was a hasp and a padlock hung off the corresponding staple. There was a little window cut in the door, at about face height, lined with chicken wire.

What the hell—the words came out of me as I turned to Randall. I was dirty and sweaty and exhausted, my good buzz was wearing off. I was, though, a little bit high. If I had any brains I wouldn't have wasted my breath asking him a question; I would've just run like hell up the stairs, making for the road. But, like I said, I was still slightly stoned.

Randall stared at me about as intently as I'd ever seen him look at anything. Sit down, he said. So while I sat on the edge of that thing—what was it, anyway? It wasn't a broom closet, and didn't I feel stupid for believing him in the first place—I listened as Randall told me his very, very weird story.

He started off by asking me if I ever heard about hitchhikers disappearing in the woods. Well, of course I had, I answered him, afraid of where he was going with this. What'dya think happens to them, he asked, as he rocked from one foot to the other. He was so intent and quiet, I wasn't sure he expected me to say anything.

Eaten by bears, I tried.

Not all of them, he said. Sometimes they're kidnapped by mountain men. You heard of mountain men, he tested me. Well, yeah, I had, I snorted, but there weren't any mountains here. You don't have to live in the mountains to be a mountain man, he replied, in a tone that implied he was disgusted by my stupidity. It's more a way of living. Uncomplicated. Taking care of yourself. He was pacing now, in a tight arc, around me and the monstrous box. What he said was true enough from what I could see; Randall had carved a pretty simple existence for himself. How kidnapped hitchhikers fit into his plans I couldn't say, but I imagined mountain men found dating a frustrating experience.

Men like *us*—he said without flinching—we take what we want. He needed a woman. He saw Gina in the woods. She was camping with two friends. He watched them for three days, for the opportunity when Gina would be alone. That's when he took her. Didn't I hear about it in the news, he asked. I reminded him that I hadn't lived in this area until a couple months ago. Apparently news of the kidnapping had not made its way four states over.

Randall went to the other box, the scarred one, and threw back the lid. There was an old stained cushion on the bottom of it, the kind of cushion you might use on lawn furniture. A greasy pillow. A pair of handcuffs, discarded, in the middle of the cushion. A yellowed plastic water bottle.

This is where she stays during the day, when I'm not home, he explained. Nobody comes out here, but I don't like to take any chances.

I don't know what I was thinking. I should've run the hell out of there, bolted for the woods, flagged down a state trooper. I should've gone for his hunting rifle, held him at gunpoint. Instead, I stared into that freaky wooden cell. I looked at the handcuffs.

Do you put a gag on her or something, while you're gone, I asked. Innate curiosity had taken over at that point.

He relaxed. He smiled knowingly. Naw. She could scream her head off; the nearest neighbor's half a mile away, he nodded.

We sat in the front room, each of us with a beer in our hand, while he explained it to me. Gina was in the kitchen, behind the swinging door, but she had to hear every word.

It's so much easier this way, he said. That is, if you pick the right one, and then it's easy. You train them to obey you. They'll do whatever you want, none of this back talk. They know who's in charge then, who's in control. Nothing I hate more than seeing a pussy-whipped man being jerked around by some ball-breaker. That ain't going to happen to me, you can bet, he said.

She'd been with him four years. Since I wasn't familiar with the story, he recounted all the facts for me: she was fourteen when she disappeared, camping with two boys from school, against her parents' wishes. She wasn't no angel when he found her, he said, as though that was his defense. A woman goes bad when the man doesn't lay down the rules, he explained. He blamed her father. She was good now.

When I was sufficiently numbed by beer, I found the nerve to ask him how he ever got the idea to do this, the kidnapping, the box, the handcuffs. He looked at me calmly, like he expected this question, had maybe even practiced it for the inevitable interrogation by the police, or the videotaped session with the reporters. He got the notion from his neighbor, when he was a boy. The neighbor had been a trucker. Picked her up hitchhiking. Kept her in a closet while he was out during the day. The wife didn't like having her loose in the house, preferred not to see her at all. You mean your neighbor kept a sex slave in his house and you never told the police, I asked him, amazed. Randall beheld me in disgust. You don't go ratting out your friends, he said. Besides, that old man would've shot me through the nuts with his Browning. He'd a killed me.

What happened to her, I prodded after another minute of silence. I mean, he couldn't have kept her hidden in his house forever.

I don't know, Randall said as he began peeling the label off his bottle. We moved away when I was sixteen. I don't know what he did with her.

That night, during my turn, I closed my eyes and poked away at Gina, just wanting to get it over with. She looked up at me. Randall was in the bathroom. We could hear him taking a leak.

You know I'm not mute, don't you, Gina muttered to me. You know I can talk?

That's when I lost it. I mean, my concentration was precarious, anyway. I just withered inside her. I climbed off, headed for the couch. Yeah, I figured that out, I said to her over my shoulder.

The ride back to the city was as tense as a heart attack. I kept waiting for him to try to kill me. Throw me out of the truck at high speed, crack my head open with a plumber's wrench. When that didn't happen, I started to seriously wonder what I should do. I mean, I knew what I *should* do, which was to turn him in. And be at the top of a fucking psychopath's list. I know most people wouldn't think that was such a big deal, but they don't have much to do with this kind of guy. For instance, you might not think these guys get set free on a technicality, but they do. Sometimes the victims won't testify against them—too scared. Sometimes they just get away. Cops make mistakes—lots of them. And how many construction workers you think are choirboys? I have personally worked with a convicted murderer, a rapist, former armed felons. More than half of the guys I've known had at least one assault-and-battery on their record. You can sit there thinking I'm some kind of morally reprehensible chickenshit, but I'm no dummy. I knew what my odds were of being shot or knifed by Randall one day.

So I was—understandably—drinking my first brewski of the morning when Randall spoke to me: so, when were we going to find a girl for me? I nearly choked; all the cold beer in the world wouldn't wash away what he said.

That's what I needed, he continued, a girl of my own. Personal pussy. Of course I'd need his help in catching one and training her right.

Come on, Randall, I tried to reason with him. I couldn't do what he'd done. I didn't even have a place to stay, let alone a house or any privacy.

That's OK, you got me. Who'dya think that new box is for, buddy, he asked, almost enthusiastic now.

That's for me? I blanched.

We'll find you a pretty one to keep in it, he said.

We took to eating our lunch—now just beer and cigarettes for me; what the hell, I was hoping they'd fire me for being drunk—near a park or at a crowded deli, and Randall would spend the entire time pointing out girls for my attention, regardless of whether I answered him or not. I didn't completely lose it on him, because I knew even Randall was not crazy enough to try to kidnap someone in the middle of the city during the day.

He didn't let me out of his sight much. I guess he didn't think I was completely trustworthy with his secret, not yet. Some nights he didn't even ask if I wanted to come up to his house, he just drove us straight there. Without fail, he brought me home with him on the weekends. I'd feel miserable until he got me stoned and drunk and laid.

As we fell into this routine, I started to convince myself that Randall wasn't serious about us taking this last step. He saw my heart wasn't in it. Maybe all he'd been looking for, I figured, was a friend. Someone to share his awful secret with. Someone to unburden himself to, so he wouldn't feel like a monster, just a guy with no social skills, a low tolerance for frustration, and a bad attitude toward women. Apparently he saw something in me that made him think I'd understand, or he thought I was such a loser that even with his shortcomings, even after his confession, he'd still feel superior to me.

If all that sounds like the desperate rationalizing of a chemically impaired mind, I'll go you one even further. I started thinking about Gina, locked in her box, in the basement. You might ask how could I not go to the police, rescue someone in that horrible situation? Hey, I told myself: it's been four years. If the girl really wanted to get away from Randall, wouldn't she have done it by now? Hell, they slept together every night, and he was usually drunk or passed out. She couldn't have used the phone in the kitchen to call the cops? Sneak out of the house under the cover of Randall's snores?

Yeah, I know. How can I look myself in the mirror. You might say that isn't a problem for me anymore.

Things didn't get better with Randall, they got worse. He started taking me to the state park, late, on the weekends. I have to admit, he was the real deal when it came to the mountain man stuff, because he could follow trails in the dark, sneak up on people in their tents without being noticed. He could probably start a campfire with two sticks and skin a squirrel, like some sadistic Daniel Boone. We even watched one couple in a sixty-nine, loving on each other. Randall got kind of mesmerized watching the girl give head. That's when I started to wonder if he wasn't into this for his own reasons. You know, that he might've been looking for a little variety. Randall thought we should bust in, carry her off, leave the guy behind all tied up. He thought I was crazy to pass on his idea.

It went on like this for two more weekends. We'd tromp through the campsites, spying on campers, Randall making suggestions, me making up excuses. Too old, too young, too fat, too ugly. I know how it sounds, but I didn't mean any of it. I was trying to spare them.

Randall was getting frustrated, but I managed to keep him at bay. Until the day we stumbled across *her*. I tried to come up with an excuse, but everything I thought of would sound like a lie. She was perfect, by Randall's standards: young, small, and delicate-looking, platinum-blonde hair pinned to the top of her head, kind of sloppily, I thought. Randall thought it was cute.

"That's it. She's the one," Randall hissed to me. At his feet were our supplies: duct tape, a length of clothesline, a set of handcuffs, a plumber's wrench—instantaneous anesthesia, if needed.

Her boyfriend had left for some reason, got in their beat-up little Jetta, and drove away. She wasn't crying, so I assumed it wasn't because of a fight. Probably went off to get some beer or something. It didn't matter; he'd be back. We couldn't debate this all night.

Thing is, I knew from the moment we started that I couldn't go through with it. Yet I let it get to this point, crouching like a madman in the woods, following Randall in the dark, now having to explain to him that I was going to let him down. Sorry dude, I'm not going to be your partner in completely-insanely-evil-crime. I thought I was going to have a fucking heart attack, I couldn't speak to him.

What the fuck, man, was all he managed to get out. I think he knew I was bailing on him just by looking at me. I had to turn away from his bulging eyes, fierce frown, tendons starting to rise on his neck like the tension cable on a clear-span bridge. I started to stand up, with every intention of walking away, thinking it was over, but I never made it to my feet.

It's probably obvious, but I will say it anyway: when you get whacked on the back of the head with a two-pound plumber's wrench, your skull is going to hurt when you wake up. *If* you wake up—I guess I should've considered myself lucky to be alive. I'm sure the skull was cracked somewhere, judging from all that matted blood in my hair. He decided to take his chances that I might die, Randall did, when he tied me up and threw me in the second box—the box I'd helped make with my own hands—and left me in the cellar.

He'd done it, he explained—sitting on top of the box when I came to God knows how much later—because I'd obviously abdicated my manhood. He'd respected me at first, suspected that I was simpatico with his completely whacked-out way of thinking because I was manly and all, climbing scaffolding, going to titty bars with him at lunch. I had revealed my gutless self to him, however. Only a dickless wuss would've refused what he was offering. It was no wonder I was such a loser. I wasn't a man and I didn't deserve to be treated like one.

No one would miss me—a fact he pointed out, as though it wasn't obvious enough. He'd tell them at work that I just up and left. I was a drifter, wasn't I? The brother of the friend would be relieved that I wasn't taking up his couch anymore. The company would happily reabsorb any pay they owed me. That would be the end of that.

The reason I was naked—he went on to explain, the lid creaking as he shifted his weight—was to make it easier to clean up after me. It would take a while for me to learn to control my bodily emissions during those long stretches in the box without access to a bedpan. Just like an animal. Besides, it was good for me to wallow in my own filth, remind me who was in charge, who would make every decision for me for the rest of my life—however long or short that would be.

It would be necessary to break me down, for me to revert back to the animal state. That way I could concentrate on the few rules that now applied and never forget them. He was the man, the master. There'd be no more lap time for me with Gina, needless to say. There'd be no food, either, unless I was docile. He'd have to starve me at first, anyway, to make me sufficiently weak for him to handle. That meant, oh, five or six straight days in the box. He went on and on, though he didn't expect me to answer, with the duct tape over my mouth.

I've almost gotten used to it now. At first I didn't know which was worse, being locked in the coffin for ten, twelve hours at a stretch, or knowing what would happen when the lid was opened. I rarely shit or piss on myself anymore, now that I've learned to pace myself on the water bottle. Randall leaves my hands cuffed in front instead of behind my back like he did in the beginning. No more duct tape over the mouth (it did pretty much rip out my mustache) but even though it's the two of us in the basement, Gina and I don't talk much to each other, as you can imagine.

I'd guess it's been about three months now. On those rare occasions when he lets me on the upper level of the house, I'm amazed at how hard it is just to climb those stairs. I can't even sit up, I have to lie on my side and watch him do his thing with Gina, as I wait for what comes next. But usually he keeps me downstairs and I only get out of the box to get hosed down, or beaten with an old canoe paddle or whatever weird shit he manages to think up while he's at work that day.

Mostly I spend my time wondering if there had ever been friendship between us, or if he had planned it to turn out this way all along. I do think he wanted a second slave all along, whether it was under the pretense of finding and training someone for me or whether he'd figured it was time to see if he could exercise mastery over another man, if he secretly wanted to do this stuff to a guy—I haven't figured that part out yet. I don't know that even he has the answer.

Randall has taken to bringing his hunting rifle with him when he comes to visit me. Maybe it's because I'm finally starting to heal and put some weight back on, maybe there's something about me that's giving Randall pause. Or it might be that he's already starting to have second thoughts. Anyway, it's a clear signal to me that I need to come up with a plan. Randall's not going to keep me around for years, like Gina. My days are numbered. Luckily, that's the one thing I have time for, in my current predicament: thinking. Long hours to lie almost absolutely still, and think. I've never been a really crafty guy, a deep thinker, but it seems to come a little easier to me now that I'm not drinking and smoking. I have to believe I'll be able to think my way out of this. It's like I said: sometimes these partnerships come down to mutual hate and loathing. It's me versus Randall.

Wendi Kaufman

Adulterer's Delight

WENDI KAUFMAN holds an MFA in English/fiction writing from George Mason University. Her fiction has appeared in various literary journals and magazines, including the *New Yorker*, *Fiction*, *New York Stories*, and *Other Voices*. She is responsible for the care and feeding of the Happy Booker (www.thehappybooker.blogs.com), a literary blog with a focus on D.C. writers and events. She has been a recipient of a fellowship from the Virginia Commission for the Arts, the winner of a Mary Roberts Rhinehart award for short fiction, and a Breadloaf Writer's Conference Scholar in Fiction. She is a frequent contributor to the *Washington Post*.

So, let me get this straight," my sister Stephanie said when I tried to explain my no-strings-attached arrangement with my lover, Sam. "You've become the *other* other woman?" We were sitting at Captain Pete's Crab Shack, empty orange carcasses piled up between us.

"The intern's on the way out," I explained. "She's headed back to school, and he's moving back into his house, into the *guest room*." But even I couldn't fight the obviousness of the situation. "Yeah," I said, conceding. "Consider it the other woman, once removed."

Stephanie rolled her eyes. At thirty-three, she is the expert on men. She has a track record that's hard to beat, a list of ex-lovers that staggers the mind. This is because of the way she was raised, she had the inside scoop at a crucial time in her life and claims to know how men really think—which, she assures me, is quite different from the way women think.

I, on the other hand, am a dismal failure, dating married men and confirmed singles, falling in love at the first whiff of unavailability: If you're married, holding a torch for someone else, or about to move out of town, here's my number, please call.

"Remember, what Sam doesn't know, can't hurt him," Stephanie said, poking at me with a crab leg. "Hurt him now. While you still have the opportunity."

This is the type of wisdom she dispenses, the truth of the ages, handed down from woman to woman, in an unbroken chain.

"You get what you ask for, Marie," she warned. Meaning, I suppose, that if I asked for nothing, that was exactly what I was going to get. Nothing.

"And that will be your future," she said. "Look closely."

The last time I saw my future, he was busy stuffing his ass into his pants, hopping on one foot searching for his other shoe.

"Out-of-town client," he said. "Delayed flight."

"You should have called her, Sam, left a message. She's not an idiot."

"Nope. I was busy working. By the time they arrived and the dinner meeting was over, it really was too late to call. How does that sound?"

"Like bullshit," I said. "Come back to bed for a few minutes."

"You're not a lot of help," he said, as he unbuttoned his shirt.

The definition of karma is helping your lover come up with a good alibi for his wife about his late-night whereabouts and then have that same excuse used on you later. That's karma. But I wasn't thinking about karma when I met Sam. At the time, he was newly separated from his wife, sleeping on a couch in his office, and in the process of ending an affair with an intern from work, a roller coaster of a summer fling that had left him tired and emotionally wrung out. "I'm not as young as I used to be, Marie," he said. He was forty-eight. "I'm not cut out for that kind of double life."

He told me all this in a confessional tone over drinks, while the intern was still in the picture, though fading on the horizon, and when he was thinking of moving back into his house because he missed living someplace with a permanent address, firm support mattress, and a hot shower. There was something vulnerable in the way he told me his story, a healthy mix of humor, shame, and ego. I was instantly attracted. I was twenty-six, looking for a quiet place to lay my head. Nothing serious, we both agreed.

It's two in the morning when I arrive at Stephanie's front door. She doesn't seem surprised to see me. She leads me through the house to the kitchen, turns on the lights, and takes out two chilled glasses from the fridge. Her dark hair is piled high on her head, her movements are brisk and efficient.

"You want me to help you—is that why you're here?" she asks, cutting lengthwise into a lime, preparing one of her legendary gin and tonics.

"Lay it on me," I say. "The works." I tell her I want to know it all, how to read the signs and give the signals; I need some basic training when it comes to men.

The last time Stephanie and I lived together as family was over twenty years ago, and it was summer. Even though I was only five, I remember the sounds of that summer: the quiet ushering in of days, the steady rotation of the neighborhood sprinklers, my father sitting alone on our deck listening to a ball game played in a distant city on a tiny radio no bigger than a child's hand.

One evening, sitting outside in the fading summer light, Stephanie laughed out loud at something, her mouth wide open, and she accidentally swallowed a firefly. I watched as she bit into the air, ensnaring it behind her teeth. I laughed then for no reason. I couldn't stop. I laughed while she gagged and gasped and stuck her tongue out and spit into her white T-shirt. She was quiet after that, her eyes wet from coughing. As the night grew dark around us, I saw it for the first time: the slight light, soft and white around the edges, that seeped out from her pores.

I look at my sister now, in jean shorts and a red cropped T-shirt, standing barefoot in her kitchen making gin and tonics, and I am sure her lovers see it. On those nights when everything is still, when they reach out for her in a languid sleep, their fingertips touching the pillow where her head had just been, the light already fading, they must know. She has a glow, an aura that makes other women instinctively reach out and touch their lovers when she passes, a protective gesture to remind them of what is theirs. For even they know: It's not so difficult to have it all, the harder part is to keep it.

"The problem with you, Marie, is that you're a romantic. You believe in happy endings." Stephanie reaches into the freezer for her secret ingredient—ice cubes made with tonic water—and fills the narrow glasses.

"Is that so wrong?" I ask. "Is lesson number one called: Why Marie Is Crazy to Think That Everything Is Going to Work Out All Right?"

"No, it would be called: Common Sense—How Do I Get Some?" She bends beneath the counter for her stock of gin. "You're smart enough to know there's always something that goes beyond 'and they lived happily ever after.' That's never the end of the story."

"What makes you so sure?" I ask.

"What makes you so dense? Look at us, look at our parents."

I pull a stool close to the granite counter and watch Stephanie squeeze the juice from an overripe lime. I think about my mom pining away and my father's string of women. "If you mean we're doomed to repeat the same stupid mistakes as our parents then shoot me now and put me out of my misery."

"It's like at the lake," she says, carefully measuring an even tablespoon of lime juice, her hands steady. "Remember that time when old Mrs. Rowen held her grandkid on her shoulder for hours while he slept? We all laughed when she walked around later with a hand outline on her back, and all the older women just smiled and nodded because they *knew* the deal."

"What deal? You're saying relationships are like tan lines—they're all going to fade over time? That's very deep."

"No. But they do leave marks. We all have them. If you knew how to read them, you might have a clue about where you're headed, or see a little bit further down the road."

I press the cool glass against my cheek. Only my sister would think she has x-ray vision, capable of reading invisible scars that build up, crisscrossing and obscuring the heart. I empty my glass and hold it out for a refill. "I am obviously not drunk enough for this conversation."

When Stephanie was twelve and I was five, she went to live with my father, a separation that was not as seamless as it sounds. That was the summer I learned that people's lives are seldom as they appear, there is a single moment in every day when things can turn around, a split second when decisions are made that can change the course of a life, the outcome of a marriage. It was in a moment like that when my father walked out the door, taking my sister with him.

There are only two things I remember from the night my father left: the careful way he placed Stephanie's duffle bag into the trunk of the car, like tucking in a sleeping child, and the bright red of the taillights as the car pulled away. My mother swears to this day that she never saw it coming. After the dust settled and the lawyers were called off, that's pretty much how things played out, the battle lines drawn: I stayed with Mom, while Stephanie moved into an apartment with Dad in the city.

At the time I blamed the house. There was a deep crack at the base of the front concrete steps, a dark spidery fissure that I imagined traveled all the way through our house, the force and pressure of it always there, threatening to sever us in half. After my parents split I wanted to go to school to study the weight and science of stone, to learn how to pour an impenetrable foundation, to build a stronger dwelling that would hold us all together.

After our house divided, Stephanie and I would meet at rest stops on the New York State Thruway; my parents would park near each other and Stephanie and I would run out and switch cars—she would go with my mom for the weekend, I would go with my father—waving at each other as we passed. The rest stops were always the same cold concrete buildings with imposing vending machines that offered stale-looking food and scalding hot beverages dispensed in Styrofoam cups. The only interesting thing was in the women's bathroom: a shiny glass display case that took up half a wall, housing sewing kits, comb and brush sets, bobby pins and hairnets, pink plastic curlers, and maxi pads in discrete white boxes with flowers on them. All the secrets of womanhood, revealed.

Stephanie once bought two small plastic Scottie dogs from the case, toys for desperate mothers looking for something to quiet and entertain the kids on those endless car rides between there and somewhere else. One was black, the other white, and they were glued to tiny magnets. Our parents were standing under a streetlamp in a darkened parking lot, having a rare conversation. "Watch this," Stephanie said, as she flipped over a greasy french fry container she'd fished from the trash. She placed one dog on top of the red-checkered box, the other below. The dog on top danced across the box by itself, spinning in easy circles and figure eights.

"How'd you do that?" I asked, reaching for the tiny dog. "Is it magic?"

"The power of opposites," she said, as if it explained everything. She gave me one of the dogs and placed the other in her pocket, and we watched in silence as our parents finished their conversation in the small circle glow of light.

A few years later Stephanie decided she was too old to spend every other weekend with my mother, preferring to stay in the city with her friends or boyfriends, and then she went off to school. I guess I also became too old around the same time because once she stopped coming, my parents stopped meeting and I rarely saw her or my father at all.

"I just need to know some simple things," I say. "Can they be trained?"

Stephanie shrugs and adds a second piece of lime to her drink. "You mean things like sit and down boy?"

"Sure," I say. "And don't forget 'Stay.' That's always an important one."

"Well, I can work with you on Sit—and Down Boy is especially useful—but Stay is a harder call; Stay is even beyond my power."

The list of my sister's ex-lovers is legendary. There was Sir Paws-a-Lot, the White Russian, Quick Draw McGraw, the King of Pop, and good old Larry and Harry—a guy who insisted on calling his penis by name, together they were a dynamic duo, though now I can't remember which was which, and that's just to name a few. She shed each of these men easily, moving on to the next, leaving behind a trail of unreturned phone calls, broken dates, and broken hearts, the detritus of relationships that have run their course.

"Tell me how you left it with Sam," she says. "Was it ugly?"

Only if you define ugly as the sound of keys grabbed quickly off the hall table; the lonely gait of a lover who favors his right leg when he trudges down the stairs; the hollow echo after the heavy front door has swung shut for the last time. But how do I explain this to Stephanie? Men don't leave her.

"Hand signals," I say. "Or the right look, or maybe even an invisible fence, the kind that sends out those tiny shock waves to discourage straying."

"You need to go to bed," she says. "We can talk about this in the morning."

"There's nothing like screwing up your life to make you feel like a grown-up," I say.

"That's why they call it adultery—emphasis on *adult,*" she says. "Go to sleep."

"My next boyfriend is going to enjoy a good spanking," I say this as if I am imparting great wisdom.

"I didn't know you were into that."

"I'm not. It's just that a rolled-up newspaper across the bridge of the nose is not having the desired effect."

"I'll keep it in mind," she says.

"Never trust a man who tells you how much he loves his wife," I say. "That's the only advice I would give, if anyone around here were asking me. One minute they're talking about their homes and their cars, lulling you into a false sense of security, the next minute their hands are between your legs and you're kissing any hope of rational thought goodbye."

A dull headache and the sickening acrid taste of lime are clear reminders of last night's conversation. I call Sam at the office and leave another message. He almost said he loved me once, letting it slip the last time we were in bed.

"What was that?" I'd asked. "Can you repeat that? I'm hard of hearing."

"Nothing," he said quickly, pulling the blanket up over my bare shoulder, tucking me in. "There are just things I love about you, that's all."

"Things?" I asked, now interested, more awake. In these moments the bed became our life raft; we were adrift, a swirling sea of darkness around us.

"Sure, I could reel off at least five things from the top of my head," he said.

Time spent with Sam had a stolen quality about it, existing only in the intersection of two very busy and different lives. Lying close together, toes touching, we carved out a tiny new world for two. "I don't know if that's such a good idea," I said.

"Why? Don't you think I can?" His voice had the tone of someone responding to a challenge. "I could name five good things right here and now. Besides, who doesn't want to hear something good?"

"We probably shouldn't get into this now." I rolled over, moving close to him.

"Into what?" He put his arm around my shoulder. "I'm not trying to get into anything here."

"You know how it goes," I said. "Once you make a list of all the good things, then you automatically start thinking about all the bad things, that's how things like this work."

Sam didn't understand; he just wanted to name his five good things, right there on the spot. "What are you talking about? What are *things like this*?"

"It's human nature," I said, trying to explain. "You can't fight it. You start with the good things and then WHAM! you go right to the bad stuff; that's how it goes."

I could tell Sam was annoyed by the way he pulled over his share of the covers. He turned to face me and told me he was going to recite his list, whether I wanted to hear it or not. He said he loved that I was dependable, that I would be there when he called, that I had the most expressive eyes he had ever seen, and that he loved the way I walked, long even strides that he could watch forever.

"What do you think about that?" he said, pleased with himself, happy to prove he wasn't heading anywhere else: he could just name good things and brave the consequences, thumbing his nose at human nature.

His smile faded when I told him that he had only listed four things, and the worst part was that he made me sound like a goddamn golden retriever. "All you left out was loyal."

I reached over and lit a cigarette. I was usually pretty careful about smoking or not wearing heavy perfume around him, not wanting to send him home to his wife smelling like me—though I could always still smell him, on my clothes, my skin, long after we were apart.

"Four things." I said, holding out four fingers. "All of which made me sound like man's best friend."

He seemed shocked that I could criticize his list. "You think it's so easy? I'd like to see you try. Let's hear your list."

I didn't want to try and I could tell by the look on his face that he was hurt. I tried to explain to him that my mind didn't work that way, that I didn't think about things in terms of lists. I moved in a little closer to him and wrapped my legs around his. "Maybe we could practice some nonverbal communication," I whispered in his ear.

"Not even one good thing?" He untangled himself and got out of bed. I watched as he ran his foot along the edge of the futon mattress, trying to retrieve a discarded sock. "You can't even think of one good goddamned thing."

His shadow flickered behind him as he stood in front of the desk lamp, making him appear larger than life and blurry around the edges. He reached for his clothes, shapes disappearing into the dark wall. It was late, he said, he had to go. A heavy feeling settled in around my chest, a cold breeze, a sea change. I knew then about the other list, the one that would form and begin to grow as he walked away from my apartment into the cold night, gaining momentum with every step.

"Salsa is not a breakfast food," I tell Stephanie, as I take out a pitcher of cold water from the fridge.

"It is when it has mango in it," she says. "Try some."

The thought of food makes my stomach lurch. I pick up the phone and dial home, checking messages. Nothing. "Tell me something," I say, hanging up the phone. "How do you keep from being the person who loves more?"

Stephanie is sitting at the kitchen table, legs crossed underneath her, flipping through the paper. The sunlight, far too bright and optimistic, leaks in around her. "Love isn't equal," she says, putting down the paper. "There is always one person who feels more, or needs more of something—security, reassurance, acceptance, whatever."

I pour water into my glass, take a moment to respond. "Do you think that was Mom's problem—do you think that's why she never realized Dad was going to leave?"

"Love had officially left the building," she says. "He was already gone."

There is a strong aroma of coffee in the room, a rich dark brew courtesy of Stephanie's French press that reminds me of my father. He was a committed coffee drinker, grinding his own beans, ordering special imported blends. His gleaming silver coffeepot sat on the counter after he left, unused, until it was replaced by an electric juicer and then later by a fat orange Crockpot. The smell of coffee catches in the back of my throat, an earthy smell that somehow reminds me of everything I'd lost.

"Sam has great hands," I say. "I loved the feel of them against my skin."

"How's the headache?" Stephanie gets up from the table and pulls open a cabinet drawer. "Are we talking simple pain relief, or do you need something with a little bit more kick?" She takes out three bottles of pills and lines them up along the counter. I watch as she opens the middle bottle, puts two tablets on her tongue, and tilts her chin to the ceiling, her neck pale and slender.

"And teeth, white but not perfectly straight. He has this great crooked smile." I am not sure at this point that it's even Sam that I'm missing—maybe it's the ways of men, or the feel of a man in the house, something I was too young to remember fully. Instead I am left with the blurry ragged edges encircling the hole in my life where my father once lived.

"You're obsessing," she says. "I hope you haven't told Sam any of this stuff. It's better to hold a little something back, keep him guessing. Don't tell him all the good stuff, it's better to have the upper hand."

She is standing by the sink, rinsing out her glass. The windows above the sink are bright squares of light. Small particles of dust swim by. Stephanie is wearing only a long white T-shirt that skims the tops of her thighs. I can see the outline of her body in the sunlight, watch it bend and move with an easy grace, Diana the huntress. I imagine the blue-veined wonder of her heart, whole and unblemished, beating out a simple pattern in a steady hush-hush rhythm. My head feels light, like it could float away, carried off like ash in the wind. "I couldn't even tell him one good thing," I say. "He asked but I didn't say a word."

"Good," she says. "That's a very good start."

Susan Land

The Somewhat Point

SUSAN LAND's fiction has appeared in many journals, including *Other Voices*, the *Florida Review*, the *Missouri Review*, the *Literary Review*, *Confrontation*, the *Washington Review*, and *So to Speak*. She has an MA from the Johns Hopkins Writing Seminars and was a Stegner Fellow at Stanford. "The Somewhat Point" is included in a collection of linked stories called "Uncommon Side Effects." She teaches at the Writer's Center in Bethesda, Maryland.

Charlotte asked the father, "Are you sad?"

The father asked, "Why do you ask?"

"To get an A."

Charlotte watched the father's reflection in the not-on TV screen. He nodded his head and his reflection face made a tall oval. He asked, "Do you get an A if I'm sad?"

"I get an A for following directions. 'Part 1: Study someone's face and guess his or her emotion. Part 2: Ask if you guessed correctly.'" Charlotte stood on her toes.

"You guessed correctly, Charlotte. I am somewhat sad. How did you know?"

"Your face does not move too much. It is easy to understand."

The father said, "I'm glad to see you're taking all those special lessons of yours so seriously."

Charlotte wobbled on her toes, but righted herself. Because of perspective, the father's fat chair looked too far away to seat him—unless he had a giant cartoon elephant butt. Charlotte asked, "Is 'somewhat sad' between the most and the least?"

"Somewhere between. Yes."

Charlotte wished she could climb on top of the television. It was the biggest television in the house. It was built into a piece of furniture with wooden legs and a square wooden top like a table top. *Climbing on furniture is rude unless there is an emergency and you have to escape.* Charlotte made her feet rest on the ground. Charlotte drew a graph in the Social Skills section of her notebook, with Least at zero and Most at one hundred. "Please write a mark to show me the somewhat point."

The father leaned forward with his round head and fat neck. He had an open oval of baldness. Some doctors on commercials put hair in bald places, but the father was not that kind of doctor.

"Thank you." The father was twenty-five percent sad. "'Part 3: Ask another question.' Are you approximately twenty-five percent sad because Baby Joshua does not live here anymore?"

"Yes. I miss my grandson. I liked having him here, Charlotte. I loved having him here. You guessed the right reason."

"I get an A even if I guess the wrong reason. And I get extra credit for being polite."

"You're being very polite."

Charlotte said, "Baby Joshua was here for fifty-three days and fifty-two nights. He has been gone for eight days."

"How about a hug for your old man?"

"What old man?"

"Me."

"You are fifty-seven, a prime number age. The oldest man in *The Guinness Book of World Records* was born in 1889."

"And you are ten, if I'm not mistaken."

"Three times three plus one."

"You still don't like to hug anyone but your mother, do you?"

"Hugging is not part of the assignment."

"Well, at least you have good taste. I like to hug your mother, too."

"Married people like to hug each other."

"That's the general idea."

"But you do not have to be married to someone to hug that person." Charlotte hugged her notebook, leaned over and pressed her forehead against her knees. Then she stood up tall and hopped one time. She said, "Ms. Segal used to be married to you."

"That's right. She's Joshua's grandmother and I'm his grandfather because we used to be married."

"Ms. Segal used to come to our house on Wednesdays and Fridays at three o'clock to visit Baby Joshua."

"You like Ms. Segal, don't you, Charlotte?"

"Yes. Did you used to like to hug Ms. Segal?"

"Yes, but we're divorced. Now I like to hug your mother."

"I never see Mommy hug you."

Charlotte balanced her notebook back on her hair/scalp/skull/neck and good-posture-climbed up the basement steps. On the landing, she stopped and stood on one foot, making a triangle by putting the bottom of the other foot against the side of the standing knee. She focused on the basement doorknob so she would not wobble and the notebook would not fall. She listened. The mother and Charlotte's sister had voices with many variations. Charlotte untriangled her legs, unnotebooked her head, and followed the voices down the hall past the bathroom that didn't have a tub. Charlotte's mother was writing something on the ballerina calendar next to the phone and Charlotte's sister Ava was eating rice cakes.

The mother said, "It has to be real satin and it has to be cut just so."

Ava said, "It has to be fake satin, Mom, and it has to be what the drama club costume designer designs."

"Ava, I know a Chinese seamstress who'll make something exquisite and provocative, but flattering."

"*But* flattering. What's that supposed to mean? That to make a dress flatter a body like mine takes some Oriental sewing genius?"

"Flatter" is always a subset of compliment and sometimes a subset of lie.

The mother said, "But you're the *lead* courtesan, Ava!"

"I certainly am," Ava said, and did something with her hips and head that made her woman parts stick out in different directions.

The mother said, "Cool it, please."

Ava made the big-breath sound. She said, "Mom, I'm fourteen years old, not some doll you can play dress-up with."

Ava had on leotard tights that made her legs look black but not African American and an XXL black shirt with a blue picture of President Clinton playing the saxophone. The mother had on a black shirt that was soft and tight and tucked into her jeans. President Clinton would not fit on the mother's shirt. The mother and Ava had the same color hair, almost black, but Ava's big hair would not fit on the mother's head.

Charlotte went into the kitchen and stood on the chair that she had permission to stand on. "Babies get hugged all the time," Charlotte told the mother. "Because they are so small and they cannot do things for themselves."

Ava said, "Duh."

Charlotte told Ava, "I am ignoring your rude noise."

Ava said, "Sorry. I shouldn't have duh-ed you. It was dumb."

Ava's apology made Charlotte dizzy. Charlotte stared at her mother, to steady herself. Charlotte's mother tilted her head to the right side. Charlotte's mother's hair fell, making an approximate right triangle from the part in her hair, to the edge of her shoulder, to the hinge at the base of her neck.

"Hello, Charlotte. Why are you thinking about babies?" the mother asked.

"Daddy is sad that Baby Joshua does not live here anymore."

"I know he is, Charlotte. But he is still Joshua's grandfather. They'll still get to see each other."

"Ms. Segal used to visit the baby at our house on Wednesdays and Fridays at three o'clock. Ms. Segal used to be Mrs. Now you are Mrs. Mrs. means married. Miss means not married. Ms. means it is no one's business if you are married or not."

"Very good," said the mother. "Charlotte, do you have any ideas for making Daddy less sad?"

Ava said, "He likes old skeletons and skulls."

Charlotte said, "Skulls are part of skeletons. The head part."

Ava said "Sorry" again, but it sounded more like *saw ree*—accent on the second syllable.

Charlotte jumped off the chair, knelt on the slate floor, and sat back on her ankles. Charlotte put her hands behind her and made an arch with her back. Her head fell back. Her hair touched the floor. She stuck her outee belly button in the direction of the ceiling like Baby Joshua's peenie when he got his diaper changed. Her upside-down mouth said, "Mommy, we should make Daddy a doll."

Ava said, "An inflatable life-size sex doll?"

"A baby boy doll like Joshua."

Ava said, "What a stupid idea!" *Mean.*

Charlotte's mother angry-voiced, "Ava!"

Ava said, "Saw ree, Mom."

Charlotte said, "Ava is stupid at geometry!" *Mean.*

Then Charlotte unarched her back and sat in a squat. Charlotte wanted her mother who was also Ava's mother to angry-voice, "Charlotte!" Charlotte wanted to say "Saw ree, Mom," so the meanness would be symmetrical and cancel out.

But the mother said, "Charlotte, you and I will make a pretend baby for you to give to your father. I know a little store that sells baby forms and baby clothes and accessories—"

Ava duh-voiced, "*Baby accessories?*"

"Yes. Pacifiers. Bibs. Even little eyelashes and human-hair wigs and special glue to affix them."

"Where do they get human hair, Mom? Concentration camps?"

"That isn't funny, Ava. Don't you have homework?"

"Nothing I can't put off."

"Well, Charlotte needs to do her eye contact exercises. Charlotte, we can practice presenting presents."

Charlotte said, "Present is a noun and a verb."

"That's right," said the mother. Then the mother stood up and took a white package out of the refrigerator. She unwrapped it. Charlotte saw blood, muscle, fat, bone.

Charlotte asked the mother, "Is that cow's meat?"

"Yes. It's delicious prime rib."

Ava said, "I used to think 'ends meat' was a kind of meat poor people ate, and when they were really poor, they couldn't afford to make end's meat." Ava actress-voiced, "Oh Lordy Lord, we'll have to have cabbage again. End's meat is up to ninety-nine cents a pound."

The mother smiled at Ava. Charlotte got down on hands and knees and crawled to the mother, meowing. The mother sat back down and patted Charlotte's shirt/skin/blood/muscles/spine. The mother asked, "Should we find a doll to dress up like Baby Joshua?"

Charlotte looked down and backwards between her legs to her feet. She purred and adjusted her feet so that each foot was perpendicular to the floor. Then she lifted her head. She said, "Yes. For Daddy. A doll with Baby Joshua hair and eyes and penis."

"Tell you what: Tomorrow while you're at school I'll start shopping around for a porcelain head. Then when you get home and Ava is at rehearsal, we'll pick out accessories." The mother was only-Charlotte's mother when Ava was away at rehearsals. Sometimes Charlotte's mother took naps and Charlotte watched her mother's dreaming-face.

Ava loud-voiced, "Mom, you're making this doll thing way more complicated than you have to."

"Why do you say that?"

"Because Charlotte doesn't notice subtlety, remember?"

"Your father notices subtlety. He's a pathologist."

"So? It's not like you're doing this for *him*."

Charlotte said, "The doll is for Daddy. To make Daddy less sad."

Ava said, "Charlotte, she doesn't deserve to get any credit for making Dad less sad about the baby."

The mother said, "Please do not refer to me as 'she' while I'm sitting right here in plain sight."

Ava said, "Charlotte, she's glad the baby is gone. Excuse me. Mom is glad the baby is gone."

Charlotte said, "I am also glad, Mommy. Baby Joshua was louder than Ava and I am related to Baby Joshua in a way that makes my head tired."

The mother said, "My head gets tired thinking about it, too."

Ava said, "I have an idea: Charlotte, I have a bunch of old baby dolls. We can make one resemble Joshua. Come on, Charlotte. Let's go!"

"Where are we going?"

"To my room."

Charlotte said, "I do not want to stay in Ava's room."

The mother said, "Ava, your room has too much visual stimulation for Charlotte."

Ava said, "Don't worry. We can get everything out of my closet and bring it to your room, Charlotte. There's more space for a project in your room. Are you with me?"

"I am with Ava!" said Charlotte, leaping to her feet.

"Ta-ta, Mama," said Ava.

The mother little-voice called, "Let me know if you need any help!"

Ava and Charlotte-and-her-notebook skipped down the hall and past the no-tub-bathroom. In a room with pictures of faces on the walls and tapestries of swirls on the ceiling and a mess of clothes and books and papers on the floor, Ava filled a big Gap bag with dolls. She said, "Charlotte, can you take my sewing kit?—over there on my desk—the black shoebox."

Charlotte balanced her notebook back on her hair/scalp/skull/neck to free her hands. She was careful to keep the bottom of the shoebox parallel to the floor under the mess.

Ava said, "Off to your cell."

"Why do you call it a cell?"

"Because it's as bare as a prison cell."

Charlotte opened the door to her cell approximately one hundred and twenty degrees.

Ava spread the dolls on Charlotte's bedspread. *Spread on the bed.*

Charlotte put the shoebox on her desk and aligned her notebook in its place on her shelf. Then she picked up the shoebox again.

Ava said, "Would you please thread a needle with beige thread?"

"I will sit on the floor with the sewing box beside me."

"Great."

"How long should the thread be?"

"Approximately a foot and a half."

"Eighteen inches." Charlotte measured and threaded and thought about the number eighteen, which was the sum of two nines, or two times three squared. She said, "Two equals a couple. Two is the only even prime number. There are seven boys and four girls in my class who are in love with prime numbers. They should marry prime numbers."

"There are like six girls in the drama club who are in love with themselves."

"Do they hug themselves and do the private thing in front of other people?"

Ava said, "Gross. Do people do that in your class?"

"I never do. I am not all closed off like a prime number. When I watch Mommy take naps, I understand her dreaming-face expressions. Mommy does not know I watch her. She assumes I am asleep. There are people in my class who do not understand the word 'assume.'"

"Does she ever look regretful?" asked Ava.

"Regretful is a subset of sad. Do you want to see my sadness diagram?"

"Maybe later, OK?"

Charlotte stood up and counted the naked bad-postured dolls leaned up against the wall behind the bed—six. They had plastic heads and hands and strands of hair and floppy cloth bodies.

"Well?" said Ava.

Charlotte wished Ms. Segal could sit at the desk and see the dolls. Ms. Segal would not say, "Well?" Ms. Segal would wait for Charlotte to want to talk.

"Charlotte, which one should we give to Daddy?"

"They are all girl dolls."

"For now. But we can cut a foot off one doll and make it a peenie and sew it on another doll."

"Yes!" Charlotte hopped.

At twelve hops, Ava said, "Settle down. You have to pick which baby gets the foot amputation."

Charlotte hopped four more times. Sixteen hops in all. Four times four. Or thirty-two, if you count both hopping feet. Two times two times two times two. Charlotte pointed to the doll with the biggest feet for the biggest peenie. "That one! Amputate that one!"

"Good choice for a donor. Now you have to pick the baby who gets the sex change."

Charlotte put the baby with the biggest feet on its belly. All the babies still facing out had blue-like-Joshua's eyes, but only three had eyelids that opened and shut. Charlotte put the two with eyelids that didn't open and shut on their bellies. Of the three babies left, one had better Joshua's-hair curls and one had better Joshua's-hair color. Charlotte turned the baby with neither of the betters on its belly. Then she didn't know how to decide between the two still facing out.

Ava said another "Well?"

Charlotte did not want to hear Ava's voice. Ava's voice had too much expression. Charlotte wanted Ava to go away. Charlotte wanted to clear the babies off her bed and lie on her belly and read about record-long beards and fingernails and toenails and do the private thing.

Ava loud-voiced, "Charlotte! Earth to Charlotte! I say we use this one here." Ava picked up the straight-haired. "It's the best one for Joshua."

Charlotte said, "But the hair is too straight."

"I can make it curl with gel."

Charlotte noticed that her right pointer finger hurt. Charlotte saw that she had made teeth marks between two knuckles.

Ava loud-voiced, "Are you ready for the operation? Are you ready?"

Charlotte said, "I want to amputate the foot. I know how to be careful like a surgeon."

"But it might take a while to cut all the way through."

Charlotte said, "The doll has no bones."

"OK. Cut through the leg at the middle of the calf. I need an extra inch or so for sewing."

Ava gave Charlotte the grown-up scissors. The foot came off with three snips. Charlotte said, "That was not hard."

Ava put out her hand, palm up, not a handshake hand, not a high-five hand. She said, "Give me the foot, please."

Charlotte put it in Ava's palm-up hand. Ava folded the toe area into a conehead and sewed. Charlotte hopped. Ava loud-voiced, "Charlotte, you're shaking the room! You're making it harder to sew!"

Charlotte stopped. Charlotte said, "Do you want me to show you my regret-subset-of-superset-sad diagram?"

"No thanks. Don't need it. Superset: Be sad about having no boyfriend. Think you love some guy, hook up with him, and find out he doesn't like the way you kiss. Regret that you kissed him and you let him feel you. Subset: Regret about a kiss and a feel."

Charlotte said, "The baby needs a diaper. I know where there is one. In the bathroom that doesn't have a tub!"

"Good. Go get it. By the time you're back, he'll be ready."

Charlotte ran down the steps two at a time. Two times seven equals fourteen. She found the diaper. She ran up the steps three at a time. Three does not divide into fourteen without a remainder. Three went into fourteen four times, remainder two. Charlotte was not afraid of remainders unless they were repeating decimals. Two was a counting number. Counting-number remainders stayed apart but were still unscary parts of the whole. Like Joshua's mother was part of the blended family even though she and Joshua's father never got married. When they made Joshua they were a couple—which is two but singular and prime.

Ava loud-voiced, "Here he is!"

The *she* was *he*. Charlotte touched the peenie tip and said, "The formula for the surface area of a cone has pi. Pi is an irrational number." Charlotte touched the cylinder and said, "The formula for a cylinder has pi twice."

Ava put the diaper on the bed and the boy-doll baby butt on the diaper. Ava taped the diaper. Ava pretended to tickle the belly. Then Ava said, "Hold his head still, so I can work on the hair." Charlotte held the head still and Ava rubbed clear gel on the doll's hair. Ava shaped the hair into little O's. Then Ava showed Charlotte her vertical palm and loud-voiced, "High-five!"

They slapped, but Charlotte felt dizzy and sat on the bed and accidentally bumped the donor baby and donor-baby stuffing spilled out of the cut leg onto Charlotte's bedspread. Charlotte jumped up, more dizzy. Charlotte wanted her mother but did not want to leave Ava and the spilling doll in her bedroom. Charlotte stood in the corner and said, "Ava, sew up the donor doll. PleaseAvapleaseAvapleaseAva. And do not breathe a loud breath."

"It's all right, Charlotte. It's all right."

Ava sewed and Ava did not do a loud breath and Charlotte quiet-voiced, "ThankyouAvathankyouAvathankyouAva."

Ava gave Charlotte the Joshua baby and said, "Go give Daddy the doll. I want to make curls on my own head!"

Ava ran out of the *cell with the gel.*

Charlotte made the dolls on her bed parallel. Then she went into the hall and down the stairs one at a time and past the no-tub bathroom and down to the basement, twenty-eight stairs in all. The father was still in his chair, watching a tennis game. He looked at Charlotte and turned the television OFF all the way. Sometimes he made it quieter but not OFF and Charlotte had to not look at it. Now she could look at it and see the not-on screen and the father in elephant-butt-chair perspective.

The father said, "To what do I owe the honor? Another assignment?"

Charlotte gave the doll to the father. Charlotte said, "It looks like Baby Joshua. You can hug it."

"Well, well, well." He sat the baby on his lap, facing the television. "Thank you, Charlotte."

Charlotte asked, "Do you want Ms. Segal to visit the baby doll? Ms. Segal visited Baby Joshua on Wednesday and Friday afternoons at three o'clock when Baby Joshua's mommy and my mommy went to do errands."

"You like Ms. Segal very much, don't you, Charlotte?"

"Yes."

"Good. Very good. Let's ask Mommy to come down and meet the baby."

"I will go get her. It is rude to yell up the stairs."

"Wait. I'll call her on the phone. She has a special line just for your specialists, did you know that?"

"You are not my specialist."

"But I know the number. I only use it for special times and this is a special time because you gave me the Joshua doll and because we are having a long conversation."

"Call Mommy!"

"I will. In just a minute. First, I want to ask you an important question. Charlotte, do you like Ms. Segal enough to let her stay in the house and take care of you for a week?"

"For seven nights and seven days?"

"Actually, six nights and six days."

"Where would she sleep?"

"I think she would sleep in the guest suite. You could also sleep in the guest suite, if you like."

"I like to sleep in my own room with my own *Guinness Book of World Records.*"

"Then you would sleep in your own room. Is that all right?"

"Yes. That is all right."

"That's great, Charlotte."

The father did not have the sad face.

Charlotte said, "Repeating decimals never sleep."

The father called the mother. Charlotte faced the stairs. Charlotte stood on her toes and made propellers with her arms. Charlotte imagined repeating decimals out in space, carried along parallel lines. Point three-three repeating and point six-six repeating would never meet, even though they are related by denominator. Ms. Segal and Charlotte were related by divorce.

The mother stopped on the number two-times-two step from the bottom. Because of perspective, the mother's feet looked too big and her hair/scalp/skull looked too small. The mother's too small mouth said, "Charlotte, are you all right?"

"Yes." Forward arm circle.

"Please stop flapping about. It is most distracting."

Reverse to be even. Charlotte stopped. The mother sat in the rocking chair that used to be in the nursery when the real Baby Joshua lived in the nursery and Ms. Segal visited on Wednesdays and Fridays at three o'clock. The mother did not rock. The father stood up and introduced the baby to the mother. "Would you like to hold him, Julia?"

"Thank you, but I don't think so. He seems so contented with you, Henry."

"He has a peenie," said Charlotte. Charlotte ran up four steps. Charlotte and the mother and the father and the baby equaled four. *Four divided by two equals two. Two equals a couple. A couple equals one. A couple of couples equals one.* Charlotte jumped down. Charlotte did a somersault and stayed in a ball on the carpet.

The father said, "Charlotte noticed that I was sad, Julia. She's actually starting to have empathy."

"Empathy?" gel-curled Ava loud-voiced from step number seven. "I'll bet Charlotte just wants an A."

Ava plus the mother plus the father plus the baby equals four plus Charlotte equals five. Ava walked down the stairs and stood with her toes touching Charlotte's toes. Charlotte angled her feet to be contiguous with Ava's feet. Ava asked, "Charlotte, why do you always have to get A's?"

"Because I do not want to be trapped between two letters."

"You could get F's."

The mother angry-voiced, "Charlotte is much too smart to get F's. And Charlotte, I would give your doll assignment an A-plus."

Charlotte said, "Making a doll was not part of the assignment. The doll was my own idea."

The mother said, "Really? That's wonderful. That's empathy. Henry, I can hardly believe it. All the special lessons and exercises are finally paying off."

The father said, "You are beaming, Mrs. Segal."

The mother said, "As well I deserve to beam."

"You beam in a lovely way."

The mother said, "And I shall beam at Charlotte's college graduation, and when she gets her Ph.D., and even at her wedding!"

Charlotte said, "Ava could get a boyfriend and have a baby."

The mother said, "No, no, no, Charlotte. Ava isn't married."

Ava did a loud breath.

Charlotte got up on her knees and said, "To have a baby you do not have to be married. And if you are married you do not have to stay married. You can go from being a Mrs. to being a Ms. to being a Mrs. again. Daddy could marry Ms. Segal again and Mommy could go from Mrs. to Ms."

The father said, "No way."

The mother stood up and moved closer to the father's chair. The mother sat on the armrest of the father's chair. *The armrest rests a butt!* The father said, "Julia, I got a great deal on two first-class tickets to Bermuda. I've already put in for the week off. Ava will be at that drama camp. Evelyn's offered to stay with Charlotte. She's perfect. She specializes in kids like Charlotte—"

"But—"

"Julia, she says she's never been interested in any girl the way she's interested in Charlotte."

"Evelyn would stay in this house?"

"In the guest suite. She thinks it's conducive to writing poetry. She used to be a poet."

"She'll write poems about Charlotte?"

"God, I hope not. Too many words have already tried to explain our Charlotte."

Charlotte rocked backwards and forwards on her shirt/skin/blood/muscles/spine.

The mother said, "Charlotte has Asperger's Syndrome."

The father said, "So you say. First she was autistic. Then she had sensory integration problems. Last week she was doing research on Dr. Asperger, which is unAsperger-ish you said so yourself."

"She's never been away from me, Henry."

Charlotte told the darkness between the knees she hugged to her chest, "Say *Charlotte* not *she*."

The father said, "She's ready to be away from you for six days and six nights."

"How would you know? Have you spoken to her psychologist? Have you even met her psychologist? Would you know any of her specialists if they walked into this basement?"

"I've talked to Evelyn, Julia."

"Evelyn is not part of Charlotte's team."

Charlotte said, "I want Ms. Segal to be on my team. Ms. Segal sat at my desk. She wrote in her notebook. Mommy never sits at my desk. Mommy does not have any notebooks, just a calendar and a message pad by the kitchen phone. Mommy is never still unless she is asleep. Mommy's face is always moving. I can only understand Mommy's face when she is asleep. Ms. Segal sat at my desk and I shut my door to seal in the quiet."

Then Charlotte was tired and Charlotte wanted to hug the mother, but the mother was sitting on the father's leg next to the doll. The mother sat like a floppy doll. Charlotte said, "Mommy is too big to be a doll for Daddy." Charlotte crawled to the fat chair. The mother looked at Charlotte and little-voiced, "Who are you?" Then the mother pressed her nose/forehead/eyelids/against the father's shirt/chest hair/chest/lungs/heart.

Charlotte said to Ava, "Mommy is hiding her sad-dream face."

Ava quiet-voiced, "Charlotte, you should say you're sorry for what you said. You hurt Mommy's feelings."

"Hurt feelings are a subset of sad."

"Charlotte, you are Mommy's whole life."

"No!" Charlotte loud-voiced. Charlotte climbed on the piece-of-furniture television and stood on parallel feet. Charlotte louder-voiced, "If Mommy does not have a life then only Ava and Daddy and I are alive and each one is a third, and a third is thirty-three point three percent forever!"

The father said, "Charlotte, if you're someone's life, it doesn't mean that person is dead!"

Ava said, "It means you're the most important job for Mommy. It's just an expression. Like making ends meet!"

The mother sad-dream-voiced, "Delicious end's meat, with mushrooms and gravy."

Ava said, "And a salad, dressing on the side."

The father asked Charlotte, "Do you know what they're talking about?" The father scratched the open oval of baldness on his head.

Charlotte said, "Zero is an oval. Zero is a whole number but not a natural number."

The father stood up and said, "My pretty little daughter, I wish you would let me help you down and set you gently on the planet."

Charlotte said, "On the carpet/floor/foundation/dirt/outer crust/mantle/molten inner core."

Charlotte balanced on her toes and watched Ava get smaller and smaller—because of perspective—climbing one step at a time. Fourteen steps. Fourteen divided by one equals fourteen, remainder zero.

The father turned to the mother and said, "Speaking of molten inner cores, what about that second honeymoon?"

The mother stood up and moved closer to the father. Charlotte said, "The moon is made of rocks."

The mother looked up at Charlotte and raised her arms. Charlotte kneeled down on the piece-of-furniture television. Charlotte's right hand held the mother's left hand and Charlotte's left hand held the mother's right hand. Charlotte and the mother made a zero-shaped perimeter of hands/wrists/elbows/shoulders and segments of chests. Charlotte's father stared at the subset of universe inside the zero-shape. Charlotte guessed that the father knew that he wasn't in the subset that was only the mother and Charlotte. But Charlotte had done her assignment already, so she did not ask the father, "Are you more or less than somewhat sad?"

E.J. Levy

My Life in Theory

E.J. Levy's short stories have been published in *Paris Review*, *Gettysburg Review*, *Missouri Review*, and elsewhere, and two have been recognized in *Best American Short Stories 2003* and *2004*. Her fiction has won national awards, including a Chicago Literary Award, an AWP Intro Journals Award, a Gesell Award, a Loft-McKnight fellowship, a Pushcart Prize nomination, and honorable mentions in the *Atlantic Monthly*'s Student Writers' Competition. Her nonfiction has appeared in *The Best American Essays 2005*, *Orion*, the *Nation*, and *Hungry Mind Review*, and, in 2001, she was named among Twenty-Five Nonfiction Writers to Watch by *Writer's Digest*. She earned a BA in history from Yale and an MFA from Ohio State University, and is currently an assistant professor of creative writing in the MFA Program at American University.

Philosophers, it would seem, have little to tell us about love; I know, because I am one. Despite the name *philosopher*—lover of wisdom—we are not known for our success in the realm of Eros. Truth is, our greatest minds have been losers when it comes to love. Søren Kierkegaard, for instance, had just one sexual experience in his life, and that a failed one, with a prostitute. Perhaps that's because philosophy seeks a system, and love—as any lover knows—is unsystematic in the extreme. Love's a messer-upper, and philosophers, on the whole, are a tidy bunch—at least I am, or was, until we met.

Kate, my girlfriend, introduced us.

I had been away at a regional APA conference, and for most of the flight home, I had been thinking about making love with Kate, the freckled expanse of her skin. So I was disappointed, when I returned home, to find her going on about a new reporter at the paper, recently transferred from one of those N-states in the West—Nebraska or New Mexico. I could tell from the way she spoke of him that she was a little infatuated, but it didn't worry me.

We liked to tell each other about our little crushes; it kept us on our toes, kept us honest. We had been together several years by then and shared a belief that we wouldn't stray so long as we kept our theoretical dalliances between us. Our revelations were like a *menage à trois* without the social awkwardness, and we always made love afterwards with the urgency of adulterers.

Kate and I had met in a Wittgenstein seminar five years before, where she'd impressed us all with her dry wit, long neck, and beautiful breasts. She is not what most people would call a beautiful woman—her expressions are too difficult, too interesting for that—but she is compelling. Although her mother is American, she grew up in South Africa, before her parents' divorce, and the African sun has left its mark—giving her eyes their squint, her mouth its premature lines. She has short copper hair and green eyes, and could talk any of us under the table. Unlike the rest of us in that seminar who fought hard for intellectual superiority, Kate didn't try to call attention to herself—but she had a way of seeing to the heart of a matter that commanded attention. In a heated debate over the nature of the good, she settled the question quietly with a quote from Adorno: "morality may well appear self-evident to those who feel themselves to be exponents of a class in the ascendant, but that doesn't mean they're right." She dated several of us that term, but I was the only one to last past qualifying exams, and I felt lucky, though luck is not a thing philosophers on the whole take an interest in. Superstition is largely outside our realm of concern. Although we traffic in abstractions, we think ourselves empiricists, skeptics; my peers and I snubbed the mystics among us (the Buberians, as we called them, seemed unrigorous, too sentimental for our taste). We favored Wittgenstein and Nietzsche. We grew up in the eighties, after all.

The night I returned from the APA, as Kate described her new friend, I tried to imagine him, the way one tests a new flavor on the tongue. I tried to see what she saw in him, my interest in him an extension of my interest in her. It was not hard to imagine; she described his face, his voice, his body. "You know the type," she said, with the air of amused and proprietary dismissal that signals a crush, "beauty and the beats—goatee, khakis, the collected work of Bukowski."

I wondered if she wanted to sleep with him. I wondered idly what he'd be like in bed. I'd slept with a few men before—in prep school and as an undergrad; there was something noncommittal in the whole exchange. We were friends, those guys and I; we didn't mistake sex for love. We were after pleasure, biding our time, until we met the right woman and settled down.

⁓

In *Philosophy Made Simple*—or PMS, as my students call it—the philosophy textbook from which I'm required to teach at the local university, love gets no mention in the index. *Remorse* does, as do *tyranny* and the *prime mover unmoved. Rewards* are mentioned, *revenge*, *respect for others*, *paradoxes*, *pain*, *lying*, *heat*, and *happiness. Suicide, socialism, abortion*, and *sexual morality*. But *love* is nowhere to be found. To learn about love, evidently, you have to do your own research.

The majority of people seem content to love by rote, to acquiesce to cant—love is true (or untrue), men are dogs, women are nuts, love is hell or makes the world go round. Most do not need to ask what love is, any more than they question what is the good or the real. They live and love and ask questions later. But I couldn't help but wonder, even as I was happy with Kate, *Is this love? Is this it? In settling down, have we merely settled*?

It occurred to me from time to time that the heart might not be the source of my troubles, but the mind.

Ever since I'd defended my dissertation in the spring, I'd felt a dull dissatisfaction. The examined life no longer seemed worth living. Kate called it postpartum depression. But I wondered if it might be something more.

My colleagues at the university were little comfort. In the grim warren of grad offices my fellow adjuncts assembled like an accusation. This—they seemed to say—is what education leads to. This is the image of the examined life: frail women in cardigans, men with unruly facial hair and glasses. I had heard that one of my colleagues was once a homeless man. Now he had a long red beard and no plans to complete his dissertation. He joked about being unmanned by the microwave, offered me herbal teas.

Times were tough and the administration had shunted together the Philosophy adjuncts with the English lecturers and Comp instructors, and there was a subtle war on among the posters: Virginia Woolf facing off against Nietzsche, Joyce against Adorno. We held in common only our disdain for our subjugated status and for our students' papers: "Marijuana should be legalized," one Comp instructor said, "so that I won't have to read another paper about it."

Kate jokingly referred to this state of affairs as the Pedagogy of the Depressed. It's the reason she left academia. Maybe it's the reason I've stayed. Despair can arrest action: I didn't act; I only thought about it. That is, until I met Kate's new friend, Jake.

Kate introduced us about a week after I returned from the APA conference. We were leaving her office when he came over to say goodnight. He was wearing a peach-colored sweater, something suggested—Kate would later tell me—by a men's magazine to which he subscribed; his hair was blonde, cut in a sloppy shag that seemed meant to say, *I am handsome without trying, I am a free spirit trapped in a day job.* He was taller than me—six foot, I'd guess—with a lanky, cowboy's build. He had, of all things, a goatee.

It was dislike at first sight.

He told me his name and offered me his hand. "Kate has told me a lot about you," he said.

"She speaks well of you," I said, taking my hand back.

He smiled with only half his mouth, as if he were too hip to bother with symmetry. While they talked, I observed his languorous slouch, his half-closed eyes, lids drooping as if he were hypnotized by Kate's presence. I wondered if this routine often worked on women. I wondered what Kate saw in him.

"We should have dinner sometime," he said, his voice mellifluous as a late-night jazz announcer's. "The three of us."

I was relieved when Kate said we had to get going, she was starved, relieved to follow her after a brief flurry of goodbyes out the door.

On the drive home, Kate fumed about her day. When we'd first gotten involved years before, sex had sustained us—we had more sex then than any three couples we knew combined—but over time our bond had become one of mutual indulgence. Sounding board more than sex partner. To be fair, she had a lot to complain about. The new features editor at the paper disliked "girl reporters," so Kate's beat had changed after his arrival. She used to cover environmental stories (illegal sewage dumping, unlawful development, environmental impact statements); lately he'd assigned her coverage of stolen fava beans and cockfights. That week it was the national gay rodeo that was coming to town. For background, Kate wanted to check out a gay, country western bar in St. Paul.

"I've invited Jake to come along," she said. "You don't mind, do you?"

"Why should I mind?" I said, knowing that a question is not an answer.

⁓

The Townhouse Country bar was packed when we arrived a little past nine. At first glance it was hard to tell from any other country western joint, with rough-hewn beams and cross rails enclosing the dance floor, a long wooden bar, and gambling in back. Men and women in cowboy boots, bolos, chaps, and spurs. But look closer and you noticed the rainbow flag pinned up on the far wall of the dance floor and that the predictable paintings of cowboys and Indians were actually beefcake pics of shirtless braves and cattlemen with well-oiled pecs beside a poster of k.d. lang, and those meaty cowboys gracefully two-stepping across the dance floor held other meaty cowboys in their arms.

As we leaned on the bar, waiting to order, a spark plug of a man with a handlebar mustache and ten-gallon hat approached and asked Jake to dance.

"I'm afraid I don't know that step," Jake said with an easy smile.

"He's *straight*," Kate shouted over the music.

"Can't blame a boy for trying," the cowboy winked, tipped his hat, disappeared in the crowd.

Around us a few people laughed in a nice way. And I began to like Jake just a little. His ease in what some might find an uneasy circumstance.

We found a table near the dance floor, a high small round table, the sort of impractical table dance bars favor in order to discourage patrons from staying seated too long. We commandeered three stools and leaned our heads together to be heard over the music.

Jake told us ranching jokes and rodeo tales from the West. He told us that in Salt Lake City they serve a beer called Polygamy Porter, whose label features a naked man embracing seven naked women and the slogan, *Why Have Just One*?

"The thing is," he said, smiling, "They'll only *serve* you *one* beer at a time. It's illegal to have more than one drink per customer on a table."

"Oh, it has a moral," Kate said. "I love an anecdote with a moral."

We laughed, and despite myself, I warmed to him. He had the appeal of the American West, a boastful self-contentment, an optimism and physical vigor that seemed at once decadent and innocent. It seemed to me that he had something like the delight that animals must take in themselves, a simple pleasure in the body, in life, which I had once taken, too.

It turned out that Jake, like Kate, had been getting a Ph.D. when he gave it up for journalism. "I don't believe in knowledge for knowledge's sake," he said. "It has to be applied."

"That's what I tell my students," I said.

"A man after your own heart," Kate said.

"So Kate tells me you're a philosopher," he shouted, when Kate went to get some more drinks.

"I teach philosophy. Just the basics: Platonic Forms, the Poetics, Ethics 101."

"So tell me," he leaned close enough that I could smell his faint cologne. "What exactly was the Greeks' position on sex?" He smiled his half smile.

I felt a charge pass between us, a thrill of desire.

"They had a lot of positions," I said, dismissing the question.

He laughed. "Is that a pun?"

"Not at all."

I looked away, watching the dancers on the floor, men in one another's arms.

When Kate returned, we drank another round, shouting over the music, but all I would remember later of that conversation was the heat between him and me, the pressure like a hand on my chest, real as the railroad ties that enclosed the dance floor.

If Kate noticed, she didn't show it.

"I'm going to go snoop around," she said. "You two OK here?"

"We're fine," he said.

"Hurry back," I said. But she was gone already into the crowd and we were left alone together, with the shock of desire arcing between us like a downed live wire and the awareness that whatever we said, we were saying something else.

⸙

I was teaching two extension classes at the local branch of the state university that term: Introduction to Platonic Thought, from three-thirty to four-forty-five Mondays and Wednesday, and a course on Ethics 101 Thursday nights. I had eight students in each, which was just enough to ensure that the administration could not cancel. Enrollment is often spotty and sometimes my classes do not make and I have to pick up a class in composition or the dreaded Study Skills, in which under-prepared students work through a soft-back manual comprising drills on procrastination and time management. I try to be philosophical about it. I take what I can get.

The extension classes with catchy titles do best: Love among the Runes—which purports to teach students about Norse mythology and how "to divine one's destiny by casting ancient runes" (which are, in fact, brand-new, American-made, plastic bits with faux Norse symbols pressed into their surface)—always has a waiting list. So does Introduction to Astrology. There is a brisk trade in divination these days—astrological columns, palm readings—people seem less interested in preparatory contemplation than in foreknowledge, which seems to me to have it backward.

After all, what good is knowing what's to come if you're ill prepared to cope with it?

ᨎ

We began to see a lot of Jake. We became a threesome. He dragged us out to obscure Mexican joints in what passes for a barrio in the Midwest, insisted we canoe from Minneapolis to St. Paul by way of a chain of city lakes. We went to foreign movies: Ken Loach films that required subtitles; a film by von Trier that required Dramamine; Almodóvar. And each time we met I felt more acutely the tension between us, like a private joke we were keeping from Kate; I noticed that he took care not to brush my hand when handling the canoe in a portage, he no longer shook my hand in greeting as he had done before. I began to think about him more and more, to find myself distracted by thoughts of him. Things he'd said. To feel an embarrassingly adolescent thrill whenever Kate came home from work with stories about him, whenever he called.

I had thought he was gay when we first met, but the thought had passed. Now I asked Kate as we sat reading on the couch one night; she seemed not to have considered it.

"I don't think so," she said, continuing to flip pages in *Vogue*, "but I can see what you mean, I guess. The peach sweater."

"And the goatee," I said.

"Goatees are gay?" she asked.

"They're defensive," I said. "All beards are an assertion of masculinity. Goatees are lowercase masculinity. Ambivalent."

"Where do you get this stuff?" she asked.

"I make it up," I said. "To amuse you."

ᨎ

We'd been seeing Jake regularly for several months when the three of us went to see *Vanya on Forty-Second Street* at the University Film Society—a film about a cast of actors rehearsing a Chekhov play and the sexual intrigues among them. I was trying to keep my mind on the movie, off of Jake, when I put my arm around Kate and my hand landed on his shoulder by mistake, and we both started.

"Shhh," Kate said, setting her hand high on my thigh, nuzzling her head against me.

I looked over at him, his profile flashing in the light from the screen, his eyes forward, refusing to meet mine.

At home that night, I told Kate that it would be better if they went out without me from now on. I told her that I had too much work these days to join them, that I found him a little tiresome.

"You never like my friends," she said.

"Don't be ridiculous," I said. "You don't have any friends." I regretted it as soon as I'd said it, but it was too late to take it back.

To my surprise, Kate laughed.

"You're right," she said. "I don't like many people. That's why I wish you liked Jake."

I told her that I did, that I was just preoccupied.

She leaned up and kissed me. "A misanthrope and a hermit, we make a great pair."

When he came by after that, I contrived to go out. When they went out, I stayed in. I heard through Kate that he often asked after me; he asked her if I played racquetball, said he'd like to play a game with me sometime, if she didn't mind. She said she'd pass on the message; I told her I'd rather not. I avoided her office, picked her up at the curb.

I still thought about him, but I thought about him less.

∽

In class, I often tell my students stories. Stories, I'm convinced, are what we remember, how we learn. Stories, like education, are a species of seduction: seducing students to care about something other than themselves. Drawing them out of their assumptions into a world of surprise.

That term, I began the class with the story of Zeno of Elea and his famous paradoxes. The fifth-century philosopher is not properly a subject for a course in ethics, but it's a favorite story of mine so I told it anyway (such are the prerogatives of the pedant). I told them about Zeno's famous paradox of the arrow—how, if you think about it, you will realize that an arrow shot at a target will never arrive; it will always be half the distance to its goal (given that an object moving from one place to another must first move half the distance toward its goal, then half that distance, etcetera, Zeno demonstrated that an arrow can never reach its mark). If you think about it, you can't get there from here. And yet we do. The arrow pierces the target, defying logic.

Zeno told the story to demonstrate the illusory nature of change by demonstrating the contradiction inherent in any description of motion. I tell it to get my students to consider the connection between philosophy and life, to test philosophical assertions against the world in which they live.

The whole point of an education, as I see it, is to help you take the world personally, to put you on a first-name basis with the culture. But most of my students seem to think that a college education is an extension of adolescence, the intellectual equivalent of training wheels; they live in a state of semi-adulthood, while parents foot the bill. When I asked one young woman recently what she was majoring in, she looked at me with frank disdain, as if choices were for losers, and said, with a shrug, "Y'know, pre-life." Life in the academy, my students seem to think, is not the real thing. This is practice. This is only life in theory.

In early March, Jake heard from his landlord that his building had been sold and that he had thirty days to move, so Kate and I agreed to help him. The morning was wet and soggy with melting. As we walked up the steps to his building, I smelled the heavy scent of wild mushrooms, the promising chill of spring. We were making good time, shuttling boxes down stairs, until Jake and I found ourselves alone in his apartment. The pale, March light poured in the French doors from the balcony and the room was very still.

"You've been avoiding me," he said.

I picked up a box. "I'm not avoiding you."

"What have I done?"

"Nothing," I laughed and pushed past him.

He caught my arm. "I must have done something."

"You haven't done anything," I said. "It's what I don't want to do."

He didn't ask me to explain. He raised his hand as if he meant to touch my face, when Kate walked in and we both stepped back. I joked that we were the prime movers unmoving. Kate said she didn't know how prime we were but we'd better move, because she wasn't doing this by herself. Afterwards, we went to Jake's new place for pizza and beer. The two of them talked and joked, while I maintained an uncompanionable silence.

On our way home, Kate was cross. She asked why I couldn't be nice to Jake, why I had to be so difficult. I watched the sparkling of the streetlights, like orange emergency flares going up one after another. I felt the terrible weight of regret that sometimes heralds a loss. I told her, as gently as I could, that I was attracted to him, that I loved her but was attracted to him. She must have sensed that this was not our usual talk about infatuation. My mouth felt dry.

"Have you fucked him?" her voice was steady, emotionless, the tone she used to use in a heated seminar debate.

I shook my head. "Don't be ridiculous."

"But you want to?"

"Look," I said. "I love you. This has nothing to do with us."

I wanted her to understand that it was like a philosophy problem. A question I needed to answer: I wanted to understand what was between me and him. Early on Kate and I had agreed that we didn't want ours to become a small love, the sort of love we saw all around us, resentful, limiting, couples whose lives were less for all the sacrifices they'd made for the other. Guys who'd given up mountain climbing, women who'd given up jobs or ambitions. We promised each other we'd never be like that. But lately I'd had my doubts about us, and my attraction to him worked on those.

She asked if he felt the same way.

I said I thought he did.

We were quiet for a while.

"The heart has its reasons," I said, quoting Pascal, "which reason knows nothing of."

"You're so full of shit," Kate said.

When I woke in the night I heard her crying beside me. In the morning I told her that I wouldn't see him again. And for a while, that seemed to be answer enough.

❧

The philosopher Iris Murdoch once called marriage a "long conversation," but before I met Kate I treated my love affairs more like a drawn-out argument in which my task was to disprove the premise that ours was a viable relationship. I have treated love like a suspect premise to be tested. My concept of courtship (a lawyer lover once told me) bears a strong resemblance to moot court.

With Kate, though, I was trying. I had my doubts, of course—trained as I was to find the flaw in the argument. But ours were not big problems, though we often fought over small things. Kate wanted us to go on drives in October to watch the leaves turn, to play miniature golf, buy a barbecue, get cable, and while there was nothing inherently sinister about any of these, I was thirty-three at the time and the thought of these things made me feel old. Acquiring the accoutrements of middle-class complacency was the last thing on my mind then. I wanted wisdom, not diversions. I believed that vital to human happiness were honesty and liberty, that reason was its own reward. I believed there was no problem we couldn't think our way through.

For a while things were better between Kate and me than they had been in a long while. We began going to parties, on long drives in the country, to yard sales on weekends and on evening walks, and between us there was a new tenderness; we were both making an effort, even if the effort weighed on us a little. Kate suggested we meet each other at home for lunch, when we could get away from work; we made love on the couch, the sunlight pouring in.

The questions didn't go away; but as a friend once said of being on Prozac, the questions were still there, but he no longer cared about the answer. I felt drugged with the effort to be happy.

When Kate told me that Jake was seeing the Sex Goddess®, a local lonely hearts columnist from a local alternative paper who emphasized toys and leather, I was happy for him and happy to find I didn't care.

When I ran into Jake at Kate's office a few months later, we were polite.

"You're looking well," he said.

"Actually," I said, smiling, "I look like you."

He laughed.

It was true. We both wore jeans and men's v-neck undershirts and suit coats. He mentioned that his birthday was that weekend, that he'd be spending it alone (things having gone awry with the Goddess). It seemed only reasonable to invite him out for a drink.

"You should never age alone," I said.

I'd forgotten that Kate was going out of town to cover the Polar Plunge in Ely, a fact I recalled only later that night at home. I considered canceling but decided it was better just not to tell her. I didn't want to upset her, and it hardly seemed worth mentioning. It was just a drink after all. So Jake and I met at the Lexington, a bar in St. Paul the three of us had liked, at the irreproachable hour of seven p.m.

We ordered martinis and sat at the bar. We discussed gin preferences. The virtues of a twist versus an olive. Slowly we relaxed. He told me about the Sex Goddess, who turned out to be a former gymnast from Cloquet, a Norwegian Lutheran with blue eyes and an uncannily flexible body. I told him about my latest idea for a *New Yorker* cartoon: If Philosophers Had Majored in Business, featuring Cartesian Waters: I Drink Therefore I Am; Platonic Girdles, For That Ideal Form, and Ecce Home Furnishings.

He laughed, raised his glass: "I drink, therefore I am."

I had forgotten how much I liked his company. I forgot the time. By one a.m., it seemed wise to accept his offer of a ride home. It seemed only polite to invite him in.

I made us coffee while he looked at the bookshelves, the volumes of Adorno, Nietzsche, Wittgenstein, Kant, German idealists, English empiricists. When I returned with the coffee, he took the cup, then set it aside and asked if I would kiss him. It was a curious locution. He did not ask if he might kiss me, but whether I would kiss him—my volition the issue at hand. And I liked him for this, even though the kiss was bland. Even though I was aware of the hard length of his tongue, the musty gin taste in my mouth, and then I was aware of none of these things, only of the lurch of desire in my stomach, his mouth, his smooth chest.

⁂

Desire confounds categories.

Systems fail us when it comes to matters of the heart. They leave out too much, lead us to false conclusions. We assume instead of know. Empiricism our only hope. To learn through experience. Kate was the one who reminded me that the phrase "the exception proves the rule" does not mean *validates* but *tests.* Desire *proves* love. *Tests* it. At least exceptional desire does, but isn't desire always exceptional to those engaged in it?

Lesbians are often accused of narcissism—our love of women blamed on a hatred of men or a hatred of our mothers or a thwarted maturation that has locked one in pursuit of an adolescent mirror image of oneself—as if a woman simply loving another woman were inexplicable without reference to aversion or impediment. But this, in my experience, could not be more wrong. I have loved women because they are beautiful, because they are tender or brilliant, because I am moved by them.

When I fall for a man, as I fell for Jake, it's because he reminds me of myself.

⁂

The next morning, while Jake was in the bathroom, I called Kate on her cell phone; I just wanted to hear her voice. I told her that I missed her. She told me that I sounded funny. *Was I OK*? "I'm fine," I said. I remembered how she used to say, whenever I was away at a conference, "You can come home now, all is forgiven." I said it to her now. She laughed. "I didn't know there was anything to forgive." I wanted to tell her everything, but I knew I couldn't. And the thought of that made me incredibly lonely. I told her that I had to go, that I had a lot of papers to grade. But I didn't work that day. After Jake left, I sat at my desk watching the wind push the leaves around outside.

ൟ

When Kate returned, I didn't tell her about the drink. But she must have sensed something. She seemed sad, and I felt a great desire to reassure her, because despite what I was about to do and had just done, I loved her. My feelings for him, I wanted to tell her, had nothing at all to do with her. I was trying to find out about love, about what it is to be human; I was after evidence, the facts of the heart. Desiring him did not detract from my love for her, anymore than reading one book detracts from enjoying another. But I could tell her none of this.

She said she was having trouble at work. Her assignments were less and less relevant. In the last year she had covered a vampire convention of Anne Rice fans at the Hyatt. The theft of the butter bust of the Dairy Queen from the State Fairgrounds. The House Rabbit Society's Easter pageant. What she called the cultural trivia of a trivial culture.

"We are the Romans," I said.

"Yeah," she said. "Look what happened to them."

Perhaps I only imagined it, with a lover's narcissism, but it seemed to me—as I debated the ethics of having an affair—that the culture egged me on. Everywhere I turned were exhortations to excess, refutations of restraint. Adultery began to seem like the amorous equivalent of second-hand smoke, a byproduct of a culture loathe to accept limits. Ford Motors, that quintessentially American company, whose slogan had once been "We're Number One," now boasted, "No Boundaries." Bus billboards pledged NO LIMIT credit cards. Hewlett-Packard insisted "Everything is possible." As if we needn't choose. As if choices had no consequences. Or as if we needn't live with them.

ൟ

Kierkegaard distinguished between the ethical and the aesthetic life, the life shaped by will and that led in pursuit of pleasure. But it seemed to me that the choice was between a life shaped by convention and that shaped by authentic desire. Morality, as its Latin root suggests, is merely a matter of custom. Moralistic, as a term, has been used pejoratively since Hölderin and the age of German idealism, long before Nietzsche's critique. Ethics, on the other hand, derives from the Greek word *ethos*, roughly translated as character or nature. To be ethical, then, is to live in accord with one's nature. What could be wrong with that? With the self as guidepost to the good life? "There's nothing wrong with feeling good," Jake had said the other night; at the time, his logic seemed irrefutable.

For a few weeks Jake and I met at his apartment in the afternoon and made love. I told Kate that I had student conferences, classes to prepare. Our meetings were largely wordless, a matter of gestures—mouths and hands, taste and touch. For hours after leaving him, I was conscious of my skin, dazed with arousal. Familiar streets took on a new brilliancy, the sky a new radiance; as I walked home along Garfield, each house, each sign seemed to possess a new significance.

But the more I desired Jake, the less we had to say to each other. Grasping at desire, it seemed to disappear. After sex, I dressed quickly, eager to get home to Kate. I began to feel closer to her, more tender, protective. I began to notice little things she'd like—a Freud action figure, a biscotti recipe, books on South African history. I recalled how Kate's stories had amazed me when we first met—stories of her work with the anti-apartheid group the Black Sash, of her visits to remote villages and her appearances before pink-faced judges to protest pass laws, of her uncle's strangulation by wire, the taste of blood oranges and olives eaten on a mountain hike. How she had wanted to be an Anglican priest because she liked the phrase "Peace be with you," passed around like a collection plate at the end of every service. I admired how she'd taken part in what Adorno termed "resistance," a refusal "to be part of the prevailing evil, a refusal that always implies resisting something stronger and hence always contains an element of despair." She seemed to carry in her the parched landscape of southern Africa, its desolation and its harsh beauty. I realized that the passion I felt for Jake was passing: our sex was a little like getting drunk, liberating at first but tedious if done too often. I was embarrassed by the boredom I felt.

A month passed and another, before I admitted to Jake that I didn't know if I could do this anymore; he appeared neither disappointed nor surprised. He simply asked if I wanted him to change my mind. I said it would be easy, but that I'd rather he didn't.

Sitting there beside him, I missed him. And more than missing him, I missed desiring him.

Kierkegaard—that failed lover—spoke of "the enthusiasm of a love that ever seeks solitude," and I wonder now if this wasn't the source of my disappointment in that affair; what I was seeking with Jake, I suspect, wasn't him—lovely as he was—but a more perfect solitude, a more complete sense of the world. I wanted the feeling that comes when you release yourself toward things—reading can do this and looking at a painting and listening to music or walking through half-empty streets almost anywhere alone at night will do this. I wanted to stand in the radiant presence of desire, when all things, the black branches of trees, light falling on brick, the strains of a violin concerto, one's own hand, seem illuminated by a loveliness musical in its intensity.

↝

When Jake called my office a few days later, I was surprised. He asked to meet at a pub in St. Paul. He sounded nervous; I noted that he didn't suggest we meet at his apartment.

When I arrived he was waiting in a booth. We ordered beers, chatted awkwardly.

"Have you run across my sweater," he asked. "The peach one?"

I had not seen the sweater in weeks.

"I thought you'd thrown it over for a tweed," I said.

He didn't laugh.

"I've checked my car," he said. "I can't find it. I thought maybe."

"I'll check."

We drank pints of ale, and he flirted with the waitress, and it was clear that whatever had been between us was over now.

⁂

Kate was the one who found the peach sweater, the hideous thing had fallen behind the radiator in our bedroom, cast off, evidently, without attention. When she told me, I blushed, stammered. Confused by the implication, which—until she saw my reaction—she had not seen. When she asked me directly what was going on, if I'd slept with him, I couldn't bring myself to lie.

Kate sat on the couch and covered her face and cried as if someone she'd loved had died. And I started to cry, too. And it occurred to me that in all my careful reasoning I had left out one key thing. My formulation of the problem had been wrong, the premise flawed. I had been so concerned with the true and the untrue, the ethical versus the moral, action and inaction, that I had failed to consider the obvious, the simple fact that I might hurt the woman I loved.

I told her that it had nothing to do with us. That it was over.

"You're right," she said, standing. "It is." And she walked out.

⁂

For a while Kate and I tried to patch things up. We got back together. Made love. Fought. Cried. Called it off and on again for a couple of months. Until finally we no longer remembered what it was we were trying to save, a time before things were over. I heard that Jake left the paper a few months later to return to school. I did not see him again.

⁂

Even now I prefer to think of ours as a temporary separation, not an ending. I take comfort in the thought that things haven't really changed, that Kate's absence is a momentary break, which time will heal—that change, as Zeno would have it, is illusory.

But every so often I remember the story in *PMS* of the follower of Zeno, who was lecturing before a crowd in Athens, gesticulating wildly as he made his points. The Zenoist was arguing that an object *cannot* move, because it cannot be in more than one place at a time. "If it moves where it *is*, it is standing still. If it moves to where it is *not*, it cannot be there," he said, when suddenly he dislocated his shoulder. A doctor was called from the crowd. Asked to fix the shoulder, the physician explained that it could not be dislocated: either the shoulder was where it had been and was not dislocated, or it had moved to where it was not, which was impossible. At which point the patient saw what should have been obvious all along: logic lies. If we rely on reason alone, the answers we seek—the obvious truth—may elude us.

I remembered the story this morning as I watched my students write their mid-term exams. It was one of those extraordinarily windy days in autumn and all manner of things were blowing past the classroom window, the flotsam of other lives—pages of newsprint, plastic bags like round white kites, twigs and cups and colored flyers—and in the midst of the maelstrom, I saw something go by, out of the corner of my eye, which must have been a twig, but which looked like a child's arrow, and I thought briefly that it could be one of Cupid's, or Zeno's—aiming for something it will never, ever, reach.

Meena Arora Nayak

Neel Taal

(Rhythms in Blue)

Meena Arora Nayak is the author of two novels, *In the Aftermath* and *About Daddy*, and a children's book, *The Puffin Book of Legendary Lives.* Her third novel, *Endless Rain*, will be released in July 2006. Her work has been included in the anthology *The City of Sin and Splendour: Writings on Lahore.* Meena also translates for *Hindi, a Literary Journal*, and writes articles and book reviews for *WorldView* magazine. She is an assistant professor of English and mythology at Northern Virginia Community College and lives in Virginia.

A blue moon. A blue moon again. And blue eyes. How much blue can a body take without capitulating to its blueness?

Here we are, sitting under the Bradford pear side by side on the garden bench, its planked wood still warm with the memory of a spring day's sun, and its wrought iron back articulating the clumps of primroses. Just sitting side by side, with me in the middle, flanked by an age-old security on one side and a tingling new warmth on the other, talking about the phenomenon of a double blue moon, the stars, music, and lottery tickets.

"It's the randomness of it all. Like the stars…you know…no pattern. They just seem to pop up whenever they please," I say.

"Actually, it happens only when all the elements are just right," Ray says. He looks away at the moon, then at me with a blue so intense it could have been the first color of creation. It is hard to inhale—that color. I have no more breath left. What little remains trapped in my heart sounds like the heartbeat of a fetus—focused, loud.

"Music. There has to be a rhythm. Compositions. Rhythms. Not possible without a rhythm of some sort," Dev says. He's a percussionist with aspirations of composing a rhythm so intricate, yet so simple, that the very firmament will be utterly explained. "The numbers, too, will naturally follow the rhythm of the stars—you know, a distinct method to the apparent randomness."

"We could start by laying down the last five years' winning numbers. I could buy a copy of the lottery gazette," Ray says.

"I think we can do this." Dev suddenly reaches across me and snatches the crumpled pack of Camels from Ray's breast pocket. "Yes," he mutters through lips clenched over the cigarette, as Ray reaches over me to light it. "I think we can crack this open." He draws quick puffs. "If this is at all logical, as it must be, all you'd have to do is find the pattern in the numbers. I'll create the music. You come up with the next logical sequence in numbers, and I'll do the same with the notes. Then we'll match them. If we both come up with the same sequence, we'll know those are our numbers—the winning numbers. What do you say? You're with me?"

"Yes..." Ray sits up a little and shifts his weight; the curve of his elbow draws away from mine, and the nip of the spring evening immediately seizes upon the warmth that has been there. He takes the pack of Camels from Dev's hand and, straightening its edges, retrieves a wrinkled, filterless cigarette and lights it. His first puff drifts away in concentric circles.

When the moonlight sits like a halo around the pinky-white blossoms of the Bradford in my yard, it transforms it into a nest of fairies. I spread out a palm to catch a blossom fairy fluttering down through the smoke, its petal wings crumbling the smoky heart of a circle.

Dev believes we draw circles around us—circles of relationships, circles of feelings, circles of intensity, circles of how much we will live and how much die—circles of rhythms, but all within a structured circumference. We start at a point and allow ourselves freedom within the circumference. But we must arrive back at the point to complete the circle. How big a circle we draw all depends on how we define fulfillment. For Dev I could be anything from his wife in seven births to a pampered child to the goddess Sarasvati inspiring centuries of tradition in music. For me Dev is my own patch of terra firma, allowing me to lift off and explore new rhythms, allowing my heart to wander away from home. But his gravity keeps me facing home, like a stripling bee who flies backwards to remember the way back to the hive. How can I love him less for allowing me to love more? It is the extension of the same love. Sometimes I wonder what will happen if our rhythms begin to seek totalities that cannot be contained within circles.

"The five numbers should be easy. They will fall within the cycle. It's the Power Ball I'm worried about," Dev says.

The lunch tables in Teaism are only ten in number. At noon, people play musical chairs. The prize is a sun-window, a view of Washington, D.C., from the fifth floor, and Teaism's famous vegetarian platter, but the establishment allows the winners only a half hour to savor their victory. I have about ten minutes left. I try to raise myself above the cackle of voices, to absorb the sun, the city, myself.

"Have you ever placed your palm against railroad tracks just before the arrival of a train?"

He is reflected in the glass of the sun-window. I lift a hand and place it against the glass, my palm flat, covering his lips, his nose, my fingers reaching towards his eyes.

"The train trembles through your whole body."

"Hi," I say, turning to look at him.

"Do you mind if I share your table?"

I absorb the trembling of the world for the next half hour. His eyes, his porous blue eyes, absorb my trembling.

Teaism at noon becomes a breathless game we play every day.

My house begins to reverberate with new rhythms. Dev creates compositions for each of the year's winning number sequences to test his theory. I sit among his tablas, giddy with the wonder of new rhythms.

"What'll you do with the money if you win?" I ask him one evening.

He looks at me puzzled, as though I have introduced a new variable into the equation. "The whole point is to crack this lottery thing wide open, to find the logical rhythm," he finally says. "The money will figure itself out."

"What's Ray going to do with his share?"

"He's got plans," he says. "He won't say what."

"Leave him. Marry me." Ray is sitting in a pile of computer paper in his apartment, each sheet a chronological tale of numbers—five years of lottery history.

"I love him," I say.

"Then what is this?"

I shake my head.

"I keep thinking it's just physical. I keep thinking if I can make love to you one time—one time only, it'll be over."

I shake my head again. "I'll have to kill myself then. Because for me it won't be over. And I'll have broken all the rules."

"Do me a favor, will you? Before you die, call me. Give me what I want." He laughs.

I laugh with him. "I'll have killed myself after the fact."

"If I win the lottery, will you marry me then? I'll be rich."

"You'll only be half-rich. The other half of the riches will be Dev's. Either way I'm a winner."

I am a good wife—the epitome of a perfect Indian wife. My house is clean and tastefully decorated. I like to watch the proud satisfaction on Dev's face when visitors to our house stop in mid-visit to exclaim, "What a beautiful house." My refrigerator is always stacked with Dev's favorite food. I have learnt to cook his favorite dish: carp, fried and spiced, the signature dish of Bengal, exactly like his mother makes, exactly like all Bengali girls learn to make to define prosperity in their house. I make sure I'm home before he gets back from work, so I can greet him at the door, wearing a fresh coat of makeup and a smile. "Forces of gravity." My mother taught me the lesson on the morning of my marriage. "A beautiful wife who is happy to see her husband is a gravitational pull that will prevent him from straying." At night I make sure all our differences are resolved. I never let him sleep with an issue weighing on his mind. At the end of the day if the apologies are all mine, so be it. "The night is treacherous." Another lesson learnt from my mother. "It whispers betrayals in his ear. Don't give him reasons." Every time he reaches for me, I make myself available. But Dev is a considerate lover, attuned to my moods, knowing instinctively when I'm really willing. Never once have I had to bear him in bed. Every time we've made love, it has been when I'm not only willing, but also wanting.

Ray and I sit drenched in sweat in the Sculpture Garden, letting the sun pour into our skin. At this time we are nothing except receptacles of the sun. Ray's pure white linen shirt stains with the golden of his chest hair. I trace a finger down the curve of his chin over his throat into the hollow at the base and stop there. Perspiration trickles like a leaky faucet between my breasts.

"What is this in me?" Ray says, his voice floundering. "You're a married woman."

"Happily married," I add.

"Why doesn't this feel wrong?"

"We owe each other something from a past birth."

"What? One day? One night? A whole lifetime? How do we know how much?"

"We'll know," I say. The sculptures in the Sculpture Garden are all immense. I hadn't realized the paucity in my world till Ray had become a part of it. I have never been a taker; I only knew how to give. Now I want to take everything he owes me. If it is one day or one night, I'll receive it like a beggar in the cupped palms of my hands.

Every night I cremate the day with meticulous rituals: remove its valuables and set them aside—legacies for posterity; bathe it—the orifices purged of earthly impurities; inhale its death-smell before I dress it—its wantonness clothed to meet the lovers' sobriety. The bed is a pyre.

Dev is stretched across the bed; his limbs spread out in a free fall like a parachutist jumping out of an airplane, bracing the air with his pressure-flattened body. I free the comforter from under his leg and arm from my side of the bed and slip in, my back towards him. He turns on his side, his face towards me, and slips an arm around my waist.

"Do you ever think of death?" he says, his voice simply a deep breath between sleep and wakefulness.

"Every night," I whisper.

"Sometimes, I grow afraid."

I pull his arm around me tighter and gather myself back into the scoop of his lap. In India women used to commit Sati, throwing themselves into their husband's pyre to die with them rather than live without them.

Ray is sitting at a cement chess table in Lafayette Park sketching the ancestor oak across from him. Behind him American Israelis and American Palestinians demonstrate ten feet away from each other. Violence has broken out in Palestine again. The Israelis made a special visit to claim the Temple Mount, and the Palestinians protested the violation of their Noble Enclosure. Twenty-eight Palestinians and four Israelis are dead.

A squirrel scampers up a branch of the oak and disappears into a hollowed nest.

"It's like a refuge," I say.

"Yes," he says. "Like a sprawling development—each new resident adding an apartment there, a condominium here, without any thought to design. And the branches keep spreading out like streets to accommodate more. All are welcome."

"It's good," I say, looking over his shoulder at the sketch.

He shakes his head. "The branches look like precarious perches rather than streets in a safe neighborhood. I'll have to draw it again." He looks up. His eyes are the skies, the oceans—unceasing blue. "This world is too insular. I want to live in this tree," he says.

I get up and walk to the oak, laying my palm flat against its wooded benignity, needing to be absorbed in its secular culture. I will him to look into my eyes, to see the revelations of blue in them. His eyes are scrunched up against the sun's rays slanting through the branches of the oak, his ridiculously long blonde eyelashes almost touching his eyebrows. Ray has the eyebrows of a little boy. They haven't learnt their own machinations. They say whatever his eyes do.

"Don't," he says. "It'll kill me. It'll kill us all."

Ray picks up his sketchpad and pencils and walks away, cutting through the demonstrators—now he's a Palestinian, now an Israeli; now he's lost in the lunch-hour crowds of 15th Street. The Palestinians and the Israelis continue to demonstrate peacefully in Lafayette Park ten feet from each other, the violence in their soil surrendering to their harvests of American dreams.

I seek blue in lunch-hour streets, errand stores, sun parks, Teaism's sun- windows—places of chance meetings that we had explored by design before.

The air, the light, the shadows whisper rumors of his being to me—a gait, an angle of shoulders, a curl of hair touching a collar, the sound of a voice. Following the rumors, I step into "Don't Walk" signs.

The sky is pervious, its blue only that of osmosis. It filters through my eyes. I want blue to define my life. Every morning I instinctively reach in my wardrobe for clothes with blue definitions. Walking down the street at lunchtime one day, I step into the corner flower shop and buy blue hydrangeas. At my ophthalmologist's, testing for new contact lenses, I try on blue.

"It suits you—the color blue," Dev says one evening.

A sob convulses in my throat. When Dev reaches for me that night, I am a shy Indian bride covered from head to toe in bridal finery. It takes him all night to disrobe me. Then I tremble at every whisper of love. He is my first lover. He is my last. I am frenzy. Then I am death. The color of love that night is blue.

At the beginning of time the primeval waters were quiescent. But in order for creation to occur, chaos was necessary. The serenity had to be disrupted and the forces of good and evil had to engage in a creative conflict. Thus the serene waters were churned, and the neutrality was transmuted into the elixirs of life—milk, butter, ambrosia—and the reversal of elixirs—poison—an extract so potent in its destructive power, it paralyzed the three worlds. Shiva, the god of destruction, the only one capable of battling the venom, took the shape of a sacred chant and held the poison in his throat like an incantation. From that time on Shiva assumed the name of Neel Kantha, blue throated. Thus it was, the color of the poison was revealed.

I banish blue. I pull out all clothes with blue definitions in my closet and fold them meticulously to put away in a drawer with clothes I have chosen to forget. I remove the blue contact lenses and make a note in my planner to call the ophthalmologist to get a pair of clear ones. At work, I carry the pot of hydrangeas to the receptionist's desk.

I sit and watch television in the evenings now—witty sitcoms with young couples alluding to love, lovers' beds, lovers' games with circular rules. Dev's rhythms still steal in from under the basement door. He has received the final tally of numbers from Ray. They met in a coffee shop near Dev's work. I've stopped waiting for crows to crow in my yard—Indian birds announcing intimations of visits from loved ones. There are no crows in the skies of my neighborhood. Ray has sworn off my streets.

There's a discordant note in Dev's final rhythm—a syllable falling down—a star dislodged from its orbit, hurtling into the black hole.

"Why don't you come and listen to me anymore?" Dev is standing beside me. "I can't get it right. There's a note I keep missing."

I shake my head.

"It's Ray, isn't it?"

I look at him. His eyes plead for a denial.

"I'm lost," I whisper. I can't find the beginning of the circle anymore. I reach out a hand to him. "Help me."

A calm settles on his face, like the silence after a slaying. He shakes his head. "I can't. You have to find your own way back."

The jackpot is a hundred and sixty-two million dollars. The lines outside lottery ticket stores stretch all the way into hope. The odds of winning this lottery are one in a million. Ray has checked his tally numerous times, but Dev's numbers still have a syllable that doesn't fit. I can hear him in the basement, repeating the rhythm like a child learning his math tables over and over again with a pause at the multiple that constantly eludes memory. He, too, has lost the point in the circle that makes the circle absolute.

It's a myth; I want to scream at him, like the myth of Moksha, of Nirvana, the Absolute, formulated only to keep us striving. Life is random—a random beginning and a random end. There are no patterns to follow, and those we design for ourselves veer off into randomness at the slightest hint of a blue.

When I was younger I used to say I'm waiting to experience that one moment of the absolute—absolute sorrow or absolute joy.

I was so wise when I was younger.

I pick up my car keys and step out of the house.

By the time I reach Ray's apartment, I'm soaked in blue.

Later that night, the phone in Ray's apartment rings. It's Dev. "Put me on the speaker phone," he says. Despite the static distances of telephone lines, the tabla bol drums into the room with the clarity of inevitability.

> DHA DHA DHIN DHIN / TITE DHIN NA /
> TITE KATA GADI GHENE / TITE DHIN NA /
> DHAGE DHIN DHIN TETE / KATA GADI GHENE /

"Twenty-one beats," he says. "That's the Power Ball—twenty-one."

> GHARANE DHAGETETE TAGETETE KARAN /
> KITETAGE TAGETETE KARAN /
> DHETE DHETE TAGE TETE / DHUMA KETE DHUM
> DHUMA KETE TAGE TETE / KREDHE TETE DHUM
> TAGENNA KETE DHUMA KETE / KATA GADI GHENE
> KAT-GHARANE KATE DHA-KITE TAKADHUMA /
> KITETAKA TAK-GHARANE TAK-GHARANE /
> DHA KITE-TAK TAK-GHARANE DHA /
> KITETAKA TAK-GHARANE TAK-GHRANE / DHA

"Twelve, seven, nineteen, and twenty-six beats. Those are the numbers," he says. "Go buy your ticket, Ray. It's yours. All of it."

When Parvati, Shiva's wife, playfully covered his three eyes with her hands, darkness fell upon the three worlds, for Shiva's eyes are the sun, the moon, and fire. A sweat bead of passion fell from Shiva's forehead and flowed into his third eye—fire. From the heat of the eye, and the seed of the sweat, a terrible child was born—Andhak—blind, for he had been born in darkness, and blue, for he had been born from passion. Parvati wished to claim him as her own, because his blueness was from the passion she aroused, and his blindness was from the darkness she invoked. And Andhak, being blind from passion and darkness, desired Parvati as soon as he was born. So Shiva, the god of doomsday, impaled Andhak on the tip of his trident and danced the Tandava—the dance of death—the dance with a rhythm as vibrant as a beginning, as terrible as an end—a rhythm of the seed of life transfixed in death.

The winner of the multi-state lottery jackpot of hundred and sixty-two million dollars is an eighty-two-year-old grandmother in Harrisburg, Pennsylvania. In an interview she says she let the computer pick out her numbers—the winning numbers—twelve, seven, nineteen, twenty-six; Power Ball—twenty-one.

Vanessa Orlando

from *Railroading the Devil*

VANESSA ORLANDO is a recipient of the Maryland Writers' Association short fiction prize. Her short story, "When Sara Looks Up," was made into a short film by Columbia College Chicago in 2004. She was also one of five writers admitted into the Manitoba Writers Guild's Emerging Writers Program in 2000. She is a former newspaper reporter and past recipient of the Georgia Associated Press feature writing award.

MORIAH – INTERLUDE

Moriah gets in all by herself and rolls up into a ball. If she stays quiet long enough, she'll win. They'll win—she and momma. They're a team and they'll win. In just a little while, momma will come around and announce that no one has found her and it is time to come out and claim the prize. Moriah sure has been in there a long time, though, and she really wants to come out, but she wants her prize, too. Wants momma to hug her and tell her how well she did and claim their prize together. Momma doesn't play with her very often so she wants to be sure to play right. To make it fun so momma will play with her again. So Moriah stays as small and silent as she can, for as long as she can, but she's young, and winning doesn't seem so important once she gets tired and thirsty, and her legs start to cramp, and sweat makes her clothes stick to her back and she has to go to the bathroom. She doesn't really need a prize. In fact, she doesn't mind letting Tina win. She just wants to get out.

"Momma, can I come out now? Momma?"

Fear comes in short, violent pulses. Each pulse lasts just an instant and then a little longer. And a little longer. Moriah shivers but just for a second. She closes her eyes and holds her breath and beats back the pulses and swallows down the tears, certain that momma will be back any second to declare this game of Hide 'n Seek over and won. Moriah starts to scream but muffles it with her own hand—then with both hands. She tells herself to stop being silly. To be quiet. Momma knows she's there. Momma put her there. She'll be back when the game's over. Win or lose, momma will be back.

Moriah hears something right outside the box—something like a cough but not loud enough, maybe a sigh but too loud for that. Someone is there, though. Maybe momma! Yes. Momma's probably right there, waiting to declare her the winner as soon as it's for sure. Oh please let it be for sure now. Moriah's ready to come out. Ready to give up. Ready to stretch her legs and get out of the dark and go to the bathroom. She's been hiding long enough. She doesn't care if Tina wins. She likes Tina. They're friends. Best friends. They'll probably share the prize no matter who wins anyway.

"Momma?!"

Louder and then abruptly softer.

"Momma!"

She tries to hum and sing. She doesn't know why that seems like the thing to do but that's what she does. Sing.

> Three blind mice. Three blind mice.
> See how they run. See how they run.
> They all run after the farmer's wife
> Who cuts off their tails with a carving knife.
> Did you ever see such a thing in your life.
> Three blind mice.

Momma knows she's there. Momma put her there. She'll be back any second.

> Twinkle, Twinkle Little Star
> How I wonder what you are.
> Up above the sky so bright
> Like a diamond in the night
> Twinkle, Twinkle Little Star
> How I wonder what you are.

The pulses of fear turn into stabs. Pulsating stabs, one after the other. And each stab causes the fear to spread, like blood into a bandage, until fear gives way to abject terror. Moriah screams from the back of her throat, where a scream is most gritty, most raw. Moriah's little stomach pushes as much volume up through her throat as she can. The muscle contractions make her sick, make her want to throw up. She begins to convulse, to retch. She begins to comprehend what's happened and yet how can she? She is a four-year-old girl, just a wisp of a little thing, imprisoned in a footlocker, screaming to be saved by the person who put her there.

Sahara used to have to grab Moriah by the arm or the elbow or the hair and drag her down the stairs; Moriah used to kick and claw and scratch and bite and screech as loud as she could. She used to punch and kick at the locker lid until she was bruised and sore. But now, Moriah walks down the stairs freely, zombie-like, without protest. She whimpers a little when Sahara tells her to open the lid and get in, and Sahara allows her that little moan of protest as long as the girl doesn't hesitate.

"That's right. Get in and whimper like a dog, if that's what you want to do. I don't care, you goddamn piece of shit."

Moriah knows she might be in the locker for an hour or two days, but she's stopped fighting and crying. Instead, she makes herself numb. Lifeless. She imagines she's dead and in a casket. Death is a place like the local mall or playground on the corner. She imagines the Harper City cemetery and thinks of all those people, terrified and living in boxes, just like her, and feels lucky that, at least, she isn't buried alive like they are. She is only in the basement.

Moriah loses track of time but during the day, at least, a little light, thin as wire, streaks through the hinge. Not enough to see or illuminate anything, but enough to know light is coming through the small basement window. In Moriah's eyes, the wire-like light comes to life and shapes itself into cartoon characters she's never seen before but she names them just the same. Fatty Catty. Soggy Doggie. Horsey Horse Horse. She sees her own laser light show, with all her cartoon creations. Sometimes she uses her finger to outline the shapes she thinks she sees, and by drawing where it will go, she makes it go there...and there...and there too. If Sahara had ever stepped quietly upon the footlocker, she might have even heard Moriah giggling at the predicaments her creations got themselves into.

At night, when there is no wire-thin light, Moriah starts to make herself see things in the dark, and everything she conjures up is bright—yellow, gold, red, white. Sometimes the things she sees are real, like sunflowers and daisies, and sometimes she just sees colors blending into a kaleidoscope of shapes and hues. When she is out of the footlocker, frightened that she might say something that will make Sahara put her back in, Moriah develops a language of color. Every thought she has, every request, every comment poses so much risk that she begins to see and then express everything as colors and shapes. It is easier to say, "blue swish" and "green stripes" than to compose a sentence with nouns and verbs, ideas and thoughts that might get her imprisoned again. She studies colors, even colors she can't imagine, and gives them meaning. Red and green are easy enough, but colors like magenta and fuchsia and periwinkle have their own meaning, depending on what she's trying to say. Coral might mean ice cream as easily as it means open window. Blue means moon except when it means puppy. Moriah knows everyone thinks she's talking gibberish. That's OK. It's better than speaking perfect English and being misunderstood anyway.

߷

Footsteps.

Moriah can tell by the speed, the cadence, the weight with which Sahara walks whether freedom will be a relief or a continuation of the darkness. If her footsteps saunter and tease, she will take her time opening the locker and enjoy the slow ballet. She will drop the keys loudly on the lid and say, "Now where did those keys go? I hope I didn't lose them. I'll never be able to get the thing open if I lost them. Wouldn't that be something." If she walks down quickly and hurriedly, Sahara is in a fury. She will pound a hammer or a pasta ladle or a two-by-four against the sides of the locker for a second or two, or even a few minutes straight as if Moriah did something wrong while she was locked up. And then she will take her fury upstairs without opening anything, and who knows how long it will be before she comes back down again.

These though…these are footsteps she's never heard.

They are too quiet. Too tentative. Moriah hears short, fast breathing, loud, almost like a gasp. She hears a click. Sees the thin wire of whiteness appear. Moriah waits, breathes out a little. That thin light, that moment of salvation is what she hopes for the moment the lid closes. Sahara, though, never takes this long to let Moriah know what's coming. Open the lid, momma. Open it now. Please.

Moriah cocks her head to listen. Something's not right. Not right at all. Moriah is sure someone is out there. She swallows, although her mouth is dry and there is no spit left to swallow.

"Momma?" she whispers.

She hears a gasp, footsteps retreating. Moriah kicks at the lid and kicks again, screaming in one long continuous note until it sounds, even to her, like a fight among feral cats. Something clangs to the ground. A garbage can top maybe. Or a chair. The kitchen door at the top of the stairs opens and slams. The footsteps disappear along with the presence that came with them.

It is during that scream that it all becomes clear—that a seed of hope she never knew she had is obliterated. Moriah kicks the lid and screams again. And again.

More footsteps.

She recognizes these as Sahara's but different.

Sahara shoves the footlocker onto its narrow side in one motion. Then shoves it again so that the lid is on the floor. She shoves it still again, onto its other narrow side, and leaves it there, one turn shy of a complete revolution. "Shut up, you little devil. Shut up now or else."

Moriah feels something wet and sticky on her face. Nose bleed. Ick.

She knows the lid will open and Sahara will pull her out sooner or later. Moriah will be blinded by the light or the continued darkness. She will be thirsty and confused, and her clothes will be encrusted with fresh piss and stale vomit. "Not a word. Not a goddamn word or the next time, I will keep you in there until you rot, do you understand?" Sahara bundles her up in a fluffy blanket, clutches onto her tightly, and rushes her to Dr. Percival's office, crying, "My baby! What's happening to my baby!"

Michele Orwin

Frequent Flyer

MICHELE ORWIN is a writer and a teacher. Her first novel, *Waiting for Next Week*, was published by Henry Holt & Co. Her articles have appeared in *McCall's Magazine*, the *Washington Post*, and the *Los Angeles Times.* She has taught creative writing at Cooper Union, NYU, American University, and the Writer's Center in Bethesda. "Frequent Flyer" is part of "The Magic Mountain B&B," a new collection of short stories. She lives in Washington, D.C., where she currently works as a senior speech writer for a large nonprofit.

THE INN OF THREE DANCING FISH
OLD SAN JUAN, PUERTO RICO

Carlos clears his throat in the mornings with a terrible cough. This cough wakes everyone else in the house while he still sleeps. He is an artist.

His pictures hang in the courtyard below my room. The Small Museum of the Three Dancing Fish, he calls it. He lives with Jorge on the ground floor. Carlos has splotches on his face, dry red patches. He must avoid the sun. This was not a problem when he lived in New York. When he was called Charlie. But he is a Puerto Rican now; a new *sanjuanero.*

He is always slipping in and out of languages. Always he speaks carefully, slowly. Always it is the ongoing present that he speaks of in the simplicity of a child. The weather is good, he says, as if he were a character in a Hemingway novel. The pineapple is sweet. It becomes hypnotic and contagious. I cannot stop myself from imitating him.

Carlos and Jorge have been running this small bed and breakfast in the Old Town for years. Even before Jorge got sick. This is what artists do here with the crumbling old houses. Part art gallery, part inn. Many cats.

You don't have to be gay to stay at the Inn of the Three Dancing Fish. No one cares anymore. And no one minds that Jorge practices "The Sound of Music" in the mornings on the old piano in the courtyard. Often he cannot find all the notes.

Maria, the maid, speaks loudly. You take coffee? she shouts to me through the door, while I am still in bed. I am the only woman here and I wake later.

You take coffee? You take milk? she shouts while I am two dreams away from being done with my sleep. The garbage truck passes, making a grinding noise so loud it rattles the perfume bottles on the dresser. There is a lizard on the wall inside my bedroom. A plate crashes and the lizard slips through a crack.

Carlos says to Jorge—What are you doing? It is an accusation. What are you doing this time? he means. Meaning, Look how stupid you are.

Too early I am driven from my bed.

Where is the coffee? Carlos yells to Maria when I come to the table. Don't you know that she takes coffee? he shouts. Everyone else has left. My last two dreams were filled with the noise from the house, the coughing and the grinding. My head feels as if spiders have danced all night behind my eyeballs and spun their webs inside my brain. I hate traveling alone.

Each time I think I will be less lonely in a strange place. I will be exotic. I will find a romance. This has never happened.

In the taxicab from the airport, the driver has told me he used to be a policeman in New York City. He has come here, now, to drive a cab. He has come home with his three brothers. All born in the States. All returned home to this island. Their *abuela* still lives in the mountains and does not speak English. It is unnatural to live so many months without sun, he tells me. You will see, he says, you will end up staying. We were all taken from our country the way the slaves were, he says. All our fathers slaves to the dream of America, he says. But it was all a lie. The dream is here, he says, with the palm trees.

At breakfast at this inn it is required that I talk. I did not learn the art of conversation over *parcha* juice and sliced mango rinsed with lime. My father was wealthy. This gave him a power he used most inside his home. He liked us quiet at the table. It still seems close to sin to talk over food.

You not tell me you take coffee, Maria shouts at me, though I am now in the room with her. You take milk? she shouts louder because Jorge is already at the piano.

Carlos and Jorge have two dogs, Yin and Yang. When Jorge plays "The Sound of Music," one dog yips, the other yaps. The three cats hide.

Jorge hits two notes at once. Neither one is in the song.

What are you doing? Carlos says. Meaning always—Look how stupid you are, again. Jorge keeps playing, the dogs keep yipping and yapping. My head is spinning.

My friend Tomas says inexpensive airfare is not enough reason to travel. A journey must have a purpose, he says. A point of departure. Then a destination. How else will you know when you've come home? I do not mean this literally, he says.

I travel when the airfare's cheap. I don't know why. I did not intend to come to this Old City but this is where I am.

A long time ago, when my father was poor, his family lived here. He has never returned. Why should I? he says. There is nothing for me there, he says. There is nothing for you either, he says.

But I am sure I shall find the home I have been sick for. I shall walk the streets with the blue cobblestones; I shall look at the bay to my left, then the ocean to my right, and know I belong halfway between them. I shall stand on the winding street between the two large forts and know my home is in a painted house with a curved iron balcony. I shall stop for coffee at the *kiosko* in the Plaza de Armas and a stranger will sit down at my table. He is a stranger but somehow we are already familiar. We share the dark *café con leche* and the sweet *mallorcas*; the powdered sugar decorates our lips. The morning passes and we continue swimming in each other's eyes. We do not need the ocean.

He tells me the streets are full of saints and miracles. Of this, he says, you are the proof.

Together we walk the Calle Cristo. Near the Parque de las Palomas, where the pigeons have decorated the sidewalks with their own white frosting. He shows me la Capilla del Cristo, the small chapel dedicated to the foolish Spanish lieutenant who accidentally jumped over the wall on his horse, tumbled to the bay, and somehow survived. A miracle, he says, like the color of your eyes.

Together we stand in front of the Catedral de San Juan and watch as a young bride in ivory satin prepares to walk the aisle. Her mother stoops in front of her to pick up the hem of her dress. Through her layered tulle crinolines, we can see her thin legs. She reaches out her small, white hand for her father to lead her into the old cathedral. I catch my breath and make a wish for her.

When we marry, he says, you will be even more beautiful.

Maria clatters in and out; she has forgotten the sugar.

Where are you from? Carlos says.

The webs are still in my head. If you could shine a light in there you would see them. Today I say Wisconsin. Though lately I have been claiming North Carolina as my home.

Sometimes I pretend I live in Maine. Near the cold, rocky coast. Really it's New Jersey, by the shore. Or else Minnesota. When my father left this country all his family knew of was New York. When he became rich, he left the crowded country of New York and moved to Connecticut. He lives now in a gated community that could be anywhere.

Do you snorkel? Carlos says. The word sounds very funny to me.

Yes, I say. Yes, of course I do. That is why I am here.

It is so easy if you do this. I am here from Wisconsin to snorkel, I say. And then we have something to talk about.

I would not have this problem with the stranger at the kiosk. We would talk without effort. We would laugh at the idea that you can make conversation the way a cobbler makes shoes. My father's father made shoes when he lived here. In New York he only repaired them. He had a small store with a metal foot turned upside down inside the window. He sold jars of shoe polish and soft cloths and yellow boxes of Chiclets. He had a machine for making keys. My father will not return to New York either. He will not leave his gated community that has plastic cards instead of keys. He does not like it that I travel. He does not like that I travel alone. That I stay in these guest houses filled mostly with gay men.

My friend Tomas says that I am more afraid of life than my father. He says I prefer the company of gay men because I feel safe. It is an illusion, he says. Outsiders are never safe.

You like too much being different, my father tells me. He has spent his whole life trying to fit in. There is nothing noble in being apart from everyone else, he says. Only loneliness. He says I act as one who has bought the inexpensive tickets for the mezzanine so I can watch life go by on the stage below me. I do not even dare to sit in the orchestra, he says. How can I tell him it is not a choice?

I love *mallorcas* in the morning, I say when Maria puts the basket on the table. This makes her smile. She has already decided I take milk with my coffee. She has found the sugar.

I love *mallorcas* and dogs and the sound of music. I love snorkeling. I love, also, the stranger at the *kiosko.* He has asked me to live with him before we marry but I have refused, after all. I must return home. I am homesick for Wisconsin. And while I sit there with my coffee in the courtyard, with the sleeping lizard and the now silent piano, it is all, for just that one moment, true.

That is why I travel, Tomas. Not the cheap airfare.

Sibbie O'Sullivan

Sharon and Toni

SIBBIE O'SULLIVAN is a native Washingtonian who enjoys writing in a variety of genres. Her poetry and prose have appeared in a number of publications. *Little Wheel*, her CD of poetry, was selected Best Poetry CD 2005 by the *Montserrat Review*. O'Sullivan has received three grants from the Maryland State Arts Council, one for her play, *The Body*, which was performed in 2004 at the Clarice Smith Performing Arts Center. She has recently collaborated with composer John Stephens, who commissioned her to write the libretto for his opera, *The Devil in the Flesh*. O'Sullivan is a senior lecturer in university honors at the University of Maryland, College Park.

Two women. Strangers. Sharon driving, Toni sitting next to her, head bobbing, voice trailing off against the car's cold window. And then a sudden alertness, as though home had become a gamble, an aphrodisiac.

"Park here," Toni said. "Wanna drink?" holding a glass out to Sharon.

"How'd they let you out with that?" Sharon asked.

"They didn't let me out. I took it. I hid it."

"Where?"

"About my person. Here. Wanna drink?"

The glass wobbled like a bubble on a stem. Sharon reached for it, but Toni's arm moved, spilling the drink in her lap.

"Oops," Toni laughed, patting her wet legs.

Sharon leaned across the car seat and began to pat the damp flesh where Toni's skirt ended.

"Men are pigs, fucking pigs," Toni sing-songed, then she poured what remained of the drink onto Sharon's hair. There wasn't much to spill and Sharon hardly felt it as she kept patting the damp flesh of Toni's legs. But she stopped patting when she felt Toni gather a strand of her hair into her mouth.

"Hair of the dog," Toni giggled, slowly sucking Sharon's hair, then releasing it.

All at once Sharon was aware of everything, the silence of the late hour, the smoke-filled car, the quiet parking lot. But most especially the closeness of the other woman. She breathed it in until she felt as though she were acquiring new flesh, as though she were changing into another person.

"You saved my life," Toni said, falling back against the window.

Then she began to bark like a dog.

"Shhh," Sharon said, covering Toni's mouth with her hand.

Toni twirled her tongue around Sharon's palm, licking off what liquor remained on it. Sharon took her hand away, brought it to her face and smelled it, then looked at Toni slumped against the car door. It was then she knew she could do anything.

So Sharon said, "Toni, take off your top please."

Toni laughed, "Right."

"I mean it. Take your top off. Please."

Toni's eyes narrowed. The evening had worn away her face and she felt off-center. Through dimness, Toni watched Sharon's hands move toward her until they rested on her shoulders. Earlier, Sharon's hands had come between Toni and the man in the red shirt, but now they came toward her.

She wasn't afraid.

"Toni, I mean it," Sharon said, resting her hands on Toni's shoulders.

"Sharon."

"Come on Toni, do this for me."

"You're crazy."

"I brought you home, didn't I?"

Toni sat still. She had been in a difficult situation, but she was all right now. She tried to think of the terrible thing that had happened, but she couldn't remember because Sharon began unbuttoning her blouse. For protection Toni put up her elbows, but Sharon spread them apart. With one hand Sharon held Toni's wrists, and with the other she finished unbuttoning the blouse. It only had three buttons.

"Are we home? How did you know where I live?" Toni's head swayed.

"You told me," Sharon said, letting go of the wrists so she could push the blouse off Toni's shoulders.

Toni lifted her head and smiled crookedly. "You're crazy, but I like you." And then a little click inside her head went off, like someone snapping their fingers. "And you saved my life."

"And I saved your life."

Sharon had never been so close to another woman before; it felt like she was looking with all her senses, not just her eyes. Back in the bar Sharon had watched Toni at a distance; back in the bar everyone had watched Toni. But now in the dark car Sharon was the only person watching and she liked that.

Toni knew that Sharon was watching her and so she waited. "Oh, I'm not pretty. I'm an ugly old bitch," and Sharon covered her mouth again.

Ugly old bitch. Earlier Toni had said that in the bathroom of the bar when Sharon and another woman had tried to calm her down. The man in the red shirt had gone, but Toni was still shaking. Toni had said, "That's all I am, an ugly old bitch, but you're so pretty, isn't Sharon pretty? And you are too, you're both so pretty, and I'm just a dog, nothing but a damn dog. I can't believe he tried to do that. In the parking lot. Oh, I don't know how I'll get home. I'm just a dog."

"I'll take you home," Sharon had answered.

Some of the glitter Toni had in her hair had fallen onto her neck and chest, and in the dim light of the car the splash of gold and silver made her skin look like wrapping paper. Sharon took her hand away from Toni's mouth and touched one of her breasts.

"Oh."

"I'm sorry." Sharon wanted to soften the moment, but she didn't want to lose it either, so she took her hand away, but just for a second.

Then she put it back.

Two hours ago she could not have imagined this moment, or the moments leading up to it. She could not have even imagined Toni. Everybody watched Toni. She was that kind of girl, hip cocked, cracking gum, looking around the bar while the man in the red shirt paid their way in. Her hair was spiked, she wore a studded collar for a necklace which shone blue under the lights. Her eyes were lined with black, her lips tinged magenta, and tiny handcuffs hung from her earlobes. She was big shouldered and wore a skimpy top. A little roll of flesh pouted over the waistband of her denim skirt. When she danced, her skirt rode up her thighs, the gold teeth of the two-way zipper widening as she thrust her hips. Out on the dance floor with her hands behind her head and her head thrown back, she was easy to notice. She danced as though she belonged to everyone.

"Watcha doin'?" slurred Toni.

A piece of glitter hung off one of Toni's nipples and Sharon wet her finger and dabbed at it.

"I saved your life, didn't I Toni?" Sharon's voice had gotten deeper. She could feel the close thick air of the car drying up her mouth. Her arms felt heavy, as though they were suddenly muscled, and her hands felt different. Earlier she had saved a woman's life, or so she liked to think, but it was really like a cartoon, words and gestures lifting off from her like queer captions, her arm weightless in the air. It moved uncommanded, it was not hers for that moment it came between Toni and the man in the red shirt. But now in the small dark space of the car, Sharon felt everything was hers.

"Take off your skirt Toni."

"Ooh," Toni's voice winced. She tried to come forward, away from the car door she was slumped against, but Sharon's hand, pressed flat upon her chest, kept her from moving. Toni looked down at the hand and her own bare breasts between them, then up at Sharon.

"Sharon," she began.

Sharon did not answer. She pressed harder on Toni's chest, feeling the muscles of her arm tense beneath her skin.

"Watcha doin' Sharon, come on, I wanna go home."

"You are home Toni. I brought you home, don't you remember?"

The two women watched each other. Then Toni burped, a dark bubble of sound.

Sharon said, "Unzip your skirt," still pressing Toni's chest with one hand while she fumbled the zipper with the other.

"Nooo, Jesus, watcha doin'," Toni struggled a little, flapping her hands about. "Lord I'm drunk," she finally said. Her head bobbled two or three times before it came to rest against the cold window. The two women sat very still, and for a moment Sharon thought Toni had passed out.

"Toni," Sharon said softly, lifting her hand off Toni's chest.

Toni raised her head and went, "Oink, oink."

"Let me take off your shoes," Sharon said, leaning back against the driver's door, allowing the dark, smoky air of the car to slip between them once again.

"My golden slippers..."

"Yes, your golden slippers." Sharon straightened one of Toni's legs and took off one high heel. Then she brought the other leg up and took off the other shoe. Then she pushed her hand along Toni's legs, up across her crumpled skirt, and up over her exposed breasts. Everything is easy, Sharon thought, all you have to do is do it.

"What happened to your necklace?" Sharon asked, passing a finger over Toni's collarbone.

"He took it, that lousy motherfucker." Toni lifted her hand to her neck where her fingers touched Sharon's. Toni's eyes closed and Sharon saw how drunk and helpless she was. "Will you help me get home," Toni said, "that pig took my car keys."

"You are home."

No one spoke for a few moments, then Toni opened her eyes, straightened up and looked around. She reached for the door handle but Sharon leaned across her.

"Take your skirt off Toni, will you do that for me?" Sharon asked, pressing against Toni.

"No."

"Please Toni. I brought you home."

"No."

"I just want to look at you."

"What for?"

"Because you're pretty."

"No I'm not. I'm just an ugly old dog."

Sharon pulled at the zipper and though Toni didn't struggle much, the zipper was hard to undo. When it came undone, the skirt came apart and Sharon saw Toni's thighs. In the smoky light of the car, Sharon saw the red marks on the tops of Toni's legs and worried for a second that maybe she had put them there.

"Where's your underpants?" she asked.

"He took 'em, remember? God."

Sharon leaned back against her door. "Why don't you lean back too, Toni."

Toni leaned back against the door. Sharon reached over and straightened Toni's legs across the car seat as much as she could. Toni was naked except for the skimpy top that hung open at her shoulders. She watched Sharon through half-closed eyes.

"I'd like my shoes," Toni finally said.

"They're on the dashboard."

But neither woman moved. Sharon thought of looking away, but she couldn't. Toni's nakedness was too compelling. She leaned closer.

"Did he do this?" Sharon asked as she touched the red marks on the tops of Toni's thighs.

Toni dropped her head and looked at where Sharon was touching her.

"I suppose. I don't know."

"Did he scare you?"

Toni kept her head down and made noises like a pig. Toni's head wobbled. She looked down at Sharon's caressing hand, then she looked wildly around the car, then back at Sharon. Then she smiled.

"No, you saved my life. Where's my shoes?"

At first Sharon was tentative, her hands awkward and heavy, but Toni's flesh was surprisingly warm and encouraging. She moved her hands over

Toni's thighs, over her belly, over the stray spots of glitter that had fallen onto her torso. She touched Toni's arms and shoulders, her ankles and hips. Toni sat still with her head down as Sharon touched her, and neither woman spoke. But when Sharon tried to push her hands between Toni's thighs, Toni balked and sat upright.

"Watcha doin'. Get out of there." Toni swatted at Sharon's hair.

"You promised," Sharon said, pressing her hands down on Toni's hips.

"Get off me you weirdo. Where's my shoes. I didn't promise nothin'."

"You said I could look Toni, remember. I brought you home and you promised." Sharon lay her face on Toni's belly, which smelled of liquor. She remembered how nice it felt when Toni licked her palm, so Sharon began to lick the skin on Toni's belly.

Things stopped turning enough for Toni to grab her shoe off the dashboard and swing it into Sharon's face. The heel caught her in the cheek. Sharon put up her hands, but Toni swung again and again.

"Stop it Toni please I'm sorry."

"You fuckin' pig, you weirdo fuckin' pig," Toni screamed as she hammered Sharon with her shoe. Then she stopped, sick and exhausted. She pushed Sharon off of her and swung her legs off the seat. Toni opened the car door and leaned outside. A little vomit squirted from her mouth and splashed onto the pavement. Then Toni was outside the car. She was on her hands and knees. Sharon had pushed her.

Toni looked behind her and saw Sharon leaning out the open door, hissing down at her. "I brought you home Toni just remember that." Then Sharon closed the door and started the car.

Toni got up on her feet and put on the shoe she was holding. She wobbled a bit as she watched Sharon back the car out of the parking place and swing it around until it pulled up beside her.

"Just look at you Toni, just look at you," Sharon said jabbing the other shoe at Toni through the car window. "You're nothing but an ugly old bitch, you know that. Nothing but a dog."

Toni stood crookedly, naked except for the skimpy top that hung open from her shoulders. Her eyes were big.

"Well, just look at you Sharon," Toni said, then turned away, limping quickly across the parking lot in the direction of the low brick apartments.

Sharon thought how funny, then how sorrowful Toni looked walking that way, and she looked down at the shoe she held in her hand, then over at the rumpled skirt beside her on the seat. She knew the right thing to do was to give them back, so she stopped the car and got out.

Sharon walked quickly but Toni seemed to get farther and farther away. She tried calling out Toni's name but was afraid to. She held tight to Toni's skirt and shoe because she didn't want to lose them. When Toni got to the door of one of the apartments, her arm raised to knock, Sharon stopped. Then she spoke: "Toni," Sharon said, but much too softly to be heard.

Toni knocked again, then yelled something. The door swung open and Sharon saw Toni standing in a narrow wedge of light. A man moved into the light and looked at Toni, then put his arm around her. As he moved Toni close to him, toward the light inside the apartment, his arm looked like a wide red blister across her back.

Saïdeh Pakravan

The Eyes of the Hunter

SAÏDEH PAKRAVAN is Iranian-born and French-educated, and lives in McLean, Virginia. A writer of both fiction and nonfiction and a poet, she was for many years the editor of a cross-cultural quarterly in English for the Iranian-American community in the United States, *Chanteh.* Her work has appeared in anthologies and in publications including the *Potomac Review*, the *Sonora Review*, *Poet Lore*, *Calyx*, and the *Baltimore Review.* She has also published a collection of short stories, *The Arrest of Hoveyda: Stories of the Iranian Revolution* (Mazda Publishers). She has received an F. Scott Fitzgerald Award and been nominated for a Pushcart Prize.

I know exactly when I stopped feeling like a woman, when I withdrew—or was withdrawn—from the playing field. I have now stopped looking at men as a woman looks at them who can be stirred by them and who knows they can be stirred by her.

A woman who is still active as a woman—not necessarily sexually active but potentially sexually active—looks at men and upon men in a particular way, even the ones most removed from her idea of what a man should be like in order to attract her. Often quite unconsciously, she sees the ugliest and the dumbest male as belonging to a sex with some other representatives of which she could have something going at some point.

Not necessarily that she will, mind you, but that she might. And—nothing new under the sun—a woman who considers men in this light sends out vibrations that representatives of the male sex will in turn catch and respond to—even those not interested in her per se—as they would respond to any sexually active woman, or any woman potentially so. Which means that in the way they look at her, in the way they may lightly touch her to stress a point or give her their attention, they will indicate (though most of the time totally unaware of doing so) that they, in point of fact, recognize her as someone who belongs to a category from which a man might pick a mate, temporary or otherwise.

Attention is the key word here. The surest way to measure the deterioration of a woman as she advances in age is the degree and quality of attention men give her. In her late teens or her second or third decade, a reasonably winsome woman will, at some level, have a man's total attention. The man may not be rolling on his back, audibly purring, or letting his eyes go dreamy, but his hormones will say hi to hers. A healthy man who responds to a young female may not even be aware of it or have the least intention of pursuing her. He may be a perfectly faithful and content husband meeting a friend's wife, a father having a heart-to-heart with his daughter, an autocratic boss berating a secretary, a writer meeting his editor. He may have a calm penis, resting motionless between his legs. But at some level, he will intimately vibrate with the knowledge that he is interacting with a young woman. She has firm breasts and buttocks, smooth lips, a vagina where a man can put the tool that nature gave him for that very purpose. (We are talking nature here, not deliberate lust or wantonness.)

In her fourth decade, a woman may or may not be sexually interesting. It depends on the extent to which she takes care of her looks, it depends on whether the natural aging process is taking place in a flattering or gross manner. It also depends on whether she is in a position of power—she's the boss—or related to someone in a position of power—she's the boss's wife. So a woman in her forties, *if* she's moderately attractive, *if* she's powerful or related to someone powerful, will keep her allure and men's attention. Also, beside her circumstances, the years will have added certain advantages to make up for the fact that her hormones are not calling out as loudly as before: she will be more amusing, more forceful, more secure, or more determined. Enough to earn a man's attention, though this last not as intense as that a younger woman might command.

Now we come to women in their fifties. Some women in their fifties keep in shape, take care of their skin and their diet, and cover the gray in their hair. But under the facials, their skin is dehydrated and men who bother can only imagine how dry the rest of her would be. Although there may be some surprises there. Individuals vary. A woman may look all right and she may remain tight and lubricated enough to accommodate a man and pleasure him. But for the most part, she will begin to be out of the game and content with a husband growing old by her side.

Not to disparage a cherished companion, but after thirty years or more of seeing her every day, the husband will not, ever, look at her with the eyes of the hunter. If the two form what is traditionally known as a good couple, asperities sanded away so that there's a snug fit and enough likes and dislikes in common, they will be happier than most. If one is difficult, or both of them are, then the bickering exploding from time to time into full-blown conflict will continue until one of them dies. But that's another story.

To come back to our woman over fifty, she will soon realize, without undue surprise, that the quality of men's attention has diminished, that sometimes, in the middle of a conversation, their eyes are drawn to what goes on beyond her, so that she will catch herself turning to throw a furtive look at whatever fascinating situation has developed behind her back. In her fifties, if a woman is in a position of power or is related to someone in a position of power, she still has a fair chance of capturing a man's undivided attention, particularly if the man's livelihood depends on the woman's appreciation of him, but the reasons will no longer be the right ones.

Of course, a man-woman contact of any sort, be it the most casual, has its subtext. But then, so does a black-white contact—or any other combination of races or nationalities—a young-old one, or a fat-thin one. Each individual will remain conscious, at some level, of the other person's difference.

The fifth decade was certainly the decisive one for me. I went so fast from being a woman to no longer being one that I didn't know what hit me. Not because of age, which would have allowed a smoother transition. No. Rejection was what undid me.

A few months after that rejection—of which more later—I was talking to my boss, Alex, when I became strongly aware of the fact that neither of us was using the indicators that I was accustomed to in any conversation with a man. The realization was so stunning that I believe I stopped in mid-sentence. We were going through spring catalogues. Alex's assistant was there, a pert, bosomy girl with extraordinary curly red hair that fell to her waist. I knew there was nothing at all between them and no intention on either side that there ever should be. Alex had just entered into a raging affair with a model and Lizzie, the assistant, was engaged. Yet, whenever Alex turned to her, a light went on in his eyes that he snuffed out whenever he turned to me.

Alex likes me. We have worked together a long time and his manner is ever friendly and courteous. But there it was. The change that came over him as he went from Lizzie to me and back to Lizzie was unbelievable. Even more startling was my realization that I'd been sitting there as aware of him as a man as I'd been aware of my chair as a chair.

Over the next few days, I gradually became aware of my new status as a non-woman or a no-longer woman. I started testing the fact with salespeople, customers, suppliers. When people came to me, or when I went out to look at the new collections to pick what we needed for our stores, I was transparent. Everybody was welcoming—after all, my position in the chain of command called for deference—but something was missing.

I, in turn, was no longer seeing the men. I heard them, saw their hands that tapped a pencil, pointed to a particularly good sketch, picked up a paper cup, held a door open, but it was all work. In the past, a shapely hand could send me, at some level, into a daydream of it cupping my breast or slipping between my thighs; a full mouth would call for a kiss even as I was discussing numbers or schedules. Or I would automatically check out a man's backside as he walked by. Now, nothing.

So what had happened? How did I go from that to this? Rejection. One morning, months before, Alex tells me that we're meeting with the company lawyer to discuss the Joel G. plagiarism issue. Alex wants me there as I was the one involved with buying the line. Though we all know that in fashion, plagiarism is next to impossible to prove, we still have to cover our ass and make sure we won't be hauled into court if the designer is.

At our lawyer's, things look the same. The watercolors haven't changed, neither has the secretary. But someone else is occupying Jack's office, Clarence something or other. I've seen him at a couple of parties and I don't like him. For one thing, he's loud. He sneezes loudly, clears his throat loudly, his voice booms, he laughs too much. I jump when his phone rings: the volume seems to be set to the maximum. Plus, he's the least subtle sort of womanizer. Even when he talks directly to Alex, his eyes move back to me, run from my throat to my breasts to my knees to my ankles, again and again.

Now I won't deny that a minimal amount of stroking—not touching, mind you, but some decent spark of admiration in a guy's eyes—does me good. In fact, I need it from time to time, dealing as I do with gorgeous models, the epitome of women men lust after. They may be vacuous, but physically, the competition is disheartening and I often feel like a lump. So male attention, when discreet, is mostly welcome. Now this man is putting it all out for my benefit. OK, he would surely do more for Kate Moss or Naomi Campbell but I don't find him repulsive and, at some level, I start responding. He, in turn, shifts into high gear. There's only the three of us. Alex, ever attuned to his surroundings, listens to Clarence then turns to me and lets his eyes rest on me, telling me he's aware of what's going on.

We have brought a portfolio of drawings and photographs. Seated next to me on the couch, Clarence looks at them, says there's no case there, and rubs his leg against mine. As if that weren't enough, every time he makes a point, he actually puts his hand on my thigh. Christ, I can't believe this guy!

And I can't believe myself. Normally, a gross come-on like that turns me off completely. Now, not because of it but in spite of it, I'm aroused. It's the guy himself. He's sexy, no denying it. I'd like nothing so much as to hitch up my skirt and hoist myself on his lap. Instead of which, as a matter of discipline, I look at my watch, say I have forgotten something important, and leave.

He calls me at my office an hour later. Discipline hasn't been working too well, though I've occupied that hour looking intently at the photographs of my family on my desk, telling myself that I've put three kids through college, that I have grandchildren, for God's sake, that I am fifty-three years old and that guy is loud, brash, a thigh-kneader, and worse, a name-dropper. In our first five minutes in his office, he mentioned three celebs. One who had called him late last night to ask for advice, one who invited him on his yacht, a third whose biography he was reading. "I have to. I'll run into her in at least a couple of places and she's bound to ask me what I think." Christ! Plus, he's probably a grandfather himself. But when he calls and asks me to dinner, I say yes. Yes, yes.

Though big and blonde and of Dutch origin, Clarence goes by the manual of the Latin lover. When he picks me up, he brings along a box of ridiculous long-stemmed red roses. And takes me to *the* restaurant. Does he think I'm impressed? (Though he does have his own table, I'll grant him that.) What impresses me is his voracious personality. He stuffs himself like a pig, his napkin stuck in his collar, drinks an enormous amount of rich burgundy, his hand at my side keeps going on my knees—I brush it away with less and less conviction (I drink a lot of burgundy myself). He wipes his lips slowly when he's done eating, first with his napkin, then with his hand, looking at me all the while. Then his eyes lock in mine, stuck in a freeze frame so prolonged I feel like fast-forwarding him.

In his eight-room pad across from the Metropolitan Museum, every wall, door, window frame surface is stark white. Everything else is black: leather couch, picture frames, the pictures themselves. The overall effect is depressing, a throwback to the sixties, like walking into a Vasarely. Smooth gray stones, round or oval, about the size of my palm, crowd the smoked-glass top of the coffee table. Clarence sees me looking at them and tells me they're the work of a world-famous Greek sculptor. A close friend of his, he adds. But of course.

Even the sheets are black, but I don't smile. My mind is entirely taken with him. Indeed, I want him more than I've ever wanted a man. That's always hard to establish after the fact, but when we get into bed, a few indications tell me that this one must be different for me. For one thing, I don't mind facing the lamp that no doubt highlights my every wrinkle. Nor do I worry about camouflaging flab but let it spread where it will, nor do I artistically drape the sheet over my breasts that have seen better days. And, a first as far as I can remember in my highly excited state, I'm not keeping count of moves and countermoves either. Not once do I think, I'll do this if he does that first. I do what I want and take what's offered in good spirit.

Not, I expect, that Clarence is aware of all the finer aspects of my emotions. He pounds away, oblivious, touching all the right spots. No delicacy, but good sturdy equipment and plenty of endurance. I don't even need to rely on fantasies but keep my eyes open and myself firmly anchored in the here and now. The here is where I want to be though I have a brief vision of rolling hills, of wild flowers, and cascading water. Is this me screaming? In the wee hours, I drop, half-dead, into an incredibly deep sleep.

He's gone when I wake up, God knows how many hours later. On the nightstand, a yellow stickie with one word on it, followed by an exclamation point, "Wow!"

Wow! is how I feel too, although I wouldn't have put it as succinctly. I roll this way and that in his bed—*his* bed I keep telling myself with glee—spreading my limbs, running my fingers and my tongue—I'm not ashamed to say—on a couple of wet stains on the black sheets. Lying on my back, legs together, my arms across my breasts, my eyes closed, I thank the dispenser of all favors for this gift. Eat your heart out, Kate Moss.

Worried that Clarence doesn't believe in rubber, saying that people like us are not at risk? No, I'm not worried.

Feeling guilty that I cheated on my husband who's with his group somewhere in the Far East? No, I don't feel guilty.

I make myself some coffee, go back to bed, pleasure myself. Then I take a shower, slip one of the smooth gray stones in my bag, and leave. He'll call me. There's no sense of urgency.

He doesn't that day, nor the next. I wait three days, then call him. He's out of town for a couple of weeks. Although Alex, still anxious about the plagiarism issue, talks to him twice and reports the conversation to me for comments.

I act *dégagé* and ask Alex if Clarence is back then. "Back?" he asks. "Back from where?"

"I don't know," I say. "Someone mentioned he was out of town."

"Maybe he was, earlier in the week. I saw him yesterday."

Over the next two weeks, I put myself through every humiliating situation that a woman, smitten and scorned, can put herself through. I threaten his secretary, whine, plead. I send him notes, gifts that I pick to reflect both my taste and my sense of humor and that he doesn't acknowledge. He's not in to take my call, he's not in to take my call, he's not in to take my call. He won't be in to take my call.

OK, OK, I can deal with this. No, I can't. I rationalize that he needs to be reminded of me, of my physicality. One evening, I waylay him outside his office building. What I can't rationalize is his annoyed pursing of lips when he sees me. Nor his greetingless, wary nod as he passes me. OK, it doesn't get any worse. Grovel I will. "Clarence," I call out.

He'd already walked past me. Now he stops and turns around. "You're a grandmother," he says. "Why don't you start acting like one?" and walks away.

Where are thunderbolts when you need them? I close my eyes, sharply breathing in. When I open them, he's nowhere in sight. Not scorched and burned to the ground, or bullet-ridden, with rivers of blood flowing from him. He's just gone.

He did die a few days later though, of a massive coronary. Sentiment is so subjective. Here I was, after a couple of weeks in the throes of binding my fate forever to this man, knowing as if the fact had been handed down with the tablets of the law on Mount Sinai that if I couldn't have him, the sky would remain dark forever and spring would never come again, yet the news of his death brought me nothing but relief. Can one smile inwardly?

Now, two years after my night of half-demented screwing and those countless orgasms that had come chasing one another like golf balls out of an Indian fakir's mouth, I'm dried up as a prune, which is to say that I still have a little flesh on me and hardly any juice to speak of. What the next avatar is, God knows. I'm entering my fifty-fifth year, one of the last legs. Outwardly, all is good. Inside is another story. I hardly remember Clarence and no longer see the smooth gray stone I use as a paperweight, but that one rejection has made everything that came before him a miserable failure. Ah, but we all live. Live long enough, and memory will go, and all memories.

Ginger Park

His Footsteps, His Whispers

Korean American author GINGER PARK writes for both children and adults. Her highly praised work has often been inspired by her heritage. She has been a guest on *Good Morning, America*, *The Diane Rehm Show*, NPR's *Weekend Edition Sunday*, Washingtonpost.com, *Between the Lines* (Associated Press), UPN's *Making a Difference*, and the *Channel 9 News*. Her work has been featured in many publications including *USA Weekend Magazine*, *Glamour*, *Dallas Morning News*, the *Washington Post*, the *Sun Sentinel*, the *San Jose Mercury News*, and the *Oregonian*. She has garnered many prestigious awards, including the 1999 International Reading Association's Children's Book Award, a Notable Books for a Global Society Award, Parents' Choice Award, and a Bank Street College Award. "His Footsteps, His Whispers" is an excerpt from her recently completed novel "Sojo's Truth." To read about her work, visit parksisters.com.

Like every weeknight following tennis practice, I was home studying while my father was out on the sea. I had a chemistry test the next day, but when I heard footsteps and whispers in the hallway, I closed my textbook.

Mother: *Shh, my son's home.*

Man: *I should go.*

Mother: *No, stay. He's in his room.*

Man: *Not a good idea, Jewel.*

Mother: *One glass of wine.*

Pause.

Man: *I think I should go.*

Mother: *Wait here.*

Silence.

My mother had been drinking. My door was shut, my jaw locked. A moment passed. Then a knock at my door. I buried my face in my textbook.

"Come in."

The door swung open. Sparkle scurried across the hall, ricocheted off the wall and into Maeve's empty bedroom. My fourteen-year-old sister was at a roller-skating birthday party, and Sparkle, her blind cat, missed her. Fool cat. Didn't she know Maeve was in a better place? My mother stood in the doorway, her cheeks rosy from too much wine.

"Why don't you go for a run, Hawthorne," she suggested.

When my mother drank, she morphed into a creature of sin. When she drank she met a friend, and sometimes he came to our home. The same friend, I think. I couldn't pick him out of a lineup; my mother made sure we never saw him, slipping him into the house like a specter in the night. But I recognized his footsteps, his whispers; they were as worn and woven into my mind as the carpet on the stairs. If I really wanted to know his identity all I had to do was open my bedroom door and look him in the eye. But I didn't want to know, I didn't want to pin a face to those footsteps, those whispers.

I couldn't say my mother's friend was a bad man, but he drove me out of my home and that said something about him.

I jogged along the streets, my shadow my only companion. It followed me down Cambridge Road, through the woods, and along Route 28. I liked it out here on the bleak streets where stray dogs and cats roamed, where bats dove dangerously low because sometimes these creatures felt like my friends, and sometimes this is where I felt I belonged.

On this night it grew particularly dark out, as if the streetlamps were flames I extinguished one by one upon my arrival. The air wasn't cool and crisp as it should be in September, but dank from the stench of rats rising from the sewers. I continued jogging, my thoughts on my father and the conversation we had had that morning.

I was in bed, eyes on the ceiling, when a *tap*, *tap*, *tap* came at my door.

"Hawthorne," my father said, knowing I would be awake. Wide awake. His eyes peered through a crack in the door. "Can I come in?"

My eyes shifted to the clock. Ten minutes past five. He was off to sea, but not before apologizing for the argument last night.

"Yeah, Pop, come on in."

My father was a fisherman, and every night he brought home the smell of the sea. His face was rugged, and I imagined he would someday be like Hemingway's Santiago; old and weathered from the elements, but more so from life.

He crossed the room and sat on the edge of my bed, wincing and clutching the small of his back from an injury in an epic battle with a five-hundred-pound bluefin tuna. It was the catch of his lifetime.

"Caught nearly a decade ago, and the back still aches," he remarked.

The room was dark. The only discernible light emanated from the clock. My father's shadow took up the wall. Sometimes it surprised me that he cast one at all.

"How was practice?" he asked me.

"It was good."

His eyes scanned the rows of tennis trophies on the wall shelf. "Would like to come out and watch you play sometime."

"I don't know, Pop. Might make me nervous."

My father solemnly nodded. "I'm glad you know how to dream, Hawthorne. I'm proud of you, son. I hope you know that."

"I know, Pop."

Long pause.

"And I'm sorry about the argument with your mother last night. You know I love that lady. Hell, I would die for that lady. But sometimes I don't know how to live for her. Does that make any sense?"

"You could spend more time with her," I said.

My father ran a tense hand through his receding brown hair. "I know, son. I know. But do you really think that would stop her from drinking?"

"I can only hope," I replied.

I can't pinpoint when my mother's social drinking developed into a serious problem; only that it seemed to slowly take over our lives like the spread of cancer. My mother was small and demure, and even when she drank she was placid and, in her own way, loving and nurturing. Though there were sins and arguments, I can only recall once when a near moment of violence passed through our home.

Thanksgiving: Five years ago. The smell of turkey and sweet potatoes in the oven will always conjure up that holiday when my mother was drunk, and taunting my father with a collection of Hummel heirlooms that had belonged to his grandmother. She juggled three in the air before allowing them to crash to the floor. Red with rage, my father raised a hand to her and muttered a profanity.

"Pop, no!" I cried before he could strike.

My father slowly lowered his hand, lip quivering. He picked up the pieces of the three Hummel heirlooms. Destroyed like the foundation of our home.

That Thanksgiving took my family down dark, disparate paths. My mother swept Maeve and Sparkle off to Aunt Maggie's in Somerville. My father took me aboard his fishing boat. We sailed a million miles away from the confusion of our home where the peaceful fog on the Boston Harbor silenced my angst. No weekend of confession or talk of the pain that divided my family that holiday. We were simply father and son on the hushed sea.

I had a dream that this Thanksgiving would be different.

I passed Saint Matthew's Church at the same time Pappy was pulling out of the parking lot. To his congregation he was Father Drake. To me he was Pappy, my tennis coach. He drove up to the curb in his gold Duster and rolled down his window, slowly keeping pace with me. He could read my mind.

"Care to talk about it?" he asked.

"I'd rather just run."

Long silence.

I climbed Chestnut Hill and turned onto Tremont, Pappy still keeping pace with me, always by my side.

"Focus on Thanksgiving weekend," he finally spoke. "Don't let things eat you up, Hawthorne. Remember, you have a dream, I have a prayer, and together we have a plan. Win Chicago and you're on your way!"

Pappy kept my dreams alive. As he put it—

"That's what coaches do, Hawthorne."

There were times when I was convinced that he was more excited than I was about the national indoor tournament held in Chicago. If I won, my spring calendar would be marked with the biggest tournament of the year: the National Boys 18s in Ann Arbor. If I won, a scholarship was sure to come my way.

I clenched my fist and roared, "I'm ready!"

Pappy winked. "That's what I want to hear. I'll see you on the practice court tomorrow, four o'clock," he said before driving off.

Pappy took me under his wing four and a half years ago after spotting me on the Brighton public tennis courts. In those days I was a scrawny boy who envied my taller and stronger peers. Now I was seventeen, nearly six feet tall and still growing.

Pappy was hammering the practice wall when my friend, Will, and I walked onto a court. I was surprised by Pappy's athletic prowess. To most, he was known as the father who gave fiery sermons. But did anyone know he could hit the ball with that same fire?

"Hey, Father Drake," I waved as we warmed up.

Pappy waved back. He took a seat on a bench, and stayed through the first set, watching intently. I was nervous by his presence, his eyes, but this nervous energy also raised the level of my game. I surprised myself with some impressive shots: whipping forehands and cross-court winners.

Pappy left before our match was over, missing a victory on my part. But that evening, a knock came at our door.

"Good evening, Father Drake," my mother greeted him.

"Jewel, we've been neighbors for years, and I had no idea the tennis talent that lived next door!" he exclaimed.

My mother was a little confused, but Pappy cleared things up with a briefing of his tennis history. "I played tennis at Stanford..."

I sat quietly, listening to their conversation.

"I would like to work with your son," Pappy said.

"With all due respect, Father, Hawthorne's hoping to play for his high school team next year," my mother told him.

"That's great. Wonderful. I encourage that endeavor. But Hawthorne will never have a chance to play in college unless he plays the USTA circuit. All the college scouts recruit their players through the United States Tennis Association. Hawthorne has natural ability, great footwork. He needs some harnessing, but with a little guidance and a little faith he could someday play college ball."

My mother's face and shoulders sagged with despair.

"What's wrong, Jewel?" Pappy asked.

"Father, you dream big. But college isn't in our budget, much less tennis lessons."

"Jewel, Jewel," Pappy addressed my mother, his voice soft with compassion. "I went to Stanford on scholarship. Granted, my parents doled out a lot of dough on tennis lessons, but I'm willing to work with Hawthorne. All I ask in return is his time and effort."

My mother sat up straight. "So you really think Hawthorne is that good?"

"I wouldn't be here if I didn't think he was *that* good. He's got raw talent. But raw talent alone will only take a player so far. There are a lot of these guys out there. A dime a dozen. The ones who succeed are the ones who work hard and dedicate themselves." Pappy turned his attention my way. I quickly learned that his gaze was never dismissed. "Are you up to such a task, Hawthorne?"

That afternoon, Pappy saw something in me that no one else had seen my whole life. There I was just out playing tennis—a game I loved—and now he was talking about college. He was giving me hope for the future. If that didn't give a person faith, nothing would.

"Yes," I replied.

Pappy's passion for the game was seen in his eyes, heard in his voice. And when he pumped his fist, it pumped my spirits. *You have a dream, I have a prayer, and together we have a plan* became our mantra.

One hot summer day as we cooled down after a two-hour practice, I watched Pappy chug water and wipe sweat off his face with his ragged T-shirt. He did it with such sacrilegious drama. I couldn't say I was ever witness to it, but I was certain there were moments when Pappy cursed his God and wiped sweat off with his sacred *cloth*.

I had never asked Pappy a personal question—the focus always on me, my game, my dream—but a philosophical sky opened up to us, and it seemed the appropriate moment to ask why he gave up his tennis dreams for priesthood.

"I once had a girl named Jessica," he began. "We met at Stanford. Jessica was my whole world."

"So where is she now?" I asked.

"In our junior year we were heading south down the coast to Laguna Beach on spring break when a drunk driver took a curve too fast and collided head-on with us. In a split second Jessica was gone."

"I'm sorry, Pappy."

Silence.

"What happened to the drunk driver?" I asked, feeling shame for my own mother's history behind the wheel.

"He walked away with a few bruises. As they say, ain't life ironic?"

Silence.

"What about you? Were you injured?"

"My knee was crushed under the weight of the dash. I couldn't walk for three months. Was on crutches for another two months or so. Over time, the knee healed, just not my head. Without Jessica I was lost."

Pappy dropped his head.

"I didn't mean to drum up sad memories," I apologized.

But Pappy wasn't listening. "She wanted to have a house full of kids. But God had decided otherwise."

"Is that when you decided you wanted to become a priest?"

Pappy shook his head. "For months after my knee healed, I did nothing but condemn the world. I couldn't focus on my studies or tennis. It all seemed so meaningless. Eventually, I dropped everything—my studies, my tennis racket—and roamed the country taking odd jobs."

"Like what?"

"Sweeping floors in markets, washing cars, peach picking. Whatever earned me a buck or got me a meal. I met kind and unusual folk along the way. The most interesting of all was an elder by the name of Kotori."

"Kotori?"

"Hopi Indian," Pappy informed me. "Which means Screech Owl Spirit."

"How did you meet a Hopi Indian?"

"In a campground above the Grand Canyon. I truly believe it was a karmic meeting. Do you believe in karma, Hawthorne?"

I shrugged. "Karma?"

"In Hinduism and Buddhism, it means the effects of a person's actions that determine his destiny in his next incarnation."

"How can you believe in karma, Pappy? You're a priest."

"True," Pappy agreed. "But let's just say I'm an open-minded priest."

"So you met Kotori in the Grand Canyon?"

"It was a cold night. The winds were blowing desert sand everywhere, causing eerie sounds. Then a knock came at my van door and there was Kotori, claiming to be a medicine man. At first, I was skeptical, but that skepticism faded over a can of Vienna sausages. Kotori told me—*In the white man's culture, I am a doctor. In my culture, I am a shaman. The difference being, I heal the sick, physically and spiritually.* The white man's doctor healed my knee. Kotori healed my spirit."

Pappy came home and went back to school. To earn extra bucks, he moonlighted as a tennis club pro. After graduating, he continued his studies at the seminary.

"Priesthood was a calling, Hawthorne," he claimed.

Pappy believed he had returned from his long journey physically *and* spiritually renewed. But sometimes I wondered. Sometimes I believed Pappy's priesthood was a safe pause from a world he was still condemning.

I lost my first USTA match, and many more thereafter.

"Everyone's so much better than me," I lamented to Pappy.

"They've got experience under their belts. That's all they've got over you, Hawthorne. Some of these boys have been on the circuit since they were eight years old. You're a late bloomer. You're going to have to work twice as hard to catch up."

Pappy's faith kept me going. He encouraged me to enter every local tournament, which I did. I forsook friends and TV and other interests such as basketball and soccer all in the name of tennis. But that first year was a disaster.

"Win or lose, each match, each tournament, is earning you experience," Pappy insisted.

And he was right. Grueling practice sessions and a year of tournament experience made the next year my year. I not only won matches, but tournaments too. My confidence was high and my sectional ranking soared to eighteen. But Pappy didn't let it go to my head.

"Keep your feet on the ground, Hawthorne," he advised me. "New England is one of the weaker sections. Focus on boosting your national ranking."

Four years later, my ranking was ninety-five; good enough to put me on the college scout radar. But I needed that scholarship; my only ticket to college.

"Chicago will change all of that," Pappy assured me. "College coaches from around the country will be there to see what I saw in you five years ago."

I prayed he was right.

Later, as I jogged up Cambridge Road, I spotted Pappy's car parked in his driveway. Peace settled over me like an angel spreading its wings. For nearly five years, Pappy had guided me on the tennis court, and now he was guiding me into my own home. I had never spoken of the troubles that plagued my family. I didn't have to; there were some things Pappy just knew. Last year he had invited me to church, something my family had forsaken long ago. I had asked my parents to come with me, but their reply—no—was less out of faith and more out of shame.

I walked inside the house, looked around. No footsteps, no whispers. My mother was sound asleep.

Soon my father would be home from work.

Like a thousand times before, he would feel the trespasser's aura everywhere. It would be all around him, but he would never speak of it. Not to anyone, not to me or Pappy, not even to himself. I think that's what broken men do; turn over in their sleep without words.

Suzanne Picard

The Witch Doctor of Love

SUZANNE PICARD graduated from Harvard College before becoming a Peace Corps volunteer in Cameroon. She is finishing her first novel, a love story between an American white woman and the heir to a West African tribal kingdom—a witch doctor, an ivory smuggler, and a polygamist expected to take thirty wives. She lives in Kensington, Maryland, with only one husband and their three children.

Turn almost any corner and you bump into someone who's not having enough sex.

Like now: I'm wiping snot from Jeff's nose and juggling children's valentines and cheap candy hearts as I round an aisle at CVS and collide, right-breast forward, with a dark-jacketed arm. The man attached to the arm backs up two steps and mumbles an apology even though it couldn't be more obvious that I'm the one at fault. I recognize him as Tom Ryder, a Sunday school teacher at Wallace Memorial, my husband Jimmy's church, and immediately wish I'd worn a bra or at least a coat.

"No need to apologize. I should look where I'm going." Thrusting the dirty tissue into my jeans pocket, I wonder if Tom's cheeks and high forehead could be reddening. This makes me fish for memories of our recent interactions, and I pull up a conversation in which we discovered that we'd both grown up in Pittsburgh. I declared my craving for a Primanti Brothers' sandwich, and he nodded, *with an icy Iron City to wash it down,* and then we laughed and said our mouths were watering. We took turns praising the Strip district, the two inclines, Carnegie Museum, the Steelers' young quarterback, and the view of the city and its three rivers when you first emerge from the Fort Pitt tunnel. Fragments of other half-forgotten, fun conversations float by, too—the theology in Philip Pullman novels, the best architectural features of Monticello, the most interesting Civil War battlefields near Washington—but now Jeff is tugging on my sweatshirt.

"Mommy, I want Spiiiiider Maaaaaan valentines, too."

"But Spider Man is so ugly. They're OK for your brother, but not for four-year-olds. Where *is* Carter anyway?" I confirm that my oldest is nowhere in sight before giving my attention back to the definitely blushing Tom. "Valentine's Day. It's so silly, isn't it? Do you know how hard it'll be to get a nine-year-old boy to address these to—" I gasp, roll my eyes, feign horror, "—a dozen girls?" I rattle packages of Spider Man cards and Necco conversation hearts, realizing too late that I'm letting loose Kiss-Me-Marry-Me-Loverboy energy waves into the air between us. Tom has a small bald spot and is a little too thick around the middle, but he doesn't have a comb-over, and long, dark lashes surround cerulean eyes. Looking at him now with fresh interest, I decide that his round face and barrel-shaped torso give him a Teddy-Roosevelt-Rough-Rider look.

"Did Jim tell you… I…I just had coffee with him yesterday, as a matter of fact." Tom shifts from one foot to the other and folds his arms across his chest.

I murmur a friendly inanity and silently increase the amount of time he hasn't been laid from the typical couple of weeks to a year or maybe two. No doubt he'd call himself happily married. I used to think infrequent-sex marriages were a Washington phenomenon, but lately I've been broadening my theory. There could be something Western and religious about them. I've made it into an equation, in case I get around to telling Jimmy. *Monogamy and Monotheism are both factors. It's simple: M x M = Morality Squared.* My point—and Jimmy was a Peace Corps volunteer in Africa too, so maybe he'll understand this—is that you never see such pinched, anxious, hungry looks on the Bekom people of Cameroon unless they're waiting for a meal of steaming *fufu* and *njamba-njamba* at the peak of dry season.

As Tom and I exchange see-you-on-Sunday farewells, I'm already a dozen years in the past and five thousand miles away, dancing to juju music with the Bekom witch doctor. We shuffle our feet and gyrate our hips, and when the music ends, he reaches for my hand. He rubs his middle finger in a slow clandestine circle on my palm. Even though his touch melts me faster than the Cameroonian sun at noon, I shake my head, tug my hand free. And for the next two years I'll have daily chats with myself: *You did the right thing. He would never have worn a condom. You would have gotten AIDS. You would have gone crazy on the nights when he played doctor with the newly abandoned first wives.*

"Did that man make you sad, Mommy?"

After years of not thinking about him, the *chongwan,* the witch doctor, glides again through my days and nights. Whenever he wants to. No matter where I am. I wish I knew why. "Mister Ryder? No, he didn't make me sad. Besides, Mommy can't be sad when she's with you."

❧

Jimmy walks into the kitchen while I'm dipping tilapia fillets into egg then bread crumbs for our typical Friday night loaves-and-fishes meal.

"I ran into poor Tom Ryder today."

"Why in the world would you call him poor?"

The arc of Jimmy's question spurs me to tell him the truth. I lean toward him in case Carter or Jefferson should bound into the kitchen. "Because he's not getting laid." Jimmy and I met in Africa not long after I declined to sleep with the witch doctor, and I start to say that Poor Tom would be getting plenty if he lived in Cameroon, but Jimmy's eyes look as startled as a hyena's in the headlights.

"You... know... how... do you know?" He's stammering as much as Tom was earlier in CVS, the incredulity obvious in his baritone preacher's voice.

I stare at him for a second before I hoot. "Shit, that's too funny!"

The minister claps a hand over my mouth as Carter slides into the kitchen on white-socked feet. "Sh-h-h—the kids."

"Is Mom laughing or crying?" Carter asks.

Jimmy heaves a sigh and shakes his head. "Laughing."

"Crying," I say. "For Tom."

"For who?" asks my son, at the same time that his father grabs me by the elbow and steers me toward his study.

He closets us in the tiny open space between his messy desk, file cabinets bulging with sermons, his U.S. presidents' collection—everything from bobble-heads to campaign buttons and bumper stickers—and the loaded bookshelves and towering stacks of religion and American history tomes. I throw my arms around his neck and nibble his lips, which he tolerates for a moment, but when I slide one hand down between us and tug on his zipper, he grunts and pushes me away. "That's not why I brought you in here, and you know it."

Backing away, I pretend-pout, although to be honest, I'm more excited about the tilapia fillets and Marvelous Market cheese bread than I am about sex. I try to remember when we'd last been naked together and decide it's been at least ten days, maybe longer. We always had sex on Sunday afternoons until Carter outgrew his afternoon nap, although back then we would have laughed at any need for once-a-week scheduling. In a few years, will Jimmy and I be equally lost in Tom's dry wilderness? Will forty days and nights seem like nothing? With two fingers I stretch and smooth the vertical wrinkles between Jimmy's eyebrows. "How long—did Tom tell you that? More than two years? It must be ages since he's fucked anybody. He'd have to be *desperate* to tell you. You can probably double whatever length of time he said. Or—wait. He's getting ready to have an affair, and—"

"No! Stop this now. He loves Lucy. She's... you know." His voice drops to a hissing whisper. "Past menopause." He looks wary, wondering if I'll let that sexism go by. "They've been married a long time. I'm sure legions of men are in his exact same situation. Come on, hon, he's a deacon—he teaches Sunday school. A great guy. Now that's it. I won't say another thing. I made a mistake—I hadn't meant to tell you. You *know* how I feel about this."

He refers to sharing parishioners' secrets, and I nod and bite my lip to restrain my lingering mirth. Jimmy has leaked secrets before, but never like this. Too distraught over stepfather incest, early teen pregnancies or abortions, parental homophobia and disgust toward an only son, he's whispered to me in bed, usually in the morning after a sleepless night. More than once he's made me cry, the stories difficult enough without his kindhearted distress.

"I am curious how you guessed, though. You're not friendly with Lucy, are you?"

"I don't remember ever meeting his wife. She doesn't come to services, does she? No, he just had that uptight, Washington look." My gaze travels over Jimmy's shelves searching for Teddy Roosevelt titles while I try to come up with possible ways a Presbyterian minister, even a charming, brilliant one like Jimmy, could help. "You didn't just quote the Bible at him—Jimmy, please tell me you didn't." I raise my eyebrows in hope. "That stuff about marital duty—a wife's body belongs to her man, blah blah blah."

Jimmy shakes his head and frowns, but his eyes twinkle. "You cannot *blah blah blah* the Bible. And yes, as a matter of fact, I did quote First Corinthians, as it's almost perfect on the subject, now isn't it? *A man should fulfill his duty as a husband, and a woman should fulfill her duty as a wife, and each should satisfy the other's needs. The wife is not the master of her own body, but the husband is; in the same way the husband is not the master of his own body, but the wife is.* You see, it's not even sexist."

I again make a play for his zipper, but he grabs my hand and squeezes before continuing his homily. *"Do not deny yourselves to each other, unless you first agree to do so for a while, in order to spend time in prayer."*

"Jesus Christ, Jimmy, you didn't tell him to pray about it. Prayers won't help!"

"They might. You never know." He winks at me and grins. "Plus I referred him to a good marriage therapist." He walks toward the door, and with one hand on the knob, turns back to me. "Sweetie, do you think... you could maybe watch the profanity? You're going to slip and embarrass yourself in church. Or in front of the boys..." He gives me the lips-together half smile that conveys his love—awareness of my strengths and tolerance for my foibles—but also a desire that I comport myself, at least occasionally, like an old-fashioned minister's wife.

"I promise to try harder." I say it as sincerely as possible because a witch doctor's plan—modified by more than a decade with Jimmy—is slipping into my brain. Maybe I could even use the Bible. I multiply Witch Doctor times Minister's Wife, and even though the only possible solution is Trouble, I ask Jimmy, "What grade does Tom teach? In Sunday school?"

"Why do you want to know?"

"Well, I can find out." I walk toward the kitchen bookshelves with the phonebooks and the Wallace Memorial directory.

Jimmy sighs. "He teaches eighth and ninth. Now, can we please forget about Tom?"

I stand on my toes in order to kiss him on the cheek. "I've forgotten." Thirteen- and fourteen-year-olds. I squirrel this information away with a vague sense that it may help.

ঌ

After dinner, Jimmy comes up behind me at the sink, slides dirty dishes into the sudsy water, and then gives me a hug. I look over my shoulder for Jeff or Carter before dropping the sponge and pressing back against him. This time I actually shiver.

I shiver again when I realize where my imagination is taking me. Juju music pulses through the Wallace sanctuary, but the arms encircling me belong to neither Jimmy nor the witch doctor. I'm with Tom, his blush coaxing my desire. I struggle to censor scenes that flow like a litany: undressing in an aisle, kneeling in front of him, casting shy glances upward at his open-mouthed gratitude. I see us on the pews, in the choir loft, our positions varying as fast as you can turn pages in the *Kama Sutra*.

I'm struggling to keep us away from the altar, when Carter returns to the kitchen with his homework. Jimmy kisses the top of my head and grabs the newspaper on his way out of the room. *Thank God.* I plunge my hands back into the warm water, shaking my head to clear away the images—too sacrilegious this time, even for me.

ঌ

I dip enameled tin plates in and out of the five-gallon bucket of cold rainwater, convincing myself that I'm washing them. The sun is setting in the fast way that it does near the equator, and I hurry to finish up. I'm ready for the quintessential Peace Corps evening—lighting a kerosene lantern, writing a letter home, and finishing Thoreau's *Walden.*

"I day go this night for *chongwan.* You day come wit me?" Dina's voice sounds plaintive. She and her husband Suboh live in the compound next to my Cameroon-government-issued cinder block house, and I've been taking my meals with them and their three children. Standing next to me in the open courtyard, she dries the dishes with a dirty rag. Several weeks ago I would have gone off in search of a cleaner towel, but now I save my revulsion for guinea worms and tumba flies living under the skin's dark veneer, rotting floorboards over too-full pit latrines, the dozens of black widows and their crazily spun webs under every piece of my furniture, the Bad Juju whose touch is a death curse...

"What's a *chongwan* again?" One of my too-numerous-to-count frustrations as a new volunteer is my inability to make any sense of Itangikom, the tribal language of the Bekom.

"*Chongwan* now doctor for bush."

I immediately know where she wants to go and why. "Listen, you don't need any doctor. Let me talk to Suboh. Maybe he'll change his mind. It isn't right, what he wants to do to you and your kids." But I know this is ridiculous even while I'm uttering the words, and when Dina turns away with the stack of plates looking ready to cry, I scrap my plans for a safe evening alone.

Before we set out, I stuff my pockets with spare batteries—the ones for sale in the local market never last—and grab a machete and flashlight. Dina shakes her head in amusement—the gibbous moon has already begun to glow—but I'm still as afraid of the African night as I'm certain about monogamy's moral superiority. Although I have yet to meet the Bekom tribal king with his two dozen wives, I'm already rebelling against kneeling and speaking only through cupped hands while I'm in his lecherous royal presence.

The *chongwan's* hut is the old-fashioned type—mud bricks with an elephant-grass-thatched roof. His bed, although constructed from raffia palm trunks, is huge and neatly covered with a gray blanket. Raffia shelves cover two walls from floor to ceiling, and I gape at their contents:

herbs, bark, bones, claws, pelts, feathers, tusks, horns, stones, shells, hollowed gourds. Splatters of candle wax decorate almost everything. Broken eggshells and dark splashes of what I assume to be blood are equally ubiquitous.

The man himself is gorgeous—broad shoulders, smooth, dark-chocolate skin, sparkling eyes, symmetrical features, full lips. He's younger than I expected. Ditto taller and more muscular. I tell myself it's the dim, kerosene-fueled lighting that's making him look like a god, and take a couple of deep breaths of the slightly excremental air to bring myself back to reality. Positioning myself under a citrus-scented bundle of herbs hanging from a beam, I try to keep my gaze on Dina as she explains her plight in Itangikom. When he responds, his voice is slow, confident, low in pitch and volume.

He'll prepare the right fetish—one that will ease her jealousy over Suboh's impending marriage to a second wife—and she can claim it the next night when she brings him a sacrificial fowl. In slow motion, his eyes travel first over Dina's body, then mine. I feel like I'm standing naked before him and am surprised when I don't feel any urge to turn from his gaze.

"You day bring *wulbongna* when you go come," he says to Dina as we depart. I assume he's reminding her to bring a chicken until I recall that w*ulbongna* means *white man*. Heat rises in me as fast as the Bad Juju can disrupt an ordinary market day.

~

All of us—Dina, Suboh, his second wife, Dina's children, the fetuses growing inside both Dina and the second wife, the *chongwan*, me—float on the slow river of time for an unquantifiable interval that is typical of bush life in Africa. Dina is once again happy. Sometimes she smiles as she touches the fetish around her neck, a tiny sack woven with palm fronds and filled with stones, seeds, and herbs. Sometimes I see her slip from the compound around midnight and take the path into the hills that we had once taken together two nights in a row. One market day, the witch doctor approaches Dina and me while we bargain for *cocoyams* and palm oil. After holding my hand for too long in greeting, he turns to Dina, and both their laughter and barely audible Itangikom make me cross my arms over my chest, trying to suppress a yearning that I thought to escape by coming to Cameroon. In spite of the midday heat, their bodies lean in toward one another, and their eyes shine brighter than the sun reflecting off the new machete blades for sale behind them.

Around four o'clock the next day, Jimmy's in his study practicing his sermon, his preacher's voice rumbling through the air ducts. Soon we'll have a light meal, the kind he likes before his high-stress Sundays. Lentil soup simmers on the stove, its garlicky aroma floating through the house. The soothing familiarity of such a Saturday almost makes me want to forget about witch doctoring, and I tell myself I'm only sitting at the big dining room table to help Jefferson and Carter. But Carter is scrawling his name across two dozen Spider Men in rapid succession, slipping them into tiny white envelopes like the ones in the church pews. Picking up more speed, he jots down his classmates' names, even the girls, crossing them methodically from his class list.

In a minute, without any need of maternal cajoling, he's done. "I'm going out to shoot hoops."

"OK, but come in when it's dark."

Jeff wants to go with him, but I can't be alone, Jimmy's rumbling baritone notwithstanding. "We're not finished. Only a few more to go." I shake a tiny box of Necco Sweethearts. It rattles like the Bad Juju's ankle bracelets, and I bite my lip. He's writing *Jeff* on the miniature pink boxes, while I address them to his preschool classmates. Soon he too sprints from the table.

"Wait. You need a jacket." After I hustle him into a fleece, I walk the circle of kitchen, dining room, living room, hallway, kitchen, making deals with myself. If Jimmy stops preaching and comes out of his study, I will not play witch doctor. If the boys come inside. If one of them comes in, if only to pee. If I see one spider web.

But I don't look in a single corner. Feeling like I've drunk too much palm wine on market day, I go to my desk, pull out a white security envelope, and then look up Tom's address in the Wallace Memorial directory. Then with the stamped, addressed envelope in hand, I return to the dining room table. I flip over a tiny card that pictures a black-webbed man squatting atop a train and declaring his ardor. The witch doctor once told me not to worry about the dozens of black widow spiders living in my cinder block house. *They won't bite you if you let them be. I have a cure for the widow's bite, but it is impossible to avoid pain and suffering.* I remember thinking that he spoke of love.

In small, rounded printing that could belong to any thirteen- or fourteen-year-old, I write on the back of Spider Man: *Let him kiss me with the kisses of his mouth: for thy love is better than wine*, and below it in miniscule letters, *Song of Solomon.* Jimmy has stopped preaching. Soon he'll be looking for his family and singing delicious hymns of praise for my soup. Ready to shred the miniscule card, I listen for the study door to open or the boys to rush back inside. *Day and night, I dream of your kisses.* The silence lies as impenetrable as the moonless nights did in Africa. *Wishing I could be…*

My spidey senses tingling, I hurry to finish: *Your valentine.*

I hear the witch doctor order me to sign my name—*you can't expect anonymous words of longing to be an improvement over Jimmy's pastoral counseling*—but my hand is shaking, and I tuck the card inside first its small envelope, and then the one I've stamped and addressed.

He'll wonder if it's from me, I argue back, *and he'll be inspired to cover Lucy in kisses. It will be aphrodisiacal, even if he doesn't know for sure.* I reassure myself that sending an anonymous valentine is the kind of prank a group of thirteen-year-old girls would play on their Sunday school teacher. I lick the envelope's bitter glue, trying not to hear the witch doctor's low laughter, and drop the valentine into my purse.

If Jimmy preaches tomorrow from *Song of Solomon*, I will not go anywhere near a mailbox.

Judith Podell

Ground Zero

JUDITH PODELL is the funniest unknown woman writer in America (according to some of her friends) and the real author of "How to Sing the Blues," which is all over the Internet but which first appeared in *WordWrights!* in 1997. Her work has appeared in numerous publications and anthologies, including the *Village Voice*, the *Crescent Review*, and the 2002 edition of *Mirth of a Nation: The Best in Contemporary Humor.* She holds an MFA in creative writing from the Stonecoast MFA program at the University of Southern Maine.

The summer of 1981, magazines were full of articles about professional women reaching career plateaus and finding themselves at dead ends with their biological clocks ticking. It was as though *Time* and *Newsweek* had turned into my mother, whose letters often included free samples of improved deodorants and the latest feminine hygiene sprays. ("Dear Lauren, this came in the mail and I thought of you. When will you bring that nice Meltzer boy home again?") My closest women friends were all married, some for the second time, with mortgages and serious furniture. I was thirty-four, still single, with a government job and a futon; a relic of the idealistic, if somewhat self-serving, Carter era. Signs of the Reagan ascendancy were all over Washington. I was tired of friends asking me when was I going to leave the government and get a "real" job, as though working for a federal regulatory agency was something to be ashamed about when you could be making big bucks defending the corporate right to sell dangerous junk. Fortunately, Government High Option Blue Cross still paid generous mental health benefits, which was why I could afford psychoanalysis, the Rolls-Royce of psychotherapy.

Not that I had much to show for it. Although I'd been seeing Dr. Freundlich four times a week for more than a year, I was still hooked on cigarettes (three packs a day) and Jake Meltzer, a divorced lawyer who said we had a mature adult relationship.

Whatever that meant.

"What are you thinking?" said Dr. Freundlich.

Jake hadn't called me in two weeks, not since the night he'd dropped in for dinner, bearing Chinese takeout; kung pao chicken, shrimp with walnuts, and crummy fortune cookies. Mine had read Your Mother Was Right.

"What are you thinking that you don't want to tell me about?" said Dr. Freundlich.

In other words, Dr. Freundlich wanted me to say whatever was on my mind "without fear or censorship."

Jake was off limits, as far as I was concerned. Too embarrassing. I searched for something safe as soap, yet sufficiently provocative so Dr. Freundlich wouldn't suspect I was holding out on him. He needed new soap in the bathroom off his waiting room. By now, the solid pink bar of Lifebouy I remembered from the start of my analysis was a melted-down puddle of beige slime. For that matter, his bathroom was dusty. I wondered what that meant, and what my noticing meant. Analysis was about little things, noticing them as if they were important, and then talking about them, even though it was embarrassing. I imagined cleaning Dr. Freundlich's bathroom up, replacing the old beige slime with a fresh bar of blue Zest, and buying him some terry cloth hand towels. That sounded too much like transference, or was it self-abasement? As far as I was concerned, they were one and the same. Or else I was turning into my mother, the Bitch-Goddess of Hygiene.

A sigh escaped me.

"Hmm-m-m?" said Dr. Freundlich.

"I've got this new nervous tic. Or else it's an old nervous tic I've noticed for the first time."

"Describe it," he said.

"I take deep breaths and sigh all the time. Sometimes I have to remind myself to exhale. I guess it's just depression."

I knew I was a bore when I talked about being depressed, which always made me feel more depressed, as well as guilty for boring Dr. Freundlich. I was on the point of apologizing to him for being a guilty boring puddle of beige slime when he said:

"You may be experiencing a loss of elasticity in your lungs, which is an early warning sign of emphysema."

We had a truce; he let me smoke in his office, but took every opportunity to remind me of its hazards to my health, which were the times when I felt free to tune him out.

This time, though, as if on command, I put out the cigarette.

Not that I wanted to. I felt suddenly split in two, half of me watching, with dread and curiosity, the act of a stranger who was also me, but who wanted to quit smoking. Idly, I wondered where the surplus nervous energy would migrate, and saw myself knitting a long, lumpy muffler while gobbling fistfuls of junk food. Within a month I'd be too fat for standard sizes. In a year I'd be sideshow material.

I could hardly remember life without the reward of cigarettes. A childhood of walking home from the orthodontist in the rain. Frantic hours of piano practice the night before piano lesson as penance for not practicing all week. Staring out of classroom windows. Staring at the clock. I fished the crumpled cigarette out of Dr. Freundlich's ashtray, ready to light up, but my hands shook too badly for matches. The rest of my life stretched before me as a series of desperate, disconnected improvisations.

"What is it you're not saying this time?" he said, but he'd seen the whole show.

He knew what it meant. I didn't have to tell him.

That summer I lived in the remnants of a group house off Dupont Circle with Rainbow, an acid casualty with good office skills and many irritating mannerisms. She'd lived in places like Big Bear and Boulder, but moved back East to be near her family and become a grown-up. (Her words, not mine.) Housemates my age who tolerated chain smoking and meat eating were hard to find. I couldn't figure out whether she was sincere or just goofing on me in a post-modern ironic way. Out of the blue, she'd say stuff like "It's OK to love your country and be a chick again," or "Capitalism is really hip, y'know?" Her wardrobe came from thrift stores, and her big ideas seemed to come off matchbook covers, the kind that said Earn Big Money Now! Learn in Your Spare Time. She was taking a correspondence course in truck driving so she could become an independent entrepreneur.

"It can't be healthy for you to live with a retarded person," Jake had said after he met her. "You have to be some kind of a moron to believe you can learn to drive a truck by mail."

Sometimes I imagined Rainbow's presence in my life was, in reality, a re-education program for sixties' holdovers underwritten by the Heritage Foundation, but I understood her better once I met her family. They lived in an excessively restored farmhouse outside Leesburg and were consumed by hobbies. Rainbow's father repaired clocks in his garage workshop. There was a congealed boyishness about him, something sinister and gauche. He wore black socks with his Bermuda shorts and his face was too old for his hair. He made a point of telling me, not that I asked, about being first trombone with the navy band until he lost his embouchure and retired early on disability. Rainbow's mother was taciturn and fidgety in a way that suggested long Midwestern winters. Each kitchen appliance had its own cover, either quilted or crocheted. She showed me her root cellar and what appeared to be a lifetime supply of homemade relishes and preserves. I never got to meet Rainbow's brother, who was reenacting the Battle of Spotsylvania that weekend with his Civil War re-enactor group.

On the way home, Rainbow told me the retired trombone story was just cover, and that her father was really a retired spy. CIA. The root cellar was cover too; it was a fallout shelter. Space was reserved for Rainbow, who hoped she would get to it in time.

"Just leave work early so you miss rush hour," I'd said, "That traffic jam around the Pentagon is a killer."

"It's no joke, Lauren," she'd said.

Her look told me she pitied my ignorance but that it would be a breach of national security to tell me more.

"You really want to live in a hole in the ground with your parents and eat pickled relish?"

"I'm a survivor," she'd said.

Not me.

I wanted to be at ground zero when the big one hit. I wanted to be vaporized.

The kitchen smelled deliciously of ginger and cinnamon.

"I'd rather die than not live under a Capitalist System," said Rainbow by way of a greeting when I got home.

She took a tray of fresh-baked cookies out of the oven. The polka-dot kerchief tied around her curly red hair and ruffled apron were straight out of *I Love Lucy.*

You twit! I wanted to say. Do you know what your life would be under Godless Communism? Pretty much the same; a shared apartment with a roommate or two in a nice part of Moscow. An office job where you typed letters and answered the phone. A few more amenities than your average Commie working girl, thanks to a daddy in the KGB.

"I just quit smoking."

"Oh wow, Lauren. You must be feeling so good about yourself right now."

"Not really," I said. "It's more like driving without brakes."

"I'll fix you some milk and cookies," she said. "The ones in the jar are cool enough."

The cookies in the jar looked like chocolate chip, but turned out to be oatmeal raisin made with too much ginger. I ate three of them, even though I normally don't like raisins, and gulped down a glass of milk.

"Any messages for me?" I asked, ever hopeful.

"Jake didn't call," she said. "Tell me you're not in love with him. Are you?"

I'd never used the word, even to myself. He was my sentimental education, my destiny. We'd grown up in adjoining suburbs that we despised and met at a progressive summer camp in Vermont when we were teenagers. He gave me my first kiss, after which he made a play for Wanda Johnson, who was my tent mate, but that didn't count. What counted was our meeting up in Washington, half a lifetime later, and connecting.

Bodies never lied. He could reduce me to a puddle of lust with a flick of his tongue. My first orgasm ever was the time Jake took me from behind on his living room floor. We shared Saturday nights and Sunday morning Naked Brunch: sex, bagels, and lox; *fresh* bagels and *fresh* lox because we were from New York and knew the difference.

"Yeah, it's love."

Together, we knew all the answers to the Sunday *Times* crossword puzzle.

"He's not good enough for you."

She looked like she wanted to say more, but thought better of it.

"That's sweet of you, but actually Jake and I are pretty well matched. He's a little lacking in social graces, but, hey, I'm not the world's best housekeeper—"

She interrupted me.

"Jake made a pass at me the last time he was here."

"You're kidding! The night he came by with the Chinese food?"

"He sort of snuck up behind me in the kitchen when my hands were full and copped a feel, so I stepped on his feet. It wasn't the first time he'd tried something like that. I would've said something sooner if I'd known you were, like, having a relationship."

I wanted to believe she was making this up, but knew better. Rainbow lived in fantasyland, but she didn't tell lies. Soon every cell would shriek betrayal. I needed something to do with my hands or put in my mouth that was not a cigarette. While I brooded, Rainbow cleaned up the kitchen.

"Men are back, and they're better than ever!" she announced brightly after she scrubbed her last pot.

Translation: she was in love again, and it was the real thing this time. The last time I'd noticed she was dating a stringer for one of the wire services, who had a phone in his car but no fixed address. Rainbow called him a reporter but he was more like a news groupie.

Before that, it was two guys named Steve.

"It's the real thing this time," she said.

"Are we talking about Marty?"

"Don't be silly. No one who lives in a Honda Accord is ready to make a commitment," she said.

His name was Henry Abernathy and he had a house in Great Falls with a Jacuzzi. When I congratulated her for landing landed gentry, she gave me a pitying look.

"That's not what it's all about. Henry's a real man. He knows how to make me feel like a real woman. I'd be a fool to let this one get away, a perfect fool."

From the low tremor in her voice, I could tell she was thrilled with the chance to use that perfect fool line. Rainbow had a hope chest stuffed with bad dialogue. Bette Davis in *Now, Voyager*? Or did Daisy Buchanan say it to the Great Gatsby? I wrapped my brain around the concept of gender realness unrelated to real estate but got distracted by thoughts of food.

Any kind, and lots of it.

Now!

"Rainbow! What did you put in these cookies besides ginger? Suddenly I'm starving."

"That's because you've been without a cigarette for how many hours?"

"Four and a half," I said.

A large, semi-transparent cigarette drifted across my field of vision on the diagonal. I blinked and it moved faster, followed by another. Not exactly a hallucination, more like subliminal advertising.

ISN'T it time you had a cigarette?

Isn't it TIME you had a cigarette?

Isn't it time YOU had a cigarette?

Isn't it time you had a CIGARETTE?

Rainbow was still yacking about Henry Abernathy.

"Henry has a trust fund, so he doesn't need a regular job."

"No real job? I thought that was part of being a real man."

"Not if you're independently wealthy," she explained.

"So where'd you guys meet, or is that classified information?"

"The Georgetown pool. He asked to borrow my Bain de Soleil."

Trust Rainbow to meet true love at Swimming Pool of the Doomed. When I went to the Georgetown pool I met teenagers with bad acne and loud radios, Arab med students with green card problems, and crazy old people who talked to themselves. I suddenly realized Rainbow wasn't an airhead at all, but a fount of feminine intuition, all that stuff I'd forfeited by going after pay equity. Maybe I could learn how to be more effective as a girl. Rule one: Use pricey cosmetics. Rule two: Never let him know you don't have a date for Friday night. Rule three involved either sticking elbows in grapefruit halves before a bath, or remembering to write your hostess a bread-and-butter note three days after the visit. I probably owed a bread-and-butter note to Rainbow's folks, the spooks.

My mind was coming unglued.

A useful rule of conduct in Washington is never do anything you wouldn't be able to justify in front of a hostile Congressional Oversight Committee, and it occurred to me I was on thin ice.

"Rainbow! Are there drugs in these cookies?"

"Don't worry, it's just reefer, not acid," she said with a shrug.

"So what," I said. "It's still illegal."

"It's better for you than tobacco," she said.

There was a reception that night for the FFA Board of Directors, and Rainbow invited me to come as her guest. The FFA stood for Friends of Firearms in America. Rainbow was filling in for their regular receptionist who was out on maternity leave. The FFA threw frequent receptions, which gave her the chance to wear her collection of thrift store cocktail dresses to work.

"Maybe you'll meet someone nice, and anyway, there's lots of food," she'd said, by way of inducement.

The spread was lavish, but in odd ways. Five kinds of bourbon but no vodka, and the hors d'oeuvres were made from wild animals shot by the membership. I sampled venison meatballs but passed on the moose Stroganoff. Rainbow introduced me to the president of the FFA, who looked like Mr. Potato Head and smelled of Brut aftershave. Over the din of drunken small talk I could hear the sounds of gunfire and laughter, and wandered down to the rifle range. Tentatively, I picked up a shotgun, but thought better of it when I noticed a man in a navy blue blazer aim his camera in my direction.

He came over to me, clearly disappointed. He wore penny loafers, and looked chipmunk cute up close, like something out of a kit, and turned out to be the FFA's official photographer.

"Say, you didn't think I was going to take your picture so I could blackmail you just in case I found out you worked for Teddy Kennedy? Most women like to have their pictures taken on the range. I bet you'd be surprised to find out how many women members we have. Why we even have a woman on our board of directors. She's some feisty lady."

He pointed to a laughing, gray-haired woman with a creased leather face, the only woman besides me in sensible shoes.

I wanted to think well of him, but his use of the "feisty" was a turn-off. It's not a real word. The only thing worse was "diminutive," a patronizing way of saying short.

Feisty, diminutive Lauren Ginsburg shot Jake "the Snake" Meltzer with FAF rifle, police report. Claims temporary sanity.

"My name's George," he said. "I'm not such a bad guy when you get to know me."

So we talked, or rather I listened. George admired Walker Evans and Ansel Adams but thought his own work would be as emblematic of the eighties as those portraits of Dust Bowl Madonnas were for the Great Depression; George's work being to photograph the guests at FFA cocktail parties just in case, for instance, someone from Teddy Kennedy's office wandered across the shooting range.

His hand rested lightly on my arm. He beat a gentle tattoo with his fingers. I recognized the rhythm as the opening bars of the *Twilight Zone* theme music.

Men are back and they're better than ever.

The image of Jake groping Rainbow in my kitchen sprung to mind. I felt exceedingly vulnerable, an old-fashioned liberal on nicotine withdrawal, but also voracious. Maybe Rainbow's way worked, in which case,

George the Photographer was a friendly dog kind of guy, rather than a polished rodent. He certainly seemed eager to please me, although he hadn't a clue. There was something Jake used to do to the back of my neck that made me eager for ravishment. Big vampire kisses that sometimes left dull raspberry marks on my neck. I wondered if George would get the general idea if I tilted my head ever so slightly. As George's lips grazed my neck, I wondered what sign he was, and hoped not Capricorn. According to Rainbow, they made lousy lovers. Jesus Christ and Richard Nixon were Capricorns. Your typical Capricorn was anal retentive, a real freak for control, as opposed to Virgos, who were anal compulsive, meaning they wash up immediately and wouldn't eat in bed. No one in Washington understood about eating in bed except Jake. Spareribs, spring rolls, and the Sunday *Times*. Jake nibbling on my ear. Orca in five letters, prick in six. Ratfink. Schmuck. Meltzer.

"You have beautiful eyes, George," I said.

"My wife thinks I look like Al Pacino."

"You're married? I'm so sorry."

I worked my mouth into a moue of despair. Time to be a cartoon.

"But let me put it like this," he said. "We have a little understanding, so long as no one brings home anything contagious, if you catch my drift."

He meant herpes. AIDS was barely a rumor back then.

"I'm a Libra," I told him. "We repel social disease."

Rainbow said Scorpios were the sexiest, but you shouldn't marry one since they could turn on you.

"How would you like to take a nice shower first," he said.

Damn, a double Virgo. We hadn't even left the shooting range.

"I'm going to look pretty silly with wet hair and streaky mascara," I said.

"Oh come now, haven't you ever made love in a shower?"

It was silly for him to call what we were about to do "making love," but probably he thought he was appealing to my feminine sensibilities.

"Could we get horizontal," I asked. "I don't balance well on slippery surfaces."

"Aw, where's your spirit of adventure?"

Having sex with strange men seemed adventurous enough for me. You could slip on a bar of soap, fall down, hit your head, and die in a shower.

"Do you have something against beds?" I asked.

"I like to push the envelope," he said.

It was nine hours and forty-nine minutes since that last cigarette. My lungs felt empty. My lips longed to wrap themselves around something smooth and tubular. I also had a sudden fierce desire to bite down hard on something. OK, not bite, just suck real hard.

This was so infantile, such infinite regress!

"Maybe you can help me out," said the strange woman who seemed to be occupying my body. "I'm an oral fixate. Would you mind giving up the shower for a really good blowjob?"

George led me down four flights of stairs to a large dimly lit room that contained rows of bunk beds, each one covered in an army blanket.

"Guess where we are," said George.

"Sleep-away camp?"

The friendly stink of old blankets made me think for a second I was back at summer camp, which led inevitably to thoughts of Jake the Snake.

"Welcome to the largest privately owned fallout shelter in the free world," said George.

He showed me his bunk, which was one of the lower ones.

"Does Rainbow get one? My roommate, she's your temporary receptionist."

"You only get a bunk if the FFA thinks you're a valuable survival resource," he explained. "We're saving spots for Sinatra and Olivia Newton-John so we can't cover clericals."

Shrieks of laughter erupted from the other side of the room. I recognized the laugh of the woman director.

"I told you she was feisty," George said.

I saw myself facing the Congressional Oversight Committee, all proceedings televised. In the visitor's gallery I could see Dr. Freundlich, my counselors from progressive summer camp, and my mother. The Chairman of the Oversight Committee addressed me with a sneer in his voice. He bore an uncanny resemblance to Jake Meltzer, except he was old, bald, and fat.

"On the night of June 24, 1981, did you or did you not commit an act of sexual congress that is illegal in the State of Georgia?"

What the hell.

I had the perfect excuse.

I would tell them I stopped smoking.

Elizabeth Poliner

Last View of the Canyon

ELIZABETH POLINER is the author of *Mutual Life & Casualty*, a novel-in-stories (Permanent Press, 2005). Her stories and poems have appeared widely in literary journals including the *Kenyon Review*, *Southern Review*, *Laurel Review*, and *Other Voices*. A recipient of numerous grants from the DC Commission on the Arts and Humanities, and fellowships to Yaddo and the Virginia Center for Creative Arts, she has also been named a Tennessee Williams Scholar in Fiction at the Sewanee Writers' Conference and a Bernard O'Keefe Scholar in Fiction at the Bread Loaf Writers' Conference. She lives in Washington, D.C.

Gray is the color of cancer. I've seen it several times before. The skin of those soon to die turns sallow in its sickness, then sinks into a gray, an alarming and unnerving shade, especially when it clings to human flesh.

When Carol told me that my ex-husband, Mike, had cancer, I was looking at something magnificently gray already: the Grand Canyon. No, the canyon's color isn't only gray, but gray hides behind the whole of it, illuminates and imbues every generation of rock that can be seen in the lines of the canyon walls and every shadow between them.

We'd taken a trail that, about a half mile down, led to an overlook. A morning haze lingered above the canyon's bowl, and we sat, our feet kicking into the rust-colored ground, our eyes fixed on the geological monstrosity before us. We sipped water and talked. I would have preferred to have been sipping coffee at that hour, but there, priorities, at least certain ones, became straightforward: hydration preempted caffeination. Below us, a line of people, their size diminished by the canyon's depths, wound their way, step by step, up the canyon wall. I had been there before, climbed to the bottom of the vast pit in my early teens when touring "America's Scenic Highlights"—a bus tour filled with rambunctious, horny adolescents—and remembered the heaviness of my legs on the return climb and my unquenchable thirst. It would be hours, I knew, before that group reached the overlook.

He'd been sick a long time already. A year and a half. The last time I'd seen Mike, in a restaurant, by accident, he'd looked his same old self: perky, telling jokes, hair tousled. We were embarrassed at first—running into each other while on dates—but he'd broken the ice with a smooth one-liner, and by the time we said goodbye we'd looked directly into each other's faces, unafraid, unashamed even of all that we couldn't fix in those last years.

Saying goodbye, he had gripped my forearm. "Are you getting your checks all right?"

"Of course," I'd said. We'd agreed to a few years of rehabilitative alimony. Though I worked throughout our six-year marriage, I still earned less than Mike, and the alimony was supposed to compensate for the post-divorce decline my standard of living was bound to experience. I smiled. "You never fail," I said.

Carol and I mulled over a lot of things that morning on the overlook, surveying our lives as much as the view. We discussed our respective jobs back in Boston, whether women really had a role in corporate America, whether we, both "successful" as that term is narrowly defined by corporate standards, would make it for the long haul. So few did, we mused. Money, power, status. These things still didn't mean the same thing to women as they did to men. As carrot sticks, money, power, and status kept only a handful of women gripping tight the corporate ladder. We wondered if the track we'd gotten on somewhere in graduate school had taken us more away from something than toward anything. Over the last few years, as we'd skated past thirty, skidding toward thirty-five, we both felt that we'd lost much of our professional ambition.

We agreed that we liked traveling in Arizona, in just the two days we'd been there, more than we liked traveling to and from our jobs back in Boston, more than we liked Boston itself. "Here it's like being on the moon," I'd suggested the night of our arrival. We stayed in Phoenix then, at an inexpensive hotel. That afternoon, we'd taken a long drive past the city's outskirts on what was known as Apache Trail. The road, a bumpy dirt-covered one, wound into the depths of yet another craggy canyon, more modest in scope than the grand one we would see next, golden in a way that reminded me—as if color could conjure up smells—of both cinnamon and clove. The land reeked of odd flavors.

Time slowed in Arizona. In just two days it had nearly stopped. Of course, most people we ran into vacationed, as we did, and that might have explained the leisure with which people moved. But it wasn't only that people moved more slowly. Days did. Time did. "That's part of the moon effect," I'd said to Carol. That was the night before, a few hours after we'd reached the canyon, while we sipped beers by our newly raised tents. "I feel like we're some zillion miles away," I'd said. "Loose and floating."

"That's how you're supposed to feel," she said.

Carol had known both Mike and myself before Mike and I knew each other. She had been at our wedding, an efficient middle-of-the-week ceremony, downtown in a twelve-story building, before a justice of the peace. She had been at our first housewarming party, a more ambitious affair, set in a two-bedroom condominium we'd bought in Cambridge near Harvard, not that we had connections there, but Mike and I both liked the idea of living amidst all that brain power. "I get a surge," he'd often say as he descended our front steps onto the sidewalk. We often walked around the university grounds, its antique, brick buildings suggesting solemnity and durability. "I get a surge," Mike would exclaim. And I'd laugh at my husband, a rather small man, slight in frame, dark in hair, who surged at the very idea of things.

Carol had been there, of course, during the months preceding the divorce and during the divorce proceeding itself. And she continued to be there, amazingly, for us both. In a way, she acted like a connection between us—one of the last we had—despite the fact that she rarely if ever mentioned the other to us. She put it simply when she did tell me. "He's sick," she said. "Cancer. Began in the lymph nodes. Now in advanced stages."

I swallowed hard and examined the expanse of landscape. Cancer. Years ago I went through a phase, afraid of it myself, but I'd stripped the illness of its awesome personality by transforming it into simple, preventative routines: monthly home breast examinations, yearly pap smears. These days, single again, my greatest health fears were AIDS and other sexually transmitted diseases. Cancer… Merely saying it felt awkward. It sounded oddly out of context, like a regressive, outdated, often even curable disease.

She went on. "He's doing badly now. I thought you should know." I watched some squirrels chase each other nearby, then I turned to Carol. Her hair, a pale, auburn color, reminded me of the cinnamon and clove smells of the Apache Trail.

"Yes," I agreed. I swallowed more water. Carol did the same. "Do you see him much?" I asked.

"Not much. He's involved now." She paused. "You *did* know?"

That much I knew. I nodded.

"He always asks about you. He wants to hear that you're OK. Getting along. That's how he puts it. Is Suzannah getting along?"

"I hope you always tell him yes," I said. "Suzannah gets along. God knows, there's not much else to tell. But get along, that I do."

We laughed. My being single again had brought my friendship with Carol to a new stage. As two lone women we were bound to each other by a layer of common experience, of common need.

I looked out once again, intoxicated for a moment by the vastness before me. "Here is everything." I pointed into the bright air, at nothing really. "As if viewed from the moon," I said.

The night before, our first at the Grand Canyon, two boys (I've heard Carol tell this story, and she'd say two young *men*) approached us. They'd met us earlier that afternoon, literally upon our arrival, and had helped us raise our tents. One had long blonde hair that hung over his shoulders. The other, smaller and skinnier, had brown hair that fell just as loosely. Our tents intact, our helpers promised to visit later that night, and I wondered if they really thought we made good pickup material. Apparently, we did. Kyle, the blonde, carried a six-pack. George, the other, smoked a cigarette. "It's the gang!" I whispered to Carol as I watched them approach. A flashlight's glow dimly illuminated them.

"Oh, good," she said, and I was surprised to hear something in her tone connoting genuine pleasure.

Kyle slammed his beer on the picnic table where we sat. "Ladies," he said. Carol's gaze instantly met mine. Since we'd been in Arizona, every hotel attendant, waiter, and park ranger had called us "ladies." We felt well respected, but helplessly old.

"Mind if we join you? How'er those tents holding up?" George sat next to me, but with a glance from Kyle he shifted to the other side of the table, by Carol.

Soon enough we learned that they were musicians. Hadn't made it yet, though. It's tough, Carol said. George played guitar and Kyle played bass and sang. Did we smoke reefer? they wanted to know. Not in a decade, Carol said. I said nothing, stunned that they were even there. I hadn't been out, hadn't put myself "out there," as Carol would say, during most of the last year. I'd forgotten about younger men, boys, possibly hoods. After several beers and cigarettes, Kyle began to sing, to me, a love ballad of some sort. He put his arm around me. About then I became less stunned. I excused myself to get a kerchief from my tent.

When I returned both George and Kyle were into another melody. And both waved their hands in the air, feigning guitar playing. Carol, always better than me at feigning interest in others, looked positively rapt. She giggled and swallowed beer, then lit a cigarette herself. I gave her a glance that said, "What the hell?" She returned one that said, "What the hell."

Kyle, who must have thought Carol and I were warming up to them, launched into a tale of his and George's travels throughout the country. No tents, just lots of luck, he said. At that, Carol's eyes grew wide. I ducked my head.

"Ladies," Kyle said from time to time as the night progressed. But he had nothing with which to follow that. He'd simply say it, every so often, then inhale from his cigarette, smile widely, and shake the loose hair that fell about his head. Two hours later, and he and George still posted themselves at our picnic table, a little drunk, a little cold—the temperature dropped significantly during the night. Kyle's eyes glowed in the lantern, and his voice sang, every so often, as if putting the word to music might imbue it with certain potencies, "Ladies."

Ever since my divorce I'd begun to ask myself in varying situations: "What if this is the last time?" For example, I was in the habit of listening every so often in the dark, in the middle of the night, to my favorite symphony since childhood, Beethoven's Fourth. It was the first symphony I'd ever heard. I'd listen, invariably when I was alone on a weekend in the two-bedroom condominium that I now solely owned, and I'd feel a contentment wash over me. This isn't so bad, I'd remember about my life. Then it would hit me. The possibility that anything could happen in the upcoming days and weeks. Anything could happen, and this could be the last time I might experience this symphony, this delicious swirl of sound, this old friend. Only I couldn't know for sure. My concern was not so much with my own impermanence as with the realization that I would have to go through life bearing losses, personal losses—personal in that I would feel the loss as a deprivation in my senses—and that I wasn't good at that task.

When Carol and I decided to vacation together I hadn't thought at all about letting anything go. My thoughts were only of getting away, of temporary flight, and of coming back refreshed, more vital, ready to start something—anything—anew. But in the airport as I waited to meet Carol at the flight gate, I'd sat down and stared blankly at some luggage—the carry-on type—and the question came to mind. I'd been to the Grand Canyon before and I wondered how it was that I could go there again, could go to a place so magnificent, and take a look at something so wondrous, so special, knowing all the while that the view might be my last of it. I might never go there again.

I was thirteen when I'd last seen it. I was young and strong. I'd walked down the whole of the canyon one bright morning and had found myself just that afternoon, and for the first time in my life, slowing down, tiring, doubting whether I would make it the rest of the way. I felt angry at the canyon then, as if it betrayed me, forced me by its very geology to experience sensations, such as the darkness of deep fatigue, that at thirteen I felt

I had no business to know. It wasn't the view I worried about not seeing again in those moments when I thought I couldn't take another step. Then it was my life I wanted back, the one I hadn't yet lived. Sweating, almost crying as I neared panic, I felt stripped of things I hadn't even owned. But of course I made it out of the canyon that time. And before I knew it I'd forgotten the anxiety of the climb and my own fatigue. Before I knew it I was a little girl again, budding into my teens, bragging in a letter to my parents that I had done it, had *done* the canyon, down and back, all in one long day.

Of course, Carol's telling me about Mike changed the tenor of the vacation. Changed it, yet intensified the sense I already had of time ceasing to move, of myself floating, suspended weightless in air, of dry, canyon-filled Arizona assuming a mysteriousness second in my mind only to life as I could never know it: beyond planet earth.

Mike sick. Somehow it seemed impossible. He was forever perky. Joking. Surging at the odd moment. On impulse, I began to review his habits. He'd sleep late on Saturdays and Sundays. Not late, but ridiculously late, I had thought then. But the fatigue that kept him wrapped in his blankets those long hours of the morning wore away as soon as he'd showered and downed two cups of coffee. The coffee, I mused. Two cups straight away each morning. A third often, right before lunch or with lunch. Another, at least one, late in the afternoon. And always, coffee, or coffee with liquor, after dinner. Coffee. Coffee and cancer. Could that be the link?

After Carol and I hiked back from the overlook, we sat at a picnic table by our tents, sipping water and staring at our neighbors. I thought then: if only he had moved more, had exercised. But he was a sitter. Sundays he'd spend quietly reading. All day reading. Even then, he felt something from life slipping, and it would be gone if he didn't try to keep up, he insisted, through reading. I wanted to move, always to move. "Walk with me," I'd beg. I'd have to beg; it took that much to get him going. Yet once going, he was a good sport. He'd undoubtedly surge. From the very start we were so different: he, reading to keep pace with something he sensed as life; me, walking, as if life hadn't happened yet, but might be there, if I just kept going, around the very next bend.

Contrary to Carol's carrying on, she did not let George, that evening before, lay a finger on her. Nor did I let Kyle, though he did manage to sing me one more love ballad.

The evening air cooled, ultimately, down to forty degrees or so. Carol and I took turns going to and from our respective tents, layering on turtlenecks and sweatshirts as the decline in temperature progressed. Apparently, drinking beer protected Kyle and George from sensing the chill. Eventually, though, they made their move, verbally. "You ladies want partners this evening?" Kyle asked it, directly enough.

"Unlikely," Carol replied. And that was all she needed to say.

They promptly asked for a ride—to a party at another campsite. I took them in our rented car, a small, two-door contraption that slowed to a scary crawl whenever we hit a steep incline. Upon driving it, I was thankful we'd chosen Arizona for our vacation, and not some place steeper, like the Rocky Mountains, my logic—or illogic—being that wherever we could have gone, Carol and I were destined for this tiny car and this car only.

Kyle sat beside me in the front seat and promptly lit a cigarette. George stationed himself in the back. There's almost nothing to tell of our ride, about five minutes long, to a nearby campsite. They knew where they wanted to go. A group, mainly of girls, younger ones, still in their teens I guessed, staged a party by a campfire. Music blared, and a fairly large crowd milled about. "This is it," Kyle said as we approached.

And that was it. Two boys who had entertained Carol and me for the duration of the evening. Call them a variation on an old theme; call them an American Scenic Highlight. Or call them nothing new. Yet I was taken by them. Not by anything that had happened during the course of the evening, but by the simplest thing that happened as I dropped them off.

George said it first. A friendly, genuine goodbye.

Goodbye, he said. You take care, Suzannah. His personable touch shocked me.

Then Kyle said it. Goodbye, Suzannah. Thanks a lot for the ride.

He looked at me as he uttered this, smiling widely, obviously pleased to have met me.

What I realized then was that I'd been less affected by the meeting than they had. I'd thought, up until that moment, that I didn't care about these two.

Kyle then leaned over and gave me a great, warm hug.

I hadn't received anything of the kind in longer than I cared to remember. It felt as good as any hug I'd ever received. He kissed my mouth then dashed out of the car.

Driving back I tried to deny that that hug meant anything to me. I tried, more assertively, to ignore the kiss. But even then I knew both meant something. If nothing else, they placed into relief the physical deprivation with which I lived.

"My God," I said to Carol when I returned. "What sweet things."

"Yes." She pulled on the hood of her sweatshirt and aimed herself for her small pup tent. "Cold night," she then said.

"Cold night," I agreed.

"You noodle."

"What? Just this morning I was full of bologna. I've always been full of bologna. We've had but one rule in this house: to argue in strict delicatessen metaphors." He sipped his coffee. "What's with you?" Mike asked.

I turned to him. I held a glass of spring water. "There's been a development in our relationship: we're talking pasta now."

It hadn't lasted. The fun, the jokes. The differences became chasms. He settled even further down into a lethargy I found distasteful; I became ever more restless, ever more uncertain of what was to come.

Of course, it had been hard once we split. The loneliness, naturally, overwhelmed. Great waves of it would take me, and I would coast, as if riding upon them, waiting to be washed, breathless, on the proverbial shore. My shore was my bed. I spent hours there, with the shades pulled, riding out the worst of the lonely episodes. Had I done the right thing, I wondered. I placed long-distance calls asking every old friend for his or her opinion. No one seemed to know.

Had I done the right thing? Up until the split, the answer seemed obvious enough. We *would* split. Get on with our respective, different lives. We would no longer have to compromise over what had seemed our most personal, most essential, of preferences.

At first I phoned Mike every so often to say hello and appease the loneliness. Hello, Suzannah, he'd say. We'd talk about nothing—how our jobs were going, what movies we had seen, and the like. Once I almost told him the extent of my doubts. I almost disclosed how I spent my weekends lying, with the shades drawn, in bed. As if he sensed as much he had asked: "Suzannah, what are you doing?"

"You mean now," I said, "or in general?"

"Now," he said. "What are you doing now?"

"Lying on my bed." I paused. "That's all."

"I can see you doing that." He paused too. "I can see you lying on your bed."

With my free arm I stretched, reaching for the bed's edge. "What are you doing?" I asked.

"Breathing," Mike said. "I'm talking to you. And besides that," his voice grew quiet, "I'm breathing," he said.

When Carol and I planned this trip, we set out for a whirlwind tour. We had no place in particular to be except for the two nights we'd spend camping at the canyon's south rim. Our plans were over-inclusive and vague. During lunchtime planning sessions we'd speak of the Painted Desert, the Navajo reservation, Phoenix, the Hopi reservation, even Las Vegas, as if they were all within our six-day grasp.

Yet upon arriving in this strange land—arid, golden, crusty, sunny—we scaled back our plans. We spent our first morning doing nothing but drowsing by the pool at our cheap hotel. We lunched downtown in Phoenix at a Sizzler's all-you-can-eat buffet. We spent the rest of day—a beautiful, clear eighty-eight-degree day—inside, unable to tear ourselves from Phoenix's Hurd Museum. I discovered something new about Carol: at a museum she read every placard placed on every display. I talked to some German tourists there while I waited for Carol to finish her most diligent of rounds.

We left Phoenix and headed straight for the canyon. We stopped once on the way up at Montezuma's Castle, the remains of an Indian village set in nothing but a ragged cliff. Simplicity. All about us the worn Arizona terrain signaled simplicity.

Like the unfailing sunshine, simplicity seeped its way into our skins, and, upon arriving at the canyon, we did the obvious thing. We parked our car, stood at a lookout, and looked.

The canyon is hard to grasp in one look. It's so wondrous, so vast, so beyond the realm of the imagination, I believe it forces a person, upon approaching it, to look, then look again. Upon seeing it I remembered instantly how, at thirteen, I'd also been taken this far aback by my first view of the canyon. "Yes!" I'd said to Carol. "It's like this. Totally unbelievable!" Then I remembered something else. I kept my eyes fixed on the vastness before me. "Until you get used to it," I said.

Our next day, our one full day at the canyon, had been equally uneventful. Early enough in the morning to avoid what could become piercing heat, Carol and I had taken that mild hike to the overlook. There, we watched tiny people wind their way on a trail that, from our perspective, looked like a pencil's scribbled line. Carol told me that Mike was sick. Later that day we ate lunch and milled about our campsite, napping, chatting, watching other people. We made a plan that before dinner we'd drive east along the rim to catch what we hoped would be a spectacular sunset.

Before sundown, the air already began to cool. We layered on ourselves long-sleeved shirts and sweaters, and took off in our little car, which felt to me, the more I drove in it, like a little home. We came to an overlook, fairly empty of other tourists and with a good view, it seemed, of the canyon and valley in its middle.

Amidst all the colors before us, the deep mauve of the canyon's walls, the emerging red and pink hues of the setting sun, the rust of the clay-like dirt at our feet, nothing compared to the shocking aqua blue of the Colorado River. It ran, like a fanciful serpent, below us. Its sight chilled. Carol and I watched it in silence, and I thought I could hear it, in the sounds of a lover, breathe and roar.

We must have sat there for an hour watching the sun go. As the canyon dimmed before us, the evening air glowed in ever-increasing iridescence. Carol snapped photographs and kept scolding herself for shooting too soon. "Peak already!" she exclaimed to the setting sun. Then she'd wait and take another photograph. Inevitably, though, the sky and the landscape would transform itself in the next moment into something more brilliant, more dense with color, more luminescent, and more mysterious than the moment before.

We stayed, growing chillier, yet unwilling to leave this sight, this particular overlook, nearly into nightfall.

"Carol," I said, turning to her after a long silence. We sat, each wrapped with our arms across our chests. "Something so small happened before I left for here, for Arizona."

"Mike," she said.

"Yes," I answered.

"You saw him?"

I stretched my legs out and pulled the arms of my sweater over my hands. I balled my hands into fists as I spoke. "No. I don't see him anymore," I said. "Haven't in a long while. It's not that. Something smaller than that."

I pulled my legs toward my chest, then folded my arms over my bent knees, my fists still clinging to the sweater's sleeves. My head fell into my arms. I felt dizzy. Too many sensations were emerging. I was heavy, tired, sad, hungry.

"You know our alimony situation," I said.

"Sure."

"Well, it's over now. I got my last check the day before we took off." I raised my head.

Carol turned to me, not saying anything. A breeze had been blowing, and Carol's auburn hair floated, as if pulled by magnets, away from her face.

"Congratulations? Is that what I should say?"

"Not really." Once again I raised my head, though my voice, I knew, remained low, as if still muffled. "It's just this. Such a small thing, really.

"It was late," I said. "Two weeks late." I paused. "He's never done that. Maybe," I paused again and looked out at the canyon, now fading before us, "maybe this time he didn't want me to 'get along.' Maybe he had trouble sending it."

Carol remained silent and still.

"I'm hoping that's what it meant," I said. "Now isn't that foolish? I'm hoping that he had a hard time mailing his last alimony check."

Carol smiled then, and I did too. "Yes," she said. "I can see why you hope that."

She didn't say anything more, and we sat for a few minutes longer, staring into what was then full darkness.

"I'm going to miss him too," Carol finally said.

Did I do the right thing? That's what I thought when I opened the envelope containing the last alimony check. This is it, I thought. And I still didn't know if I'd done the right thing.

I'd been asking myself that question throughout the vacation. It had been there, in my mind, as Carol and I drowsed that first morning by the pool. It had been there during that long trek around the exhibits at the Hurd Museum. It circled in my mind as I circled our tiny car around the steep bends of the Apache Trail.

It had been there, most poignantly, those minutes alone in the car after I'd said goodbye to Kyle and George. Goodbye, Suzannah, they'd each said. The words echoed in my ears, as if off the canyon walls. Goodbye, they'd said, and they'd called me by my name, Suzannah.

It had been there that next morning as Carol and I walked to the overlook. Then Carol had told me that Mike was sick. Cancer. Advanced stages.

It had been there, but then it didn't matter anymore.

An older, more familiar question surfaced.

How do you say goodbye?

I was looking then at the canyon as it stood, rusty in color, and steeping like tea in the morning's haze. How do you say goodbye, I wanted to ask it. And I still sought to ask it that the next morning, after Carol and I rolled our tents and packed our little car.

We stopped for one last view. Carol was driving and she pulled off to one of the nearby overlooks. I was drinking coffee from a Styrofoam cup. With my hands wrapped around the warm container, I took the few steps from the car to the rim's iron railing. One last look. It seemed an impossible thing to do.

But then, the canyon was there to be looked at. That morning the scene appeared less amazing, almost familiar in its sea of variegated tones. The sun wasn't yet shining, and the canyon emerged, as if from out of nowhere, a huge sleepy mass. Lines of brick-colored rust comprised the closest sections and they were spotted with the green tips of trees. Beyond that, the canyon became a hazy sea of color, all muted in tone, shifting in swirls and half circles from mauve to the dullest green to, at the edges, an ephemeral light blue. Contained within each color lay the color gray, muting the green, brightening the rust, transforming the blue into something barely distinguishable from the early morning air.

I've tried so many times in the months since I've returned to Boston—to my routine, my job, my friends—to describe the canyon, the lines that sweep around it, telling its geological life story. Often I've asked myself whether it's comprised, layer upon layer, of merely rock, or is it something more: rock and color, color and air, air and time?

I looked that morning with all the intensity I could muster, knowing full well that this could be my last view of the canyon. I might never return, I thought then. With hindsight's help, I've tried to simplify my impressions: it's endlessly interesting, I've said. It changes, each moment that you stare. It dulls the senses as much as it awakens the one sense of wonder. It's old; it's cracked and lined; it's rough in texture. Like a human face, it's vastly complex and simply beautiful.

I sipped my coffee as Carol pointed our car south, away from the canyon's rim. The moment that I turned my gaze wasn't as hard as I imagined. In fact, like the moment before sleep, when you slide from a roaming dreamworld into something deeper and more obscure, I find that I can't recollect the transference at all.

Judy Pomeranz

People Don't Fly

JUDY POMERANZ is a freelance writer, lecturer, and art critic. Her articles have appeared in a wide range of newspapers and magazines, and her short stories and essays have been published in literary journals including *Santa Barbara Review*, *Potomac Review*, *Crescent Review*, *Fodderwing*, and *MassAve Review*, as well as in the anthologies *Great Writers, Great Stories*, *Chesapeake Crimes*, and *Chesapeake Crimes II*. Her novella, *On the Far Edge of Love*, is currently being serialized in *élan* magazine, which also serialized her earlier novellas, *Lies Beneath the Surface* and *Elegy*. She holds an MA in writing from Johns Hopkins University, teaches writing at Georgetown University, and has won prizes and recognition in fiction contests sponsored by the National Press Club, the D.C. Bar, and *élan*.

People don't fly. That was my first supremely inappropriate thought when I saw Mr. Jacobson shoot past my window on a downward trajectory. *People don't fly.*

I remember being surprised, maybe even a little shocked, or jolted—yes, jolted's a better word for it—at the time, but not horrified like I probably should have been. I've replayed the scene a thousand times now and it's always the same. I'm sitting at my desk in my BVDs getting ready to write a check for the minimum balance due on my Visa bill when I catch a glimpse of this red and black thing zooming past my window.

The window was grimy, so I didn't have a very clear view of what the thing was. Besides, I wasn't really looking. I just barely saw this streak of red and black. I've thought a lot about this lately—way too much, actually—and I've concluded that the brain does something weird to avoid making sense of this kind of thing. Basically, your brain doesn't figure out what it's all about right away because it doesn't want to. But at the same time, you do sort of know. So, I think I knew it was a body—or a person—and I think I may have even known it was Mr. Jacobson wearing those stupid black jeans he was much too old for and that silky red shirt that reminded me of Wayne Newton.

Yeah, I think I knew right from the get-go what was going on, but it didn't *strike* me, as they say. I saw it and I thought something like, *that couldn't be Mr. Jacobson because people don't fly.*

It was probably, like, maybe a couple seconds later—maybe a half second—when I bolted out of my chair and ran to the window to see what he would look like splatted on the ground. So, I must have known what it was—and who it was—because I'm pretty sure when I ran over there, I knew what I was going to see on the pavement.

Then I stared; I swear that's all I could do. I just stared at that mess of a person who resembled a little pile of doll parts or something. It wasn't gross; I didn't see much blood, though it would have been hard to say, considering the red shirt and all. It's not like there were brains splattered all over the place or anything. He mostly just looked messy. And kind of unhappy.

❧

I first saw Mr. Jacobson the day I moved into the building, right after I split up with Amanda. When she and her new *inamorata* (her word, needless to say) decided to take over the rent-controlled one-bedroom she and I had shared on Columbus Avenue, I moved down here to the East Village because it was cheap and about as far away as I could get from the two of them.

I didn't have much to move, and had managed to get it all into the back end of my buddy Jeff's pickup. I kept thinking about the lead-in to those old *Beverly Hillbillies* reruns as we drove that damn truck through Manhattan, with my puke-green armchair that smelled like stale beer, a mattress and box springs Jeff had scared up from his group house in Brooklyn, a huge torn khaki duffle bag, and maybe fifteen boxes of general junk in the open truck bed behind us. We even sang the theme song as we drove.

We parked on the street in front of the building, in the *No Parking: Entrance* zone, and carried the stuff through the so-called lobby where we tried to shove it into the so-called freight elevator, which is really just an ordinary elevator that's more dented and scratched up than the other one. Just as we were trying to cram the mattress into the elevator car, I saw old Mr. Jacobson behind me.

He stood and watched us as we maneuvered and manipulated the way-too-large thing into the way-too-small space. We were pushing and shoving and sweating and swearing and yelling and grunting and making a whole big deal about this project, and all the while Mr. Jacobson—whose name I of course didn't know at the time—just stood there watching.

"Jesus *Christ*, man," Jeff finally said to him, "either do something to help us out here or get out of the way."

The old man was not actually in the way, but I guess he was giving Jeff the creeps, the way he stood there staring, kind of into space and kind of at us, and not saying or doing anything. Anyway, Mr. J turned around, kind of shuffled over to the front door, and walked out. Just like that. He wasn't mad, wasn't anything, really. Just basically vacant. Nobody home.

"Asshole," Jeff muttered.

"Yeah," I agreed, for no particular reason.

I didn't see him again until a couple months later, nor did I think about him. He's not really the kind of guy you tend to think much about.

I had just come in from work; we'd gotten off early because of one of those freak snowstorms that completely paralyze the city. I was in the elevator and the doors were beginning to close behind me when I heard this little voice say, "Hold it!" It was a Minnie Mouse voice. Not squeaky really, but high pitched and funny. I stuck my hand into the space between the doors and when they snapped back open, the owner of the little voice joined me in the car.

"Thanks," she said, pulling off a red and blue knit stocking cap. I noticed she was wearing sneakers—the old Keds kind, not the new *athletic footwear* kind. They were soaking wet and made squishy noises when she shifted her weight. She smiled up at me. "Even with cold feet, I love snow."

"I hate it," I said, just to be perverse.

"I'm from Minnesota," she said, as if that explained everything.

I nodded, and just about then the door opened onto the sixth floor. My floor.

"We're practically neighbors," she said with a kind of excitement I thought was a little ridiculous since what did she *think* we were, for God's sake, living in the same building and all. "I'm in 7G."

"I'm in 6F," I said.

"I'm going to make some cocoa. Want to come up?"

I'm not a big cocoa fan, but I liked the way she looked. Blonde and tiny and very cute in a pug-nosed, Gidget kind of way. I guess you'd have to call her spunky. Something like that. I don't often hang out with spunky people but she just looked good to me at that moment. It was nasty and gray outside, I knew my apartment would be cold, I was pissed from being bossed around all day at work, and this little, spunky, red-cheeked person who was making cocoa kind of appealed to me. It's not something I can explain.

So I said sure. "Let me just drop off my coat." I started down the hall toward my apartment. "I'll be right up."

"7G," she repeated, as if I'd already forgotten.

꩜

When I got upstairs, I knocked on her door, trying to "rap smartly," a line I remembered from an English whodunit I once read. I do read from time to time, even though most people I know find that hard to believe. I figured a "smart rap" would be something a spunky individual would appreciate. And sure enough, she opened the door with a big smile.

"I'm Loretta Homer," she said, sticking out her hand as I walked into her apartment.

"Lance Barker," I said. "Nice to meet you."

Then she looked past me, out into the hall, and kind of craned her neck to the left.

"Mr. Jacobson," she said. "How nice to see you."

When I looked back to see who she was talking to, I saw the crazy guy Jeff and I had seen in the lobby. He didn't respond, didn't even acknowledge her.

"Mr. Jacobson, this is Lance," Loretta said.

I nodded in his direction, but he still didn't respond. He just stared at me, kind of the way he had before. Maybe he nodded a little bit; it's hard to say now. Anyway, that was the conversation.

"Would you like some cocoa?" Loretta asked him.

This spunky thing was turning a little spooky now, as far as I was concerned. What was the *deal* asking everyone in sight if they wanted cocoa. Anyway, he didn't answer.

"I'll bring you some," she said.

Then he went into an apartment across the hall, just above mine, and we went into Loretta's where she made that cocoa. After delivering the promised mug to Mr. Jacobson, she proceeded to prove to me that chocolate-making farm girls from Minnesota are not necessarily the virginal little prudes you might imagine. It was a very good evening.

After that, I spent a lot of time with Loretta. Turns out she was an artist; she had a studio in an old warehouse in the Bowery where she made huge paintings of things I was never able to recognize or respond to in any reasonable way. Still, I used to tell her how much I liked them.

But what I really liked was her. She was sweet and, like I said, spunky and, most of all, lonely. She had been in New York for six or eight months and had met very few people. She said I gave her a nice, warm feeling, and I can tell you for sure, she gave me one. She was only about twenty-five, I think, but had this kind of grown-up, confident way about her. She was easy with herself and with people. And she honestly, genuinely liked people, which made her very different from me.

As far as I'm concerned, most people are just in the way. They're in line ahead of you; they're in cars creating gridlock and driving like maniacs; they're buying the last onion bagel; they're kicking up a fit because you're double parked; they're talking in the movie theater; they're always asking stupid questions; they're jostling you in the street; they're screaming for you to work twice as hard and fast as any human being possibly can. They're just in the way.

But to Loretta, people were something magical. All these damn people. She used to tell me how each one had a value and a spark (that's the word she used, a spark) all his own. She liked to talk to people and see where they were from, what they were interested in, what they liked and all that. She even liked to *incorporate their spirits* (her expression, obviously) into her paintings. She got some kind of kick out of that, though I never understood it myself. I'd much rather have a good TV show and a beer, say, than a conversation.

But I did like talking to Loretta, and I especially liked what we did after we talked.

⁓

"Why do you bother with him?" I asked her one night when she was making me spaghetti for dinner. Loretta wasn't much of a cook, truth be told, but she did do a few things quite well, and spaghetti was one of them.

"Bother with who?" she asked as she ladled red sauce over the pile of pasta in front of her and covered the whole thing with a piece of tin foil.

"Mr. Jacobson. Why do you bother with him?"

"He's sweet," she said.

"He's not sweet," I said. "He's never said a word to you."

"He doesn't have to talk," she said. "It's in his eyes. He has lovely eyes."

"He has vacant eyes," I said, pleased with my choice of words. It was very rare for the right one to pop into my mouth that way. "He has eyes like a dead person. He doesn't talk, he doesn't react, he doesn't do anything but roam the halls and stare at people. He gives me the creeps."

"He's lonely," she said, as if that ended the conversation, then she left the apartment to deliver Mr. Jacobson's spaghetti dinner.

⁓

Loretta talked to old Mr. J like you would talk to a person in a coma. She would chatter on about the weather, her work, the Mets, whatever.

She would talk and talk and never expect a word from him. She brought him dinner now and again, not every night, just once in a while. And if she didn't see him for a few days, she would tap on his door to see how he was doing. He would open the door, grunt at her, and she'd go home happy.

I was there at her apartment, watching the evening news one night, when she did just that. "I'm going to check on Mr. Jacobson. I'll be right back."

I nodded and kept watching Dan Rather.

She came back to the apartment a few minutes later and sat down on the ottoman in front of my chair. She was blushing and smiling as big a smile as I'd ever seen on her.

"What's up?"

"He talked." She said it almost breathlessly.

"He *talked*?" I felt like we were in that part of *Heidi* where the girl hops out of her wheelchair and walks. "Jesus Christ," I said. "What'd he say?"

"He thanked me for the spaghetti."

"You mean, just like that? He said all those words?"

"Yes."

"What brought it on?" I asked. "Why would he talk all of a sudden? And, if he can talk, why didn't he do it before this?"

"I don't know," she said, "but I'm so excited. I've waited so long for this."

"Why?"

"I guess just because I always believed there was someone inside that body, but I wanted some proof." She turned her little elf face up toward mine and fixed those big blue eyes on mine. "Does that sound crazy?"

"Maybe a little," I said. I pretended to be joking, but I meant it. It was a little crazy, but it was so *her* that it was also kind of cute.

"If I ever leave here, will you take care of him?" she asked, suddenly very serious.

"Where are you going?"

"Nowhere," she said quickly. "I just meant in case... I can't stand thinking of him all alone here, with no one to visit him."

"What did he do before you came along? He got along, right?"

She seemed to ponder the question before answering. Finally she nodded slowly, "I suppose he did."

And so I managed to end the conversation without having to make a commitment.

⁓

But of course, Loretta did leave. She moved back to Minnesota maybe six months after we met. She decided she didn't like New York, even though her art was going places and she was getting noticed, which was just what she had hoped for when she moved here. But she just didn't like it. *It's not me*, is the way she put it. That made me wonder what kind of a place would be *me*, I mean in my own case. It was a new concept, this idea that there might be me-places and not-me-places. I thought you just were where you were and made do with that.

Anyway, when I look back on the whole thing, her leaving was inevitable. She was one of those people who pops into your life like a fly or a mosquito, and then buzzes right out again. One of those people who leaves a little mark on you, like a bug leaves a welt, a mark that goes away about as fast as a mosquito bite even though the bug-juice might hang around in your system a little longer. But that's neither here nor there, as they say; the bottom line is, these people do not stay. And she didn't.

⁓

After Loretta left New York, I saw a lot of Mr. Jacobson, not that I wanted to. It seemed like he was out there wandering around more than ever; after all, he'd lost his only visitor. I would see him on the sidewalk in front of the building, just standing there, staring. I would see him in our sorry excuse for a lobby, the scrungy little place outside the elevators. A few times I saw him in the park across the street, sitting on a bench, watching kids play. And a couple of times I even saw him on *my* floor, the sixth, where he had no business being. I never did know whether he was lost or just kind of lurking.

Of course, I never spoke to him. I'm definitely not the kind of guy who smiles at someone, or winks, or says a friendly or witty thing. Whenever I saw him, I'd try to get out of the vicinity before he could spot me. When he did catch sight of me, he'd stare, as usual. That's all, just stare. I never found those eyes to be kind, the way Loretta did. Just spooky.

I remember the very last time I saw him, not counting the day he went flying. He was standing next to the elevator on the ground floor when I came in the door. Something about him made me think of my father, who is not a guy I have good feelings about—and that's putting it mildly. I guess it was the way he just hung out there that suddenly reminded me of my old man who also used to hang out while my mother worked and I went to school or did whatever the hell I did in those days. My dad would hang out on the sofa with a brew, or with a fifth if times were really good. He would stare too, kind of like Mr. J, but at the TV so it wasn't as bizarre. At least he was watching something, as opposed to watching nothing.

Anyway, I basically just walked past him the way I always did, and he basically stared at me, the way he always did. But something seemed just the tiniest bit different. It was like he looked at me more carefully than usual, if that makes any damn sense at all. He didn't seem quite so vacant. It was almost like he was about to say something or do something.

Of course, I didn't hang around to find out if he would. I really didn't want it to happen because I didn't want to have to deal with it. In fact, thinking back on it, I'm wondering if I might have even smirked at him or looked disgusted because, you know, I really was. I hated the guy. He represented everything about New York that sent Loretta back to Minnesota, and that really pissed me off. It's not like I expected her to be here forever, like I said, but without people like Mr. J around this hellhole, she might have lasted a little longer. So I suppose I might have shot him some kind of a dirty look, but it wouldn't have been on purpose.

It was just a couple of hours later that I saw him fly past my window, and then all hell broke loose in this place. The cops came by and talked to everyone they could find, including yours truly.

Did you know him well?

Did he have family or friends that you know about?

Did he seem unhappy?

Do you think he would have jumped? Any reason to think he might have been pushed?

My answers were, like, no; no; not any more than anyone else; yes; and no.

Of course he wasn't pushed. Who the hell would bother? There was no one on this earth, I'm pretty sure, who cared enough about Mr. J to have pushed him. Or to have saved him, for that matter. Sure, he might have jumped. Why the hell not? What did he have going on here that would have made him want to stick around? What do any of us have going on here, for that matter?

He had Loretta for a while; so did I. She was the kind of person who made a difference in things like this, whatever that means. But I wasn't about to get into that with the cops. She was long gone, and it wouldn't have been fair to bring her into this. Actually, I was starting to wonder if she'd ever really been here. I mean, there was no trace of her at all anymore. It's not like she had left anything behind. Maybe she was one of these mirage things, like something from the *Twilight Zone* or one of those visions people at Bellevue have. Maybe I'm as nuts as old Mr. J.

Anyway, I finally told one of the cops, maybe the third one who came by asking the same stupid questions, to butt out. I told him that Mr. J did what he did. No one did it to him, and it was no one else's business. Anybody has a right to jump out his window. As I said it, I realized I kind of admired the old bastard for doing it, for just taking matters into his own damn hands and doing something with his life. He was a lot gutsier than I'd given him credit for being, a hell of a lot gutsier than I was or anyone else I knew. Gutsy or nutsy, I thought, and kind of chuckled to myself at my poetry.

◆

The next day, I looked at the weather forecast for Minneapolis in the *Times*. That made the place seem real to me and made me feel like Loretta might really be out there somewhere. For a little while after Mr. J took his flight, I just wanted to believe she was somewhere in the world, though I felt like a complete asshole for thinking that and would never have said it out loud. And don't get me wrong, mostly I still think people are just in the way.

Anyway, I never heard anything more about Mr. Jacobson, and I really don't care to. I don't know if he had a decent burial or if he had any family. I don't know where he came from or how he ended up here. I don't know why he did what he did, and I don't need to know; I never made any commitment.

The crazy thing is, he was probably less in the way than most people, for what that's worth, which isn't much. But still, it's kind of a funny thing to think about and kind of makes the whole thing about him a little sad.

Stephanie Siciarz

Nest Egg

STEPHANIE SICIARZ is a student in the graduate writing program at Johns Hopkins University. She lives outside Washington but travels often to faraway islands. Her favorite, and the novel series it has inspired, takes up most of her time.

Rain.

The name had never suited her.

Rains were free spirits. Bohemians. Surely *she* came from the womb already nudging a pair of reading glasses up the bridge of her nose and demanding to be rinsed of her mother's fluids. A Gertrude. An Althea. A Bea.

Definitely not a Rain.

Rains liked to go camping. They wrote poetry and had sex on the first date. Rains were *not* financial planners who kept antibacterial towelettes in the glove box and who, at the age of forty-three, could still count all their lovers on one hand.

She had tried to settle into the name, tried to become what she thought a Rain should be. Social smoker, geology major, vegetarian. Once she took a trip to Greece without even booking a hotel. Just a passport, a few bucks, and a two-piece in a backpack.

She had never been so terrified.

She decided—there, on a Greek isle whose name was forgotten with some coins at the bottom of her pack—decided: no more "settling into" anything. Not a name, not a relationship, not a vegetarian pizza. She couldn't—and wouldn't—deny her urges one minute more. She liked plans. She liked steak. She liked her blouses ironed and she liked to be taken seriously.

She donned her likes, a bright yellow slicker with latches fastened right up to her chin, and went back home.

Once she decided that she wasn't who she was, everything fell into place. She breezed through grad school, snatched up a husband and an MBA, and hung a shingle "Financial Advice." Her husband was good—not for a Rain (his hands were too small and his demeanor too big), but for her he was good—and her marriage thrived. The business, too, was a smashing success, clients drawn to her as if by magic spell.

Her favorite client was a forty-something surgeon, a workaholic and accidental playboy named Jack. Jack fell in love too quickly and too often, and two ex-wives now pecked away at his nest egg. He was her favorite because he lacked the time to question what she said. He did what she told him and signed what she sent him, at least on a trial basis. When the trial was over and his money had grown in spite of his pecking exes, impressed, he took her on indefinitely and gave in to her every suggestion. He sold his house and bought something smaller, drove used cars instead of brand-new, and watched his nest egg grow.

So much had she multiplied his small fortune in a few short years, and earned herself handsome fees, that Jack became seduced, and she did too. Not seduced by each other, but each by the profit that the other inspired. He began to call her more and more frequently, to seek her approval of even insignificant outlays: dinner with Rita at Foie d'Or, a silk scarf for Judith, tickets to the theater for him and a surgical nurse. When his calls came through, her palms got sweaty and she always told him no.

"What about the future?" she would say. "What about your hungry ex-wives?" And the nest egg grew with every syllable she spoke.

Because she had so limited Jack's expenditures, the Ritas and the Judiths and the nurses got bored, and soon Jack spent most of his free time alone. Not that he had much free time, for she encouraged him to work all he could. He went from home to hospital and back, like a pendulum unable to stray from its arc.

Jack's family amounted to little more than his ex-wives, so on holidays she invited him to dinner with her and her husband. They had plenty of room. She always cooked a turkey, with dressing and cranberry sauce.

"Nice place," Jack would say. He said it every time he went to her house, as if the times before he had never seen it. As if he had never noticed the flooring or the layout of the walls. It *was* a nice place—not for a Rain (the garden was too small and the mortgage too big), but for her it was nice—and there she and her husband thrived.

For ten years they shared their Christmas turkeys, she and Jack. For ten years she invested Jack's money and fed her growing business. For ten years Jack worked as hard as he could and forgot about Ritas and Judiths. The nest egg swelled to grotesque proportions, she and Jack both as proud of it as if it were their very own child, fattened and made strong by their sacrifice and sweat.

One day, when she was forty-three and Jack was forty-four, the future she helped him save for finally arrived. It didn't crash through Jack's front door during a violent, midnight storm, didn't thrust its bags and cases on the landing and demand a room indefinitely. It trickled, rather, like a leak in the ceiling above his favorite chair, the drops falling right into his eyes.

They didn't sting at first. The drops just blurred his vision a bit, and not even that all the time. Most days Jack was as good as ever. But a month or so passed, and with it the leak grew heavier and Jack's vision grew worse. Every morning he woke up, his first thought to look at his hands. He did it even before climbing out of bed. Some days they looked like the hands he remembered. Other days the lithe, healing fingers that snipped and tied, that mingled with veins and arteries, looked to Jack's dripping eyes like raw and swollen sausages, the lines between them lost or frayed.

He spent part of his nest egg on specialists and procedures. He traveled to famous clinics and underwent experimental treatments. Three more months passed, but nothing could be done.

Jack's vision remained unforecastable, cloudy one minute, clear the next. Too unforecastable to schedule surgeries or to hold sharp instruments near delicate organs. Too unforecastable to drive his used cars or to take ski trips now that work no longer occupied his time. He went fishing sometimes or to a movie, but mostly his days were as thin as his nest egg still was plump.

He didn't call her as much anymore. He didn't call her at all. The allure that each had exercised upon the other melted away with the future that no longer needed saving for, the thirsty seduction of all those years before now sated by what had come to pass. At his pace, the nest egg would sustain both him and his hungry ex-wives for a long time to come.

She was glad he stopped calling because she didn't know what to say to him. She had merely done her job, and done it well. It wasn't her fault if the gamble hadn't paid off; if he had sacrificed ten years of the present for a future that arrived fuzzy and blurred. Hers were only suggestions. She couldn't be blamed if he took her too seriously.

Without Jack's money, her business faltered. Not for lack of capital, but for lack of conviction. Jack's blurred vision had contaminated hers as well, distorted her neat resolutions into ugly beings, empty but bloated, who haunted her at home and at work. She couldn't eat, or sleep, or conduct her business. She no longer knew who she was.

Her husband bought her a ticket to take a trip. He saw that she wasn't herself and decided a change of scenery would do her good. He would stay home and mind her business while she was away.

"Good idea," she told him. She would escape from the guilt that had trickled into her eyes, free herself from the ghosts that blocked her view.

They packed her bags and he put her on a plane. More than ten years had passed since last she traveled alone. When she arrived, she found a taxi and asked the driver to take her to a hotel. Any hotel but the one her husband had booked her in. She thought she might better avoid the ghosts that way, by changing the plans. The driver left her at a clean and comfortable two-star, two-story establishment. Not the hotel she would have chosen on her own. But, still, it was good, for her.

She showered for a long time. Unresolved and wrapped in a towel, she stared out the room's long windows. She stared at the clouds, which transformed themselves into the ghosts she couldn't elude, Jack's wasted years, and her own, her business, and the name she had made for herself, the blinded life she had settled into. She stared them down, faced their pale, flimsy nakedness, and her own, until their reproofs finally dissipated into vapors billowed and shaped by the changing, forgiving air. She stared until she felt hungry and then she dressed.

Her luggage was lost, but Rain had put a spare shirt in the bottom of her carry-on bag. She pulled it on now and checked herself in the mirror as her hand reached for the door. The top buttons undone, the shirt exposed the lacy edge of her bra. She stopped and studied its reflection, as if the white material against her skin were unfamiliar. As if both bra and skin belonged to someone else, not to her.

Her eyes moved quickly over the rest of her image, over the crisp, cutting wrinkles her travels had left imprinted in the fabric of her shirt. She studied those, too, the way they sliced their way across her stomach, her heart, her arms. She flicked her hand over them lightly, futilely, and went out—out, into the dusk that suppressed the nameless clouds, and blew them out to sea before night could fall.

Rozanne Gooding Silverwood

Little Miss Anarchist

ROZANNE GOODING SILVERWOOD lives in Reston, Virginia, with her husband and three teenage daughters. She is a creative writing instructor at several Fairfax County public schools, teaching elementary school students to write for, edit, and self-publish school literary journals. An excerpt from her novel-in-progress, "Hunting Prayers," was published in *Gargoyle* and her young adult short story, "The Star That Fell to Earth and Became a Tree," will soon appear in *Cricket*.

The express checkout lane is backed up ten deep and an old lady smelling of baby powder and cat piss empties twenty-five cans of Fancy Feast cat food, one at a time, from her grocery cart out onto the conveyor belt. My PETA membership is what temporarily spares the lady from my typical teenage scowl. That is, until she heaves up her next grocery item, a jumbo package of Depends. I draw the line at adult diapers and reach for a red plastic dividing rod, a hasty grab that puts me squarely in line with the cat lover's final purchase, a grocery store tabloid. And here's where, after ten years of teasing the public's imagination with a story that should be as dull as an Elvis sighting, a familiar black-and-white glamour shot stops me cold.

"Poor JonBenet," the cat lover clucks, handing the cashier her coupons and a Bonus Savings Card. "How could anyone hurt such a cute little kitten of a girl?"

I'm hardly listening though, not even remembering my mom who's outside with the Volvo running, her fingers drumming on the steering wheel.

During my kindergarten years, I was a princess wannabe, and it was JonBenet, not Princess Di, that fueled my fantasies of beauty queen titles and tiaras. My mom had spared me from the fine print below the headlines, the details about rope burns and duct tape. This tragic back story was kept under wraps, only later disclosed, vaguely, like evidence police detectives forever allude to uncovering in the Ramseys' basement closet.

All teenagers must have at least one pathetic imitation that causes them to cringe. Mine involves a frilly pink chiffon dress with tiny bells sewn onto the hem and my eyelash-flutteringly demure JonBenet mimicry. I can see myself leaving the grocery store, being buckled securely, double-checked for extra precaution, into a built-in rear safety seat that boosted me just high enough to catch my reflection in the rearview mirror. And my imagination was like a photographer's gel lens, reducing my sharp nose to buttonlike cuteness, softening my muddy freckles to powder-puff pink, smoothing my tangled mat of dishwater dull hair to a halo of shining curls. But what lies outside the lens frame of that rearview mirror's lower rim, is my crooked grin, more snarl than smile—the severely scarred reminder of an earlier child safety seat, a forty-mile-per-hour head-on encounter with crushed plastic, a now-deceased father, and a carload of drunken teenagers. In this memory the garish grimace that dominates the lower left side of my face has been trimmed from view along with the tattered edges of the bodice ribbon on that favorite party dress, worn to utter limpness, seven days a week, party or not, until the sad morning when I awaken to find in its place, a tie-dyed T-shirt and a pair of blue denim shorts laid out like a truce. This would be the same day that my mom would explain, with carefully chosen words, the unfortunate fate of that blonde poster girl; this would be the same day that I stopped looking into rearview mirrors.

I've since strangled the life out of my naïve beauty queen fantasies and channeled my remaining idealistic tendencies into the defense of defenseless creatures. Meanwhile I view life through the stark, unforgiving lens of facial disfigurement and teenage angst and having developed a cynical acceptance of my unexceptional figure—flat chest, flat butt, flat feet—I've adopted a utilitarian fashion formula, jeans and T-shirt, accessorized by torn and tattered thrift store castoffs, otherwise known as "vintage." As for my facial scars, currently accentuated by the artistry of orthodontia, I try to carry off the offense with an air of defiance, alluding to all pity-mongers that the whole mess is the result of a back alley tussle involving switchblades and broken bottles, with my departing the scene in much better shape than my sorry opponent.

The cat lover with the Depends is counting out her last nickels and pennies when the cashier comments on the tabloid's headlines: New DNA Tests Identify Killer!

"It's the mother's fault," the cashier offers with a throaty croak, volunteering this information as if she's just reviewed the crime report during her last cigarette break. "Dolling that little girl up with mascara and lipstick, for pete's sake. Why not just invite all the child molesters in the neighborhood over for coffee?"

The cat lover takes her change and, leaning the full weight of her frail shoulders into the task, she wheels her grocery cart toward the exit, out of range of the clerk's perverse accusations.

"Paper or plastic?" the clerk asks me the essential question of the twenty-first century.

"Plastic," I say, choosing the consumption of petroleum products over killing a tree.

My flat package of poster boards glides along the conveyor toward her reach. "School assignment?" she asks, stuffing the plastic-encased cardboard sheets into yet another plastic bag while blankly staring across the aisles as if calculating the minutes until her next cigarette break.

"It's for a school field trip," I answer, making note of the cashier's lapel pin, a red-white-and-blue enameled crucifix. "My political science class is going into DC for tomorrow's Inaugural Parade."

"What a great learning experience!" the cashier says, keeping her eyes on the register screen as she slides my assortment of items across the glass scanning plate.

Blip! Sharpie Felt Tip Marker, Color-Black Jumbo-Size...$1.49. *Blip!* 10-Count Package Latex Balloons-Multi-colored, Medium...$1.99. *Blip!* Super-Saver Tempera Paint, 16 fl. oz, Red...$1.99.

"That'll be $8.63," she announces, finally taking her eyes from the scanner, assessing my chrome-studded vegan leather belt and the ragged thumb holes cut into my sweatshop-free jacket. My thrift store scarf at my throat, a red Chinese print of cute little kittens licking their paws, holds her momentarily or maybe it's the maroon streaks that peek through my tangle of greasy brown hair, but when she comes to my face, she blinks—I'm used to this response—and desperate for a comfort zone, she settles on my lapel pin, "Meat Is Murder!" Here's where her lips purse, and in a manner that I'm thinking she mostly reserves for those fresh-faced teenage jocks with six-packs who try to pass themselves off as twenty-one, she shakes her head in disapproval.

The cashier makes change for my ten and I take it, gathering my purchases to leave. "God Bless America!" I say, flashing a peace sign.

A whoosh of freezing air sucks the breath from my lungs as I pass through the electronic doors. My mom has the car idling in the fire lane and from her look I can tell that she's still fuming. I slide into the front seat, bracing for her complaint.

"Kate, when will you stop waiting until the eleventh hour to ask me to drive you somewhere?" She asks this a lot.

My reply, "When you let me get my driver's license. I'm almost eighteen, for Chrissake." Here's where that discussion always ends. "And it wasn't my fault. Some old woman who smelled like a litter box had to count out her pennies."

"Don't be so mean, Kate," my mom scolds. "You, too, will be old someday and some wisecracking teenagers will be making snide comments about you."

"Oh, but they already do," I say, but immediately feel guilty. My mom takes it personal when I make fun of my face. "I caught up on the latest tabloids, though. There's a story about a Bermuda Triangle toilet bowl where people simply vanish? They say that it leaves you 'feeling a little flushed.'"

My mom is laughing and this is how we cope with conflict. "Buckle up," she says, checking the rearview mirror, cautiously pulling into the busy intersection.

"JonBenet is still in the news. Remember how I used to want to be just like her?"

"Yeah, well, she was cute," my mom says. "But cute didn't keep her from getting killed."

The wintry mix predicted for Inauguration Day has, thankfully, not materialized, although the temperature is still in the low thirties. But my mom's in a better humor driving me to the Metro station and it's my turn to be annoyed.

"Didn't you pack a lunch? At least something hot to drink?" she nags.

"Mom! I'll buy something when we get there. Besides, where would I put it? No backpacks, no cans, no fruit allowed. And certainly no thermos bottles—*Ahem, excuse me miss, but is that hot chocolate a bomb?*"

"One day your sarcasm will land you in jail," she says and proceeds to ask for the fifth time this morning if I'm wearing layers under my sweatshirt.

"I'm warm as toast," I answer, revealing nothing about what's hidden beneath my oversized jacket. Placards larger than a postage stamp have been listed as security threats and will be confiscated, so my "unlawful" protest poster is folded and duct taped to my stomach. This makes it almost impossible for me to bend at the waist and frankly, I'm surprised that my mom hasn't commented on the sudden improvement in my posture.

"Hypothermia is no joke," she says. "If you get into trouble, call me. You have your cell phone?"

I give her a thumbs up. My shoulder bag is just big enough for my phone, wallet, and a pack of gum, and I'd decided on it, instead of my larger canvas tote, after measuring both purses carefully against the template in the morning's newspaper, a six-by-eight-inch square that read *Prohibited Items: Does Your Bag Fit in the Box?*

"We're meeting at the east entrance. Pull over and let me out here," I say, and before I can get out the door, my mom has me by the half-inch safety pin dangling from the tie string of my sweatshirt hood. A good luck charm she made me promise to wear.

"Remember…" She tugs at the pin. *"Be safe!"*

"I'll try not to get my face smashed in," I tease.

"Stop making yourself the butt of your own jokes. It's not funny or cute."

"Whoever said I was trying to be cute?" I shimmy out the car door while trying not to bend, the stiff edge of the poster board digging into my groin.

I find my classmates shoving dollar bills into the farecard dispenser, purchasing their Commemorative Inaugural Day Metro cards, while my teacher looks on. Her black, ankle-length cape whirls around her and, illuminated by the stark lighting of the tunnel, gives her a witchlike appearance. She has all the earmarks of an aging flower child, tremulous voice, vegetarian emaciation, and Birkenstocks. The loose-fitting tie-dyed caftans she likes to wear, reeking of sandalwood incense, and her distinctive gliding walk creates a sort of billowing effect and this is why we call her "Billow," instead of "Bill," which is short for Wilhelmina.

Billow teaches political science at my school, and her classroom is like a flashback to the sixties and her heyday at UC Berkeley. Papered with psychedelic posters—anti-war, women's lib, black power—it also epitomizing the Bohemian atmosphere of my school, Brookstone Academy, a progressive institution of higher learning, bankrolled by semi-wealthy, liberal-leaning parents who encourage field trips such as this Inaugural Day protest.

We began planning this trip on the heels of November's presidential election. Billow has assigned each of us to arrive at positions of dissent—no willy-nilly against anything allowed—with all viewpoints thoroughly researched and presented via weekly five-page essays. Only two parents voiced concern to the school administration, but, when approached by Headmaster Stephenson, Billow explained that we were studying a unit entitled "Democracy and the People's Voice" and we would conclude the quarter with a ten-page written essay, or fifteen-minute PowerPoint demonstration, which any parent would be welcome to evaluate. Our projects are to include a poster to be graded on originality and impact. Mine reads, "4 MORE YEARS OF HOMELAND IN-SECURITY," with a Sharpie rendering of Munch's *Scream* and to be honest, when I worked on it last night, it was meant as more of a commentary on my mother's hovering than on matters of the state. But I'm hoping to find a way to tie the slogan into my thesis topic, "Democracy or Police State?" selected via *eeny-meeny-miny-mo* method from Billow's long list of essay options. I've yet to come up with my opening argument, and since it's due the day after this field trip, I'd say I'm a tad behind schedule.

Billow is at the turnstile now, counting heads, and everyone is present and accounted for, except Jeremy Stallings. No surprise, Jeremy is always late, if he bothers to show up at all. His absences are always excused by his bad boy charisma and spectacular good looks. He's a pencil-thin boy with delicate features, green, copper-speckled eyes, long eyelashes, and wispy blonde hair. If not for the cigarette he keeps tucked behind one ear, alluding to world-weary innocence, he would be almost too pretty.

Our classroom debates reveal that Jeremy's politics are shaped by two primary influences, Brad Pitt's character in *Fight Club,* and the more incendiary sections of the *Anarchist Cookbook.* Meaning Jeremy's a rebel, but he's no revolutionary. Still, everyone seems to adore him, wants to play along with his Bolshevik game, particularly Billow, who is completely undone by his soulful, James Dean-like squints. She is the first to soothe and coddle him through every inconvenience.

Shannon Nicholson-Palmer has her camera phone aimed toward the west entrance. "There's Jeremy," she shouts, snapping his picture.

Shannon recently transferred from Dalton Prep, for undisclosed reasons, and while she's not particularly attractive, her parents have the finances to keep her outfitted with the latest technology. She's sixteen years old and drives herself to school in a pimped-out BMW convertible. This is why I hate her—that she drives. All of the boys, including Jeremy, are smitten with her BMW.

Jeremy's studying the wall-sized Metro map and he takes one last drag on his cigarette before tossing it to the ground, snuffing it out with the toe of his scuffed Doc Marten. The tattered hems of his oversized cargo pants sweep the pavement as he shuffles toward us.

"Now that we've discussed our game plan..." Billow says, looking mostly at Jeremy, her pet, who stands off to the side, shoulders hunched, hands shoved into the pockets of his wool navy pea coat. "Are there any more questions?"

The class shrugs. Jeremy, likewise, shrugs.

"OK, then let's get going. Democracy beckons!" Billow shouts, attempting to stir our enthusiasm. We follow behind her flowing cape, a sleepy crew of disinterested eleventh graders, in search of little more from this presidential fanfare than a passing grade.

I manage to snag an empty aisle seat, three rows from the door, and am surprised when Jeremy skooches in front of me, taking the window seat to my right. He nudges me with his elbow. "Did Billow mention which stop we're getting off at?" he asks, pulling a cigarette from his pocket, tamping it on the metal stud of his black leather wrist cuff.

"Dunno. I got here just before you did," I shrug, wondering why he isn't sitting with Shannon.

Jeremy and I hear, "Yoo-hoo!" and we both turn to see Shannon sitting two rows behind us. "Say cheese!" She snaps our photo and waves, giving Jeremy a little pout, then goes back to giggling with her latest BFF, Delia Crofton. They pose together for a self-portrait which Shannon will use in her PowerPoint presentation, entitled "Parade Memories."

Jeremy tucks the cigarette behind his ear and asks about my essay, how it's coming. I'm utterly surprised by my awkwardness, how I'm fumbling for words and bringing my hand up to cover the left side of my mouth in a stupid, self-conscious gesture which I hope Jeremy doesn't recognize for what it is.

I'm unprepared when the train takes a curve and am briefly thrown off balance and into Jeremy. He smells of pine soap and nicotine, a lethal mix of wholesomeness and vice, the effects of which give birth to a newfound wave of pheromone-induced courage. I assume the hushed tone of a co-conspirator and tease, "Billow said there might be undercover cops lurking about."

"Yeah, right! And I'd say she's suffering from conspiracy delusions."

I begin to assess the passengers and swivel to look behind us. Shannon and Delia are still snapping photos of each other with their posters. In the next row behind them, Bernard Nimms, the class technophile, is tapping furiously at the keys of his laptop, most likely revising the final draft of his essay, "Digital Warfare and the Use of Surveillance Practices for Social

Control in the Post-Cyborg Era." The remaining members of my class appear to have been lulled to sleep by the rocking motion of the train.

A few rows further back, Billow stands, keeping a watchful eye on her flock of students. Beside her, a rather short man clutches the same metal bar that she does. He's dressed in a gray business suit and black wool overcoat, but his navy baseball cap with the NYC logo looks oddly out of place. I give a little wave and smile at Billow, who is now making nervous eye movements in the man's direction and just as the train brakes for an approaching Metro stop, the man adjusts his weight. Here's when I notice the earpiece, the curled plastic cord tucked behind the curve of his ear.

I face forward and whisper to Jeremy, "The guy standing next to Billow seems to be our man. Take a look, but try not to be too obvious."

Jeremy pretends a yawn and stretch. He brings one arm down, around my shoulder, turning to look behind us, and the fresh soapy scent intensifies.

Jeremy snorts. "That's just his cell phone!"

"Then why is the cord going down the *back* of his shirt?"

Jeremy looks again. "Dude! That's *awesome!*" He almost shouts this while I'm trying not to notice that his arm is still slung along the back of my seat.

"Good thing I concealed this before I got on the train then," he says, knocking on the side of his calf with his fist. A hollow thunk is muffled by the pant leg. "PVC pipe! Might've come in handy to hold up my poster...if I hadn't forgotten to bring it."

I lift up the front of my sweatshirt, just enough to reveal a portion of the folded cardboard tucked into my pants. "My poster didn't meet the size requirements. We can share." Smoothing the lumpy shirt back over my stomach inadvertently reveals evidence of my other secreted contraband and suddenly Jeremy is staring at my chest.

One of the deeper scars below my left cheek begins to throb as a rush of blood flushes my face. "Let's just say the President's motorcade is in for a surprise." I say, pulling at the sweatshirt to restore its original frumpiness, camouflaging my increased bust size. I readjust my mom's Victoria Secret push-up bra, each paint-filled balloon still safely nestled within the spongy nylon cups. I'm surprised by how strangely sexy it feels with the added weight on my chest and I'll never admit to how long I'd studied my reflection in the bathroom mirror, admiring my improved profile.

"I ruined two towels cleaning paint off the bathroom counter," I say. "It's just a little something I learned from ALF."

"Who's he?"

"Animal Liberation Front. I don't endorse them blowing up research labs, but I can understand why. They rescue the medical rats."

"So you have some cute little mice in there?" Jeremy points at my chest, giggling. "Can I pet one?"

"Don't be such a freak!" I shove him away, but smiling so that he knows I'm game for this flirtation.

"You think you've got a surprise. Feel this." Jeremy takes hold of my hand and pulls it toward his crotch.

I jerk back, laughing. "Hey, I may like *cute little things*, but I'm not that easy!"

"*Touché!* But I promise, I am a complete gentleman," he pouts, mocking me. "Besides, it's not what you think."

The passengers within our view all seem to be deeply absorbed in their morning rituals, reading newspapers, working the crosswords, updating Palm Pilots, so I let my hand inch across his thigh toward that forbidden zone. Something firm bulges beneath the thick khaki. My fingers gingerly explore the object, finding it uniformly round, the size of a... "Tennis ball?" I whisper.

Jeremy is nodding and grinning. I've heard enough of his classroom braggadocio to know that his favorite homemade explosive is assembled by cutting a tiny slit into a tennis ball and stuffing it with "Strikes Anywhere" match heads. One bounce and—BOOM!

"Jeremy, you're nuts!" I hiss under my breath.

"Exactly!"

Worried that our undercover man has overheard, I turn, but find he's not in sight and Billow is now weaving her way through the crowded aisle. "We're getting off at this next stop," Billow tells us, adding, "Hopefully that undercover agent will leave us alone. But if he doesn't, remember, this is just the sort of thing we've been discussing in class. Do not let covert surveillance tactics keep your political voice subdued. You are the future leaders of this nation! OK, class, it's a long walk to Pennsylvania Avenue, so bundle up. Everyone should already have my cell phone number in case we get separated...which we won't, right?"

We all nod in unison, and begin collecting our belongings, getting to our feet as we hear the unintelligible static of the station announcement. The brakes squeal and the train jerks to a stop. A flood of passengers, including the man in the NYC hat, shove their way through the doors. Billow signals for everyone to exit, but when I make my move to follow, Jeremy takes my arm and holds me back.

"Hey? What's the deal?" I say, laughing, noticing that his grip is firm, insistent, but not thuggish. Billow is on the platform, now, counting heads.

"Trust me," Jeremy says, and as if understanding just what it will take to get me to comply, he tilts his head forward and kisses me on the lips. It's just the barest peck, tentative enough to cause me to mistake it for tenderness, and not just a reflexive response to my scars.

The doors close and through the smudged glass, we watch as our absence dawns upon Billow. Her eyes grow wide. She's mouthing words at us, arms outstretched from her cape as the train lurches forward. Jeremy waves to her, sheepishly, and shrugs, making a hand signal that we'll call her.

"Next stop," Jeremy says, gently squeezing my arm. "That's where the action is."

"What about Billow?"

"No worries. We'll catch up with them later. You've got her number, right?"

I mentally backtrack to that cavalier moment in class when I stupidly decided that it was *way* too much trouble to put Billow's number into my cell phone's memory.

At the next stop, a dozen other commuters get off and we hurry with them toward the broken escalator. The freezing air quickly cuts through my cotton T-shirt and sweatshirt, past the tape and double-layered cardboard until I'm begrudging my mom for being right about my needing a few more layers. At street level the cluster of people disperses in different directions while Jeremy and I, holding hands and out of breath, get our bearings. An eerie silence hangs in the air as if the whole city has been shut down. No cars or buses, no sign of activity, save for the snipers armed with rifles, stationed on the rooftops of office buildings. Their menacing presence fails to convey that sense of homeland security that they claim to be armed in the interest of and I'm reminded of Billow's talk in class about surveillance as a tool for political intimidation. But she hadn't mentioned M9s and I'm beginning to think that I'm out of my league; this *is* an adults-only game.

The rumbling of drums and voices guides us toward the nexus of dissent and when we turn a corner we come upon a mob of hundreds of people, young and old, all milling about, corralled in by a series of wooden barricades. Their mood is jumpy and agitated, as if on their mark for the starting shot of a marathon, while further down the street several dozen police, in full riot gear—clubs, shields, helmets, face guards—seem just as anxious for the race to begin. They have secured their post behind temporary wire fences erected for the express purpose of separating the riffraff from the paying customers.

"Not quite what Billow had in mind, eh?" Jeremy comments, now pointing at the posters and effigies being waved by the crowd. I notice a lady dressed in a clown suit. She's pacing and shouting into her cell phone.

"Shit!" I say, suddenly remembering Billow. I fumble to pull my cell phone from my bag. Flipping it open, the screen lights up and reads, "NO SERVICE."

"Let's stand over there." Jeremy takes my elbow, leading us further from the security gates, past the sour-faced, black-clad anarchists, unfurling their banner, complaining about the lack of a coordinated plan.

Here's when we notice the cheerleader. She's waving pom-poms, leading the crowd in a holler-back chant. She's dressed in orange satin short-shorts and a tight-fitting green turtleneck top with a large black "A" appliquéd to its front. Her blonde, punk hairdo is topped off with a dime-store tiara.

"ONE-TWO-THREE-FOUR..." she shouts.

"WE DON'T WANT YOUR FUCKING WAR!" the crowd hollers back with contagious enthusiasm.

I unzip my sweatshirt and free the poster from my waistband. Jeremy is bending to fold up the leg of his pants, but his eyes are locked on the cheerleader. She stretches her arms out wide, the A on her chest buoyant and bouncing. She makes a leg-splitting leap into the air, with the tiara barely hanging on, and here's where Jeremy, true to gender, becomes distracted.

"Man, what I wouldn't give to have her cheer at my lacrosse game," he says, wincing as the tape rips off a swatch of his blonde leg hair.

I notice that everyone's wearing a face mask. Luckily, I've got on my scarf, the one with the cute Chinese kittens, and I start to reposition it. "Do you have a bandana?" I ask Jeremy.

"Why? Does my fair maiden desire her beloved's kerchief before this duel?" Jeremy says in a phony English accent.

"Pepper spray," I say, retying the triangle of fabric so that it covers my nose and mouth. I get the hood of my sweatshirt lifted back over my head until all that remains visible are my eyes.

Jeremy is staring at me.

"What?" I ask, self-consciously.

"You're actually kind of cute...with just your eyes showing like that!"

And before I can recover from this sucker punch to further review my fashion options for this budding romance—burqa or paper bag?—a group of college students gather beneath an American flag draped from a pole. Some guy with a lighter is climbing onto the shoulders of another, bigger guy. The flag's corner catches fire and flames rise to consume the stripes of red and white fabric. This is where the riot police move in. This is when the cheerleader does a cartwheel. Here's where Jeremy lets the PVC pipe slide off his leg and fall, clunking to the sidewalk.

I turn toward the sound of pipe hitting pavement, and see Jeremy sprawled on the gray concrete. A black leather glove belonging to a man sporting a shiny black helmet with a Plexiglas face shield is now gripping the pipe, taking aim. Meanwhile the double-layered cup of a smelly jockstrap holds a tennis ball awaiting sulfuric detonation.

Later I can puzzle over my impulsive leap, deciding if it stemmed from my altruistic concern for a dumb and defenseless creature or if there was something more personal and pathetic at stake. But either way, I find myself diving, not out of harm's way, but headlong into the dangerous fray, as if it's my fate to return once again to that space between a piece of plastic and the combustive consequences of teenage folly.

And here's when my mom's safety-pin talisman, as if on cue, fulfills its mission to serve and protect. It springs open and digs into my chest, well, not my chest, actually, but a balloon pretending to be something more. A spray of red liquid gushes up from my T-shirt, soaking my mask until I have to rip the scarf away from my face in order to breathe. Still lying on top of Jeremy, I'm gulping for air and ready for the next blow, or to explode, when I see the cop's expression through the glare and smear of red on his face shield. His face says it all—a wince, a gaping mouth, another assumption shattered by my disfigurement. The PVC pipe drops from his hand and I believe that I've just pulled the trump card in this rock-paper-scissors game—scarred flesh pierces bulletproof vests.

Aroused by the exhortations of the cheerleader, and before Jeremy and I can recover to our feet, the crowd is charging through one of the barricades and rushing down the street toward the distant gated security checkpoint. Our assailant and his team of Darth Vader clones set off in hot pursuit, chasing the young protesters. The pepper spray and billy clubs of democracy now spring into action, defending and protecting the sanctity of a far distant presidential motorcade.

"Shit! Let's get out of here!" Jeremy says, rolling out from under me, pulling me to my feet. We dash toward a side street, deserted but for the scatter of discarded leaflets, soda cans, and fast food containers. In the distance, I spy a CVS drugstore's lights flickering like a beacon.

"I'm going to clean up," I say, leaving Jeremy near an overflowing trash receptacle. He's reaching down into his pants and I'm thinking this is where he's giving up on any dreams of a grand slam.

Entering the store, I'm greeted by a cushion of warm air and a fat olive-skinned man in a turban who's reaching under the counter, most likely feeling for the unregistered handgun kept handy regardless of DC gun laws. Both of my hands instinctively fly up into the air, as I attempt to convey an attitude of compliance, smiling and nodding. I point to my face and mumble something about a nose bleed and the clerk motions toward the door with the "Employees Only" sign.

"Do not get blood on my floor!" he shouts after me, while I grab a black T-shirt bearing the bold white initials, "FBI," from the souvenir display. I promise to settle up on my way out and quickly shut and lock the door behind me.

My eyes burn from the paint and the caustic aroma of a toilet that lacks ten years' worth of scrubbing, but one look in the mirror explains the clerk's eagerness to dispose of me. The tempera paint has thickened into a goopy mess, although it appears that my sweatshirt has been spared from the splatter. I peel down to my mother's bra. One balloon is still intact, safely nestled within the confines of the bra, giving me the lopsided look of a botched mastectomy. I free the slippery red orb from its soggy nest and, using my safety-pin good luck charm, jab and puncture the stretched latex, reducing my WMD to a thin, impotent stream of red paint that swirls down a rusty drainpipe.

After using an entire roll of paper towels, my chest and face are clean, and I stuff all evidence of my criminal intent into a daisy-patterned waste-basket under the sink. And so I emerge, my mortal wounds miraculously healed, while the clerk offers no sympathy or comment. He simply takes my money for the T-shirt and points me toward the door.

Once outside, Jeremy is nowhere in sight. I could return to the deserted main street, where the flag burners and riot police have disappeared in a trail of posters and pepper spray. And I would probably find Jeremy there, standing by the overturned barricade, with the cheerleader at his side. She would be animated and impossibly adorable wearing his pea coat over her skimpy shorts, but somehow I don't think that she would've taken the tackle, like I did. Cute tends to keep to the safety zones, cheering on the sidelines, and while damaged goods like me can enjoy a certain reckless freedom, it's the cheerleaders that always get the quarterbacks in the end. Now she would be leaning into Jeremy as he lights her cigarette and their smoky exhalations will mingle and rise into the gray afternoon chill. I settle for a coveted kiss and a backhanded compliment about my eyes and I steal toward the Metro. Later, in the privacy of my room, I'll pull out these mementos and try them on with the "vintage" pink chiffon gown I recently snagged from the Salvation Army remainders bin. Meanwhile, the debris of dissent—flyers, placards, Starbucks coffee cups—litters the street and sidewalk. A gust of wind scatters some orange flyers, advertisements for a *Counter*Inaugural Ball, and I catch sight of the glittering, molded plastic of the cheerleader's tiara, most likely lost during one of her crowd-pleasing cartwheels. Here I place it on my head, the sharp plastic combs catching hold in my tangled hair, and I lift the hood of my sweatshirt to conceal my trophy.

After going two blocks, my cell phone screen shows a signal and indicates twenty-three missed calls, all from Billow. I punch the send button and Billow answers, with her normally breathy voice now reduced to a frantic series of hoarse squawks, demanding to know my whereabouts. Here's where Patty Hearst becomes inspiration, the hostage princess of radical politics. I claim that the whole affair was Jeremy's idea, and am happily surprised by Billow's response to my defensive use of the Stockholm syndrome. She coos and consoles me and by the end of my remorseful assurances to return to the flock, the question of Jeremy's whereabouts becomes almost a footnote.

"He told me to tell you he'd catch a ride home with friends," I say. Billow seems to accept this.

The bleachers for the high-ticket donors are almost empty, but for the few stalwart and shivering Republicans whose couture seems to consist of Stetsons, Burberry scarves, and full-length fur coats. Here's where I regret my haste, a well-placed lob of my balloon could have served a greater cause. The motorcade has already come and gone and people are making their way back through the now unmanned security gates. I find Billow and the class just in time for us to leave, and on the Metro ride home, Shannon explains how the President's caravan, flanked by ten SUVs and a posse of more than two dozen Secret Service men on foot, traveled past their observation post at a high speed, missing every regulation-sized poster my classmates had worked so hard to produce. Shannon shows me the blurred images she managed to capture on her camera phone and she brags how these photos will guarantee her an A+.

At the Metro station, my mom's silver Volvo is idling in the taxi lane and she pokes her head out the window to make sure I see her. When I slide into the passenger seat, I pull back my hood, revealing the tiara perched upon my head.

"Tah-dah!" I laugh, striking a dramatic pose.

"Cute!" my mom says, only slightly amused at my latest fashion accessory.

"Yeah, but cute almost got me killed," I blurt, forgetting that I'd promised Billow to keep mum about my Black Bloc abduction. "But your pin protected me!" I add quickly—her cue to not take me seriously—and I'm dangling the twisted metal amulet in her face, mocking her superstitious vigilance. Here's where my mom realizes that this is the most she'll get from me during our field trip debriefing.

"Buckle up," she says, pulling into the commuter traffic. And for a while longer I allow her to rest in the comfort of her maternal delusions of "homeland security" while I'm busy putting my thoughts toward crafting the opening lines of that essay due on Billow's desk tomorrow morning. *"Washington DC is a military state, an occupied nation where freedom rings from the rooftops, guarded by bulletproof vests, long-range scopes and sniper silhouettes..."*

Julia Slavin

Last Rights

JULIA SLAVIN is the author of *The Woman Who Cut Off Her Leg at the Maidstone Club and Other Stories* (Henry Holt, 1999) and the novel *Carnivore Diet* (W.W. Norton, 2005).

Hammy came home.

Late that afternoon, I watched our handsome brother step out of the Mount Shasta blue Merkur he rented at the airport. I ran down the steps of the porch. "You look beautiful." I threw my arms around his neck. Hammy and I looked exactly alike. Growing up, people had thought we were twins. Sadly for me, our features worked better on a man than a woman. Hammy looked like a movie star. I looked like Hammy in drag. But I was forty-three and had become comfortable with who I was. I'd never be a traffic-stopper like Hammy and that was OK.

Gene leaned on the door frame with his arms crossed. "Little Brother."

"Big Brother."

"What's this?" Gene picked up Hammy's ponytail between his thumb and index finger like it was a dead opossum.

"What's this?" Hammy poked Gene in the gut. Then they wrestled on the porch like brothers.

"Boys!" I went in to check the orange-poppy cake.

Hammy dropped himself in the chair where our father died. He could be insensitive. He was, after all, the baby and Mom and I had spoiled him. I walked over and rearranged the plastic cover on the Louis XV reproduction our mother died in instants after our father. I was hoping Hammy would get the point. He didn't. Instead, he pushed down on the arms of the lounger so the foot stool would pop out. Our parents passed immediately after two police officers sat down on the Duncan Phyfe and told them their son Tim was the Fox Gap Career Girl Murderer. Mom had offered the officers limeade and frosted shaggy dogs and they'd accepted, which struck me as strange, given they were about to advise our parents that their son had mutilated three short-haired career girls who vaguely resembled our mother and me.

We moved out on the deck and drank iced tea and Hammy regaled us with stories from the Left Coast. There was the shrink who skinny-dipped with his patients. "Boy, people are weird out there," Gene said. The actor with seven Ferraris. "Some serious cake out there." Gene rubbed his fingers together. There was the Raiderette who did the StairMaster at the gym and Hammy wanted to make his move. "You're so L.A.," Gene said after each of Hammy's anecdotes. "This guy is so L.A." I imagined Hammy out West, soaring through the sunny world in a red Miata, the Raiderette by his side, pushing it to ninety down Mulholland Drive. Hammy adjusted well to our tragedy. He'd really carved out a meaningful place for himself in California. My life went to pieces after they caught Tim. I kept seeing images of those poor girls wherever I went. I worked as a dancer at the Camelot in Shapsburg and married a Formica counter installer who liked my act but punched out my teeth. Three hours after we lowered Mom and Dad into the Mintwood Country Cemetery and Mausoleum, Hammy drove westward in a tan Delta 88. But now our baby had come home; home to the brother and sister who loved him. I felt happy and safe.

I'd marinated a top round two days for sauerbraten and served it alongside nutted wild rice, sweet & sour red cabbage and sautéed carrots mixed with snow peas. I asked Gene to slice.

"No meat for me, just the rice and vegetables." Hammy held out his plate. Gene looked up from the beef. "I'm a vegetarian."

"Since when?" Gene asked.

"Well, actually, since they got Tim."

Gene let the carving fork and knife drop on the platter.

"Gene," I cautioned.

"What the hell does Tim have to do with a perfectly fine piece of sauerbraten?"

"It's all right," I said.

"It's not all right. Your sister spends two days cooking for you and you show no appreciation. How dare you impose your morals on others."

"Gene, could it be that you're reacting so strongly because of your own doubts about eating meat?" Hammy asked.

"Don't give me any of that L.A. nutrition-action-psycho-babble, hippie."

"At least I've done something with my life."

"You're a scuba instructor."

"At least I'm not living off my inheritance in Mom and Dad's house." Hammy then pointed at me. "Or spreading out for a bunch of hard hats like they were a gynecologist convention."

"I wore a G-string," I cried, my hand over my heart. "I was tasteful."

"Like that husband who fucked up your face and made you more ridiculous looking than ever?"

I sank to the floor.

Gene slammed the table with his fist. "This house takes enormous effort to maintain. And Trix and I have committed our lives to helping others."

"Helping others?"

"Trix volunteers at the Community Center and I have my work with Tutor Tots."

"So you can twiddle little boys."

Gene shot up from his chair and flipped the oak table. "You," he said through clenched teeth. "You."

Hammy locked his fingers behind his neck and crossed his feet at the ankles. "Yes, Gene?" he said. "Me?"

"I don't have to take this from a, from a, from a, from a," Gene turned purple and lumbered to the back door with his arms out and his legs apart like a matinee mummy. Hammy and I watched from the dining room window as he staggered around the patio.

"It wasn't supposed to be this way," I said. "This was supposed to be a nice time. Family time. You were coming home to build on that."

"Family time?" Hammy said. "I'm on my way to New York to pick up my advance on the book I'm writing about Tim."

"You're w-w-what?"

"'Last Rites: A Killer among Us.'"

"No."

"Shit yeah. I'm gonna blow life into that son-of-a-bitch."

I let out a scream that was so guttural, loud, and blood curdling that I thought it was coming from someone else.

"Trix, Mom and Dad have any records? You know, from shrinks, report cards, clippings? Oh, I'll need to take those photo albums. How 'bout it, Trix? Any documents or reports?" I'd been sitting in Mom's rocking chair all morning, laconic. Gene stayed outside and hit himself. "Trix?"

It seemed too big an effort to talk. "I...don't...want...the...pictures...to...leave...the house."

"Growing up, you kept diaries," Hammy said. "I'll need a look-see."

"They're personal."

"I'm not interested in your love life or lack thereof, Trix. Just the goods on Tim. The seeds. Where it all began. Is violence hereditary? Is it learned? Some specialists believe deviant behavior can be traced in DNA samples. It boggles the mind, Trix. There's a neurologist in Quebec who says the violent brain has an excess of metal manganese."

"I thought I'd bake a broccoli millet casserole from *The Tassahara Cookbook*. Would that be satisfactory?"

"Make whatever you and Gene like and I'll eat around it. Anyway, I've got miles of microfiche to zip through at the library. Don't know that I'll make it to chow."

Over the next week Hammy was in and out with stacks of old clippings, books, and essays on deviant behavior, case studies that resembled Tim. "Yow, I never knew what happens to you when you get electrocuted. You sort of burn up from the inside out. And it usually takes a few tries." He held up an article he'd Xeroxed at the library. "Tim's eyes popped out."

He went through the attic and basement, artifact by artifact, document by document, memento by memento. "Remember this?" He'd come across a grainy old photograph of himself sitting on a duck raft at the Fox Gap Lake Pool. He couldn't have been more than seven. It was the Hammy I'd always remembered. A happy-looking boy with a closed mouth smile and deep dimples.

"I was a pretty cute kid," Hammy said.

"You were adorable." Old pictures affect me like old songs. They make me sad. I wanted to put my hand into the print and pull out the boy I loved so much. Then I saw the blurry image of Tim on the left side of the photo, crouching down in the pool, water all the way up to his eyes like an alligator, staring into the camera. I could barely make him out, but there was no mistaking Tim. I was glad Hammy didn't notice.

He interviewed me. "You said in your April 15, 1957, entry that Tim and Tony Saterswhite quote, *seized and searched* you. Can you explain?"

"I don't remember."

Hammy slid forward in his chair. "Trix, sometimes we say we don't remember because we don't want to remember. But it's all up here." He tapped his forehead. "It doesn't go away... *September 11, 1959. Tim played the same note over and over on the piano for two hours and when I asked him to please play something else, he came at me with the beat wand from the metronome.* Comment?" My jaw began to quiver. "Trix, is this about the money?" Hammy took my hands in his. "Because thirty percent is yours, Trix. This book's gonna soar."

"It's not about the money. I don't want the money. It's about our name. I can't have the family name besmirched anymore." I broke down.

"Besmirched? You kidding? We're gonna be on *Larry King*!" I started hitting him. "Not the face, not the nuts." No, I wouldn't hit him in his beautiful face and I certainly wouldn't knee him in the nuts. I'd missed my chance having babies but I still had hope in my heart for a niece or a nephew. I kicked him in the shins over and over with my espadrilles and then Gene came in, red from the sun, eyes slanted and puffy like a big mad pig.

"There are rotting floor boards on the side porch. It's not like when Mom and Dad were here to take care of everything, Gene. Old homes need attention and care."

"I'm the one who wanted to close that room off fifteen years ago," Gene said, cutting through Hammy's ulna and radial artery with a number four scalpel.

"That 'I told you so' attitude is unhelpful." I held open a lawn & leaf bag.

"I'll call Dale Veeth in the morning."

"There's got to be another contractor in this Godforsaken town."

"Dale's had a rough time. I want to help him out."

"We're always helping everybody out," I said under my breath.

"What did you say?" Gene asked. Hammy's eyes and mouth opened wide when Gene picked up the head by the ponytail.

"Nothing."

"Is someone being a Little Miss Me, Myself, and I selfish bug?"

"He does bad work and he steals."

"What's that?" He cupped his ear with a bloody work glove and looked around the rec room. "Did I just hear a Little Miss Walk-All-Over-Appalachian-Children? No? Must have been the bug zapper by the Fieldings' pool."

"All right, enough." I looked down at Hammy's torso and felt ashamed of what I'd said about Dale. "Call him in the morning."

We tidied up and went for a walk. It was a humid night. Everything felt dreamy and achey and the hot air seemed to go right through us. Gene and I talked and laughed and I felt better than I'd felt in a long time. He gave me hip-checks into the bushes and I took out my teeth and did my Zira impression from *Planet of the Apes.* We stopped for refreshment at the Fox Gap Lounge.

"Two more Sad Slammers, Kevin," Gene told the bartender.

"No, Gene, three's my limit. Oh, what the heck. Two more Sad Slammers, Kev."

The place was full for the Lounge. Usually the proprietors only made money off the alcoholic fathers of kids we grew up with, but that night there were a few office parties, clear fresh faces, and a lot of laughter. The jukebox, usually dark, played one Top Forty hit from the fifties, sixties, and seventies after another and people were dancing.

"What's going on tonight?" I asked Kevin.

"The heat," Kevin yelled over Moby Grape. "Make native yo-yo loco." He moved his index finger in circles around his ear.

Then I noticed everyone in the Lounge was looking at us. Fear gripped me. They know, I thought. They know, *they know.* "Gene." I grabbed his arm. "They're all staring. Look around."

Gene laughed and patted my hand. "I noticed when we walked in. They're not looking at us. They're looking at you."

"Why?"

"Because you're beautiful."

I looked in the mirror over the bar. He was right. The heat of July had dried up the froth of spittle that perpetually bubbled through my dentures and somehow with Hammy gone, there was no one to compare me to. The only person our features flattered now was me. Then I knew what Hammy felt all his life, felt it myself in the gazes from the men at the Lounge. I knew how the head cheerleader felt, pursued by the quarterback and the science teacher.

"May I have this dance?" Gene offered his hand. There was an orchestrated intro, then Shirley Owens Alston fronting the Shirelles. I wasn't a good dancer. I kept stepping on Gene's feet and saying, "Oops, sorry. Oops, sorry." But it felt great to dance with clothes on.

That night Gene jolted up in bed and switched on the floor lamp with the blue bulb. I could see his white fleshy back tinted blue, the folds on his bald head and the elastic waistband of his Ward's briefs.

"What is it?"

"Hammy's book." Gene was short of breath.

"It's gone. Forever."

Gene turned to face me. With his thick puffy fat and alopecia, he looked more like beluga than a forty-six-year-old man. Perhaps Hammy was right. I needed to cook with less animal fat. At least cut back on butter and oils. "Does it have to be?" He asked. "I mean, what if you and I were to..."

"No." I leapt out of bed and stormed into the bathroom.

Gene stood outside the door. "Trix, it could be good for us. It could be cathartic. Hear me out."

"No," I screamed.

"To hell with the family name, Trix. You think Tim's a big secret? You think people don't cross the street when they see us coming?" He was sounding like Hammy.

"I won't have this." I pounded the back of the bathroom door. "I will not besmirch the memory of our mother and father. I will not climb down into hell." I heard Gene move away from the door and the creaking of Mom and Dad's sleigh bed as he got back in.

I woke up at five. Gene was already downstairs in the kitchen. He'd made coffee and there were cinnamon buns heating in the oven. "Smells good," I said. Then I saw the white legal pad.

"Trix, please, just look at the outline." I grabbed the pad and rushed out of the house clutching it to my chest. I threw it in the back of Hammy's car and screeched out of the driveway. Gene chased the car halfway down our street in his underwear. I floored the Merkur up Monte Avenue, the legal pad in the backseat, and buried the document with Hammy in his shallow grave behind the Fox Gap Mall. Then I drove home, scrubbed the dirt out of my nails, and made a sandwich. Gene crept up behind me. "It's all up here, Trix," he said in a gravelly whisper and tapped his skull. "I don't need a synopsis. I got it *all* up here." I spread some Hellmann's, rolled up a Kraft slice, and gently folded over a piece of Levi's Rye Bread, just the way I like it.

Gene was asleep on his side with the covers pushed to the bottom of the bed. I mixed some crystal Drano with warm water in the bathroom and filled a syringe. I watched him sleep for a moment. His lips moved silently the same way he read the newspaper. I leaned over, moved the elastic band of his briefs aside, and stuck the needle in the top of his right buttock. He leapt up, complaining of a charley horse and ran to the bathroom.

"Zowie, that smarts!"

It was wrong to have attempted the injection during the light sleep of the morning hours. At three or four in the morning Gene was usually out cold, so I waited up the next night. But Gene watched one video after another and never went to bed.

"Aren't ya tired?" I kept asking.

"Nope," he said, rewinding *Darn Pets!* Around dinner time it became clear that Gene had some ideas of his own about me.

We stayed awake three nights. I went to five doctors for five prescriptions of Benzedrine but Gene had his own Rolodex of prescription-friendly doctors. On the fourth day we began to hallucinate. Gene bought dog food and fed Smarty-Pants, the springer spaniel we had back in the fifties. Hammy was all over the house. He shoved his leg under his arm and marched room to room like a soldier with a bayonet. His head was the Water Pik Shower Massager and told me I was ugly every time I got in the tub. And it was true. My stream of spittle had returned with the cold front from Canada and black circles had formed under my eyes. I looked like a sad, ridiculous Hammy.

On the fifth day, Gene foolishly accepted a bowl of my homemade vichyssoise which I'd thickened with 10,000 milligrams of Unisom. Now that he was out, I felt I could relax. That was the wrong thing to do. I did the laundry and watched *The Frugal Gourmet.* While the sheets were drying, I went upstairs to get the Drano and syringe and blacked out on the steps.

Two days later I woke up in a pool of urine with my dress up to my neck and no feeling in my legs because I'd been lying upside down. I heard Gene moving around the kitchen tidying up and singing the Lemon Pledge commercial.

"Hello?" I called out.

"Hello!" He rushed to the stairs. I looked up and saw his large glabrous head. "Trix, the most amazing thing. You're not going to believe it." His hand was behind his back and I was certain he had a knife. "Brace yourself." He whipped his arm around and showed me something extraordinary. "A double banana!" Two fruits in one skin, like a pair of edible Siamese twins emerging from the Botticelli scallop shell. "How did it happen, Trix? A freak of nature gone sublime." I reached my hand up to touch the pulpy twins and he let me hold them, their yellow peel draped over my fist like a mink stole. Then we both cried from the sheer beauty of the fruit. "I've decided not to write the book, Trix. You were right. Our family name has been besmirched enough. We need to move on." I smiled, happy to have my brother back. Then he wrinkled his forehead. "Trix, don't you think you oughta go upstairs and sponge off?"

The next few weeks were happy ones. Gene worked hard at cleaning out the basement and organizing our parents' things in the attic. Dale Veeth replaced the rotting floor boards on the side porch and stole our mother's jewelry. "If he didn't need it, he wouldn't have taken it," Gene made me repeat with him over and over. But sometime in late August, Gene came across Tim's death certificate which I'd haphazardly shoved into a shoe box many years before. Then he found the clippings and printouts Hammy'd made at the library and got the book bug back.

"Independence Day, 1961," Gene began. *"Tim locked Kathy Prig and me in a wicker trunk and said he wouldn't let us out until we agreed to blow on his sparkler.* Could you explain?"

"I thought I'd make a grilled skirt steak," I said. "With a coriander garlic sauce and a side of herbed tomato chutney..."

"November 7, 1964... Fortunately, we had Indian Summer while I was tied to the old Maple behind the Neilsons' garage. Where was I during all this?"

"For dessert, fresh plum parfaits sprinkled with amaretti crumbs and ruby port..."

"New Year's Day, 1966..."

"And for starters, a nice cold vichyssoise."

To hell with my dentures. I call the hotel from the car and ask the concierge to have a warm slice of their scrumptious blueberry pie waiting in my room *s'il vous plait.*

"Thirty Rock," I tell my driver. "Wait, Harvey. Pull over."

"You sure, Ms. Humford?"

"Of course I'm sure. They're children." I press down the window switch.

"Ms. Humford?" A small towheaded boy tiptoes up to the car with a much larger boy. "Will you sign our book?"

"Certainly, boys."

"I'm Edward and he's Petey. He's shy. Our brother Gary killed a nun."

"Oh, for heaven's sake. Petey," I say. "I'm willing to bet fifteen percent of my royalties you've got a set of dimples a fairy princess could eat custard out of." This gets to him. He tries to fight it but breaks out in a wide grin exposing the dimples I predicted.

"Could you do that thing you did on that TV show?" Petey asks in a voice that's tiny for a boy his size. "From *Planet of the Apes?*"

"Oh, all right. But then we've got to dash." I take out my teeth and crane my neck towards the roof of the car. "Cornelius!" The boys laugh so hard they fall down on the sidewalk, their book on the ground, back cover up with a picture of *me!*, spittle airbrushed, false teeth twinkling through a star filter, hair like Kathleen Turner.

Rose Solari

from *Between Earth & Air*

ROSE SOLARI is the author of two full-length collections of poetry, *Orpheus in the Park* and *Difficult Weather*. Her writing awards include the Randall Jarrell Poetry Prize, grants from the DC Commission on the Arts and Humanities and the Maryland State Arts Council, and an EMMA Award for excellence in journalism from the National Women's Political Caucus. She is a longtime faculty member of the Writer's Center in Bethesda, Maryland.

DOVE ABBEY, OXFORD, 1182

The two women sit in the small bare room that serves as their scriptorium, facing each other across a wooden table covered with sheets of parchment, some written on, some still blank. Those sisters who can read the language of the Church used to have their lessons here, on the floor above the abbey's modest library. But despite his distance, in every sense, from Dove Abbey, Brother Martin had persuaded the abbess that Margaret's gift must be given room and time to develop.

"She will need a sister who can read and write to record what she sees," he had said. "That person must translate, as they go, from our tongue to Latin. She might, along the way, teach it to Margaret, too. They will need a room where they can work together, unmolested by other tasks or curious eyes."

He paused, went on.

"Margaret might have, as well, a separate place of her own to sleep, apart from the cloister. That would be ideal. She will need quiet."

The abbess had dismissed the last notion. No, she was sure that Margaret needed the company of the other sisters; to set her apart would be to make too much of her, too soon, and create envy in the other girls. But after much scrambling—for their quarters were less than ample as it was, and despite her efforts to educate her girls, there were few in the abbey with a firm command of the language, and fewer still among them whom the abbess could fully trust—a scribe was selected and a room given over to the recording of Margaret's visions.

That was a little more than two years ago. Now, once again, Margaret has sent for Christina.

They have moved their table to the northeast corner of the room, where the light, what little there is of it this time of year, makes its way through the narrow casements unblocked by trees. Margaret would prefer the south wall, overlooking the newly completed Lady Chapel, and the forest beyond. But the days are short, now, and the light, precious. Christina insists they forego the pleasures of scene, of stone and leaf and sky, for the sake of the longest light.

She is right, of course. She is right about many things, as Margaret has to remind herself, sometimes, when the older nun's strictures and complaints grow oppressive. And surely, Christina's job is the harder one. Margaret has some leave from almost every aspect of the Rule in order to pursue her God-sent night and day dreams, while for Christina, the job of writing down what her more blessed sister sees is now her first priority but not her only duty. There is all the rest—and Margaret has heard the list often enough—strict observance of the Rule, as well as the running of the infirmary, and now the abbey accounts as well, Mother Elizabeth's eyes having grown, so fast, too weak to read the ledger or record what the abbey must pay for stone and for wheat, or what they had taken in, somehow never enough, from the sale of the sisters' thick, long-burning candles and embroidered cloth.

"Shall we begin?" Christina says, taking up a new reed, dipping it into coarse-ground black ink. She would work it more finely, make it smooth as water, if she had the time.

"It was just here. I could just see it," Margaret says, her voice quiet. She is talking to herself.

She rests her head in her cupped hands, elbows propped on the table, and closes her eyes.

"Not yet. Be patient. Wait."

Brother Martin told her early on that patience was the greatest of virtues, and one she particularly needed to learn.

"I have seen some very young novices all aflame for God, bearing witness to Him in the most extraordinary ways," he had said, at one of their first meetings. He was doing most of the talking, as always.

"Then they became greedy. Perhaps they thought they could summon Him up at any time. Indeed, you might say that they forgot who was serving Whom."

He paused, looked at her. *You are supposed to ask me what happened to them,* he thought. *Curiosity. Questions and answers. That is how we learn.*

"So you have known many, then." Her girl's voice was low, a little hoarse. Years of sore throats, he thought, and never enough food.

"Known many..."

"Who have this—these fits. These dreams." She tossed her head from side to side, as if to shake something out of it.

"These visions," he corrected. "These showings from the Lord."

"There is a lady, sometimes," she said.

"Of course. His Lady Mother. The Mother of our Church."

"You are sure of that."

"Yes, my dear. I have built my life on that."

"And you have known others like me, and helped them."

"Yes, and yes. More times than it would take the fingers of one hand to count."

Margaret looked down at her hand as if assessing the number of fingers on it for the first time.

Then she looked back up at him, straight and speculative. He could see her weigh his words in her mind.

"Then," she said, "I will believe you."

Now, despite the earthly and impatient body of Christina across from her, Margaret can scarcely be said to be in the room at all. She is in a field of stubby grass, arranging a pile of brown and white stones into an oblong ring. Once set in place, each stone begins to glow, as if absorbing and spreading the light of the one before it. She is careful not to leave too much space between them, not to hurry.

Christina sighs. Margaret fights to keep herself from opening her eyes, though in her mind she can see, now, Christina's face and form. The circle of stones flickers behind it, fading. And Christina is there, not as she is now but as she will be, an old, old woman whose face is grooved with perpetual discontent, and who is also unmistakably present in the Christina who sits across from her now, sighing at the imperfections of her ink. And as the older Christina presses a hand to her side, and sighs again, Margaret sees outlined beneath the hand a small, irregular dark circle, growing beneath the flesh. It pulses with bad intent.

This is the worst of it, the second edge of her gift's blade. For it is one thing to touch the hand of the Lord's Mother, or repeat the piece of a prayer she taught you. But it is another thing to look at a woman you have lived with every day and know, sudden and sure, her end. It is another matter to see that the smith will lose a hand tomorrow to the blow of his own hammer, and to carry that knowledge inside of you, like the stone at the center of a piece of fruit. Her mother had made a living from time to time of knowing what others did not; it had brought her a certain power, yes, over certain kinds of people, but look where that had led.

Margaret has, at least, learned from her sad example. Only Brother Martin knows of these matters, of how she sees, sometimes, premonitions of the fates of those around her. He and she had quickly agreed on this: No one else, not even the abbess, need know.

In all these thoughts, the near-completed ring of stones is almost lost, and now Margaret shakes herself, calls herself back to it again. Her body is suddenly restless; she must get up, she must move.

She pushes her hard chair back from the table. Her eyes only slightly opened, as if she is walking in her sleep, she moves to the south casement, presses her head against the cold stone, and allows herself a sliver, a glimpse of the forest beyond the Lady Chapel.

There, in the air above the treetops, she sees it all forming again. A field of green. A ring of stones. Her hand reaches out to place the last one in its position.

"Margaret?" Christina says.

"Wait, wait. It is almost here."

And so Christina waits, stirring her ink.

"Tell me," the abbess had asked Martin, in the beginning. "Do you think that recording all of it is wise? Should we perhaps wait to see just what it is that Margaret has to tell us, before committing time and care and another sister to this project?"

"With respect, Madam, I must say that it is better to work quickly. In some cases, these visitations only come in youth. I have known boys of ten or eleven years to be full of such matter. And then a year passes, and then another—their faces sprout hair, and their voices deepen—and the Lord does not visit them so directly anymore."

"If it is the Lord," Mother Elizabeth had said. "The boy who knew her—"

"Benedict."

"Yes. He said her mother was a witch."

"He said the people of her town thought the mother was a witch," Martin corrected gently. The lady was easily insulted; he had to watch his step.

"The poor and uneducated often mistake good for evil, gifts with curses. Her mother may have had something of Margaret's gift, but no light to see it for what it was, no instruction. No one like you, lady, to love and trust."

He paused, went on.

"She is devoted to you," he said, softly. "She wears it on her face. Such a pure love."

"She has always been a good girl," the abbess said. "But you must understand. She came here with no dowry. She cannot stitch or sing or read aloud to the other sisters, or make cheese or butter, or bake. She is—she was—like a piece of parchment with no writing on it.

"I thought we had time. I thought she might be made into something. But to place her above the other sisters, to bend the Rule just for her, to give her sway over another who must write down whatever she says—"

Martin sighed, shaking his head. All the young monks in Glastonbury were lettered.

"It is a pity she has no language now."

"Sister Agatha gives lessons for those who have need of them," Elizabeth said sharply. "Margaret seemed too young, too frail to be forced to take part just yet."

"If she is what we think she is, she will require strength beyond our imagining. Perhaps it would be best to find out just what she is made of now."

She was, she is my girl, the abbess thought. *She came here with nothing, and I gave her a home and love and life and she trusted me, she was devoted only to me. Must I sacrifice this all to you, to this idea of yours? Was it not simply an accident, that you were here the night when she ran wild in the grass, feverish, talking to herself, and gathering stones?*

I asked for his help, the abbess chided herself. I had no one else to ask, after William.

"Besides," Martin went on, "she needs to be ready for what might happen next, if—and I still say *if*—these seeings of hers last beyond her childhood."

"So she will need to read and write?"

"Yes, lady, but that is so little of it. What will she do when the faithful hear of her power?"

"I thought we had agreed," Elizabeth said, "to keep this matter inside the abbey walls, at least for a time."

"And so we did," Martin said. "But the holy will find their followers, and pilgrims will seek a place of pilgrimage. All it takes is a voice to say, *See what they have in Dove Abbey. A seer. Perhaps a prophetess. Let us go and ask her to bless our barley, our pigs, our unborn children. Let us hear what she has to tell of the life everlasting.*"

"And in that order."

"Yes, Madam, I believe it will be in that order."

"We must prevent such a thing."

"We can try to prevent such a thing from happening too soon, or for no reason," Martin said. "But if she is—"

He waved his hand in the air.

"What we think she is," Elizabeth continued.

"Well, then," he said, "we must be assured that those in need of whatever it is she has to tell will surely find her."

ණ

It would be a mistake to think that she was unaware of the way others thought of her. She felt the glances of her sisters as she walked across the abbey grounds, or reached, at supper, for the portion of bread and lentils she never finished. She could hear, as if they were spoken, the many thoughts that clung to her like dust, like burrs. And so, as she walks through the thickly falling snow with Christina at her side, the two of them carving out a twinned set of footprints in the whiteness, toward the guest house where Benedict is waiting, Margaret knows too well how many whispers follow her, the conjectures, the threads of gossip spun from anything but truth. The abbess has sworn both she and Christina to silence, but the public version of their task—that she and Christina are engaged in some kind of advanced scriptural study, directed by the abbey at Glastonbury—cannot have fooled, say, someone as wise and experienced as Sister Agatha for very long. Margaret longs for the day when she will be allowed to tell her sisters of her visions.

In the meantime, it would be going too far to say that Margaret does not care what her sisters think. But she does not care enough to let it alter what she is.

As a cluster of four novices passes by, she does not try to hide from them the anger in her face, still visible in the days since she and Christina met with the abbess and were informed that all Margaret has labored over must be pushed aside. Too many of the sisters are sick now; they will have to return to the duties of abbey life, Christina to the infirmary, and Margaret back to the sewing, baking, and scrubbing that were the lot of all the others.

"Your work for Brother Martin," she had said pointedly, "will have to stop, at least for a time."

"For how long must we stop?" Margaret had asked, and the abbess had scolded her for impertinence. It had been the first time the abbess had ever taken that tone with her, and since then Elizabeth had been chilly, selecting other girls to sit at her right at supper, scarcely talking to or looking at Margaret. It stung, yes, but it also made the younger woman wary. Now she and Christina were to hand over the last of their work for the year, and to tell Benedict that no one could say when it might resume. Each of them carries in her hand a rolled pile of parchments tied with string.

"I am sorry, Sister," Christina offers quietly, as they walk. "I wanted to go on as well, you know."

"You might have told her that," Margaret replies. "She would have listened to you, I am certain."

"I would not tax my vow of obedience so far," Christina says. "I am sure that Mother Elizabeth knows better than we do what is right for all of us."

"You are sure of that?"

"Yes, of course. She is so wise. She has been, she is so kind."

Margaret looks at the older woman, her gray eyes nearly expressionless. Again, Christina is reminded of how much Margaret has changed. Why, she had been devoted to the abbess, before Brother Martin came.

"Wise," Margaret says slowly. "Kind."

"She was kind to take you in, you know," Christina replies, suddenly angry on the abbess's behalf, as well as for herself.

"You came with nothing. No dowry, no skills, no learning. She could easily have sent you away."

"No, she could not," Margaret says, shaking her head. "It is an obligation of the Rule. St. Benedict says that the abbey must offer shelter to any in need. Besides, the Lord Himself tells us of the importance of hospitality when he visits Lazarus—"

"I do not need lecture on the scriptures, Sister," Christina says, though inwardly she is surprised. Margaret can barely read the vernacular, and nothing of the language of the Church at all. How had she absorbed so much?

"What I do know is that Mother Elizabeth rescued you from the worst sort of filth imaginable. Remember, I was there, the day you came. I saw the woman who brought you to the gates."

"My aunt," Margaret says. "Not a wise woman, no. But kind, very kind."

Christina hears the knife edge in her voice. *Sarcastic with me, indeed, my girl,* she thinks. *After all that we have been through.*

But she does not say that. Instead, she tries another tack.

"I am sure it will be just for a little while," she tells Margaret. "Just until a few more sisters are well."

Margaret shrugs, but does not speak.

"It happens every year, you know," she says, gently. "There are some who cannot take this weather. They will recover. We will—you will have your time again."

She smiles at Margaret now, and adds, softly, "The Lady will understand."

"You sound so sure," Margaret says. "I wish that I could share your certainty. Every time she comes to me, I am afraid that it will be the last time. Perhaps she will think that I have given up on her now."

"Why, I am sure that she will not think that. Who better than she to understand the obligations of our lives? She knows you will not forsake her, or she would never have come to you."

Hearing the certainty in Christina's voice, Margaret stops walking, clutching the older woman's arm so that she stops, too. The snow has begun to fall again, lightly now, sifting down between bare branches, and between the low stone buildings of the abbey.

"Sister," she says, and it is as if she is seeing Christina for the first time, "Do you truly believe that our Lady, the Lord's mother, comes to me?"

"Why, yes, of course, Sister. Of course I do."

Christina moves to pull her arm away, but Margaret will not let her. The softly falling snow begins to cling to their robes, to their veils, to their eyelashes.

"You are very sure of that?" Margaret asks.

"Of course. I have been there, when she comes to you. I have seen the difference between that and the rest of life. You would have to be a fool not to see it."

"I always thought that you disliked me," she says, letting go of Christina's arm. Her voice is flat, not self-pitying.

"I thought it was only for obedience's sake that you did it. Wrote down the words. Copied it all out again."

Christina feels an unexpected rush of tenderness. She hesitates, and then begins.

"I have been angry at you, sometimes," she says, "when you would not do as you were told. And sometimes, when I felt that you did not respect me properly, but treated me like a servant, subject to your whim."

"I did not mean to—I am sorry—"

"I know. It does not matter. But I believe in what you have seen, and in what you will see."

"You are with me, then. I was not sure. I had to know."

The snow is falling harder, now; thick veins of it have settled into the folds of their robes as they stand there, each full of many thoughts.

"Yes, Margaret," Christina says, "I am with you."

Sally Steenland

Sometimes It Takes a Little Longer

Sally Steenland's short stories have appeared in *Colorado Review*, *Antietam Review*, *Hawaii Review*, *Cottonwood*, *West Branch*, and other journals. She's written two best-selling books, *The Magnetic Poetry Book of Poetry* and the award-winning *Kids' Magnetic Book of Poetry*. Her short story collection, *Skin and Bones*, was a finalist in the 2004 Bakeless Literary Prize for Fiction.

When Joanna was growing up, she thought that when she got married, she'd want to have a baby. But after she married Ed, she thought, *not yet*. She watched him playing with the babies of their friends—something few men liked to do—and saw how eager he was to be a father, and what a good one he would be. He had the patience and openness, the curiosity and sturdiness to do it.

"When?" he asked. "Soon," she said and meant it. She gave herself reasons. She loved Ed and wanted him to be happy. She didn't want to be selfish or considered defective.

Another reason was this: if they had a child, Ed wouldn't look so much to her for attention. Already she worried that she was too quiet and aloof for him, and that though he claimed to love her reticent nature, it was only a matter of time before he grew impatient with her lack of exuberance and accused her of having a diminished capacity for life.

She found out she was pregnant from a kit. For a little while, she didn't say anything. It was early, and things happened. But one morning while Ed was taking a shower, she threw up in the downstairs bathroom. That evening, she told him. He didn't whoop with joy or twirl her around, which was what she'd been bracing for.

Instead, he shook his head slightly and rested his hand gently on her flat stomach. "Our baby—our new little child." His voice was quiet and reverent, as if the miracle had already happened.

In the early weeks, she was exhausted and sick. It's normal, friends said. They were eager to welcome her into the tribe, and brought offerings of advice, warnings, and used baby clothes. She put their carefully marked boxes in the nursery and closed the door. She could feel it growing, pushing out, spreading inside her. She felt as if she were being choked. She didn't say this to friends, or to Ed. She knew what was allowed. Negative feelings had to be intermittent, and balanced by happy ones. Excitement, hope—even awe. She didn't have them.

In the evenings when they lay in bed, Ed talked to the baby. He whispered his warm breath into her skin and caressed her growing belly. He rubbed her feet and asked where else she ached. Everywhere, she said. He rubbed her back and legs until he fell asleep.

When they found out it was a boy, he asked if they could call him Thomas, which was his father's name. Of course, she said, relieved that here was one thing she could do.

Gifts arrived. A set of Peter Rabbit dishes and a panda bear puppet from his parents. Hand-woven blankets in soft pastels from hers. She dreamed she gave the gifts to strangers. She dreamed she dropped the baby on rocks.

She worked as an editor for an academic journal. It was an office of women, mostly mothers. One day Sue stopped at her doorway to ask how she was feeling.

"Terrified," Joanna said. "Panicked."

Sue nodded and smiled. "I know exactly what you mean. Remember what a mess I was? How certifiably insane?" Her baby had been sick with colic, screaming inconsolably night and day. She'd rocked him, carried him, pushed him in the stroller. She'd wanted to push him down the stairs or leave him in the yard like an old couch for strangers to take.

Sue made her ordeal seem funny, even reassuring, because here she was, the crazy mother—nicely dressed in a pink sweater, wearing makeup and shoes. Ryan was in third grade now, and pictures of him, a happy boy, filled her office.

Joanna stopped confessing. The words she used—panic, terror, rage—made other women nod their heads. Yes, yes, they'd felt that way too. Exactly like that. But they hadn't. In a corner of her mind, she glimpsed the vast difference. It was the difference between getting wet and drowning.

All her life, she had gone along like a pebble in a brook, carried by what other people wanted and did. She had gone to camp and ballet, learned how to play tennis and the flute. She couldn't remember wanting to do these things, only that they had been presented and she had said yes. Whether she'd wanted to or not, she had done them well. But this was beyond her capacity.

In her last months of pregnancy, Ed sometimes looked at her with concern. *You're so quiet. Are you all right?* She could feel his attention roving like a searchlight over her swollen body. She closed her eyes against the glare. "I'm tired," she said. "I've lost my balance." Then she said quietly, "I'll be a bad mother."

Ed quickly took her in his arms and said, no, no—she would be a wonderful mother—how could she not? She was tender even to spiders and their webs. She had a loving heart, but an anxious nature—that was the problem. In fact, her worrying proved she'd be fine.

When Tommy was born, the nurse wrapped him in a blanket and gave him to Ed. His voice broke as he held Tommy for her to see. *Here's our baby, he's perfect.* She saw a red-faced, squalling creature wearing a hat. So that's it, she thought, and turned away.

After the doctor finished his work, the nurse put Tommy at her breast and rubbed his cheeks. He began sucking her nipple. "He's a strong little guy," the nurse said. It was her job to make breast-feeding a successful experience. "Sometimes it takes a little longer," she said when Tommy barely got a trickle. "Let's try the other one."

The hospital released Joanna with a basket of supplies. Stuck inside was a pamphlet on post-partum depression, listing numbers to call. But experts couldn't change her into someone who wanted a child. They couldn't erase the dismal awareness of the years dragging forward. School, camp, sports, college. None of it mattered to her.

One morning she took Tommy for a walk. It was cold and the park was deserted, except for a woman wearing a red jacket over a bright yellow sari, holding a toddler on her lap. They were face to face, playing a clapping game and singing a cheery jingle. The sight of them made her dizzy. What if the woman spread her legs and the baby fell to the ground. What if the woman stood up and walked away.

When she got home, she put Tommy down for his nap. Snow was falling outside the kitchen window, and she watched it drift up against the sill. When the monitor crackled, she went upstairs. In the darkened nursery, a strip of light from a gap between the curtains fell on the rug like a line on a highway. She picked Tommy up and felt his soggy diaper. As she bent over to change him, his fingers skidded across her cheek.

Now it was late afternoon. The room was darkening, as the gray winter sky emptied to black. She sat in the rocking chair and Tommy slept in her lap. On a nearby table was an envelope. Inside were pictures Ed had taken of the three of them. In each shot, he'd set the timer and hurried to join them before the flash. They had to choose one for Christmas cards.

In all the pictures, she was holding Tommy. In some, he was propped up, head against her neck, her arms crossing his body like straps. Ed was freckled and smiling, as if surprised he'd made it back to them in time. Her dark bangs were overgrown and hung in her eyes. Her face looked like a stranger's. The picture Ed liked best was the one where they spilled into each other, arms and torsos merged. A family, she thought.

Tommy was fifteen weeks old and every day demanded more from her. She was supposed to talk to him, play with him, stimulate his brain. They were supposed to bond.

People on the outside watched to see if she was doing these things. She could feel them watching.

Now she heard Ed's car in the driveway. He'd bound into the house and ask what they'd been up to today. A nap, a walk, lunch. That's what she would say. After dinner, he'd stick the panda bear puppet over his hand and swoop it through the air as Tommy shrieked and tried to grab the big rubbery nose.

Later they would stretch out on the bed. Ed would ask Tommy about his day, and Tommy would babble and wave his arms. Such affection made her feel cold as a stone. "I need to run to the mall," she'd say. "I won't be gone long."

She'd drive fast on the highway, following a wavery stream of car lights ahead. On and on they flowed, as far as the eye could see.

Across the room, the panda bear puppet was poking through the bars of the crib. She thought of animals caught in traps, gnawing off their flesh. Tommy was heavy, and she'd been sitting in the rocker too long. Her legs felt dead. She closed her eyes and pictured the numbness rising up through her body.

Blood and water turning to ice. Each day colder, as she kept on.

Venus Thrash

Cast Away Stones

VENUS THRASH received her bachelor's and master's degrees from American University. She is a Cave Canem, Lannan, and Soul Mountain fellow. Her poetry has appeared in the literary journals *Gargoyle*, *Catalyst*, and *Folio*, and in the Cave Canem anthology *Gathering Ground*. She is currently hard at work on a short story collection, "Soul of a Man," and a novel, "Hole."

"You know what I did soon as I got out of prison for killing that bitch? I went and found out where she was buried and right there under the broad sun, with God and the dearly departed as witness, I pissed all over her fucking grave. And I ain't sorry I did it."

Owen looked long and hard at Patrick and couldn't decide if he was for real or totally talking himself up. "Man, you lying. No way you peed on your wife's grave."

"Yeah I did, too. Made me feel a lot better about her. Less jealous. Less angry. I forgave her for all her wrongs and I wasn't mad anymore that she made me slip up and choke the ever-living daylights out of her and then had to do all that time on top of it. When I let go of all that beer, I let Sherrie go, too. It was like crying my heart out in reverse."

Owen shifted his weight on the bunk and wondered if pissing on some damn grave would give him the peace of mind he had never found in his life so far. If pissing on Sherrie's grave had given Patrick the satisfaction he claimed, then why did Patrick go and kill Sherrie all over again in the form of Michelle? Now his dumb ass would rot in prison. Still, Owen wasn't buying it, but he let Patrick go on blabbing off at the mouth because Owen didn't give a damn one way or the other.

If there was any one person in the world whose grave Owen would take aim at, it would be Idella Lovings's. He pictured himself standing over Idella's grave and letting it rip. All she ever gave him was birth.

Although his father, who drove a cement truck for a living, often told Owen he was proud of him, Owen still seemed to need encouragement more from Idella than from anyone else. He was sure that if she had shown him some simple act of love, had spoken one kind word to him, hugged him, or even patted him on the back every now and then, that he would not be behind bars today. Instead, he would be a famous artist known all over the world. Now, as it stood, he was famous for his elaborate jailhouse tattoos.

He had learned quickly to be creative after Oak Tree knocked him dead in his mouth when he added an extra S to Trellis—Oak Tree's boyfriend's name—on Oak's two-by-four muscled forearm. Owen almost let fag slip from his mouth in a rush of anger and blood. But that was seventeen years and one missing front tooth ago. He and Oak got to be good friends after Owen plucked the loose tooth from his mouth, swallowed the blood, and turned the extra S into a heart. Five years later, both Oak and Trellis died from AIDS. Owen accepted a long time ago that it wouldn't be prison if there wasn't death everywhere you looked.

Owen had seen enough sex, violence, and death to put one hundred Charles Bronson movies and two hundred John Holmes flicks to shame. He had seen Tommy push his intestines back inside himself after Nick tried to take him out with a roughshod knife shaped from the handle end of a toothbrush. He had seen Chris X with his head nearly cut off with plumbing wire that Hitman Jackson had smuggled into the joint. He had seen Steve "Twitch-Eye" Williams suck off Joe-Joe Kennedy, Psycho Sam, and Captain Grogan within a forty-five-minute time span for a pack of cigarettes, extra telephone time, and dining hall privileges. Hell, even Owen got some head from time to time, but that's as far as he was willing to go.

Twenty-two years of a twenty-five-year sentence for first-degree manslaughter and Owen had seen all the ugly there was to see of prison life—nothing to look at but the same hard-edged faces each and every day, performing the same rusty routine, staring down the same crusty walls, eating the same rotten food. He would be fifty in three years and God knows he didn't want to turn fifty behind bars. He was up for parole in two years. If he could just stay away from trouble, which was harder to do in here than the time itself, for twenty-four more months, he would be free.

Owen could still remember what freedom tasted like in a flaky-crust beef patty from the Kingston Carryout on the street corner where he grew up and what freedom sounded like coming out of Al Green's silky throat and Aretha's soulful treble on his stereo and what freedom felt like slapping cold and icy against his face in winter. Owen remembered how soft and supple a woman's breast felt cupped in his hands, how smooth the curve of her hips when he traced them with the tips of his fingers, and the cherry-flavored gloss of her lips savored on his. Owen was tired of remembering. He wanted the rottenness of green bologna gone from his mouth forever, and the everyday beatboxing and rapping to quit thumping against his brain. He wanted the women in his mind to become real again—to touch and feel and smell them again.

Although he had no skills other than drawing and tattooing, he could still try to make a honest living out of that. At least he had his high school diploma. But Idella didn't even bother to show up to his graduation. She had to work that day, his father reminded him, but did nothing to comfort Owen, as upset as he was. That night, he clocked some dude over the head with a tire iron and stole his car. He tried to drive as fast and as far to anywhere as he could before the pigs caught up to him and threw his ass in jail. That was his first run-in with the law. He did five out of eight for that. Idella never visited him once. Never even wrote. But she was there in the courtroom at his sentencing—the first time he could remember her showing up for anything important in his life.

"Let me say goodbye to my Mama," he told the guard who had just cuffed him. He hoped Idella would at least lean over the wooden railing, open her arms and hug him goodbye.

"I'm ashamed to call you my son, Owen. I hope you have plenty of time to think about what an embarrassment you are to me and your family," she said, and walked away and never looked back.

"I know that, Mama," Owen shouted behind her. "I've known that for the last eighteen years. Tell me something I don't know," Owen spat out as he was led away. That was the last thing they had said to each other and that was almost thirty years ago.

Her words stabbed deep into Owen's mind, his heart, his soul. At that moment, there was no other place he'd rather be than jail. Or dead.

Owen would sit and stew in jail trying to figure out why Idella Lovings hated him as much as she did. Perhaps Owen was the son who came instead of the first-born daughter Idella prayed for. She had had two girls after Owen's birth and Owen had watched her be less cold and less uncaring toward them, yet still distant and uninvolved. And Owen would have settled for less than a third of the love she showed them but he never got it.

Owen had tried to outshine his sisters. He had tried to prove to Idella he was worthy of her love. He spent most of his years between nine and eighteen trying to do everything right—grades, sports, school band, community volunteering—but Idella never patted his back, never said good job, never uttered the words "I love you."

There was no making sense of Idella's hate. It came as natural to her as the mother hamster that out of hunger, or no sense of obligation to offspring, and no natural mother's instinct to protect, often ate her young.

Owen found he still loved his Mama in spite of herself. The yearning he felt at night was his need to have her love him too, and the more Owen had reached out to Idella and found himself unembraced, the more resentful he'd grown. But at lights out, lying face up in his bunk, staring at the cracked, water-stained ceiling, annoyed at the friction of security buzzers, the clink-clank of bars sliding and locking into place, entombing him alive, and the clack-shuffle-clack-shuffle of the prison guards' steady pacing from one end to the other, keeping him awake most nights, Owen sobbed violently for the love Idella never gave him.

"What, if anything new, can you offer in your statement today that will grant you a different outcome from your previous two appearances before the Parole Board?"

Owen had nothing new to say. He felt the same now as he did the first time he found himself begging a bunch of strangers who knew nothing of the hell of prison life to grant him his freedom. They wanted to hear Owen say he'd been a good boy in prison and he'd be a good boy on the outside, too. That he'd learned his lesson, he'd never do it again, and that he was sorry.

Owen wasn't sorry. Dude jumped in his face over some goddamn ten dollars Owen owed him. Owen kept telling the MF he was gonnna get his money but dude tried to jump bad anyway and Owen had to show he was a bad muthafucka, too. He was only trying to tell the dude to back the fuck up when he pulled the .45 from the back of his waistband and pointed it at the man's chest. Dude kept coming and Owen shot. If push came to shove, Owen would do it again in a heartbeat. No. He wasn't sorry. Dude got what he had coming.

Now these bloodsuckers wanted him to beg. He'd tell them all they wanted to hear. He would cup his hands together pleading, let tears roll down his face, remorseful as hell, and cast his eyes down to the filthy floor to show he was ashamed.

"And finally, Mr. Lovings, if you were to be released, the Board is curious as to who would be the first person you would want to see?"

This was the easiest question Owen had so far. One he didn't have to lie on. He had thought about it every wakeful day and night over the last two years since Patrick told him the only thing that helped him get over all his balled-up anger was pissing on his wife's grave. Owen had dismissed the act as stupid-crazy but just a few days later, whenever Owen stood over the stainless steel toilet bowl to relieve himself, it was Idella Lovings's stern face he saw reflecting in the water. The very idea made Owen feel better about himself, and he looked forward to the day when he would walk through those prison doors for good. He began to picture himself full of beer, walking among the dead, treading the close-cropped grass, searching the headstones for the one who had caused him so much grief. "Chairperson, other members of the board, there is only one person I would love to see and talk to once I get out of here. My Mama. But since she died while I was serving my time, the first place I'd want to go is where they laid her down so I can say a proper goodbye."

ﾕ

Owen had no woman, no sister or brother waiting outside those prison gates when he walked out. He boarded the white prison bus with its darkened, caged windows and was anxious to be finally and completely free. It had become an ex-con tradition for the Virginia State Prison bus to drop off its newly released right outside Washington, D.C. The walk across the 14th Street Bridge was a kind of ritual, a rite of passage for reentry into the world.

"See you when you get back," the prison bus driver yelled to Owen, then shut the door and laughed as he pulled off.

"Fuck you," Owen shouted over his shoulder.

Owen walked across 14th Street Bridge on wobbly legs. He was aware only of the blinking hand at the other end. He wasn't sure. He couldn't remember. Walk now while it's blinking? Stop? He couldn't remember. He darted across the street just as the hand stopped flashing and stayed into a pattern of bright orange lights.

He walked unsteadily down the sidewalk and tried not to be startled by the passing cars, the blowing horns, the way the whole city seemed to brisk by him in a flash of red and white lights. Had it always moved so fast?

With each step, he grew surer, and the sidewalk under his feet began to feel like cement again instead of quicksand.

The smell of roasting coffee drifted from the corner of 14th and P. He didn't remember Starbucks. He continued to walk along 14th Street. He didn't remember the Fuddruckers, the Quiznos, or the Duke Ellington condos. He didn't remember there being so many goddamn dogs, or people whose pale or olive-skinned faces he couldn't recognize. Where were his boys from the old pool hall on the corner of 14th and U?

Owen's pace slowed along the U Street corridor. He was amazed at all the changes. The last time he strolled through here in the seventies, the place was still gutted from the riots.

Owen was happy to see Ben's Chili Bowl still there. Thirty good, solid, U.S. prison bucks in his pocket, might as well make it good. He could barely get inside Ben's 'cause the line was almost out the door. Man, there were some pretty browns sitting up in there. They all looked out of Owen's league. Owen licked his lips when he got to the counter and ordered one chili dog with onions. Three dollars and seventeen cents? For one goddamn chili dog? Weren't they fifty or sixty cents when he went in? As much as Owen wanted to, he didn't stop at the Tropicana Jamaican Restaurant. At this rate, a beef patty would be fifteen dollars. He walked to the corner of Georgia and Florida. He could always find a smart, pretty university woman walking past Howard on Georgia Avenue, but Owen kept going straight on Florida anyway. There were a few places with new paint but for the most part, the buildings and the people were starting to look like the ones Owen remembered. Owen stopped in the new Joe Caplan Liquor store, bought a Miller Draft twelve-pack—he didn't remember twelve-packs either. He walked all the way up Florida past the new Burger King which was once a Roy Rogers, past the wholesale district that still looked dirty and busy. He nodded at the lady pumping gas at the Hess gas station, which he also did not remember. He strode past Gallaudet University and past all the deaf students standing around flicking their fingers back and forth in fast, jerky movements. The familiar scene put Owen more at ease. He hooked a left on West Virginia Avenue and then right on Mt. Olivet Road. He knew Idella was buried somewhere in Mt. Olivet Cemetery.

❧

Owen followed the concrete path along the back fence just as the woman in the cemetery office, which was a small trailer off to the side near the back entrance, had told him. He kept his head up and did not look at the names on the markers or headstones as he passed them by. Owen did not like cemeteries and imagined dead people to be much like the zombies in the *Night of the Living Dead* movies he used to love watching so much. He walked over a tiny hill just as the woman said he would and past a blooming dogwood tree Owen guessed Idella would have liked. He counted off five graves then turned right past ten more before he came to Idella's. He stood over her and muttered at the ground. "Goddamn you, old lady, for not giving me the satisfaction of cussing you out to your face." Owen wiped his feet on the grass above where Idella's casket should be, plucked a warm beer from the case, popped the cap, and chugged it down almost in one long swallow, then drank a second right behind it. He could piss all over her right now if he wanted. Instead, he waited. He wanted to make it a good one. He popped open another bottle and drank.

Owen was still standing over Idella's grave by the time he started on his fifth beer. But he couldn't finish it. The ground was starting to spin and Owen felt it would cave in beneath him and bring him down to meet Idella face to face. He leaned over and grabbed the headstone, and glanced up only long enough to read the blurry words. *Idella Lovings, Loving Wife and Mother, 1930–1990.*

"Loving mother, my ass." Owen slurred his words and felt as though he might throw up. He stood up straight and read the words on her headstone again. He shook his head and grabbed for his zipper just as he heard footsteps behind him along the path. He turned to see a woman pass underneath the dogwood tree. She was tall and wore huge silver hoop earrings.

Owen rubbed the blurriness from his eyes. He watched the woman stop a few rows ahead of him, then kneel down to place flowers on a grave. She was shapely and curvy like Pam Grier in the *Foxy Brown* and *Coffy* movies. He slid his hand down the crotch of his pants and cupped his dick in his hand. Owen hadn't had pussy in over twenty years.

The woman had on dark shades, a blue denim skirt just above the knee, and a pinkish cotton blouse. A blue knitted shoulder bag, the size of Owen's large palm, swung slowly at her side. Owen thought she might be in her late twenties, early thirties. He watched her remove the shades and put them on the ground next to her knee. She began to brush her fingers along the etched words on the nameplate embedded in the ground and began to speak to it like the person buried there was still alive and right in front of her. Owen could not hear what the woman was saying, but he thought he heard the words *I love you* whispered between her lips.

Owen moved closer to the woman. He watched her wipe at her eyes and cheeks. She brushed dead grass, loose dirt, and pebbles away from the nameplate. As he came closer, he could hear the woman speak.

"We love you, Larry. We miss you. Mama misses you. Your daughter is doing fine. We know you'd be proud of her. You know she'll be twenty-seven soon. Same age as you. She was just a baby when you left us. I wish we'd had more time."

Owen was close enough now to peek over the woman's shoulder and read the name on the plate. *Laurence Maurice Reynolds, Beloved Son, Devoted Husband, and Doting Dad. 1953–1980.*

It struck Owen that Larry was the man's name he shot dead some twenty-six odd years ago. But Owen was sure this wasn't the same Larry. He stood near the woman for several minutes and watched her clear more dead grass from around the nameplate as dusk slowly covered the cemetery grounds. He wiped his hands through his salt-and-pepper hair and cleared his throat twice before he spoke. "You Larry's wife?"

The woman did not seem startled. "No. I'm his sister, but I was just a kid when he died. He was fifteen years older."

"You still remember him?"

"Why wouldn't I? He was always nice to me and used to buy me dolls and bring me candy and jump rope with me all the time. I remember enough to know that I loved him then, and still do."

"Oh," was all Owen could say.

"Did you know Larry?"

"No. I'm just here to say hello to my Mama."

"That's nice. It's good to know some men still love their mothers."

"Yeah," Owen stared at the ground.

The woman stood and knocked grass and dirt from her skirt and knees. She held out her hand. "I'm Anne Reynolds."

Owen's hand trembled as he held it out to shake the woman's hand. "I'm John."

"Good to meet you." The woman turned and started to walk away.

Owen watched the woman pass back underneath the dogwood and disappear over the hill. In twenty-five years, Owen had never thought of the man he'd killed. Did Owen snatch the man away from a grieving little sister or brother? A daughter? Son? Did the man's mother love her son? Did she hate Owen for taking her son away?

Owen zigzagged back over to Idella's grave and began to zip down. "You know, I really did love you, old lady. As hard as you made it, I really did." Owen kicked away a small rock that had come to rest at the edge of Idella's headstone. He knocked loose dirt from the top of it. "I really loved you," he said again before falling to his knees. He knocked another stone away and another.

Owen cried wildly and easily. His shoulders heaved up and down as he sobbed his words. He cried out again until he found himself spread out across Idella's grave. His face was messy with snot and tears. Owen pounded his fist so hard into the dirt that he believed Idella could hear him. He curled himself up into a tight ball and felt the wet warmth of urine fill his underwear and pants, and Owen Lovings could not keep from crying.

Julie Wakeman-Linn

Sex and Corvettes

JULIE WAKEMAN-LINN is the editor of the *Potomac Review*. She teaches creative writing at Montgomery College and is the program co-chair for the F. Scott Fitzgerald literary conference. Her fiction has appeared in small literary journals including *WordWrights!* and the *Larcom Review*.

Ellen fiddled with her hair, staring out her office window at the two teenage boys smoking under the elm tree. The sunlight soaked the street like syrup of a warm, sweet berry compote. Her toe tickled her mate's rib cage, rumpling his pressed chambray shirt.

"Ellen, you need to concentrate." Matthew straightened his review notes, flapping them at her.

"I'd rather play." Her toe wiggled into his pants pocket. Sometimes Matthew was too ready to help her train.

"'Time is the stream I go a'fishin in'... explicate." He massaged the sole of her foot. "I'm so proud you were chosen by the Elders."

"Let's review on a less perfect June day. Look at them," Ellen said, pointing to the two boys now blissfully stoned, stretched out on the grass. "Wouldn't you rather be outside?"

"Those days are behind us—well—almost behind us." He tapped the sole of her foot. "Come on. Explicate the prophecy."

Voices, a pleasant baritone and a shrill soprano, carried up from the boat dock.

"Take me to who's in charge." The female voice, unnecessarily loud, echoed between Ellen's bungalow office and the big square communal house across the street.

Derrick, the zone's nineteen-year-old and the leader of the cargo crew, tugged a strange girl up the cobblestone street. She was wearing a short pink dress, certainly not one of the twenty Youth assigned to Ellen's work zone.

"What's happening out there?" Matthew asked from his end of the sofa. Ellen liked how his chin jutted out more attractively when he was afraid.

Ellen quickly twisted her hair into a bun before she leaned out the window. "Derrick, who's this?"

"This girl, AmeliaNickerson, was hiding in a cargo hold," Derrick said. "When we started to play, she kicked and screamed at us."

Two names. One—a patronymic. Then the girl was an outsider. How remarkable—she'd never seen an outsider. Sometimes the Elders traveled to the mainland, but no one ever came here. Only last year, she'd heard they traveled to Washington to renew the treaty. This girl, hiding in the cargo hold, must have missed the notice of the Censor station.

"Play? You were going to rape me!" The girl yelled at poor Derrick.

"Rape?" asked Derrick. "What's that?"

Language difficulties, even though Amelia Nickerson spoke English. Ellen said, "Please come inside, Outsider Youth. You must be tired from your journey."

"An outsider?" Matthew whispered, peering out the window next to her. "What if she brought one of their weapons?" His long brown eyelashes fluttered as he scanned the street.

"She's not carrying any heavy metal objects, darling," Ellen spoke softly, straightening his collar and thinking the pink dress was too short and too tight to hide anything. "I'm curious to find out why she came here."

"Shouldn't you call the Council?" Matthew asked. "I'll raise the operator for you."

"I'll call, but I want to know what the situation is first," she said. From Matthew's shrug, she knew he objected, but his respect for her new position as Elder in Training prevented any opposition, even in this extraordinary situation.

Derrick barreled into her office, the girl in tow.

"Simplicity be with you, Youth," Ellen said, opening her arms.

Cutting off the girl, Derrick slid into Ellen's arms, saying, "Simplify with the dawn."

Ellen kissed his check and disentangled him. She loved the physical contact with the Youth under her charge. Sweet Derrick, his voice as warm as his heart. Ellen extended her hands to the girl, whose blue eyes were wild as a rabbit's, ready to bolt at a moment's fright. "Where are you from, Amelia Nickerson?"

"Call me Amelia. I'm from Boston." Dirt streaked the girl's cheeks, smudging around freckles. Her wavy reddish hair fuzzed out of her braid. "I'm sorry I yelled. I slept badly on the boat, but," she said as she wheeled on Matthew, "I want to complain about the treatment I've received, landing here in Martha's Vineyard."

"Martha? Don't you mean Margaret?" Ellen asked.

"You're in charge?" Amelia stood directly over Matthew, ignoring Ellen.

Matthew seemed to shrink into the couch cushions, saying, "Of course not. Ellen is in charge. She is the Philosopher of this zone. I assist her."

"Her?" Amelia pivoted to face Ellen. "You're hardly older than me."

"I'm thirty-two." Ellen felt prickly, being challenged by this snippet of a girl, badly clothed and in need of a wash-up. Prickly, being reminded of Maturity. "How old are you?"

"I'm eighteen." Amelia glared down at Matthew. "What are you going to do to punish them?"

Amelia wouldn't listen, Ellen thought, as long as Matthew was in the room. This outsider showed such a strong patriarchal orientation, turning to the mature man. "Why did you come here?" Ellen asked.

"I got lost," Amelia said, her lips stretched thin.

"I see." Ellen said. A Youth could not get lost in a cargo hold. Amelia lied easily, if poorly. What if her arrival were some crazy Outsider dare? Would more of them visit? The Elders wouldn't like it.

"Darling, could you double check the boat's manifest for me?" Ellen said. With Matthew gone, the girl might relax and stop lying.

"You know best," he murmured, rising to his feet with such manly grace. "I'll be right next door, if you need me."

Maybe she did prefer males to females, especially handsome ones like Matthew with his curly brown hair and his deep brown eyes. At Maturity, sexual preference was set. He'd make a good father, like her own father, when it was time. If her role as an elder ever permitted her time to have a child. She faced the girl. "Amelia, would you like something after your journey?"

Digging in his cargo short pockets, Derrick offered his hip flask of fresh raspberry wine and a joint.

Amelia's hands flapped at him. "Are you trying to entrap me?"

"Eleven o'clock is early." Ellen put her arm around Derrick's shoulder, thinking she'd like a smoke herself and Matthew was out of sight, so she extended her hand. "May I?"

Derrick lay the joint in her palm and lovingly closed her fingers over it, whispering, "What's entrap?"

She must get this innocent boy out of here, away from this confusion. "Is your crew finished unloading the shipment of car parts?"

He nodded, but he whispered, "Why is she in a dress like the Elders? Why is her hair all tied up like that? She's only a Youth, isn't she?"

"I'll explain later," she said. She opened the key cabinet. "What would you like to select for your fun after Conversation Circle? A truck, a sports car?"

"The penis extender!" he positively chortled.

"The Mustang or the Corvette?" Ellen asked, handing Derrick the breathalyzer tube. She watched the readout while he breathed. Safe, only point oh-two. Moderation in consumption was an early sign of Maturity.

"The Mustang. I need a backseat. Sandi and Sally and I are going to go trio."

Ellen tossed him the keys, wishing she could go along. "Have fun. Simplify."

"Blest simplicity." Derrick spun the keys on his thumb and began to whistle. As he closed the door, he called to Amelia, "I'll be back later if you're bored."

The girl tossed her braid over her shoulder. "What's going on here? I saw three girls with magenta and orange and blue hair necking with three boys, all of them in boxer shorts."

Ellen wondered at the odd things Amelia noticed. "Here, Youth do all the labor. They have the greatest strength so they should have the fun of sex, cars, weed, and wine," Ellen wondered what Amelia did for fun.

"You gave sports car keys to that crazy Derrick? And now he's going to have a *ménage à trois*?"

"Is that, um France, that not's the right word. You speak French?" Ellen asked. This Amelia spoke another language. Amazing. Ellen would love to explore that, but unfortunately French had to wait until the main questions were answered.

"It means three people having sex. Don't you know?" Amelia stomped to the window, her platform shoes clomping on the wood floor. "Ghastly."

Ellen stacked Matthew's prophecy notes for *Walden*. Was the girl more frightened of her own body than anything else? "Rape. That's an ancient and ugly word. Does it happen where you come from?"

"It nearly happened to me just now." Her arms folded over her mid-section, nudging her breasts against the gathered neckline of her dress. She was slim without being muscular like the Youth girls.

"Here, the boys and girls merely play, that's all." Ellen dimly recognized the source of the girl's fear—something about sex.

"Play! Sex is not about play," Amelia shouted.

"Why don't you tell me about Boston." Ellen guided her to the blue overstuffed couch and started to rub her back in spiraling circles. "The Great Mother came from there."

"Hey," Amelia said, wiggling.

"Massage will relax you," Ellen said. If she rubbed slow and steady as she spoke the litany, all Youth calmed down. "Find our place. Join the circle. Open the paradoxes. Great Mother, free us from sexual duality."

"Dual sex. Bisexual is bad enough but worse—two girls and a guy. Disgusting."

"The young are animals still, their minds undeveloped. Why fight a natural stage of growth?" Ellen swayed—massaging pleases the giver as well as the receiver.

"You must have a terrible problem with…" Amelia stopped.

"Problem with sex?" Ellen said. She smiled at the memory of her own raging hormones. She'd had sex three times a day for a while. "Why would we? The Youth must play, must try out different pairings. The prophecies cannot be understood until..."

Amelia bolted off the couch. She retched in the trash can behind the desk.

Ellen offered her water and wiped her mouth with a tissue. The cold in the boat probably upset her stomach. "We're very different from the Mainland. We find peace through the prophecies of Waldo and Henry David."

"What're those?" Amelia asked, curling up on the blue couch. Her pale skin was less green.

"The sacred teachings enable us to be self-reliant. To be a noble village of men, governed by women." Finally, the girl relaxed; now Ellen could ask for the truth. Ellen's fingers stroked the girl's neck, her skin smelling of roses. "Is that why you came to us? To hear the prophecies?"

"Women governors?" she asked, but her breathing steadied. "Sure, that's why."

"Great Mother Margaret escaped death off Fire Island." Ellen made her voice singsong. "No prophet is ever understood in her native land. Your world rejected the wisdom of her Conversation Circles. Over a hundred and fifty years ago, she brought us enlightenment. We 'go into the woods to live deliberately.'"

As Amelia's eyes closed again, she murmured, "I saw a Hallmark card like that once."

"Is that how your land interprets the sacred texts?" Ellen almost laughed. What an ignorant place the mainland was to mistreat such a delightful morsel of a girl. She'd love to teach her how to simplify, loosen her tawny wavy hair.

"Why do you remind me of my sophomore English teacher, Mr. Barnes?" Amelia asked, her eyes reflecting Ellen's hazel ones. Then she fell asleep.

Ellen slipped out to her front porch. This girl could teach her French. She had always wanted to learn another language, but no one knew them anymore. Sitting in her wooden rocking chair, she lit the joint. She hadn't had one since the training began.

The Youth trickled down the street, waving and bowing to her. The pairings and threesomes began dancing to a mainland radio station floating out of the communal house across the street. Ellen liked how this year's music's repetition naturally encouraged the pelvis thrusts, teaching Youth lovely foreplay. Matthew had abandoned his Youth status too quickly. She wanted to dance, too, but Matthew wouldn't join her anymore. Maybe Amelia would dance.

Amelia's screams pierced her blue haze. Ellen ran in, grabbing a patchwork quilt off her desk chair. She swaddled Amelia's arms tight to her torso and began rocking her, whispering, "The mass of men lead lives of quiet desperation" over and over.

"Stop. I'm awake now," Amelia said, her head popping up from Ellen's shoulder. "I had a nightmare."

"What's wrong? Let me help you," Ellen said, wanting to play, to comfort her, but stimulation was out of the question, Amelia was too frightened.

"I'm afraid I'm pregnant. My parents will kill me if I..."

"You're what?" Ellen said. Stranger and stranger from this girl.

"I'm pregnant. Preggers. Cake in the oven." Amelia's head dropped onto Ellen's shoulder. "A couple of fun nights in a Chevy van, and my life is over."

"That's not possible," Ellen said, cradling her. Poor scared little thing—she needed the facts of life. Truth always reassured those in fear. "You're a silly billy girl. You won't be fertile for fifteen to eighteen more years. You must have mixed too much weed and wine. Did you drink Derrick's raspberry? It's too tart for most Youth, although I like it."

"I'm not drunk." Amelia struggled against the quilt. "Of course, I'm fertile. The condom broke."

"Condom?" Ellen asked. "What a bizarre word."

"You've never heard of it?" Amelia's mouth hung open. "What do you use here, with everybody screwing all the time?"

"'Everybody screws 'all the time' to explore their psyches." Ellen unwrapped the red quilt, her fingers brushing against Amelia's breastbone. "No one can conceive until they reach full Maturity, in January of their thirty-third year after their hair color changes. I can't conceive yet although my hair is reverting to its old color."

"Can't conceive? No sticky condoms, no stupid foam, no lectures on 'No sex until marriage'?" Amelia's perfect white teeth clamped together. "What are you talking about hair color for? I don't get it."

"No sex until…? How would anyone know what they liked?" Ellen didn't get her either. Amelia's eyes, wide open, were pretty when she wasn't lying. "Your people didn't rinse in your red color when you turned twelve?"

"I do not dye my hair—it's natural." Amelia tossed her braid over her shoulder. "So all those teenagers out there bumping and grinding, having fun, aren't going to get in trouble?"

"Our rinses are natural, nothing dies." Ellen didn't understand why Amelia didn't understand. "I used to have the most wonderful blue streaks."

Amelia pointed at the Youth dancing. "You're not going to stop them from freaking?"

"Why would I?" Ellen said, wondering what this girl would say next. "I was going to join them. Would you like to—"

"So I could have sex here, couldn't I?" Amelia cut in. "This could be great. You know, I could go for your guy. He's a hunk. And you're his boss, even though you're a woman? I feel like I can really trust you, a woman in charge."

"Yes, I'm his superior—" Ellen started.

"Actually, I like sex. My orgasms are terrific. I really like being on top, you know."

"Matthew always has to be on top," Ellen said quickly, amazed at how easily she lied. She never lied. Amelia would confuse Matthew and oddly, Ellen didn't want to share her with him or him with her.

"OK, Derrick then. But no threesomes." Amelia chattered on about her sexual activities.

Ellen wondered why this girl was obsessed with sex. All this talk of sex stirred her own hormones again, but she still didn't know why Amelia had come here. "Tell me about your country."

"Boston's an all right place. It's a great time for women—if you don't get caught, get pregnant. After high school, after college, I think I want to go to law school."

Ellen didn't understand these words. School was a place of learning, but the Prophet Henry David wrote experience was the best teacher. She had always wished to learn more language, more logic. How could law require a school? The Elder Council made any decisions that were needed, protected them all. Pregnancy, law, school. Intriguing as this girl was, she was too much to handle alone. "I need to call the Elders," she said, dialing the phone.

As Ellen said, "Blest be the mothers" to the Elder who answered, Amelia began reading Ellen's needlepoint samplers hung on the office walls. When Ellen was a little girl, her mother had stitched their favorite prophesies. Amelia laughed out loud at "Consistency is the hobgoblin of small minds." Ellen ignored her, confirming a tea-time meeting. "We'll go to the Elders. I don't know what effect a pregnancy will have on one so young."

"I am perfectly..." Amelia started, when Derrick's head popped in the window.

"Is she OK? Somebody heard screaming." His long leg swung in the open window and stepped on the couch. Blushing, he stopped halfway in. "I'm sorry. Simplify Ellen."

"Derrick, you have the soul of a poet." His empathy, one of his best traits, he had learned to use from her guidance. "Would you like to drive us to Flint's Pond? Matthew can take charge in my absence. Where is Matthew anyway?" Ellen asked. She didn't really want complications with him and Amelia now.

"He's already accounting for the manifest for tonight's boat. I would be honored to drive you. How are you, Amelia?" He finished climbing in the window. When he offered her a hug, she let him.

Ellen put back the keys to her old Ford Tempo. She'd rather ride in the sports car. In the convertible, she'd get Amelia talking, hopefully telling the truth. After all, her greatest strength was her understanding of Youth. Amelia would tell her about Boston, French, everything from her world. She'd share in Amelia's knowledge and in her Youth. "Let's take the Mustang."

Even Amelia smiled, her thin lips so kissable.

"Can we stop and see my mom, Ellen?" Derrick asked.

"If she is not serving the Elders today." Ellen stroked his sleek black hair.

The Mustang hugged the curves of the winding gravel road. Ellen loosened her long black hair. As the breeze whipped it, the air on the back of her neck felt wonderful again. Scrunched down in the corner, Amelia held her braid close to her chest. They could correct the mistake of Amelia's people and rinse her hair now. Over her shoulder, Ellen suggested blue highlights would be perfect for Amelia's tawny hair, but Amelia didn't hear or didn't understand.

Fingering her straight hair, Ellen wished she hadn't already given up her blue highlights. Natural hair color was another marker that Maturity approached, part of preparation for the acceptance of gray.

Traveling from the coastal dunes to the edge of the farm zone, Ellen and Derrick talked about different drummers. Ellen pushed him for the correct answers to the paradoxes, hoping Amelia would join in the conversation. Amelia ignored them, staring out at the rolling fields.

"'The swiftest traveler goes on foot...'" Ellen said.

Derrick began, "'The train runs over the majority of...'"

"That doesn't make any sense," Amelia cut in. "We're in a car, after all."

As Derrick laughed, Ellen thought, this girl had come a long way for nothing, if she rejected their beliefs. Amelia was a paradox, an odd combination of a sexy mature body and an infant brain.

In the farm zone, as they drove under an arch of the white apple-tree blossoms, Ellen waved to the men weeding the strawberry fields or walking in orchards.

Derrick stopped the Mustang by a square gray-shingled house, its porch and trim a faded utility gray, plopped in a green field. The red berries peeked around the deep green frilly leaves. From a rocking chair on the porch, a plump middle-aged woman with salt-and-pepper hair waved.

"Mom!" Derrick yelled. He opened the door, practically before cutting the engine.

"Simplify, Olive," Ellen sang out. "We'll stay for a short rest, Amelia."

"Simplify with the dawn, Ellen," Olive said. "How's my baby boy doing?"

"Less and less a baby," Ellen answered, watching Olive rise with an easy grace, her green linen shift floating to her ankles.

"You know, Derrick, Ellen's mother was my Philosopher when I was a Youth," Olive said.

"Was she as much fun as Ellen is?" Derrick said. "Not too serious?"

Shaking her head at his giggles, Ellen patted his cheek. Her own mother had been about Olive's current age when she drowned. She should be here relaxing among the strawberries, not dead; Ellen tucked that thought away.

They all embraced in greeting; Derrick took his mother's hands and bowed his head to be kissed. Amelia insinuated her little body into their circle.

"This is Amelia, a visitor to us," Ellen said.

Olive paused. Then she reached for Amelia's head, smoothly kissing the top.

"Simplify," Amelia whispered. Ellen was proud of her until Amelia continued, "I need to pee. Where's the bathroom?" This girl had no sense of polite behavior.

"Derrick, show Amelia around." If Olive was shocked by the girl's rudeness, she didn't react. When the two Youth disappeared into the house, Olive picked up a flat of blushing strawberries, saying, "So, this is the girl with the sad business from the mainland."

"What I didn't say over the party line is how inexperienced she is. They don't season their Youth at all. The words she uses are so harsh, so angry," Ellen said, tapping the porch railing, "but then she will offer the most unique interpretation of the sacred texts."

"She knows them, does she? Well, that's the reason why she came to us, certainly."

"I'm not so sure." Ellen didn't want to say how Amelia sneered at some of their ideas and was mostly interested in sex.

Olive lifted the lid on a blue stock pot and dipped in a spoon, offering it to Ellen. "I was going to add more berries for sweetness. What do you think?"

"Tart, but then I like jam that way." Ellen pressed the strawberry pulp to the roof of her mouth. The taste and the tiny seeds meant the ease of summer, her mother's hands over hers as they stirred the pot together.

"Mainlainders like things extra sweet, don't they? I'll save some of this batch for you, special," Olive said. "Why do you think she came here, if not for the sacred texts?"

"She's looking for peace, I think. Her world offers her too many choices," Ellen said, thinking if she taught Amelia the prophecies, at the same time she'd learn about those interesting choices. "She said the oddest thing about law and school."

"I'm afraid her people still write them all down. The prophets warned us against that." Olive bowed her head for a moment, murmuring "'Unjust laws exist.'"

Ellen answered, "'Let your life be a counter friction to stop the machine.'"

"Strange—a Youth with child, but the child matures us." Olive began plucking stems. "You'll understand with your own child, but your training comes first."

"I wish training didn't come in strawberry season," Ellen said, rolling a red ripe berry in her fingers.

"You probably feel that way because you were born out of the ordinary season. It's always made you different," Olive patted her arm, leaving a tiny strawberry stain. "Your mother would be so proud of you."

Ellen popped a berry in her mouth, squelching the memory of her mother that swam up in her head, how her mother had celebrated her April birthday, particularly because everyone else's birthday fell in September. "Today, I'd like to 'know' strawberries, instead of beans, like the Prophet Henry David. Instead of prophecies."

"What, you'd rather be like me, a farmer? I'm surprised at you." Olive took Ellen's hand. "Has this girl confused you?"

"She's so different." Ellen couldn't explain how Amelia was fascinating, both more and less mature than herself, than she'd ever be. How cute she was with her perfect straight teeth and her creamy pale skin. She hadn't been with a girl since Matthew.

Derrick's voice rang out behind them. "Here in my mom's parlor, I read every afternoon, after Circle."

"You must take her soon." Olive peered at the two Youth, lounging together on her braided rug. "They'll be expecting you."

"Thank you for letting me help with the jam," Ellen said. The farm was like an oasis in her conflicting desires, of wanting to cling to Youth, and wanting to gain the respect that Maturity would give her.

"You look like your mother, you know," Olive said. "Remember what she wanted for you, even if it is hard for you to mature quickly. She always wanted a girl child of hers to sit on the Council."

Ellen nodded. Everyone, Matthew, Olive, even her father from his apple orchard wanted her to mature quickly, ascend to the Council by the time she was forty. She knew her mother's wishes; she just wished her mother was here to help.

"But I know how you feel—I loved the Mustangs, too." Olive laughed so hard, her chins wagged.

Derrick appeared to receive his farewell blessing. Amelia tried to shake Olive's hand, saying, "Thank you for your hospitality, Ma'am." Olive patted the girl's head.

"Blest simplicity," Olive said, taking Ellen's face in her hands.

"Blest be the mothers," Ellen said. Their foreheads touched.

As the Youth climbed into the Mustang, Olive whispered to Ellen, "Come by and share a joint sometime." She laid a finger across her lips. Ellen grinned, wishing it were possible, but Elders didn't do that.

After the farm, Derrick drove more quickly, whistling a cradle tune. Leaving the squares of green fields and apple orchards, they drove through a wall of tall oak trees where the afternoon sunlight slanted through the dark forest. The ferns barely sighed at their passing.

They emerged into a stand of elm trees that ringed Flint Pond, the clearest pond in all of their island. On the green grass which wrapped the pond, the Elders' circle of adirondack chairs stood, empty.

Ellen and Derrick bowed, Ellen intoning "'Living poetry like the leaves of a tree.'"

"The morning sun is the day star! The year beginning with younger hope than ever,'" Derrick chanted back.

Two steps behind them, Amelia said, "Who is that wrinkly old lady in the funny hat?"

"Hush, it's an Elder," Derrick said. "Let Ellen speak."

An older lady in a loose pink jumper approached, spreading her hands open in greeting. "Simplicity be with you."

"Simplify," Derrick said, catching Amelia's arm, and bowed his lowest bow, his nose almost touching his knees. Amelia bobbed her head and shoulders.

"Simplicity be with you, Elder. I bring you a troubled young Outsider with an amazing problem." Ellen wished she'd taken time to dress Amelia more appropriately in Youth clothes like boxer shorts and a sports bra.

"So the Council has been informed. Now we must try to help her." The Elder's wrinkles widened when she smiled.

"You'll help me terminate the pregnancy?" Amelia rocked up onto the tips of her toes.

The way the Elder looked at Amelia made Ellen wanted to crawl under the grass. Ellen feared a medical solution was the help Amelia was searching for, not peace. "She knows nothing of our ways. She has never heard of Great Mother Margaret, Elder."

"Excuse me, please stop about this dead mother person," Amelia said. "What about me?"

Ellen blushed all the way down her neck.

Finally the Elder said, "The Great Mother was Margaret Fuller. She came to us from your world, bringing the words of Emerson and Thoreau."

"Those guys?" Amelia said. "I get it, that's why Ellen reminds me of my sophomore English teacher. Transcendentalists!"

"We call ourselves Dialists to honor the Great Mother who freed us from sexual chains and taught us how to simplify our lives," the Elder said.

"Walden Pond. The Great Lawsuit. I know this stuff! This is cool. Women are in charge here, not the white shirts and ties like at home. I love the free sex and hot cars, although I don't like wine. I prefer beer." Amelia paused when Ellen loudly cleared her throat. "I'm sorry to interrupt. You'll help me?"

"We don't know how to terminate pregnancies because there is never one that is—what word did you use?—unwanted," the Elder said.

Ellen put a hand on Amelia's shoulder, trying to prevent any more outbursts.

"I don't think I want to stay pregnant." Amelia twisted the end of her braid. "I ran away from my parents. They'll probably make me marry my boyfriend or keep the baby and I don't want to. I want to study law."

"You have run away from your people?" the Elder asked. "Ellen, I was not told this. Study of law—Another ridiculous failing of Mainlanders."

"She was so frightened. I thought they had abused her physically in Boston," Ellen babbled. How had she overlooked the runaway part of Amelia's story?

"Boston? This Youth is not from Boston. She doesn't have the right speech." The Elder folded her arms. "You do not say the words like the Prophets did. You do not pronounce vowel sounds appropriately for a Bostonian!"

"I'm sorry. I lied. I'm from Virginia. I came here thinking I could get work or hide or something. Please help me," Amelia pleaded.

"Ellen, you made a bad decision to withhold the information of her arrival. Her lies complicate matters," the Elder said. "I must ask the Council."

"Yes, Elder. Blest be the mothers," Ellen said, feeling angry at Amelia's lies and embarrassed at her own blindness. Her foolishness, her attraction to this girl now jeopardized her position in training.

On the grass in the circle of adirondack chairs, the Council of Elders had assembled. Twenty old gray-haired women, all in long loose pink or blue or purple dresses with big floppy straw hats, listened to the one who had spoken to Ellen and Amelia and Derrick. Their voices hummed softly like distant bees.

Amelia reached to hold Derrick's and Ellen's hands, murmuring how she'd like to drive a Corvette, she'd like to have sex with him, she wanted to stay.

Derrick whispering he'd like to play with her, too, he'd teach her the prophecies, maybe they could both stay with his mom.

"Your mother didn't volunteer," Ellen interrupted them. Their mothers, between thirty-five and fifty, not eighteen, lacked a Youth's hormones and energy and would not be interested in Amelia as a playmate either. Ellen picked at her thumbnail, considering options. If Amelia stayed with her, maybe she could stop her lying. "Maybe you could stay with me," she said.

"I'd like that. Much better than another mother." Amelia squeezed Ellen's arm, whispering, "Maybe I'm not really pregnant. I'm only a few days late on my cycle. I was, you know, scared. My boyfriend's Jewish and his mom insisted he break up with me because I'm Catholic, you know?"

"You practice the dead religions?" Ellen asked. This was most shocking of all. This girl, however appealing, was too much with her lies, her bizarre physical condition, her dependence on outmoded belief systems. "You're not even sure you're pregnant?"

"What are the dead religions?" Derrick's voice cracked. "Do they make you lie?"

"I had my reasons!" Amelia said. "I didn't know if I could trust you."

Ellen walked apart from them, lingering by a tall elm. Youth was enthroned here in her land, playing and working, but all the teachings required them to grow through experience. She knew it was time to give up Youth and accept Maturity. Fighting the natural order would keep her from the Oversoul and make her irrational like beautiful, deceitful Amelia. Her desire for Amelia had been her desire to cling to her Youth. Protecting Amelia would only bring chaos.

The Elder approached. "Ellen, you are young and not always wise, but your heart is good. 'There is no odor so bad as that which arises from a goodness tainted.'"

"I am sorry, Elder." Ellen lowered her head; she was so ashamed.

The Elder lay her hand on Ellen's cheek. "The Youth's lies tainted your goodness. Walk with me, Youth. I would speak with you and Ellen."

"Yes, Elder—Ma'am—Mother." Amelia hurried to step in between them.

"I have visited your capital in the spring. It..."

"Washington?" Amelia cut in.

"Try not to interrupt, Youth. It is a terrible place. Bad architecture erupting in every cornfield, awful drivers always pushing in," the old woman's hand on Amelia's shoulder kept her at arm's length, "...like you."

"Elder, I can learn. Derrick said he would teach me." Amelia clasped her hands together. "Ellen and Derrick like me."

Amelia was trying her best sweetness, her wide thin smile, Ellen thought, but it wasn't going to work.

"No, Youth, you are not right for us," the Elder said.

"But you're right for me. I like it here, especially in this park." Amelia extended her hands, palms open. "Here on Martha's Vineyard, everyone waves, smiles. You're right—everybody pushes at home."

"We are not on Martha's Vineyard. We are on Margaret's Vineyard," the Elder said. "You got on the wrong boat. You must go back."

"Margaret's? Not Martha's? I wondered where all the rich people were, but I don't want to go back. I came hoping to work as a waitress. I want to stay." Amelia opened her mouth as if she were going to scream, but she stopped. "My parents..."

"Your parents will be very worried about you, young one," the Elder interrupted. "Whether you are pregnant or just willful, you 'would labor here under a mistake.' As the prophet says, 'Explore thyself.'"

Ellen knew Amelia was never going to be self-reliant. Maybe the worst part of this escapade was that somewhere on the mainland was a mother who feared for the safety of her child. If Ellen felt more concern for that mother than for this girl, she must be ready to mature.

"You can't just order me around. I'm eighteen and I can vote," Amelia announced. "I'm staying."

"No, you can't vote here. Not for another twelve years." The Elder rested her hands on her belly. "The prophet also said, 'I left the woods because I had several more lives to live.' You can't stay here. Go live your life."

"My life could be here." Amelia's eyes were wild, as when she first arrived. "Is there anything I can do, Elder? Ellen, please?"

Ellen shook her head, realizing she must live her life here with her beliefs, her Matthew, her future as an Elder. Ellen kissed Amelia's temple and said gently, "You are too much an 'embryo woman' for our civilized society."

"'Our whole life is startlingly moral. There is never an instant's truce between virtue and vice.'" The Elder chanted, adding, "You, young one, lie too regularly for us. Too easily. Ellen, there is a lovely shipment of strawberries going to the Mainland. Put her on tonight's boat."

"Yes, Elder, I will see to it," Ellen said. Too bad, she would like to have learned French.

After a deep bow to the Elder, Derrick offered Amelia his arm and Amelia mumbled, "I blew it—the old biddy is sending me away."

"Blest be the mothers," Ellen said to the Elder. "My training is going well."

"We are following your progress," said the Elder. "'Simplify,' my dear."

In the backseat of the Mustang, Amelia finally undid her braid. "Could I come back sometime?"

"No, I don't think so." Ellen didn't let herself pause to consider it, knowing that tomorrow she would likely find her first gray hair in her hairbrush.

Sarah Louise Williams

Dirt

Sarah Louise Williams's fiction has appeared in *StoryQuarterly* and *Gargoyle* and her nonfiction in *Grand Street* and *Vogue*. "Dirt" is part of a series of stories set on Maryland's Eastern Shore. Sarah has a BA from Yale and an MFA from Sarah Lawrence College. She has taught creative writing at Deerfield Academy and George Washington University. She lives in Maryland with her husband and sons.

Jeff Langford dreamed of Pompeii. His world history teacher had not yet led the eleventh grade to the chapters on Rome, but Jeff had already highlighted in his textbook the entire section on the eruption of Mount Vesuvius. Jeff fretted over the inevitable creases and smudges to these special pages. He did not trust the book to be safe if crammed into his backpack. Instead, he carried the book in his left hand. The book went with him to all his classes, to the echoing, metallic cafeteria, to the poorly attended meetings of the Birder Club, and to the colorfully tiled bathrooms of his immense high school, one of two schools that served all of Dorchester County, Maryland. Jeff dropped his book only once, while crossing the wide and often empty Route 331 that ran between school and his home. He stood in the middle of the road, stunned at his own clumsiness and momentarily unable to move to rescue the book from the hot asphalt. In spite of his care, a crack had developed in the binding from so much handling, so the dropped book opened easily to the photographs of plaster casts of the Pompeii victims. A stiff breeze coming off the Chesapeake Bay pushed those well-worn pages around, bringing the bodies to life for a moment. Jeff studied the poses as if they were an ancient's cryptic signal intended just for him. The breeze died, the pages flipped and stopped at the pyramids, just as a white pickup swerved and honked as it sped around him. "Dooooorrrrrkkkkk," yelled the passengers, their disappearing voices in the wind sounding like a distressed whale.

At home, Jeff couldn't stop thinking about the poses: a mother and child face down, the woman's palms turned up toward the ceiling of her villa, the man writhing on his back, suffocating in the ash, another man squatting with his hands clasped across his chest in prayer, a curled-up dog. Before Jeff went to sleep each night, he lay in the dark gesturing and freezing in the poses of Pompeii. He was well aware the Eastern Shore of Maryland was one of the flattest, least volcanic places on earth, but even so, he waited in bed, both terrified of and hoping for a dramatic eruption in the night. When he closed his eyes, he could see so easily his befuddled, pajama-clad neighbors shrieking, dragging their keepsakes and reluctant pets around on their lawns, the whole community illuminated by lava glow. Having made it through numerous hurricanes, his parents would stay calm and pile into the bathtub, but Jeff knew he'd be unable to stay indoors. He'd want to see for himself the ash descending, and he'd keep the panic down by trying to find the right way to die for posterity. *Dear God, I don't mind dying, but please let me be one who is found, Amen.* He'd squirm and squirm unable to decide who he was and how exactly his body would be discovered, until he'd finally fall asleep.

When his alarm went off in the morning, he tried not to move until he could take note of what position he was in. It was hard to do since his hand instinctively lurched toward the alarm. He found he most often woke on his side, semi-fetal, with the lower part of one leg—calf, ankle, and foot—hanging over the edge of the bed. The pose was not all that noteworthy, and this disappointed him. To cheer himself up, he'd move into a more classic Pompeii grimace before turning off his alarm and beginning his day.

Jeff grew up around collections and preservation. His mother collected crystal fairy-tale figurines, Snow White, all seven dwarves, Sleeping Beauty, even some from fairy tales Jeff had never heard of. Though her figurines were fragile, his mother never told him not to play with them. Jeff had never shown interest in anything athletic, and he was both proud and ashamed once to hear his mother say to someone on the phone how Jeff had "never broken a glass, a dish, a bone, or a tooth, a real neatnik I've raised here."

The Langfords lived directly across the street from the high school in a new housing complex in a row of nearly identical three-bedroom ranchers, each with a patio and grill pad. Jeff's father was a taxidermist specializing in waterfowl and other game. Unlike the other fathers in the subdivision who drove into downtown Cambridge or to Easton for work in offices, Jeff's father's workshop was attached to the house. Jeff didn't think his father ever got the birds' eyes right—they were too wide-eyed. He wished his dad could capture more of the birds' nobility in their final struggles, like the plaster casts did of those people in Pompeii. Yet his father had won many awards for his birds at the Easton Waterfowl Festival. The plaques hung on the wall near his favorite wood ducks and turkeys. There was a reverence and silence his father had for his work that Jeff didn't quite understand, but that he knew to respect.

At the end of the day, his father would wash his hands in a special disinfectant, then get very involved in oiling his shotguns from the gun case. He took great care of his guns even though he never used them anymore. He had wrenched his knees too many times while hunting in the marshes so, instead of having surgery, he surprised everyone when he opted to stop hunting and just focus on stuffing the birds. After the guns were clean and back on the wall, he'd sit quietly with the lights very low until it was time for dinner. "Decompression," his mother told Jeff as an explanation for his father's habits. "Everyone has to have it one way or another."

Mornings, Jeff would eat his Cheerios while watching his mother move about the kitchen. He was able to carry on a conversation with her while secretly freezing her in ash at the sink, the refrigerator, the garbage can, and the pantry. Even in winter, his mother wore shorts and a sleeveless shirt inside the house. She was from Florida originally and could not discard her love of beachwear even though she'd left Florida twenty years ago. She'd met Jeff's father on the beach in Ocean City when they were both just a year out of high school. They married young and could never get pregnant again after Jeff was born, but they were happy enough and well off compared to many in Cambridge and Cole's Island. Unlike some of the mothers Jeff had seen around town, his mother was trim thanks to the exercise bike in the basement. His mother loved Elton John, would do the hustle in the kitchen to "Don't Go Breaking My Heart," her broom in hand. She was one of those rare natural blondes who tans easily and never burns, even after a scorching summer outing on the Bay. She had beautiful green eyes and bad teeth she had never bothered to fix once she had the money. Neither she nor her husband had a clue where their bright, studious son had come from, but they loved him and wanted to love what he loved, even if they didn't understand it. When his father told Jeff that someday they might all go to Europe on a package tour so Jeff could see for himself all these places he was studying, Jeff was speechless. His father reached out his hand to Jeff just as Jeff imagined the ash coming down on the two of them, shaping them forever as they were at that moment: Jeff oddly without his textbook, without his pocket-size *Birds of America* guide, without his compass; his father without the bifocals he wore while preserving ducks and geese, without his red toolbox, without the outline of a tobacco tin showing through his shirt pocket—all the things that Jeff thought represented them both best. But it was only another daydream, no ash cloud yet, just a wordless handshake that morphed into a quick hug, then parting.

In late spring of junior year, Jeff was in the hot backseat of Mr. Early's Driver's Ed hatchback. Reid Freeman, Jeff's classmate, was driving. Jeff didn't know Reid, but he knew his nickname, Dirt. It was true that Reid wasn't very clean, but some of the other kids at school were just as smelly. Jeff recalled the stories that led to the nickname. In middle school, everyone said Reid closed down a pool because he'd taken a crap in it. In ninth grade, a popular boy, Tommy Parsons, befriended Reid for a few weeks just to see what Reid would do on Tommy's dares. Tommy persuaded Reid to fuck a hole in a mattress at a party they'd crashed. After Reid was thrown out of the party, he rolled around nude in a mud puddle oinking—not part of the dare—and that act cemented Reid's reputation. At a summer job he had at an Easton seafood restaurant, he was fired when caught pissing on the crabcakes. Reid yelled, "Secret Family Recipe!"

in his defense to the customers, and then he was pushed out the door. There was something inspiring to Jeff about how much Reid didn't care. He was his own clique of one and that was something Jeff liked to think about himself. He vowed not to call him Dirt even though at this point in his high school career, Jeff assumed Reid had accepted, perhaps even embraced, the name.

Reid began his regular practice of slamming the brakes too suddenly at stop signs, sending Mr. Early and his clipboard into the dash. Jeff learned to anticipate the stops by bracing himself against the backseat. He thought it was fun because he didn't like how Mr. Early was so complimentary to Jeff about his driving, followed by sighs and groans when Reid took the wheel. Mr. Early was heavy and took up more than half of the front seat, the folds of flesh pressed over the edge of the seat back. Jeff found the folds distracting, and he wanted to push them down back over the front seat, but he resisted the temptation.

While Reid played his braking game with Mr. Early, Jeff was free to think about going to college out West so he could go to Yosemite, Yellowstone, and Joshua Tree on weekends. He dreamed of being a park ranger, NASA scientist, deep sea explorer, logger working on a fire crew, an ER doctor. When he imagined himself accomplishing these goals, he hoped he would be tall enough to no longer need to sit on a blanket to drive. When he thought Mr. Early and Reid were not looking, Jeff froze himself in Pompeii poses all his own: slouching and drooling against the streaked window where former driving students had smashed mosquitoes; reaching out to grab the back of Mr. Early's balding head; picking his nose, about to eat it, then looking up stunned to see the cloud of ash descending. "What if, what if, what if?" he wanted to yell out to his companions, "what if it happened again, to us?" How would all the people I know be caught for eternity, Jeff wondered. He imagined Mr. Early just as he was at that moment, filling out paperwork, clipboard in one hand, a double cheeseburger in the other. Reid would be found on the toilet or throwing rocks at cars.

"That's enough, Reid, pull over and get out, I can't take it anymore," Mr. Early said.

Reid sighed and kicked open his car door. He got out and pulled the seat back forward so Jeff could exit. Jeff pulled his folded blanket from his backpack. The blanket would give him a few extra inches in height so he'd be able to see fully out the windshield and mirrors. Mr. Early, now exasperated with any delay, told Jeff to leave his books and other stuff in the backseat. Reid stood waiting for Jeff to squeeze out of the backseat.

"All yours, dude," Reid said to Jeff.

"Thanks, Reid," Jeff said, while holding his blanket and nervously looking back into the car at his abandoned history book. Even after three weeks of driving lessons together, this was the first time the boys had said anything directly to each other. Reid looked hard at Jeff as if he weren't sure to punch or thank him for not calling him Dirt.

Even though Jeff was nervous about Reid and the book being in such close proximity, he was glad to get behind the wheel. He found driving to be a good time to imagine his career at NASA, and he was able to focus on both safety and Mr. Early's commands while also checking on the various pressure gauges and landing gear, taking pictures of alien life, sending the film back to base. The wetlands were a perfect otherworld. Jeff could easily make the marsh grass glow red instead of green. The herons and egrets they scared as they drove past were transformed instantly into never-before-seen inhabitants of a distant moon. Only occasionally would his fingers flicker on the steering wheel while turning imaginary dials.

In the rearview mirror, Jeff could see Reid's face buried in the history book. After a few laps up and down 331, some turns and a parallel parking session, Jeff pulled into the high school parking lot and stopped the car. Mr. Early waved them both off in disgust and said that Jeff was ready, but he doubted Reid would ever pass the test. As Reid popped out of the backseat, he rolled his eyes at Mr. Early, then handed Jeff his backpack. "See ya."

Jeff stayed by the car frantically thumbing through his book to find the Vesuvius chapter. The pages looked intact except for a smear of what Jeff thought could be a booger not his own. Then he saw where Reid had written with dull pencil in big sloppy print, "Cool volcano," and then down lower, near the pictures of the body casts, "Cool dead people." He looked up to see Reid walking toward the idling school bus that would take him back down toward the island. Jeff wanted to ride the bus with him, to hear more of what he thought of the plaster casts.

"Yes, cool volcano!" Jeff shouted to Reid's back, but Reid didn't hear him.

The following week, Jeff passed his driving test. He didn't have a car, so it didn't really matter to him. He wondered if he'd ever talk to Reid again.

⁓

They were in Spanish class in the early afternoon. Jeff was finished with his vocabulary test, but he had learned a painful lesson back in middle school not to turn his tests in too early. He looked up from his test and saw Reid staring at him from across the room. Reid was moving his hands and arms in an unusual way, close to his chest, then away. At first Jeff thought Reid was just goofing around, dancing in his desk. Then Jeff could tell that Reid was switching positions and holding them in some kind of specific order that seemed familiar to Jeff, but he still couldn't decipher. He thought maybe Reid had burnt his tongue and was unable to speak. Or maybe it was something about Mr. Early and driving? Reid's gyrations were making his desk scrape loudly on the floor. His message to Jeff was something about being surprised, stuck, afraid, helpless, then resigned to fate. The other students were wincing with each scrape of Reid's desk against the floor.

"Cut it out!" someone yelled.

The teacher began saying Reid's name in a low voice, repeating it over and over, each time louder, but Reid wouldn't stop his movements. The scraping got louder and the teacher got up from her desk. Jeff was still baffled. Now students were staring at Jeff, waiting for him to answer Reid with a word or gesture, anything to get him to stop the scraping. Jeff was ashamed at the attention at first, but then he was too intrigued with solving the puzzle to care. Reid would break character occasionally and stare at Jeff in frustration. Reid resorted to panting like a dog, hands bent at the wrist, tongue hanging down and whimpering. The dog looked up to a darkening sky, cowered and curled himself up as best he could, then froze in the position.

"The dog! The casts! Pompeii!" Jeff yelled out, shoving his arms high into the air as if he'd won a game show. Reid and Jeff began laughing and couldn't stop. The teacher grabbed their tests from their desks and told them to leave the room immediately.

"Let's go," Reid said, once out in the hallway. He had one hand in his back pocket, the other pointing down the hall.

Jeff stopped laughing. He tried to swing his overloaded backpack over one shoulder, but it was too heavy. "Go where?"

"Go, you know, *mi casa es su casa*, come on." Reid was already turning toward the main entrance.

"But school's not out yet," Jeff said. "Aren't we supposed to go to detention or something?"

Reid snorted and started walking toward the double doors. Jeff followed him.

~

"You got your license?" Jeff asked when he watched Reid get into the driver's seat of a red, used, two-door Camaro.

"Well, I got a car, don't I? I got a C+ in English so my mom got it for me. Get in."

Jeff hesitated and then did, still unsure if Reid had a license or not.

They headed south on 331, away from school, Jeff's house, and all things with which Jeff felt most familiar. He assumed they were going down to Cole's Island, where he was pretty sure Reid lived. The road stretched out in long curves, and the closer they got to the island, there was so little shoulder that Jeff hoped Reid would be careful not to send the car down the gravel bank into the encroaching marsh.

As Jeff watched the road, he thought of the biology lab he was missing. His class was to dissect a fetal pig that afternoon, something Jeff had been looking forward to, even though his lab partner was often late or absent, and Jeff usually wrote up the reports that she then copied. It wasn't quite hot enough yet for air conditioning so when Reid rolled down his window, Jeff did the same. He took a deep breath of the rushing air and thought he could smell the formaldehyde from the lab. He looked behind him, half expecting to see his disapproving science teacher sprinting after them with the fetal pig slopping around in a tray. But there was no one there, just the empty road and, in the distance, rows of skinny loblolly pines looking down on them.

The imagined smell of formaldehyde changed to something else that was overwhelming.

"Do you smell that? What is it?" he asked Reid.

Reid shrugged. Jeff noticed that a tattoo on Reid's right upper arm said, "So?"

"Egret. Possum. Something got smashed," Reid said, keeping his eyes on the road.

"So. So, so. So what? So be it," Jeff mumbled. There was the homework he could be completing in study hall, his last class of the day. Then right after school, the Birder Club would be meeting and, since he was president, secretary, and treasurer, he knew he'd be missed. By five-thirty, his mother would begin to wonder where he was and would perhaps call the school. Reid sped up and leaned forward a little more, moving his torso side to side with each curve, as if he were waterskiing. He seemed to Jeff to be in his own world, as if he had forgotten that he and Jeff barely knew each other.

"Wait, Reid. Where are we going?" Jeff heard his voice get tight and high. He swallowed a few times and waited for Reid to respond.

But Reid kept driving, even sped up some more, and seemed to be closer to the center line than Mr. Early said was safe. Reid stuck his left arm out the window and pointed into the marsh.

"Relax, Grandma, I'll show you something cool," he said.

Reid slowed suddenly and drove the car down into a shallow ditch running alongside the road. There was no splash of water, so Jeff realized some of these ditches were more solid than they looked. Reid stopped the car and got out. Jeff decided to take his backpack and history book with him in case he got stranded out there. By the time Jeff shut his door,

Reid was already cutting through the marsh, zigzagging a bit to keep his feet on the tufts of grass and out of the water holes. He never took his hands out of his pockets. Even though Jeff knew all about the biology of Eastern Shore waterfowl, he'd never really been out in the marsh. He put his history book into his backpack as carefully as he could, rolled up his pant legs, tightened the straps on his backpack, and entered the marsh.

To Jeff, it looked as if Reid were already out to where open water began, yet Reid kept walking. Jeff followed the path of bent-grass blades that Reid had created with his body. Reid was a big guy: big head, big shoulders, big hands. Not fat, but everything oversize, out of place and clumsy, especially when crammed into a desk at school. Out here, Jeff noticed, Reid seemed more at ease.

Jeff did not feel so comfortable. Mosquitoes began attacking. From his backpack, he took a travel-size bottle of bug spray and swiped some on his neck, cheeks, and forearms. He wondered if his bug bites would swell so much he'd even need a Benadryl by the time he got home. Just the smell of the spray made him feel better. There was an occasional salty breeze that swept the bugs away, the sun was still high, and there were no clouds. Jeff got the hang of picking up his feet before the water soaked into his shoes. He understood now how to choose his spots, and he even liked the uneven rhythm of marsh walking. If only he had his binoculars and the walking stick his father gave him for Christmas, he'd be all set. He decided that whatever was going to happen that day was going to be OK. He was training to be a scientist, an explorer, an astronaut, a rescuer after all, and this unexpected journey with Reid was its own kind of grand outdoor lab.

Jeff surprised a great blue heron and made the mistake of continuing to walk as he watched the bird fly off to the north. He twisted his ankle, then fell into a dark brown pool of water with yellow scum on top, like cooled chicken soup. When he recovered, he saw that Reid had changed directions and was now heading north again, almost directly toward Jeff. Reid signaled just with his head for Jeff to keep following Reid's path through the grass. Jeff did, and, without comprehending how he'd arrived there, he found the grass had ended, and he and Reid were looking down on a small sliver of inlet in the wider marsh.

He looked at Reid, who was studying something on the bank.

"Here it is," Reid said.

A blue crab dipped down below the surface, some grasshoppers jumped, but Jeff didn't see anything unusual. Maybe Reid was going to pull out a magnifying glass, and they would analyze some insects.

"Where my dad died. Right here," Reid said, his finger pointing down to the steep bank.

"Your dad died? When did your dad die? I thought your dad was a waterman, or something." Even the lingo of Cole's Island felt wrong in Jeff's mouth. He was hot and embarrassed, and the fetid smell of the marsh mud was starting to make him sick.

"He was. A crabber. And oysters. But he wasn't working. This was two years ago. In the fall. I don't know why he was out here. Sometimes he just went off in the boat. Everyone said it was a third heart attack that got him, or maybe he drowned. But I think it was both. He was right there in his boat, right there."

"How'd a boat get all the way up here? Too shallow, isn't it?" Jeff asked, hoping it wasn't a stupid question.

"You've seen them, haven't you? The flat-bottomed kind. They can run up all these inlets, no problem. He was in waders and a big sweater, it was just starting to get cold. At the funeral, everybody said it was such a blessing it was quick, but they didn't see his body the way I did. My idea is that he tried to jump to the bank, but his waders took on water and yanked him down. But it's shallow here, and he was strong, so maybe it was a heart attack. There are the claw marks from where he tried to get up the bank. There was all this blood and mud under his nails. The undertaker couldn't get it all out, so my mom told him to close the casket. She didn't want people seeing the nails. The marks are fading, but you can still see."

Reid bent down, and Jeff understood he was to do the same. They leaned over the edge of the bank. Jeff was precariously balanced on the balls of his feet. He put a hand down to steady himself.

"You have to get upside down like this to really see them. From the other side, it's too far away." Jeff looked at Reid who was bent over so far that the tips of his greasy hair were hanging down in the water. The blood had rushed to his head and veins bulged in his temples. Jeff tried to follow Reid's lead, but he was shorter and could tell he'd end up falling in. From what he could see, there were some vertical lines in the bank, but with two years' worth of tides, Jeff was skeptical that the marks could still be there.

"How about this?" Reid asked Jeff, while still hanging his head upside down. "We take turns being my dad and having the heart attack and trying to crawl up the bank." Before Jeff could say yes or no, Reid had stepped into the water. "See, it's not deep. I'll go first."

Jeff watched Reid pretend to be his father sitting in a boat, messing with something at his feet, adjusting a baseball cap, picking his butt. They both laughed at that. Reid had a smile on his face that made Jeff relax a bit. Reid clutched at his arm, his chest, then lurched toward the bank so suddenly, Jeff thought maybe there was something wrong with him. Reid squirmed up the bank, frantically grabbing at the slick grass. He couldn't get a hold of anything solid so he started clawing the bank in such a way that Jeff jumped back as if Reid were going to yank Jeff's toes off. Then, just as suddenly, Reid stopped moving and slid down on the bank.

Jeff clapped, and waited.

Reid lay still for a moment, then sprung out of the water with grass strands stuck to his face. He smiled at Jeff. There was mud on his teeth.

"Your turn."

Jeff slid his backpack off his shoulders, emptied his pockets into the outer pouch of the backpack, folded his glasses into their carrying case, rolled his pants up a few more inches, and stepped in. The bottom was flatter, more solid than he thought it would be. Reid sat cross-legged on the bank, his wet hair sticking straight up in the air.

Jeff had trouble at first. He couldn't determine which way to turn, or which way the boat would have been facing. He tried to figure out where the sun would be at that time of day—it was morning when his dad died, Jeff confirmed with Reid. He took a deep breath and began.

He spent a few minutes killing an imaginary bug, poured some steaming coffee out of a thermos, stared out at the water thinking a waterman's thoughts, took off his hat and gave his scalp a good scratching, tapped his fingers on his knee to a favorite song, took a brief snooze, stood up in the boat without a wobble, quite manly and confident, then bent down to dig through a storage container while waving off some gnats. And then he began looking uncomfortably around the boat, the marsh, the horizon. He unbuttoned his shirt, tried unsuccessfully to take off his sweater, unhooked one side of his waders, clutched at his throat as if dying of thirst, moaned and groaned before he threw himself out of the boat. He fought gravity, digging his hands into the bank as hard as he could. Beaten back by pain, he slid slowly down and stopped moving, face up to the sky, eyes vacant, face loose, dead.

Jeff sat up and turned around to find Reid glaring at him. Nothing. Jeff panicked for a moment and thought maybe he'd pushed it too far. It was Reid's dad, after all, and he was gone. This was all your idea, Jeff was about to yell. But then Reid started clapping slowly, and bowed his head. He stood up, and extended a hand to help Jeff up the bank.

"Shit, Jeff, you are not normal. Academy Award time."

Jeff beamed, grabbed Reid's hand, and scampered up the bank.

⁓

A ramshackle wooden bridge signaled the end of Cambridge and the entry onto Upper Cole's Island, a blob of fortified marsh dotted with crab-picking factories, slanting houses in need of paint, and white people. One restaurant, Old Ned's, served frozen fish to the dwindling population of watermen and their families. The fresh catch was sent out to Cambridge, Easton, and Annapolis. In places, the island was so narrow you could see the Honga River on one side and the Chesapeake Bay on the other, with just the slightest turn of the head.

Linking Upper to Middle Cole's was a spare, arcing bridge, high enough for large boats to pass under from the Honga and Wicomico Rivers into the Bay. Middle Cole's had more structures—sagging churches, abandoned graveyards, a trio of trailers in the middle of an overgrown field—than residents. And the residents were black with the exception of Reid and his mother. The Freemans lived at the end of Middle Cole's in a small yellow house set close to the road. Below them was Lower Cole's Island, but there was no way to get there on foot or by car since 1933 when a hurricane took out the bridge. The residents of Lower Cole's had long ago moved up the island.

By the time they arrived at Reid's house, little streams of sweat had created a wormlike pattern in the caked mud on Jeff's forearms. He was exhausted, hungry, and disoriented, but he felt he had to play this adventure out before he could go home. Maybe he could take a shower here.

Reid's mother wasn't back from work yet. Jeff remembered something about her cleaning houses, vacation homes mostly, all over the Eastern Shore. There was a rumor about her stealing money, and Jeff wondered if that was how she had paid for Reid's car. Reid threw Jeff a towel and pointed him down the hall toward the bathroom. Jeff showered as quickly as he could, and hoped Reid's mother would be there by the time he got out, maybe even with a sandwich for him and an offer of a ride home with her instead of Reid. No sandwich, but there was a folded T-shirt on the sink counter. It smelled clean, and he liked that Reid had picked it out for Jeff to wear. It was black, and when he opened it up to see the face of Ozzy Osbourne staring at him, he laughed. He put it on and turned around in the mirror to see that the back of the shirt said, "Get Crazy on the Crazy Train" in neon-green block print. It was way too big for Jeff, but softer and more comfortable than the button-down, short-sleeved shirts he usually wore.

When he emerged from the bathroom, the house was quiet. He crept down the hall in the direction he saw Reid go. A television flickered from a room at the end of the dark hallway. Jeff stopped in front of the open door. There he saw Reid sitting on a shag carpet. It was a small room with an oversized television, a striped futon, and a child's desk. Baskets of folded laundry were on the futon. Reid motioned Jeff into the room. He was fumbling with a video, squinting to see if it had been rewound already. Jeff stepped into the room, conscious that his pants were still filthy even if his body and shirt were clean. There was nowhere else to sit so he sat on the floor next to Reid. Soon the screen went blue and there they were: the body casts from Pompeii, up close and in detail.

"I got it from the library at school. Some documentary. The guy's voice is stupid, but I keep the sound down. It's all those ash people, same as the ones in the book."

Reid and Jeff scooted closer to the screen. Reid pushed an ottoman out of the way, and Jeff took off his shoes. Jeff realized Reid hadn't showered. Maybe they only had one bathroom, he thought, but he decided to ignore the smell. He couldn't believe he hadn't thought to go to the library himself. They watched without saying a word. The Pompeii section ended, and Reid immediately rewound the tape and pressed play.

There was no signal to start the game, but each knew what to do. Reid was the dog, then Jeff was the dog. Reid was the man leaning against a building with hands over his eyes, then Jeff. Since Jeff was smaller than Reid, Jeff was the little child curled under his mother's body. From the hesitant look in Reid's eyes, it was clear to Jeff that Reid also wanted to be the little child curled up, so Reid fit his big body under Jeff's tiny one. They giggled and Jeff could smell Reid's armpits. The game was so odd but thrilling that Jeff felt that if either of them spoke, they'd have to stop. After the roll in the marsh, there was comfort in just lying there, resting, eyes closed but not sleeping. Jeff protected Reid as best he could, his thin arm draped over Reid's torso. Jeff wanted to keep watching the video but moving now would disturb the scene. He feared that if he moved, Reid would move, the casts would crack, the spell would be broken, and the people would pop out, showing the world their sudden deaths were all an elaborate hoax fabricated by archaeologists. Jeff needed to believe that the casts were real and that they contained real people, as real as Reid's odor and Jeff's loneliness.

Just then Reid's mother came through the door and turned the lights on.

"Oop! Did I wokest ya? Hi, who are you?" she asked, smiling at Jeff.

"It's Jeff, from school. We're studying. Have to act out this tomorrow in class. This big volcano a long time ago," Reid explained.

His mom nodded, dropped her purse on the desk and left. Jeff could hear her humming as she moved down the hall. Her hair was an orange tint of blonde. She looked nothing like Reid except for her slumped heavy walk. Jeff wondered what she thought of the muck drying in Reid's hair, or the mud stains from their clothes on the beige rug. The rest of the house was clean enough, but she didn't seem to care about their mess. He liked her, and his gut told him that she did not steal money from her clients' homes, that the car was some kind of present for Reid because of his dad, and that she and Reid were doing the best they could.

Jeff's watch alarm went off, indicating he had ten minutes to get home for dinner at six. He'd meant to call his mother as soon as he got to Reid's house.

"I have to go home. Now."

"Don't worry, you'll get there in time. We'll even have enough time to drive by Early's house and flip him off."

Jeff didn't say anything, just grabbed his backpack, left the house, and got in the car.

Reid was going too fast.

Just after Jeff said, "Slow down," his voice lower and louder than he'd ever made it go, the car failed to follow a curve.

The length of a football field, the car flew that far: a red, body-shopped rocket, all wheels spinning, leaving the pavement, launching away from the shoulder, arcing out over the brackish Bay. What Jeff and Reid needed was the magic of a close call that might have taken the car up over the water, twisting and aching for earth in mid-air, righting itself just in time, somehow swerving back to concrete for a perfect landing, all wheels down, speeding off without a scratch. Instead, the car spun halfway to upside down, then landed right-side up just where the crabgrass stopped and the true current began.

As Jeff flew through the air, the view was so much better than the map his mother had bought him of the Eastern Shore. From here, he could see how the land was meted out from above like fallen drops of wet sand, how the soggy land fought off the water that moved in everywhere, threatened everything, the way the loblolly pines towered incongruously over the desperately flat earth. Wordless knowledge of his home and his fleeting place in it came to him in flashes of desolate beauty and a chaos of colorful, skewed perspectives: the greens of the marsh, everywhere then gone; the interchangeable blue grays of water and fading sky; the whites of wave caps and church steeples. And then the car was no longer rising, but falling back down.

After the car slammed into the water, Jeff couldn't open his door. The water came in, and he sat there, blinking quickly, feeling sharp pains in his eyes. "What happened to my eyes?" he asked, but Reid's eyes were shut. Blood trickled down Reid's ear, and his chest was caved into the steering wheel. There was no answer to Jeff's question. The car was sinking, and Jeff was going to die. He thought about his mother waiting at home for him, and his father just washing up for dinner, and the two of them wondering what to do next. He remembered how he knew he was growing up because he no longer bristled when his mother mispronounced Pompeii as, "Pom-pee-ee." He desperately wanted to be there with them at the table just then, but he wasn't and he couldn't, so he took off his glasses, tried to slide them into his shirt pocket, then looked down to see Ozzy's deranged eyes looking at him upside down. No pocket. He folded his glasses into his right hand, placed his history book on his lap, then put his other hand on Reid's thick shoulder. Jeff closed his eyes.

C. Jenise Wriston

The Fiddler's Wife

C. JENISE WRISTON (née Williamson) received her MFA in fiction from the University of Maryland at College Park. Her fiction has been published in *Satire*, *Painted Bride Quarterly*, and several other literary magazines. She is the founding director of the creative writing program at Bowie State University and lives with her husband in Greenbelt, Maryland. Her interest in fiddle music, especially Cape Breton style, began while learning Scottish country dancing.

Lie doon," he said. His name was McKay but everyone, even his wife, called him Tocher. So Tocher made her a bed with his coat and pulled off his T-shirt to make her a pillow. His jeans were already open and she could see him. She was his wife, and her name was Fiona but everyone called her Fay. So Fay, the fiddler's wife, reached out to touch him but he stopped her and placed his hands on her hips and raised her blouse above her head, and her shoulders caught in the cloth pulling back her breasts. She was wearing nothing else beneath the cotton cloth her skirt was made of, and he buried his head and lowered her with him.

"That's a fantasy for even an unmarried man."

"I was thinking it was more of a woman's story."

"Either way."

"Aren't you still hungry?"

"No, I've had enough."

That night at dinner Tocher sat with Fay at the dinner table. Their two sons had a lot to tell.

"Da, I won the go-cart race last weekend," Ned said.

Fay raised her eyebrows at Tocher McKay and nodded toward Ned.

Tocher looked away from her and wiped his mouth with his napkin, revealing a smile. He turned his attention to Ned. "And how did ye do that, then?" he asked.

He was sure of himself, and as for his playing, he knew only music. With his sons, he could speak about automobiles and construction jobs, the land over which they rode their dirt bikes, and the lack of change in the weather. The weather in the north stayed for a long time. "What exactly hae ye done to win that race, Neddie?" he asked.

Tocher was home now but no telling for how long. His music was becoming popular and his plan to leave construction five years from now was no length of five years away. He was that good.

"We'd better clear the dishes."

"They haven't raised the window yet."

"Oh."

"Is that the signal?"

"That's the signal."

"Good. I can get some tea."

Fay sighed and cleared the dishes.

"They hae odd sayings o'er there," Tocher said. "Like 'getting over.'"

"What's that mean?" Ned asked.

"It means ye did no really win that race."

"I did!" Ned insisted.

"He did!" their other son Mark said. Then the boys realized that Tocher was only teasing them.

He didn't speak of his music. He heard it in his mind and left the table to play his fiddle.

Fay took out her woodcuts. She had just started a series of wild flowers.

"Da, can we see the video?"

When he was away for a long time to countries he'd never been to, Tocher made videos.

"It's in the closet somewhere, Ned," he said. The fiddle was still under his chin.

Fay was anxious to see it too but kept silent. She always stayed at home with the boys even on the long trips. She had a stoic patience that one might have contributed to the climate, but being from the north, one looked for other reasons.

"I think it's time to go."

"The window's still not up."

"I just want to do a good job."

"It's OK. It's relaxed here."

Fay didn't want to go. She enjoyed staying at home with Ned and Mark and she enjoyed working quietly on her prints.

She smiled because she had waited for him and there he was. He always returned. She always hoped he would give her that peace, a look like that first look, smiling at her, with his fiddle tucked beneath his chin and his bow pulling a hornpipe from Scotland out of the wood. She hoped it would last for as long as he might be away.

"Do we have time for more dessert?"

"How would they say it?"

"Maybe they'd say, 'Do we no hae time for so' puddin'?'"

"Oh, the window's up."

"We'd better get some work done."

Tocher put down the fiddle. "Why would ye no go wi' me, Fay?" he asked.

Fay didn't know what to say at first. Her printmaking was important and he didn't understand the reason behind it.

"Ye here all day with yourself," Tocher said.

"'Tis my work, Tocher," she said. "I no can work if I be travelin' wi' ye."

There was dancing and music on the video.

"Ah, 'tis lovely, Toch," Fay said.

Tocher left the room and closed the door loudly when he stepped outside. He loved her and he loved their two sons and he loved his music and he heard it in his mind throughout the whole day but when he looked at his wife, this beautiful woman expecting him, who had waited for him to return from far away, he could think of only her and his mind was quiet. Now he was frustrated and walked in the mist toward the cairn at the end of the road.

"Ma, Da's famous now, isn't he?" Mark asked. Mark was the younger of the two boys.

"In a way," Fay said. "Whenever he's playing, he's famous in a way with the dancers."

"Look! They love 'im," Mark said.

"In a way," she said.

She traced some lines onto the wood block. "They hae 'im all to themselves," she thought. "When he's there wi' them, he could no be wi' me."

Tocher came in wet from the rain.

"You're getting me all wet."

"Sorry."

"If you could just stay on that side of the dishwasher."

"Sorry."

Tocher shook the rainwater off his jacket and hung it behind the door.

"Hey, hae ye no seen enough of me already?" he asked.

"Ye famous, aren't you, Da?"

"No, Mark," he said. "Fame doesn't mean anything. Ye see how they be dancin'? How they be smilin'? That's what the music means. That's what's important, boys."

Fay put her cutting tool away in its leather case and stood up. "Is this what ye mean?" she asked.

"What are they listening to?"

"'Flowers of Edinburgh' maybe."

"That's a nice one."

"It's on tonight's program, I think."

"It's an easy one."

"That's good. I'm still so new at this."

Fay locked her hand in Tocher's and turned him. Mark and Ned began to jump up and down as if they were doing a *pas de basque* but they never pointed their toes; they just kicked their feet out on the third beat, maybe the second beat too.

"Ow! That's hot!"

"You should keep your gloves on 'til you're done."

"OK, I'm done. I'm ready to dance."

"Right. I've got to go back to my cabin to get my ghillies."

"Meet you on the path after I use the toilet."

"That's the benefit of getting the dishwashing job. Everyone's out of the bathrooms by the time we're done."

"That was a nice story. Is it true?"

"In a way."

RICHARD PEABODY, a prolific poet, fiction writer, and editor, is an experienced teacher and important activist in the Washington, D.C., community of letters. He is the founder and co-editor of *Gargoyle* magazine and editor (or co-editor) of fourteen anthologies including *Mondo Barbie*, *Conversations with Gore Vidal*, *A Different Beat: Writings by Women of the Beat Generation*, *Alice Redux*, *Sex & Chocolate*, and *Grace and Gravity: Fiction by Washington Area Women*. He is the author of the novella *Sugar Mountain*, two short story collections, and six poetry collections including *Last of the Red Hot Magnetos* and *I'm in Love with the Morton Salt Girl*. He teaches at the Writer's Center and at Johns Hopkins, where he has been presented the Faculty Award for Distinguished Professional Achievement. Peabody lives and works in the Washington, D.C., area. You can find out more at www.wikipedia.org and www.gargoylemagazine.com.

Cover artist JODY MUSSOFF has been exhibiting her drawings for over twenty-five years and is represented in various museums and collections in the United States and abroad. More recently, she has been working in ceramics as well. She lives outside Washington, D.C.; her website is www.artworkphotographer.com/jodym/home.htm.